EVERYMAN, I will go with thee,

and be thy guide,

In thy most need to go by thy side

NATHANIEL HAWTHORNE

Born at Salem, Mass., on 4th July 1804. Educated at Bowdoin College, Brunswick, Maine, 1821–5. Returned to Salem to try to make living as writer for magazines and gift books and as editor. After working as a custom-house official he married Sophia Peabody in July 1841, and was made U.S. consul at Liverpool in 1853. In 1857 he went to Italy, afterwards residing at Whitby, Redcar and Leamington. He returned to America in 1860, and died at Plymouth, New Hampshire, on 19th May 1864.

NATHANIEL HAWTHORNE

The House
of the Seven Gables

INTRODUCTION BY
ROY HARVEY PEARCE
Professor of American Literature
The University of California, San Diego

DENT: LONDON AND TORONTO
EVERYMAN'S LIBRARY
DUTTON: NEW YORK

All rights reserved
Made in Great Britain
at the
Aldine Press · Letchworth · Herts
for
J. M. DENT & SONS LTD
Aldine House · Albemarle Street · London
This edition was first published in
Everyman's Library in 1907
Last reprinted 1977

Published in the U.S.A. by arrangement
with J. M. Dent & Sons Ltd

No. 176   Hardback ISBN 0 460 00176 0
No. 1176   Paperback ISBN 0 460 01176 6

INTRODUCTION

In *The House of the Seven Gables* Hawthorne began to move out of the intensity and confinement of the tale toward the relative ease and freedom of the novel. True enough, we can say this of *The House of the Seven Gables* only if we view it as it anticipates the work which came after, chiefly *The Blithedale Romance*, *The Marble Faun*, and the abortive *Dr Grimshawe's Secret* and *The Dolliver Romance*. These later fictions clearly partake of the form and concept of the novel. The life of the people in them is meant to derive chiefly from their relations to the world in which they live and to each other, not from the symbolic purposes which they are to serve. Their 'meaning' is, in effect, made to rise out of their actions, and not vice versa, as in the tales and in a novella like *The Scarlet Letter*. So it is too, I think, with *The House of the Seven Gables*, though admittedly not so clearly as with the later work. Therein, indeed, lies its peculiar attraction and importance for readers of Hawthorne. If it is not quite a novel, still it aspires to be one. If it is a novel, still it is informed by the techniques, the concept, and the spirit—and thus the characteristic understanding and insight—of the tales and *The Scarlet Letter*.

I should surmise that some such notion as this lies behind Hawthorne's prefatory insistence that this is a romance and not a novel—as we would put it, primarily a 'symbolic' fiction and not a 'realistic' one. He wanted his work to be judged as holding to 'the truth of the human heart,' not as representing a minute fidelity to that side of nature that is open to common-sense observation. His work was essentially moral; and for him—unlike, say, his contemporary Emerson—morality lay not in the nature of things in general but in the nature of man as he lived amidst things in particular; thus man had to give organization to his world; thus man had to relate himself symbolically to

his world, to derive a meaning from his world in so far
as it might project the meaning he found in himself.
If for Emerson man symbolized the world, for Hawthorne the world could be made to symbolize man. So
The House of the Seven Gables centres on a series of
symbolical revelations discovering the interrelatedness
and continuity of evil in one small portion of the world,
a New England community of the nineteenth century.
This is characteristic, in essence, of the pattern of the
tales and *The Scarlet Letter*. Yet final emphasis in *The
House of the Seven Gables* is on the community itself.
And such emphasis pushes Hawthorne—willy-nilly, one
might say, looking back on the record of his writing—
into trying to achieve the compass and effect of the novel.

To look at this matter in another, related way: if
we can regard the primary theme in all of Hawthorne's
fictions as being the burden of discovery of self, with
its potentialities for good or evil; and if further we can
see the archetypal plot of his fictions as one in which the
individual is isolated (or isolates himself) from his
community, discovers what he is, and then struggles to
return and live with his newly discovered self as well
as with his neighbours—then we can say that in *The
House of the Seven Gables* Hawthorne's emphasis begins
to be placed on the community and on its history, and
how it got to be what it is. He remarked in the preface
that the moral of this work was 'that the wrong-doing
of one generation lives into the successive ones. . . .'
We note that the important word is 'generation,' that
here, above all, the theme must be, in the words of the
Puritan rhyme, 'In Adam's fall/We sinned all.' The
task for the writer is to invent a story which will register
the authentic human possibility of such a doctrine
manifesting itself in history. The central figure is not
Adam, or a symbolic projection of Adam, but Adam's
descendants and the world they have made. Original
sin, in Hawthorne's interpretation, becomes not a
subject, something which governs the form of the story,
something so firmly granted that it is a means of in-
terpreting and projecting life symbolically; rather does
it become an object, something to be discovered in the
very texture of life-in-society, something which makes
imaginative sense only in so far as it derives that sense
from a reader's awareness of the life of the society in
which it is discovered. In *The House of the Seven Gables,*

then, Hawthorne's archetypal plot is given a new
direction, new scope and richness; the individual discovers his true relation to the community; original sin
is made to achieve its expression through cultural
history.

In the novel (the word is here used with qualification,
of course) the history of the Pyncheon family ends and
begins again. It ends because Maule's curse descends
on the family for (presumably) the last time; it begins
because the sin of the family is exposed, expiated, and
the non-Pyncheon world is accepted for what it is.
Thus the crucial figures in the novel are Phoebe and
Holgrave. She is a pre-lapsarian Eve, a Pyncheon who
has enough non-Pyncheon blood in her at once to love
and reject her past. He is a post-lapsarian Adam, a
Maule who is so deeply caught by the injustice done to
his family that he would reject his past, all past, and
love no one. In their union each saves the other.
Explicitly, Hawthorne makes Holgrave out to be a
young intellectual, like so many other young intellectuals
in nineteenth-century America, at once mobile, unstable,
rationalistic, disinterested, liberal, and eager for change.
And Phoebe is the little girl fresh from the country, whose
very freshness, however delightful, must, in this post-
Adamic age of *felix culpa*, mark a certain inadequacy of
character. Her experience with the Pyncheons, her
view of what Maule's curse has done to Hepzibah,
Clifford, and Judge Pyncheon—these are said to mature
her and to make her such a one as Holgrave, waiting
disinterestedly for the destruction of the Pyncheons,
needs so desperately. In their union, which is that of
two young Americans who have borne the weight of
their past while at the same time being touched by and
drawn to the variegated life of the present, lies their
hope of the future. In them—as they make and are
made by the life that surrounds them—lies Hawthorne's
expression of his sense at once of the burden of history
and the hope of community.

To sketch out the novel thus is perhaps a little unfair.
It is to emphasize the novelistic, as opposed to the strictly
symbolic, aspects. But it is none the less necessary, I
think—since what is crucially significant in the novel is
that Hawthorne was trying to do something new for
him, to conceive of and express life somewhat more
broadly and richly than he had heretofore. The fact

remains that a reader cannot but be aware of the two-fold nature of *The House of the Seven Gables*: that it is, in spite of Hawthorne's words to the contrary, at once a romance and a novel. So Hawthorne's friend Melville seemed to view it also, in his celebrated letter to Hawthorne of *c*. April 1851. Noting the novel's engaging variety, warmth, and fullness, Melville first pointed out, in effect, that this was new for Hawthorne, and proceeded to compare it to 'a fine old chamber, abundantly, but still judiciously, furnished with precisely that sort of furniture best fitted to furnish it.' And then, a little later in his letter, he noted that Hawthorne was yet the same, that his essential theme was still there: 'There is a certain tragic phase of humanity which, in our opinion, was never more powerfully embodied than by Hawthorne. We mean the tragedies of human thought in its own unbiassed, native, and profounder workings. We think that into no recorded mind has the intense feeling of the visible truth ever entered more deeply than into this man's. By visible truth, we mean the apprehension of the absolute condition of present things as they strike the eye of the man who fears them not. . . .' 'Visible' (Melville's hand was careless enough to allow the possibility that the word is 'usable') truth must be, in this sense, symbolic truth—or rather, truth known symbolically. The writer who would discover such a truth would discover it by virtue of his certainty that it pre-existed, that it was there for the finding and recording. He would be the writer of the tales and *The Scarlet Letter*. But what if he should set himself to move beyond, or at least, apart from, his symbols—even if he was so constituted that he would have, inevitably, to return to them? I suggest that he would move from romance toward the novel—from a relatively bare and single room to one abundantly, but judiciously, furnished. He would write, perhaps, a *House of the Seven Gables*.

ROY HARVEY PEARCE

The Ohio State University,
    March 1954.

SELECT BIBLIOGRAPHY

SEPARATE WORKS. *Fanshawe*, published anonymously, 1828; *Twice-Told Tales*, 1st series, 1837; 2nd series, 1842; *Grandfather's Chair*, a history for youth, 1841; *Famous Old People* (*Grandfather's Chair*), 1841; *Liberty Tree: with the last words of Grandfather's Chair*, 1842; *Biographical Stories for Children*, 1842; *Mosses from an Old Manse*, 1846; *The Scarlet Letter*, 1850; *The House of the Seven Gables*, 1851; *True Stories from History and Biography* (*the whole History of Grandfather's Chair*), 1851; *A Wonder Book for Girls and Boys*, 1851; *The Snow Image and other Tales*, 1851; *The Blithedale Romance*, 1852; *Life of Franklin Pierce*, 1852; *Tanglewood Tales* (2nd series of the *Wonder Book*), 1853; *A Rill from the Town Pump, with remarks by Telba*, 1857; *The Marble Faun; or, the Romance of Monte Beni* (published in England under the title of *Transformation*), 1860; *Our Old Home*, 1863; *Dolliver Romance* (1st part in *Atlantic Monthly*), 1864; in 3 parts, 1876; *Pansie*, a fragment, Hawthorne's last literary effort, 1864; *American Note-Books*, 1868; *English Note-Books*, edited by Sophia Hawthorne, 1870; *French and Italian Note-Books*, 1871; *Septimius Felton; or, the Elixir of Life* (from the *Atlantic Monthly*), 1872; *Doctor Grimshawe's Secret*, with Preface and Notes by Julian Hawthorne, 1882; re-edited from MSS. by E. Davidson, 1954.

Tales of the White Hills, Legends of New England, Legends of the Province House, 1877, contain tales which had already been printed in book form in *Twice-Told Tales* and the *Mosses*; *Sketches and Studies*, 1883.

Hawthorne's contributions to magazines were numerous, and most of his tales appeared first in periodicals, chiefly in *The Token*, 1831–8; *New England Magazine*, 1834, 1835; *Knickerbocker*, 1837–9; *Democratic Review*, 1838–46; *Atlantic Monthly*, 1860–72 (scenes from the *Dolliver Romance*, *Septimius Felton*, and passages from Hawthorne's *Note-Books*).

COLLECTED EDITIONS. In 24 vols., 1879; Riverside Edition, 12 vols. (with introductory notes by G. P. Lathrop), 1883; Standard Library Edition, 15 vols., 1891; New Wayside Edition, 13 vols., 1902; Centenary Edition, 5 vols., 1962–70; *The American Note-Books*, ed. Randall Stewart, 1932; *The English Note-Books*, ed. Randall Stewart, 1941.

BIOGRAPHY AND CRITICISM. Henry James, *Nathaniel Hawthorne*, 1879; Julian Hawthorne, *Nathaniel Hawthorne and His Wife*, 2 vols., 1885; N. Arvin, *Hawthorne*, 1929; R. Stewart, *Nathaniel Hawthorne*, 1948; H. H. Waggoner, *Hawthorne*, 1955; R. R. Male, *Hawthorne's Tragic Vision*, 1957; M. Van Doren, *Nathaniel Hawthorne*, 1957; H. H. Hoeltze, *Inward Sky; the Mind and Heart of Nathaniel Hawthorne*, 1962; R. H. Pearce, ed., *Hawthorne Centenary Essays*, 1964; F. C. Crews, *The Sins of the Fathers: Hawthorne's Psychological Themes*, 1966; R. H. Fogle, *Hawthorne's Imagery*, 1969; J. D. Crowley, ed., *Hawthorne: the Critical Heritage*, 1970.

x   Select Bibliography

GENERAL WORKS. The following works on American literature contain interesting chapters or sections on Hawthorne:

D. H. Lawrence, *Studies in Classic American Literature*, 1923; Y. Winters, *Maule's Curse*, 1938; F. O. Matthiessen, *American Renaissance*, 1941; M. Bewley, *The Complex Fate*, 1952; C. Feidelson, *Symbolism and American Literature*, 1953; R. W. B. Lewis, *The American Adam*, 1955; R. Chase, *The American Novel and Its Tradition*, 1958; H. Levin, *The Power of Blackness*, 1958; M. Bewley, *The Eccentric Design*, 1959; L. Fiedler, *Love and Death in the American Novel*, 1960; M. Green, *Reappraisals*, 1963; L. Marx, *The Machine in the Garden*, 1964; E. Fussell, *Frontier: American Literature and the American West*, 1965; R. Poirier, *A World Elsewhere*, 1966; R. H. Pearce, *Historicism Once More*, 1969.

PREFACE

WHEN a writer calls his work a Romance, it need hardly be observed that he wishes to claim a certain latitude, both as to its fashion and material, which he would not have felt himself entitled to assume, had he professed to be writing a Novel. The latter form of composition is presumed to aim at a very minute fidelity, not merely to the possible, but to the probable and ordinary course of man's experience. The former—while, as a work of art, it must rigidly subject itself to laws, and while it sins unpardonably so far as it may swerve aside from the truth of the human heart—has fairly a right to present that truth under circumstances, to a great extent, of the writer's own choosing or creation. If he think fit, also, he may so manage his atmospherical medium as to bring out or mellow the lights, and deepen and enrich the shadows, of the picture. He will be wise, no doubt, to make a very moderate use of the privileges here stated, and especially to mingle the Marvellous rather as a slight, delicate and evanescent flavour, than as any portion of the actual substance of the dish offered to the public. He can hardly be said, however, to commit a literary crime, even if he disregard this caution.

In the present work, the author has proposed to himself—but with what success, fortunately, it is not for him to judge—to keep undeviatingly within his immunities. The point of view in which this tale comes under the Romantic definition lies in the attempt to connect a by-gone time with the very present that is flitting away from us. It is a legend, prolonging itself from an epoch now gray in the distance, down into our own broad daylight, and bringing along with it some of its legendary mist, which the reader, according to his pleasure, may either disregard, or allow it to float almost imperceptibly about the characters and events, for the sake of a picturesque effect. The narrative, it may be, is woven of so humble a texture as to require this advantage, and, at the same time, to render it the more difficult of attainment.

Many writers lay very great stress upon some definite Moral purpose, at which they profess to aim their works. Not to be deficient in this particular, the author has provided himself with a moral ;—the truth, namely, that the wrong-doing of one generation lives into the successive ones, and, divesting itself of every temporary advantage, becomes a pure and uncontrollable mischief ; and he would feel it a singular gratification, if this romance might effectually convince mankind—or, indeed, any one man—of the folly of tumbling down an avalanche of ill-gotten gold, or real estate, on the heads of an unfortunate posterity, thereby to maim and crush them, until the accumulated mass shall be scattered abroad in its original atoms. In good faith, however, he is not sufficiently imaginative to flatter himself with the slightest hope of this kind. When romances do really teach anything, or produce any effective operation, it is usually hrough a far more subtile process than the ostensible one The author has considered it hardly worth his while, therefore, relentlessly to impale the story with its moral, as with an iron rod—or rather as by sticking a pin through a butterfly—thus at once depriving it of life, and causing it to stiffen in an ungainly and unnatural attitude. A high truth, indeed, fairly, finely, and skilfully wrought out, brightening at every step, and crowning the final development of a work of fiction, may add an artistic glory, but is never any truer, and seldom any more evident, at the last page than at the first.

The reader may perhaps choose to assign an actual locality to the imaginary events of this narrative. If permitted by the historical connection—which, though slight, was essential to his plan—the author would very willingly have avoided anything of this nature. Not to speak of other objections, it exposes the romance to an inflexible and exceeding dangerous species of criticism, by bringing his fancy pictures almost into positive contact with the realities of the moment. It has been no part of his object, however, to describe local manners, nor in any way to meddle with the characteristics of a community for whom he cherishes a proper respect and a natural regard. He trusts not to be considered as unpardonably offending, by laying out a street that infringes upon nobody's private rights, and appropriating a lot of land which had no visible owner, and building a house of materials long in use for constructing castles in the air. The personages of the tale—though they give themselves out to be of ancient stability and considerable prominence—are really of the author's own making, or, at all events, of his own mixing; their virtues can shed no lustre, nor their defects redound, in the remotest degree, to the discredit of the venerable town of which they profess to be inhabitants. He would be glad, therefore, if—especially in the quarter to which he alludes—the book may be read strictly as a Romance, having a great deal more to do with the clouds overhead than with any portion of the actual soil of the County of Essex.

LENOX,
January 27, 1851.

CONTENTS

I

THE OLD PYNCHEON FAMILY

HALF-WAY down a bye-street of one of our New England towns stands a rusty wooden house, with seven acutely-peaked gables, facing towards various points of the compass, and a huge clustered chimney in the midst. The street is Pyncheon-street; the house is the old Pyncheon-house; and an elm-tree, of wide circumference, rooted before the door, is familiar to every town-born child by the title of the Pyncheon-elm. On my occasional visits to the town aforesaid, I seldom fail to turn down Pyncheon-street, for the sake of passing through the shadow of these two antiquities,—the great elm-tree, and the weather-beaten edifice.

The aspect of the venerable mansion has always affected me like a human countenance, bearing the traces not merely of outward storm and sunshine, but expressive, also, of the long lapse of mortal life, and accompanying vicissitudes that have passed within. Were these to be worthily recounted, they would form a narrative of no small interest and instruction, and possessing, moreover, a certain remarkable unity, which might almost seem the result of artistic arrangement. But the story would include a chain of events extending over the better part of two centuries, and written out with reasonable amplitude, would fill a bigger folio volume, or a longer series of duodecimos, than could prudently be appropriated to the annals of all New England during a similar period. It consequently becomes imperative to make short work with most of the traditional lore of which the old Pyncheon-house, otherwise known as the House of the Seven Gables, has been the theme. With a brief sketch, therefore, of the circumstances amid which the foundation of the house was laid, and a rapid glimpse at its quaint exterior, as it grew black in the prevalent east wind,—pointing too, here and there, at some spot of more verdant mossiness on its roof and walls,—we shall commence the real action of our tale at an epoch not very remote from the present day. Still there will be a connection with the long past—a reference to forgotten events and personages, and to manners, feelings, and opinions almost or wholly obsolete— which, if adequately translated to the reader, would serve to illustrate how much of old material goes to make up the freshest novelty of human life. Hence, too, might be drawn a weighty lesson from the little-regarded truth, that the act of the passing generation is the germ which may and must produce good or evil fruit, in a far distant time; that, together with the seed of the merely temporary crop, which mortals term expediency, they inevitably sow the acorns of a more enduring growth, which may darkly overshadow their posterity.

The House of the Seven Gables, antique as it now looks, was not the first habitation erected by civilized man on precisely the same spot of ground. Pyncheon-street formerly bore the humbler appellation of Maule's-lane, from the name of the original occupant of the soil, before whose cottage-door it was a cow-path. A natural spring of soft and pleasant water— a rare treasure on the sea-girt peninsula where the Puritan settlement was made—had early induced Matthew Maule to build a hut, shaggy with thatch, at this point, although somewhat too remote from what was then the centre of the village. In the

growth of the town, however, after some thirty or
forty years, the site covered by this rude hovel had
become exceedingly desirable in the eyes of a prominent and powerful personage, who asserted plausible
claims to the proprietorship of this and a large
adjacent tract of land, on the strength of a grant
from the legislature. Colonel Pyncheon, the claimant,
as we gather from whatever traits of him are preserved,
was characterized by an iron energy of purpose.
Matthew Maule, on the other hand, though an obscure
man, was stubborn in the defence of what he considered his right; and, for several years, he succeeded
in protecting the acre or two of earth which, with his
own toil, he had hewn out of the primæval forest, to
be his garden-ground and homestead. No written
record of this dispute is known to be in existence.
Our acquaintance with the whole subject is derived
chiefly from tradition. It would be bold, therefore,
and possibly unjust to venture a decisive opinion as
to its merits; although it appears to have been at
least a matter of doubt, whether Colonel Pyncheon's
claim were not unduly stretched, in order to make
it cover the small metes and bounds of Matthew
Maule. What greatly strengthens such a suspicion
is the fact that this controversy between two ill-
matched antagonists—at a period, moreover, laud
it as we may, when personal influence had far more
weight than now—remained for years undecided, and
came to a close only with the death of the party
occupying the disputed soil. The mode of his death,
too, affects the mind differently in our day, from
what it did a century and a half ago. It was a death
that blasted with strange horror the humble name of
the dweller in the cottage, and made it seem almost a
religious act to drive the plough over the little area
of his habitation, and obliterate his place and memory
from among men.

Old Matthew Maule, in a word, was executed for
the crime of witchcraft. He was one of the martyrs
to that terrible delusion which should teach us, among

its other morals, that the influential classes, and those
who take upon themselves to be leaders of the people,
are fully liable to all the passionate error that has
ever characterized the maddest mob.   Clergymen,
judges, statesmen,—the wisest, calmest, holiest
persons of their day,—stood in the inner circle round
about the gallows, loudest to applaud the work of
blood, latest to confess themselves miserably deceived.
If any one part of their proceedings can be said to
deserve less blame than another, it was the singular
indiscrimination with which they persecuted, not
merely the poor and aged, as in former judicial
massacres, but people of all ranks; their own equals,
brethren and wives.   Amid the disorder of such
various ruin, it is not strange that a man of incon-
siderable note, like Maule, should have trodden the
martyr's path to the hill of execution almost unre-
marked in the throng of his fellow-sufferers.   But, in
after days, when the frenzy of that hideous epoch had
subsided, it was remembered how loudly Colonel
Pyncheon had joined in the general cry, to purge the
land from witchcraft; nor did it fail to be whispered
that there was an invidious acrimony in the zeal with
which he had sought the condemnation of Matthew
Maule.   It was well known that the victim had recognized the bitterness of personal enmity in his persecutor's conduct towards him, and that he declared
himself hunted to death for his spoil.   At the moment
of execution—with the halter about his neck, and
while Colonel Pyncheon sat on horseback grimly
gazing at the scene—Maule had addressed him from
the scaffold, and uttered a prophecy, of which history,
as well as fireside tradition, has preserved the very
words.   "God," said the dying man, pointing his
finger, with a ghastly look, at the undismayed countenance of his enemy, "God will give him blood to
drink!"

After the reputed wizard's death, his humble homestead had fallen an easy spoil into Colonel Pyncheon's
grasp.   When it was understood, however, that the

colonel intended to erect a family mansion—spacious, ponderously framed of oaken timber, and calculated to endure for many generations of his prosperity—over the spot first covered by the log-built hut of Matthew Maule, there was much shaking of the head among the village gossips. Without absolutely expressing a doubt whether the stalwart Puritan had acted as a man of conscience and integrity, throughout the proceedings which have been sketched, they, nevertheless, hinted that he was about to build his house over an unquiet grave. His home would include the home of the dead and buried wizard, and would thus afford the ghost of the latter a kind of privilege to haunt its new apartments, and the chambers into which future bridegrooms were to lead their brides, and where children of the Pyncheon blood were to be born. The terror and ugliness of Maule's crime, and the wretchedness of his punishment, would darken the freshly-plastered walls, and infect them early with the scent of an old and melancholy house. Why, then,—while so much of the soil around him was bestrewn with the virgin forest-leaves,—why should Colonel Pyncheon prefer a site that had already been accurst?

But the Puritan soldier and magistrate was not a man to be turned aside from his well-considered scheme, either by dread of the wizard's ghost, or by flimsy sentimentalities of any kind, however specious. Had he been told of a bad air, it might have moved him somewhat; but he was ready to encounter an evil spirit on his own ground. Endowed with common sense, as massive and hard as blocks of granite, fastened together by stern rigidity of purpose, as with iron clamps, he followed out his original design, probably without so much as imagining an objection to it. On the score of delicacy, or any scrupulousness which a finer sensibility might have taught him, the colonel, like most of his breed and generation, was impenetrable. He, therefore, dug his cellar, and laid the deep foundations of his mansion, on the square of earth whence Matthew Maule, forty years before, had first swept away the fallen leaves. It was a curious, and, as some people thought, an ominous fact, that, very soon after the workmen began their operations, the spring of water, above mentioned, entirely lost the deliciousness of its pristine quality. Whether its sources were disturbed by the depth of the new cellar, or whatever subtler cause might lurk at the bottom, it is certain that the water of Maule's Well, as it continued to be called, grew hard and brackish. Even such we find it now; and any old woman of the neighbourhood will certify that it is productive of intestinal mischief to those who quench their thirst there.

The reader may deem it singular that the head carpenter of the new edifice was no other than the son of the very man from whose dead gripe the property of the soil had been wrested. Not improbably he was the best workman of his time; or, perhaps, the colonel thought it expedient, or was impelled by some better feeling, thus openly to cast aside all animosity against the race of his fallen antagonist. Nor was it out of keeping with the general coarseness and matter-of-fact character of the age, that the son should be willing to earn an honest penny, or, rather, a weighty amount of sterling pounds, from the purse of his father's deadly enemy. At all events, Thomas Maule became the architect of the House of the Seven Gables, and performed his duty so faithfully that the timber framework, fastened by his hands, still holds together.

Thus the great house was built. Familiar as it stands in the writer's recollection,—for it has been an object of curiosity with him from boyhood, both as a specimen of the best and stateliest architecture of a long-past epoch, and as the scene of events more full of human interest, perhaps, than those of a gray feudal castle,—familiar as it stands, in its rusty old age, it is therefore only the more difficult to imagine the bright novelty with which it first caught the sun-

shine. The impression of its actual state, at this
distance of a hundred and sixty years, darkens, inevitably, through the picture which we would fain
give of its appearance on the morning when the Puritan magnate bade all the town to be his guests. A
ceremony of consecration, festive as well as religious,
was now to be performed. A prayer and discourse
from the Rev. Mr. Higginson, and the outpouring
of a psalm from the general throat of the community,
was to be made acceptable to the grosser sense by
ale, cider, wine, and brandy, in copious effusion, and,
as some authorities aver, by an ox, roasted whole,
or, at least, by the weight and substance of an ox, in
more manageable joints and sirloins. The carcass
of a deer, shot within twenty miles, had supplied
material for the vast circumference of a pasty. A
cod-fish, of sixty pounds, caught in the bay, had been
dissolved into the rich liquid of a chowder. The
chimney of the new house, in short, belching forth its
kitchen-smoke, impregnated the whole air with the
scent of meats, fowls, and fishes, spicily concocted
with odoriferous herbs, and onions in abundance. The
mere smell of such festivity, making its way to everybody's nostrils, was at once an invitation and appetite.

Maule's-lane, or Pyncheon-street, as it were now
more decorous to call it, was thronged, at the ap-
pointed hour, as with a congregation on its way to
church. All, as they approached, looked upward at
the imposing edifice, which was henceforth to assume
its rank among the habitations of mankind. There
it rose, a little withdrawn from the life of the street,
but in pride, not modesty. Its whole visible exterior
was ornamented with quaint figures, conceived in
the grotesqueness of a gothic fancy, and drawn or
stamped in the glittering plaster, composed of lime,
pebbles, and bits of glass, with which the wood-work
of the walls was overspread. On every side, the
seven gables pointed sharply towards the sky, and
presented the aspect of a whole sisterhood of

edifices, breathing through the spiracles of one great
chimney.   The many lattices, with their small,
diamond-shaped panes, admitted the sunlight into hall
and chamber, while, nevertheless, the second story,
projecting far over the base, and itself retiring beneath the third, threw a shadow and thoughtful gloom
into the lower rooms.   Carved globes of wood were
affixed under the jutting stories.   Little spiral rods of
iron beautified each of the seven peaks.   On the
triangular portion of the gable that fronted next the
street, was a dial, put up that very morning, and on
which the sun was still marking the passage of the
first bright hour in a history that was not destined to
be all so bright.   All around were scattered shavings,
chips, shingles, and broken halves of bricks ; these,
together with the lately turned earth, on which the
grass had not begun to grow, contributed to the impression of strangeness and novelty proper to a house
that had yet its place to make among men's daily
interests.

The principal entrance, which had almost the
breadth of a church-door, was in the angle between
the two front gables, and was covered by an open
porch, with benches beneath its shelter.   Under this
arched door-way, scraping their feet on the unworn
threshold, now trod the clergymen, the elders, the
magistrates, the deacons, and whatever of aristocracy
there was in town or country.   Thither, too, thronged
the plebeian classes, as freely as their betters, and in
larger number.   Just within the entrance, however,
stood two serving-men, pointing some of the guests
to the neighbourhood of the kitchen, and ushering
others into the statelier rooms,—hospitable alike to
all, but still with a scrutinizing regard to the high or
low degree of each.   Velvet garments, sombre but
rich, stiffly-plaited ruffs and bands, embroidered
gloves, venerable beards, the mien and countenance
of authority, made it easy to distinguish the gentleman of worship, at that period, from the tradesman,
with his plodding air, or the labourer, in his leathern

jerkin, stealing awe-stricken into the house which he had perhaps helped to build.

One inauspicious circumstance there was, which awakened a hardly-concealed displeasure in the breasts of a few of the more punctilious visitors. The founder of this stately mansion—a gentleman noted for the square and ponderous courtesy of his demeanour—ought surely to have stood in his own hall, and to have offered the first welcome to so many eminent personages as here presented themselves in honour of his solemn festival. He was as yet invisible; the most favoured of the guests had not beheld him. This sluggishness on Colonel Pyncheon's part became still more unaccountable, when the second dignitary of the province made his appearance, and found no more ceremonious a reception. The lieutenant-governor, although his visit was one of the anticipated glories of the day, had alighted from his horse, and assisted his lady from her side-saddle, and crossed the colonel's threshold, without other greeting than that of the principal domestic.

This person—a gray-headed man, of quiet and most respectful deportment—found it necessary to explain that his master still remained in his study, or private apartment; on entering which, an hour before, he had expressed a wish on no account to be disturbed.

"Do not you see, fellow," said the high sheriff of the county, taking the servant aside, "that this is no less a man than the lieutenant-governor? Summon Colonel Pyncheon at once! I know that he received letters from England this morning; and, in the perusal and consideration of them, an hour may have passed away without his noticing it. But he will be ill-pleased, I judge, if you suffer him to neglect the courtesy due to one of our chief rulers, and who may be said to represent King William, in the absence of the governor himself. Call your master instantly!"

"Nay, please your worship," answered the man,

in much perplexity, but with a backwardness that strikingly indicated the hard and severe character of Colonel Pyncheon's domestic rule; " my master's orders were exceedingly strict; and, as your worship knows, he permits of no discretion in the obedience of those who owe him service. Let who list open yonder door; I dare not, though the governor's own voice should bid me do it!"

" Pooh, pooh, master high sheriff!" cried the lieutenant-governor, who had overheard the fore-going discussion, and felt himself high enough in station to play a little with his dignity. " I will take the matter into my own hands. It is time that the good colonel came forth to greet his friends; else we shall be apt to suspect that he has taken a sip too much of his Canary wine, in his extreme deliberation which cask it were best to broach, in honour of the day! But since he is so much behindhand, I will give him a remembrancer myself!"

Accordingly, with such a tramp of his ponderous riding-boots as might of itself have been audible in the remotest of the seven gables, he advanced to the door, which the servant pointed out, and made its new panels re-echo with a loud, free knock. Then, looking round, with a smile, to the spectators, he awaited a response. As none came, however, he knocked again, but with the same unsatisfactory result as at first. And now, being a trifle choleric in his temperament, the lieutenant-governor uplifted the heavy hilt of his sword, wherewith he so beat and banged upon the door, that, as some of the by-standers whispered, the racket might have disturbed the dead. Be that as it might, it seemed to produce no awakening effect on Colonel Pyncheon. When the sound subsided, the silence through the house was deep, dreary, and oppressive, notwithstanding that the tongues of many of the guests had already been loosened by a surreptitious cup or two of wine or spirits.

" Strange, forsooth!—very strange!" cried the

lieutenant-governor, whose smile was changed to a frown. "But seeing that our host sets us the good example of forgetting ceremony, I shall likewise throw it aside, and make free to intrude on his privacy!"

He tried the door, which yielded to his hand, and was flung wide open by a sudden gust of wind that passed, as with a loud sigh, from the outermost portal, through all the passages and apartments of the new house. It rustled the silken garments of the ladies, and waved the long curls of the gentlemen's wigs, and shook the window-hangings and the curtains of the bed-chambers; causing everywhere a singular stir, which was yet more like a hush. A shadow of awe and half-fearful anticipation—nobody knew wherefore, nor of what—had all at once fallen over the company.

They thronged, however, to the now open door, pressing the lieutenant-governor, in the eagerness of their curiosity, into the room in advance of them. At the first glimpse, they beheld nothing extraordinary; a handsomely-furnished room, of moderate size, somewhat darkened by curtains; books arranged on shelves; a large map on the wall, and likewise a portrait of Colonel Pyncheon, beneath which sat the original colonel himself, in an oaken elbow-chair, with a pen in his hand. Letters, parchments, and blank sheets of paper were on the table before him. He appeared to gaze at the curious crowd, in front of which stood the lieutenant-governor; and there was a frown on his dark and massive countenance, as if sternly resentful of the boldness that had impelled them into his private retirement.

A little boy—the colonel's grandchild, and the only human being that ever dared to be familiar with him—now made his way among the guests, and ran towards the seated figure; then pausing half-way, he began to shriek with terror. The company, tremulous as the leaves of a tree, when all are shaking together, drew nearer, and perceived that there was an unnatural distortion in the fixedness of Colonel Pyncheon's stare; that there was blood on his ruff, and that his hoary beard was saturated with it. It was too late to give assistance. The iron-hearted Puritan, the relentless persecutor, the grasping and strong-willed man, was dead! Dead, in his new house! There is a tradition, only worth alluding to as lending a tinge of superstitious awe to a scene perhaps gloomy enough without it, that a voice spoke loudly among the guests, the tones of which were like those of old Matthew Maule, the executed wizard,—" God hath given him blood to drink!"

Thus early had that one guest—the only guest who is certain, at one time or another, to find his way into every human dwelling—thus early had Death stepped across the threshold of the House of the Seven Gables!

Colonel Pyncheon's sudden and mysterious end made a vast deal of noise in its day. There were many rumours, some of which have vaguely drifted down to the present time, how that appearances indicated violence; that there were the marks of fingers on his throat, and the print of a bloody hand on his plaited ruff; and that his peaked beard was dishevelled, as if it had been fiercely clutched and pulled. It was averred, likewise, that the lattice-window, near the Colonel's chair, was open; and that, only a few minutes before the fatal occurrence, the figure of a man had been seen clambering over the garden-fence, in the rear of the house. But it were folly to lay any stress on stories of this kind, which are sure to spring up around such an event as that now related, and which, as in the present case, sometimes prolong themselves for ages afterwards, like the toadstools that indicate where the fallen and buried trunk of a tree has long since mouldered into the earth. For our own part, we allow them just as little credence as to that other fable of the skeleton hand which the lieutenant-governor was said to have

seen at the colonel's throat, but which vanished
away as he advanced further into the room.   Certain
it is, however, that there was a great consultation
and dispute of doctors over the dead body.   One—
John Swinnerton by name—who appears to have
been a man of eminence, upheld it, if we have rightly
understood his terms of art, to be a case of apoplexy.
His professional brethren, each for himself, adopted
various hypotheses, more or less plausible, but all
dressed out in a perplexing mystery of phrase, which,
if it do not show a bewilderment of mind in these
erudite physicians, certainly causes it in the unlearned
peruser of their opinions.   The coroner's jury sat
upon the corpse, and, like sensible men, returned an
unassailable verdict of " Sudden Death !"

It is indeed difficult to imagine that there could
have been a serious suspicion of murder, or the
slightest grounds for implicating any particular individual as the perpetrator.   The rank, wealth, and
eminent character of the deceased, must have insured
the strictest scrutiny into every ambiguous circumstance.   As none such is on record, it is safe to
assume that none existed.   Tradition—which sometimes brings down truth that history has let slip,
but is oftener the wild babble of the time, such as
was formerly spoken at the fireside, and now con-
geals in newspapers—tradition is responsible for all
contrary averments.   In Colonel Pyncheon's funeral
sermon, which was printed, and is still extant, the
Rev. Mr. Higginson enumerates among the many
felicities of his distinguished parishioner's earthly
career, the happy seasonableness of his death.   His
duties all performed,—the highest prosperity attained,—his race and future generations fixed on a
stable basis, and with a stately roof to shelter them,
for centuries to come,—what other upward step
remained for this good man to take, save the final
step from earth to the golden gate of heaven !   The
pious clergyman surely would not have uttered words
like these, had he in the least suspected that the

colonel had been thrust into the other world with the clutch of violence upon his throat.

The family of Colonel Pyncheon, at the epoch of his death, seemed destined to as fortunate a permanence as can anywise consist with the inherent instability of human affairs. It might fairly be anticipated that the progress of time would rather increase and ripen their prosperity, than wear away and destroy it. For, not only had his son and heir come into immediate enjoyment of a rich estate, but there was a claim, through an Indian deed, confirmed by a subsequent grant of the General Court, to a vast and as yet unexplored and unmeasured tract of eastern lands. These possessions—for as such they might almost certainly be reckoned—comprised the greater part of what is now known as Waldo County, in the State of Maine, and were more extensive than many a dukedom, or even a reigning prince's territory, on European soil. When the pathless forest, that still covered this wild principality, should give place—as it inevitably must, though perhaps not till ages hence—to the golden fertility of human culture, it would be the source of incalculable wealth to the Pyncheon blood. Had the colonel survived only a few weeks longer, it is probable that his great political influence, and powerful connections, at home and abroad, would have consummated all that was necessary to render the claim available. But, in spite of good Mr. Higginson's congratulatory eloquence, this appeared to be the one thing which Colonel Pyncheon, provident and sagacious as he was, had allowed to go at loose ends. So far as the prospective territory was concerned, he unquestionably died too soon. His son lacked not merely the father's eminent position, but the talent and force of character to achieve it : he could, therefore, effect nothing by dint of political interest; and the bare justice or legality of the claim was not so apparent, after the colonel's decease, as it had been pronounced in his lifetime. Some connecting link had slipped

out of the evidence, and could not anywhere be
found.

Efforts, it is true, were made by the Pyncheons,
not only then, but at various periods for nearly a
hundred years afterwards, to obtain what they stub-
bornly persisted in deeming their right. But, in
course of time, the territory was partly re-granted
to more favoured individuals, and partly cleared and
occupied by actual settlers. These last, if they ever
heard of the Pyncheon title, would have laughed at
the idea of any man's asserting a right—on the
strength of mouldy parchments, signed with the
faded autographs of governors and legislators long
dead and forgotten—to the lands which they or their
fathers had wrested from the wild hand of nature,
by their own sturdy toil. This impalpable claim,
therefore, resulted in nothing more solid than to
cherish, from generation to generation, an absurd
delusion of family importance, which all along characterized the Pyncheons. It caused the poorest member
of the race to feel as if he inherited a kind of nobility,
and might yet come into the possession of princely
wealth to support it. In the better specimens of the
breed, this peculiarity threw an ideal grace over the
hard material of human life, without stealing away
any truly valuable quality. In the baser sort, its
effect was to increase the liability to sluggishness
and dependence, and induce the victim of a shadowy
hope to remit all self-effort, while awaiting the
realization of his dreams. Years and years after
their claim had passed out of the public memory,
the Pyncheons were accustomed to consult the
colonel's ancient map, which had been projected
while Waldo County was still an unbroken wilderness. Where the old land-surveyor had put down
woods, lakes, and rivers, they marked out the cleared
spaces, and dotted the villages and towns, and calculated the progressively increasing value of the
territory, as if there were yet a prospect of its ultimately forming a princedom for themselves.

In almost every generation, nevertheless, there happened to be some one descendant of the family gifted with a portion of the hard, keen sense and practical energy, that had so remarkably distinguished the original founder.   His character, indeed, might be traced all the way down, as distinctly as if the colonel himself, a little diluted, had been gifted with a sort of intermittent immortality on earth.   At two or three epochs, when the fortunes of the family were low, this representative of hereditary qualities had made his appearance, and caused the traditionary gossips of the town to whisper among themselves: —" Here is the old Pyncheon come again ! Now the Seven Gables will be new shingled !"   From father to son, they clung to the ancestral house, with singular tenacity of home attachment.   For various reasons, however, and from impressions often too vaguely founded to be put on paper, the writer cherishes the belief that many, if not most, of the successive proprietors of this estate, were troubled with doubts as to their moral right to hold it.   Of their legal tenure there could be no question ; but old Matthew Maule, it is to be feared, trod downward from his own age to a far later one, planting a heavy footstep, all the way, on the conscience of a Pyncheon.   If so, we are left to dispose of the awful query, whether each inheritor of the property— conscious of wrong, and failing to rectify it—did not commit anew the great guilt of his ancestor, and incur all its original responsibilities.   And supposing such to be the case, would it not be a far truer mode of expression to say, of the Pyncheon family, that they inherited a great misfortune, than the reverse?

We have already hinted, that it is not our purpose to trace down the history of the Pyncheon family, in its unbroken connection with the House of the Seven Gables ; nor to show, as in a magic picture, how the rustiness and infirmity of age gathered over the venerable house itself.   As regards its interior life, a large, dim looking-glass used to hang in one of the

rooms, and was fabled to contain within its depths
all the shapes that had ever been reflected there,—
the old colonel himself, and his many descendants,
some in the garb of antique babyhood, and others
in the bloom of feminine beauty or manly prime, or
saddened with the wrinkles of frosty age. Had we
the secret of that mirror, we would gladly sit down
before it, and transfer its revelations to our page.
But there was a story, for which it is difficult to
conceive any foundation, that the posterity of
Matthew Maule had some connection with the
mystery of the looking-glass, and that, by what
appears to have been a sort of mesmeric process,
they could make its inner region all alive with the
departed Pyncheons; not as they had shown themselves to the world, nor in their better and happier
hours, but as doing over again some deed of sin, or
in the crisis of life's bitterest sorrow. The popular
imagination, indeed, long kept itself busy with the
affair of the old Puritan Pyncheon and the wizard
Maule; the curse, which the latter flung from his
scaffold, was remembered, with the very important
addition, that it had become a part of the Pyncheon
inheritance. If one of the family did but gurgle in
his throat, a bystander would be likely enough to
whisper, between jest and earnest,—" He has
Maule's blood to drink !" The sudden death of a
Pyncheon about a hundred years ago, with circumstances very similar to what have been related of
the colonel's exit, was held as giving additional probability to the received opinion on this topic. It was
considered, moveover, an ugly and ominous circumstance, that Colonel Pyncheon's picture—in obedience, it was said, to a provision of his will—remained
affixed to the wall of the room in which he died.
Those stern, immitigable features seemed to symbolize an evil influence, and so darkly to mingle the
shadow of their presence with the sunshine of the
passing hour, that no good thoughts or purposes
could ever spring up and blossom there. To the

thoughtful mind, there will be no tinge of superstition in what we figuratively express, by affirming that the ghost of a dead progenitor—perhaps as a portion of his own punishment—is often doomed to become the Evil Genius of his family.

The Pyncheons, in brief, lived along, for the better part of two centuries, with perhaps less of outward vicissitude than has attended most other New England families, during the same period of time. Possessing very distinctive traits of their own, they nevertheless took the general characteristics of the little community in which they dwelt; a town noted for its frugal, discreet, well-ordered, and home-loving inhabitants, as well as for the somewhat confined scope of its sympathies; but in which, be it said, there are odder individuals, and now and then stranger occurrences, than one meets with almost anywhere else. During the Revolution, the Pyncheon of that epoch, adopting the royal side, became a refugee; but repented, and made his reappearance, just at the point of time to preserve the House of the Seven Gables from confiscation. For the last seventy years, the most noted event in the Pyncheon annals had been likewise the heaviest calamity that ever befell the race; no less than the violent death—for so it was adjudged—of one member of the family, by the criminal act of another. Certain circumstances, attending this fatal occurrence, had brought the deed irresistibly home to a nephew of the deceased Pyncheon. The young man was tried and convicted of the crime; but either the circumstantial nature of the evidence, and possibly some lurking doubt in the breast of the executive, or lastly,—an argument of greater weight in a republic than it could have been under a monarchy,—the high respectability and political influence of the criminal's connections, had availed to mitigate his doom from death to perpetual imprisonment. This sad affair had chanced about thirty years before the action of our story commences. Latterly, there were rumours (which few believed, and only one or two felt greatly interested in) that this long-buried man was likely, for some reason or other, to be summoned forth from his living tomb.

It is essential to say a few words respecting the victim of this now almost forgotten murder. He was an old bachelor, and possessed of great wealth, in addition to the house and real estate which constituted what remained of the ancient Pyncheon property. Being of an eccentric and melancholy turn of mind, and greatly given to rummaging old records, and hearkening to old traditions, he had brought himself, it is averred, to the conclusion, that Matthew Maule, the wizard, had been foully wronged out of his homestead, if not out of his life. Such being the case, and he, the old bachelor, in possession of the ill-gotten spoil—with the black stain of blood sunken deep into it, and still to be scented by conscientious nostrils—the question occurred, whether it were not imperative upon him, even at this late hour, to make restitution to Maule's posterity. To a man living so much in the past, and so little in the present, as the secluded and antiquarian old bachelor, a century and a half seemed not so vast a period as to obviate the propriety of substituting right for wrong. It was the belief of those who knew him best, that he would positively have taken the very singular step of giving up the House of the Seven Gables to the representative of Matthew Maule, but for the unspeakable tumult which a suspicion of the old gentleman's project awakened among his Pyncheon relatives. Their exertions had the effect of suspending his purpose; but it was feared that he would perform, after death, by the operation of his last will, what he had so hardly been prevented from doing in his proper lifetime. But there is no one thing which men so rarely do, whatever the provocation or inducement, as to bequeath patrimonial property away from their own blood. They may love other individuals far better than their relatives,—they may even cherish dislike or positive hatred to the latter;

but yet, in view of death, the strong prejudice of propinquity revives, and impels the testator to send down his estate in the line marked out by custom so immemorial that it looks like nature. In all the Pyncheons, this feeling had the energy of disease. It was too powerful for the conscientious scruples of the old bachelor; at whose death, accordingly, the mansion-house, together with most of his other riches, passed into the possession of his next legal representative.

This was a nephew, the cousin of the miserable young man who had been convicted of the uncle's murder. The new heir, up to the period of his accession, was reckoned rather a dissipated youth, but had at once reformed, and made himself an exceedingly respectable member of society. In fact, he showed more of the Pyncheon quality, and had won higher eminence in the world, than any of his race, since the time of the original Puritan. Applying himself in earlier manhood to the study of the law, and having a natural tendency towards office, he had attained, many years ago, to a judicial situation in some inferior court, which gave him for life the very desirable and imposing title of judge. Later, he had engaged in politics, and served a part of two terms in Congress, besides making a considerable figure in both branches of the state legislature. Judge Pyncheon was unquestionably an honour to his race. He had built himself a country seat within a few miles of his native town, and there spent such portions of his time as could be spared from public service in the display of every grace and virtue—as a newspaper phrased it on the eve of an election— befitting the Christian, the good citizen, the horticulturalist, and the gentleman.

There were few of the Pyncheons left to sun themselves in the glow of the judge's prosperity. In respect to natural increase, the breed had not thriven; it appeared rather to be dying out. The only members of the family known to be extant were, first, the judge himself, and a single surviving son, who was now travelling in Europe; next, the thirty years' prisoner, already alluded to, and a sister of the latter, who occupied, in an extremely retired manner, the House of the Seven Gables, in which she had a life-estate by the will of the old bachelor. She was understood to be wretchedly poor, and seemed to make it her choice to remain so; inasmuch as her affluent cousin, the judge, had repeatedly offered her all the comforts of life, either in the old mansion or his own modern residence. The last and youngest Pyncheon was a little country-girl of seventeen, the daughter of another of the judge's cousins, who had married a young woman of no family or property, and died early, and in poor circumstances. His widow had recently taken another husband.

As for Matthew Maule's posterity, it was supposed now to be extinct. For a very long period after the witchcraft delusion, however, the Maules had continued to inhabit the town where their progenitor had suffered so unjust a death. To all appearance, they were a quiet, honest, well-meaning race of people, cherishing no malice against individuals or the public, for the wrong which had been done them; or if, at their own fireside, they transmitted, from father to child, any hostile recollections of the wizard's fate, and their lost patrimony, it was never acted upon, nor openly expressed. Nor would it have been singular had they ceased to remember that the House of the Seven Gables was resting its heavy frame-work on a foundation that was rightfully their own. There is something so massive, stable, and almost irresistibly imposing, in the exterior present-ment of established rank and great possessions, that their very existence seems to give them a right to exist; at least, so excellent a counterfeit of right, that few poor and humble men have moral force enough to question it, even in their secret minds. Such is the case now, after so many ancient pre-judices have been overthrown; and it was far more so in ante-revolutionary days, when the aristocracy could venture to be proud, and the low were content to be abased. Thus the Maules, at all events, kept their resentments within their own breasts. They were generally poverty-stricken; always plebeian and obscure; working with unsuccessful diligence at handicrafts; labouring on the wharves, or following the sea, as sailors before the mast; living here and there about the town, in hired tenements, and coming finally to the almshouse, as the natural home of their old age. At last, after creeping, as it were, for such a length of time, along the utmost verge of the opaque puddle of obscurity, they had taken that downright plunge, which, sooner or later, is the destiny of all families, whether princely or plebeian. For thirty years past, neither town-record, nor gravestone, nor the directory, nor the knowledge or memory of man, bore any trace of Matthew Maule's descendants. His blood might possibly exist elsewhere; here, where its lowly current could be traced so far back, it had ceased to keep an onward course.

So long as any of the race were to be found, they had been marked out from other men—not strikingly, nor as with a sharp line, but with an effect that was felt, rather than spoken of—by an hereditary character of reserve. Their companions, or those who endeavoured to become such, grew conscious of a circle round about the Maules, within the sanctity or the spell of which, in spite of an exterior of sufficient frankness and good-fellowship, it was impossible for any man to step. It was this indefinable peculiarity, perhaps, that, by insulating them from human aid, kept them always so unfortunate in life. It certainly operated to prolong, in their case, and to confirm to them, as their only inheritance, those feelings of repugnance and superstitious terror with which the people of the town, even after awakening from their frenzy, continued to regard the memory of the reputed witches. The mantle, or rather the ragged cloak, of old Matthew

Maule, had fallen upon his children. They were half believed to inherit mysterious attributes; the family eye was said to possess strange power. Among other good-for-nothing properties and privileges, one was especially assigned them : of exercising an influence over people's dreams. The Pyncheons, if all stories were true, haughtily as they bore themselves in the noon-day streets of their native town, were no better than bond-servants to those plebeian Maules, on entering the topsy-turvy commonwealth of sleep. Modern psychology, it may be, will endeavour to reduce these alleged necromancies within a system, instead of rejecting them as altogether fabulous.

A descriptive paragraph or two, treating of the seven-gabled mansion in its more recent aspect, will bring this preliminary chapter to a close. The street in which it upreared its venerable peaks has long ceased to be a fashionable quarter of the town ; so that, though the old edifice was surrounded by habitations of modern date, they were mostly small, built entirely of wood, and typical of the most plodding uniformity of common life. Doubtless, however, the whole story of human existence may be latent in each of them, but with no picturesqueness, externally, that can attract the imagination or sympathy to seek it there. But as for the old structure of our story, its white-oak frame, and its boards, shingles, and crumbling plaster, and even the huge clustered chimney in the midst, seemed to constitute only the least and meanest part of its reality. So much of mankind's varied experience had passed there,—so much had been suffered, and something, too, enjoyed,—that the very timbers were oozy, as with the moisture of a heart. It was itself like a great human heart, with a life of its own, and full of rich and sombre reminiscences.

The deep projection of the second story gave the house such a meditative look, that you could not pass it without the idea that it had secrets to keep, and an eventful history to moralize upon.   In front, just on the edge of the unpaved sidewalk, grew the Pyncheon-elm, which, in reference to such trees as one usually meets with, might well be termed gigantic.   It had been planted by a great-grandson of the first Pyncheon, and, though now fourscore years of age, or perhaps nearer a hundred, was still in its strong and broad maturity, throwing its shadow from side to side of the street, overtopping the seven gables, and sweeping the whole black roof with its pendent foliage.   It gave beauty to the old edifice, and seemed to make it a part of nature.   The street having been widened about forty years ago, the front gable was now precisely on a line with it.   On either side extended a ruinous wooden fence, of open lattice-work, through which could be seen a grassy yard, and, especially in the angles of the building, an enormous fertility of burdocks, with leaves, it is hardly an exaggeration to say, two or three feet long.   Behind the house there appeared to be a garden, which undoubtedly had once been extensive, but was now infringed upon by other enclosures, or shut in by habitations and out-buildings that stood on another street.   It would be an omission, trifling indeed, but unpardonable, were we to forget the green moss that had long since gathered over the projections of the windows, and on the slopes of the roof ; nor must we fail to direct the reader's eye to a crop, not of weeds, but flower-shrubs, which were growing aloft in the air, not a great way from the chimney, in the nook between two of the gables.   They were called Alice's Posies.   The tradition was, that a certain Alice Pyncheon had flung up the seeds in sport, and that the dust of the street and the decay of the roof gradually formed a kind of soil for them, out of which they grew, when Alice had long been in her grave. However the flowers might have come there, it was both sad and sweet to observe how nature adopted to herself this desolate, decaying, gusty, rusty old house of the Pyncheon family; and how the ever-returning summer did her best to gladden it with tender beauty, and grew melancholy in the effort.

There is one other feature, very essential to be noticed, but which, we greatly fear, may damage any picturesque and romantic impression which we have been willing to throw over our sketch of this respectable edifice. In the front gable, under the impending brow of the second story, and contiguous to the street, was a shop-door, divided horizontally in the midst, and with a window for its upper segment, such as is often seen in dwellings of a somewhat ancient date. This same shop-door had been a subject of no slight mortification to the present occupant of the august Pyncheon-house, as well as to some of her predecessors. The matter is disagreeably delicate to handle; but, since the reader must needs be let into the secret, he will please to understand, that about a century ago, the head of the Pyncheons found himself involved in serious financial difficulties. The fellow (gentleman, as he styled himself) can hardly have been other than a spurious interloper; for, instead of seeking office from the king or the royal governor, or urging his hereditary claim to eastern lands, he bethought himself of no better avenue to wealth than by cutting a shop-door through the side of his ancestral residence. It was the custom of the time, indeed, for merchants to store their goods and transact business in their own dwellings. But there was something pitifully small in this old Pyncheon's mode of setting about his commercial operations; it was whispered, that, with his own hands, all be-ruffled as they were, he used to give change for a shilling, and would turn a half-penny twice over, to make sure that it was a good one. Beyond all question, he had the blood of a petty huckster in his veins, through whatever channel it may have found its way there.

Immediately on his death, the shop-door had been locked, bolted, and barred, and, down to the period of our story, had probably never once been opened.

The old counter, shelves, and other fixtures of the little shop remained just as he had left them. It used to be affirmed, that the dead shopkeeper, in a white wig, a faded velvet coat, an apron at his waist, and his ruffles carefully turned back from his wrists, might be seen through the chinks of the shutters, any night of the year, ransacking his till, or poring over the dingy pages of his day-book. From the look of unutterable woe upon his face, it appeared to be his doom to spend eternity in a vain effort to make his accounts balance.

And now—in a very humble way, as will be seen —we proceed to open our narrative.

II

THE LITTLE SHOP-WINDOW

It still lacked half-an-hour of sunrise, when Miss Hepzibah Pyncheon—we will not say awoke; it being doubtful whether the poor lady had so much as closed her eyes, during the brief night of midsummer—but, at all events, arose from her solitary pillow, and began what it would be mockery to term the adornment of her person. Far from us be the indecorum of assisting, even in imagination, at a maiden lady's toilet! Our story must therefore await Miss Hepzibah at the threshold of her chamber; only presuming, meanwhile to note some of the heavy sighs that laboured from her bosom, with little restraint as to their lugubrious depth and volume of sound, inasmuch as they could be audible to nobody, save a disembodied listener like ourself. The Old Maid was alone in the old house. Alone, except for a certain respectable and orderly young man, an artist in the daguerreotype line, who, for about three months back, had been a lodger in a remote gable,—quite a house by itself, indeed,—with locks, bolts, and oaken bars, on all the intervening doors. Inaudible, consequently, were poor Miss Hepzibah's gusty sighs. Inaudible, the creaking joints of her stiffened knees, as she knelt down by the bedside. And inaudible, too, by mortal ear, but heard with all-comprehending love and pity in the furthest heaven, that almost agony of prayer—now whispered, now a groan, now a struggling silence—wherewith she besought the Divine assistance through the day! Evidently, this is to be a day of more than ordinary trial to Miss Hepzibah, who, for above a quarter of a century gone by, has dwelt in strict seclusion, taking no part in the business of life, and just as little in its intercourse and pleasures. Not with such fervour prays the torpid recluse, looking forward to the cold, sunless, stagnant calm of a day that is to be like innumerable yesterdays!

The maiden lady's devotions are concluded. Will she now issue forth over the threshold of our story? Not yet, by many moments. First, every drawer in the tall, old-fashioned bureau is to be opened, with difficulty, and with a succession of spasmodic jerks; then, all must close again, with the same fidgety reluctance. There is a rustling of stiff silks; a tread of backward and forward footsteps, to and fro, across the chamber. We suspect Miss Hepzibah, moreover, of taking a step upward into a chair, in order to give heedful regard to her appearance, on all sides, and at full length, in the oval, dingy-framed toilet glass, that hangs above her table. Truly! well, indeed! who would have thought it! Is all this precious time to be lavished on the matutinal repair and beautifying of an elderly person, who never goes abroad, whom nobody ever visits, and from whom, when she shall have done her utmost, it were the best charity to turn one's eyes another way?

Now she is almost ready. Let us pardon her one other pause; for it is given to the sole sentiment,

or, we might better say—heightened and rendered
intense, as it has been, by sorrow and seclusion—
to the strong passion, of her life. We heard the
turning of a key in a small lock; she has opened
a secret drawer of an escritoir, and is probably looking at a certain miniature, done in Malbone's most
perfect style, and representing a face worthy of no
less delicate a pencil. It was once our good fortune
to see this picture. It is a likeness of a young man,
in a silken dressing-gown of an old fashion, the soft
richness of which is well adapted to the countenance
of reverie, with its full, tender lips, and beautiful
eyes, that seem to indicate not so much capacity of
thought, as gentle and voluptuous emotion. Of the
possessor of such features we shall have a right to
ask nothing, except that he would take the rude
world easily, and make himself happy in it. Can
it have been an early lover of Miss Hepzibah? No!
she never had a lover—poor thing, how could she?
—nor ever knew, by her own experience, what love
technically means. And yet, her undying faith and
trust, her fresh remembrance, and continual devoted-
ness towards the original of that miniature, have
been the only substance for her heart to feed upon.

She seems to have put aside the miniature, and
is standing again before the toilet-glass. There
are tears to be wiped off. A few more footsteps to
and fro; and here, at last—with another pitiful sigh,
like a gust of chill, damp wind out of a long-closed
vault, the door of which has accidentally been set
ajar—here comes Miss Hepzibah Pyncheon! Forth
she steps into the dusky, time-darkened passage;
a tall figure, clad in black silk, with a long and
shrunken waist, feeling her way towards the stairs
like a near-sighted person, as in truth she is.

The sun, meanwhile, if not already above the
horizon, was ascending nearer and nearer to its
verge. A few clouds, floating high upward, caught
some of the earliest light, and threw down its
golden gleam on the windows of all the houses in

the street, not forgetting the House of the Seven
Gables, which—many such sunrises as it had witnessed—looked cheerfully at the present one. The
reflected radiance served to show, pretty distinctly,
the aspect and arrangement of the room which
Hepzibah entered, after descending the stairs. It
was a low-studded room, with a beam across the
ceiling, panelled with dark wood, and having a large
chimney-piece, set round with pictured tiles, but now
closed by an iron fire-board, through which ran the
funnel of a modern stove. There was a carpet on
the floor, originally of rich texture, but so worn and
faded, in these latter years, that its once brilliant
figure had quite vanished into one indistinguishable
hue. In the way of furniture, there were two tables;
one, constructed with perplexing intricacy, and ex-
hibiting as many feet as a centipede; the other, most
delicately wrought, with four long and slender legs,
so apparently frail that it was almost incredible what
a length of time the ancient tea-table had stood upon
them. Half-a-dozen chairs stood about the room,
straight and stiff, and so ingeniously contrived for
the discomfort of the human person that they were
irksome even to sight, and conveyed the ugliest
possible idea of the state of society to which they
could have been adapted. One exception there was,
however, in a very antique elbow-chair, with a high
back, carved elaborately in oak, and a roomy depth
within its arms, that made up, by its spacious com-
prehensiveness, for the lack of any of those artistic
curves which abound in a modern chair.

As for ornamental articles of furniture, we recollect
but two, if such they may be called. One was a map
of the Pyncheon territory at the eastward, not engraved, but the handiwork of some skilful old
draughtsman, and grotesquely illuminated with pictures of Indians and wild beasts, among which was
seen a lion; the natural history of the region being
as little known as its geography, which was put
down most fantastically awry. The other adornment

was the portrait of old Colonel Pyncheon, at two-thirds length, representing the stern features of a puritanic-looking personage, in a skull-cap, with a laced band and a grizzly beard; holding a Bible with one hand, and in the other uplifting an iron sword-hilt. The latter object, being more successfully depicted by the artist, stood out in far greater prominence than the sacred volume. Face to face with this picture, on entering the apartment, Miss Hepzibah Pyncheon came to a pause; regarding it with a singular scowl, a strange contortion of the brow, which by people who did not know her, would probably have been interpreted as an expression of bitter anger and ill-will. But it was no such thing. She, in fact, felt a reverence for the pictured visage of which only a far-descended and time-stricken virgin could be susceptible; and this forbidding scowl was the innocent result of her near-sightedness, and an effort so to concentrate her powers of vision as to substitute a firm outline of the object instead of a vague one.

We must linger a moment on this unfortunate expression of poor Hepzibah's brow. Her scowl—as the world, or such part of it as sometimes caught a transitory glimpse of her at the window, wickedly persisted in calling it—her scowl had done Miss Hepzibah a very ill office, in establishing her character as an ill-tempered old maid; nor does it appear improbable, that, by often gazing at herself in a dim looking-glass, and perpetually encountering her own frown within its ghostly sphere, she had been led to interpret the expression almost as unjustly as the world did. "How miserably cross I look!" she must often have whispered to herself;—and ultimately have fancied herself so, by a sense of inevitable doom. But her heart never frowned. It was naturally tender, sensitive, and full of little tremors and palpitations; all of which weaknesses it retained, while her visage was growing so perversely stern, and even fierce. Nor had Hepzibah ever any hardihood except what came from the very warmest nook in her affections.

All this time, however, we are loitering faint-heartedly on the threshold of our story. In very truth, we have an invincible reluctance to disclose what Miss Hepzibah Pyncheon was about to do.

It has already been observed, that, in the basement storey of the gable fronting on the street, an unworthy ancestor, nearly a century ago, had fitted up a shop. Every since the old gentleman retired from trade, and fell asleep under his coffin-lid, not only the shop-door, but the inner arrangements, had been suffered to remain unchanged; while the dust of ages gathered inch-deep over the shelves and counter, and partly filled an old pair of scales, as if it were of value enough to be weighed. It treasured itself up, too, in the half-open till, where there still lingered a base sixpence, worth neither more nor less than the hereditary pride which had here been put to shame. Such had been the state and condition of the little shop in old Hepzibah's childhood, when she and her brother used to play at hide-and-seek in its forsaken precincts. So it had remained, until within a few days past.

But now, though the shop-window was still closely curtained from the public gaze, a remarkable change had taken place in its interior. The rich and heavy festoons of cob-web, which it had cost a long ances-tral succession of spiders their life's labour to spin and weave, had been carefully brushed away from the ceiling. The counter, shelves, and floor had all been scoured, and the latter was overstrewn with fresh blue sand. The brown scales, too, had evi-dently undergone rigid discipline, in an unavailing effort to rub off the rust, which, alas! had eaten through and through their substance. Neither was the little old shop any longer empty of merchantable goods. A curious eye privileged to take an account of stock, and investigate behind the counter, would have discovered a barrel,—yea, two or three barrels and half ditto,—one containing flour, another apples, and a third, perhaps, Indian meal. There was likewise a square box of pine-wood, full of soap in bars; also, another of the same size, in which were tallow candles, ten to the pound. A small stock of brown sugar, some white beans and split peas, and a few other commodities of low price, and such as are constantly in demand, made up the bulkier portion of the merchandise. It might have been taken for a ghostly or phantasmagoric reflection of the old shopkeeper Pyncheon's shabbily-provided shelves, save that some of the articles were of a description and outward form which could hardly have been known in his day. For instance, there was a glass pickle jar, filled with fragments of Gibraltar rock; not, indeed, splinters of the veritable stone foundation of the famous fortress, but bits of delectable candy, neatly done up in white paper. Jim Crow, moreover, was seen executing his world-renowned dance, in ginger-bread. A party of leaden dragoons were galloping along one of the shelves, in equipments and uniform of modern cut; and there were some sugar figures, with no strong resemblance to the humanity of any epoch, but less unsatisfactorily representing our own fashions than those of a hundred years ago. Another phenomenon, still more strikingly modern, was a package of lucifer matches, which, in old times, would have been thought actually to borrow their instantaneous flame from the nether fires of Tophet.

In short, to bring the matter at once to a point, it was incontrovertibly evident that somebody had taken the shop and fixtures of the long-retired and forgotten Mr. Pyncheon, and was about to renew the enterprise of that departed worthy, with a different set of customers. Who could this bold adventurer be? And, of all places in the world, why had he chosen the House of the Seven Gables as the scene of his commercial speculations?

We return to the elderly maiden. She at length

withdrew her eyes from the dark countenance of the
colonel's portrait, heaved a sigh,—indeed her breast
was a very cave of Æolus, that morning,—and stept
across the room on tip-toe, as is the customary gait
of elderly women. Passing through an intervening
passage, she opened a door that communicated with
the shop, just now so elaborately described. Owing
to the projection of the upper storey—and still more
to the thick shadow of the Pyncheon-elm, which stood
almost directly in front of the gable—the twilight,
here, was still as much akin to night as morning.
Another heavy sigh from Miss Hepzibah! After a
moment's pause on the threshold, peering towards
the window with her near-sighted scowl, as if frowning down some bitter enemy, she suddenly projected
herself into the shop. The haste, and, as it were,
the galvanic impulse of the movement, were really
quite startling.

Nervously—in a sort of frenzy, we might almost
say she began to busy herself in arranging some
children's playthings, and other little wares, on the
shelves and at the shop-window. In the aspect of
this dark-arrayed, pale-faced, lady-like old figure,
there was a deeply-tragic character, that contrasted
irreconcilably with the ludicrous pettiness of her
employment. It seemed a queer anomaly, that so
gaunt and dismal a personage should take a toy
in hand; a miracle, that the toy did not vanish in
her grasp; a miserably absurd idea, that she should
go on perplexing her stiff and sombre intellect with
the question how to tempt little boys into her
premises! Yet such is undoubtedly her object.
Now she places a gingerbread elephant against the
window, but with so tremulous a touch that it tumbles
upon the floor, with the dismemberment of three legs
and its trunk; it has ceased to be an elephant, and
has become a few bits of musty gingerbread. There,
again, she has upset a tumbler of marbles, all of
which roll different ways, and each individual marble,
devil-directed, into the most difficult obscurity that

it can find.   Heaven help our poor old Hepzibah,
and forgive us for taking a ludicrous view of her
position !   As her rigid and rusty frame goes down
upon its hands and knees, in quest of the abscond-
ing marbles, we positively feel so much the more
inclined to shed tears of sympathy, from the very
fact that we must needs turn aside and laugh at her.
For here—and if we fail to impress it suitably upon
the reader, it is our own fault, not that of the theme
—here is one of the truest points of melancholy
interest that occur in ordinary life.   It was the final
throe of what called itself old gentility.   A lady—
who had fed herself from childhood with the shadowy
food of aristocratic reminiscences, and whose religion
it was that a lady's hand soils itself irremediably by
doing aught for bread—this born lady, after sixty
years of narrowing means, is fain to step down from
her pedestal of imaginary rank.   Poverty, treading
closely at her heels for a lifetime, has come up with
her at last.   She must earn her own food, or starve !
And we have stolen upon Miss Hepzibah Pyncheon,
too irreverently, at the instant of time when the
patrician lady is to be transformed into the plebeian
woman.

In this republican country, amid the fluctuating
waves of our social life, somebody is always at the
drowning-point.   The tragedy is enacted with as
continual a repetition as that of a popular drama on
a holiday ; and, nevertheless, is felt as deeply, perhaps, as when an hereditary noble sinks below his
order.   More deeply ; since, with us, rank is the
grosser substance of wealth and a splendid establishment, and has no spiritual existence after the death
of these, but dies hopelessly along with them.   And,
therefore, since we have been unfortunate enough to
introduce our heroine at so inauspicious a juncture,
we would entreat for a mood of due solemnity in the
spectators of her fate.   Let us behold, in poor
Hepzibah, the immemorial lady,—two hundred years
old, on this side of the water, and thrice as many

on the other,—with her antique portraits, pedigrees,
coats of arms, records and traditions, and her claim,
as joint heiress, to that princely territory at the eastward, no longer a wilderness but a populous fertility,
—born, too, in Pyncheon-street, under the Pyncheon-
elm, and in the Pyncheon-house, where she has spent
all her days,—reduced now, in that very house, to
be the hucksteress of a cent-shop !

This business of setting up a petty shop is almost
the only resource of women, in circumstances at all
similar to those of our unfortunate recluse.   With
her near-sightedness, and those tremulous fingers of
hers, at once inflexible and delicate, she could not be
a seamstress ; although her sampler of fifty years
gone by exhibited some of the most recondite specimens of ornamental needle-work.   A school for little
children had been often in her thoughts ; and, at one
time, she had begun a review of her early studies
in the New England primer, with a view to prepare
herself for the office of instructress.   But the love of
children had never been quickened in Hepzibah's
heart, and was now torpid, if not extinct ; she
watched the little people of the neighbourhood from
her chamber-window, and doubted whether she could
tolerate a more intimate acquaintance with them.
Besides, in our day, the very A B C has become a
science, greatly too abstruse to be any longer taught
by pointing a pin from letter to letter.   A modern
child could teach old Hepzibah more than old Hepzibah could teach the child.   So—with many a cold,
deep heart-quake at the idea of at last coming into
sordid contact with the world, from which she had so
long kept aloof, while every added day of seclusion
had rolled another stone against the cavern-door
of her hermitage—the poor thing bethought herself of the ancient shop-window, the rusty scales,
and dusty till.   She might have held back a little
longer ; but another circumstance, not yet hinted at,
had somewhat hastened her decision.   Her humble
preparations, therefore, were duly made, and the

enterprise was now to be commenced. Nor was she entitled to complain of any remarkable singularity in her fate; for, in the town of her nativity, we might point to several little shops of a similar description; some of them in houses as ancient as that of the seven gables; and one or two, it may be, where a decayed gentlewoman stands behind the counter, as grim an image of family pride as Miss Hepzibah Pyncheon herself.

It was overpoweringly ridiculous—we must honestly confess it—the deportment of the maiden lady while setting her shop in order for the public eye. She stole on tiptoe to the window, as cautiously as if she conceived some bloody-minded villain to be watching behind the elm-tree, with intent to take her life. Stretching out her long, lank arm, she put a paper of pearl-buttons, a Jew's-harp, or whatever the small article might be, in its destined place, and straightway vanished back into the dusk, as if the world need never hope for another glimpse of her. It might have been fancied, indeed, that she expected to minister to the wants of the community unseen, like a disembodied divinity, or enchantress, holding forth her bargains to the reverential and awe-stricken purchaser, in an invisible hand. But Hepzibah had no such flattering dream. She was well aware that she must ultimately come forward, and stand revealed in her proper individuality; but, like other sensitive persons, she could not bear to be observed in the gradual process, and chose rather to flash forth on the world's astonished gaze at once.

The inevitable moment was not much longer to be delayed. The sunshine might now be seen stealing down the front of the opposite house, from the windows of which came a reflected gleam, struggling through the boughs of the elm-tree, and enlightening the interior of the shop more distinctly than heretofore. The town appeared to be waking up. A baker's cart had already rattled through the street, chasing away the latest vestige of night's sanctity with the jingle-jangle of its dissonant bells. A milk-man was distributing the contents of his cans from door to door; and the harsh peal of a fisherman's conch-shell was heard far off, around the corner. None of these tokens escaped Hepzibah's notice. The moment had arrived. To delay longer would be only to lengthen out her misery. Nothing remained, except to take down the bar from the shop-door, leaving the entrance free—more than free—welcome, as if all were household friends—to every passer-by, whose eyes might be attracted by the commodities at the window. This last act Hepzibah now performed, letting the bar fall with what smote upon her excited nerves as a most astounding clatter. Then—as if the only barrier betwixt herself and the world had been thrown down, and a flood of evil con-sequences would come tumbling through the gap—she fled into the inner parlour, threw herself into the ancestral elbow-chair, and wept.

Our miserable old Hepzibah! It is a heavy annoy-ance to a writer, who endeavours to represent nature, its various attitudes and circumstances, in a reason-ably correct outline and true colouring, that so much of the mean and ludicrous should be hopelessly mixed up with the purest pathos which life anywhere sup-plies to him. What tragic dignity, for example, can be wrought into a scene like this! How can we elevate our history of retribution for the sin of long ago, when, as one of our most prominent figures, we are compelled to introduce—not a young and lovely woman, nor even the stately remains of beauty, storm-shattered by affliction—but a gaunt, sallow, rusty-jointed maiden, in a long-waisted silk gown, and with the strange horror of a turban on her head! Her visage is not even ugly. It is redeemed from insignificance only by the contraction of her eyebrows into a near-sighted scowl. And finally, her great life-trial seems to be that, after sixty years of idle-ness, she finds it convenient to earn comfortable bread by setting up a shop in a small way. Nevertheless,

if we look through all the heroic fortunes of mankind, we shall find this same entanglement of something mean and trivial with whatever is noblest in
joy or sorrow.   Life is made up of marble and mud.
And without all the deeper trust in a comprehensive
sympathy above us, we might hence be led to suspect
the insult of a sneer, as well as an immitigable frown,
on the iron countenance of fate.   What is called
poetic insight is the gift of discerning, in this sphere
of strangely-mingled elements, the beauty and the
majesty which are compelled to assume a garb so
sordid.

III

THE FIRST CUSTOMER

Miss Hepzibah Pyncheon sat in the oaken elbow-
chair, with her hands over her face, giving way to
that heavy down-sinking of the heart which most
persons have experienced, when the image of hope
itself seems ponderously moulded of lead, on the
eve of an enterprise at once doubtful and momentous.   She was suddenly startled by the tinkling
alarum—high, sharp, and irregular—of a little bell.
The maiden lady arose upon her feet, as pale as a
ghost at cockcrow; for she was an enslaved spirit,
and this the talisman to which she owed obedience.
This little bell—to speak in plainer terms—being
fastened over the shop-door, was so contrived as to
vibrate by means of a steel spring, and thus convey
notice to the inner regions of the house, when any
customer should cross the threshold.   Its ugly and
spiteful little din (heard now for the first time, perhaps, since Hepzibah's periwigged predecessor had
retired from trade) at once set every nerve of her

body in responsive and tumultuous vibration. The crisis was upon her! Her first customer was at the door!

Without giving herself time for a second thought, she rushed into the shop, pale, wild, desperate in gesture and expression, scowling portentously, and looking far better qualified to do fierce battle with a housebreaker, than to stand smiling behind the counter, bartering small wares for a copper recompense. Any ordinary customer, indeed, would have turned his back and fled. And yet there was nothing fierce in Hepzibah's poor old heart; nor had she, at the moment, a single bitter thought against the world at large, or one individual man or woman. She wished them all well, but wished, too, that she herself were done with them, and in her quiet grave.

The applicant by this time stood within the doorway. Coming freshly, as he did, out of the morning light, he appeared to have brought some of its cheery influences into the shop along with him. It was a slender young man, not more than one or two and twenty years old, with rather a grave and thoughtful expression, for his years, but likewise a springy alacrity and vigour. These qualities were not only perceptible physically, in his make and motions, but made themselves felt almost immediately in his character. A brown beard, not too silken in its texture, fringed his chin, but as yet without completely hiding it; he wore a short moustache, too, and his dark, high-featured countenance looked all the better for these natural ornaments. As for his dress, it was of the simplest kind; a summer sack of cheap and ordinary material, thin, checkered pantaloons, and a straw hat, by no means of the finest braid. Oak Hall might have supplied his entire equipment. He was chiefly marked as a gentleman—if such, indeed, he made any claim to be—by the rather remarkable whiteness and nicety of his clean linen.

He met the scowl of old Hepzibah without apparent

alarm, as having heretofore encountered it, and found it harmless.

"So, my dear Miss Pyncheon," said the daguerreo-typist,—for it was that sole other occupant of the seven-gabled mansion,—"I am glad to see that you have not shrunk from your good purpose. I merely look in to offer my best wishes, and to ask if I can assist you any further in your preparations."

People in difficulty and distress, or in any manner at odds with the world, can endure a vast amount of harsh treatment, and perhaps be only the stronger for it; whereas, they give way at once before the simplest expression of what they perceive to be genuine sympathy. So it proved with poor Hepzibah; for, when she saw the young man's smile,— looking so much the brighter on a thoughtful face,— and heard his kindly tone, she broke first into a hysteric giggle, and then began to sob.

"Ah, Mr. Holgrave," cried she, as soon as she could speak, "I never can go through with it! Never, never, never! I wish I were dead, and in the old family-tomb, with all my forefathers! With my father, and my mother, and my sister! Yes, and with my brother, who had far better find me there than here! The world is too chill and hard,—and I am too old, and too feeble, and too hopeless!"

"O, believe me, Miss Hepzibah," said the young man, quietly, "these feelings will not trouble you any longer, after you are once fairly in the midst of your enterprise. They are unavoidable at this moment, standing, as you do, on the outer verge of your long seclusion, and peopling the world with ugly shapes, which you will soon find to be as unreal as the giants and ogres of a child's story book. I find nothing so singular in life, as that everything appears to lose its substance, the instant one actually grapples with it. So it will be with what you think so terrible."

"But I am a woman!" said Hepzibah, piteously.

" I was going to say, a lady,—but I consider that as past."

" Well; no matter if it be past !" answered the artist, a strange gleam of half-hidden sarcasm flashing through the kindliness of his manner. " Let it go ! You are the better without it. I speak frankly, my dear Miss Pyncheon : for are we not friends ? I look upon this as one of the fortunate days of your life. It ends an epoch and begins one. Hitherto, the life-blood has been gradually chilling in your veins, as you sat aloof, within your circle of gentility, while the rest of the world was fighting out its battle with one kind of necessity or another. Henceforth you will at least have the sense of healthy and natural effort for a purpose, and of lending your strength—be it great or small—to the united struggle of mankind. This is success—all the success that anybody meets with !"

" It is natural enough, Mr. Holgrave, that you should have ideas like these," rejoined Hepzibah, drawing up her gaunt figure, with slightly offended dignity. " You are a man, a young man, and brought up, I suppose, as almost everybody is now-a-days, with a view to seeking your fortune. But I was born a lady, and have always lived one; no matter in what narrowness of means, always a lady !"

" But I was not born a gentleman ; neither have I lived like one," said Holgrave, slightly smiling ; " so, my dear madam, you will hardly expect me to sympathize with sensibilities of this kind; though, unless I deceive myself, I have some imperfect comprehension of them. These names of gentleman and lady had a meaning, in the past history of the world, and conferred privileges, desirable or otherwise, on those entitled to bear them. In the present—and still more in the future condition of society—they imply, not privilege, but restriction !"

" These are new notions," said the old gentle-woman, shaking her head. " I shall never understand them; neither do I wish it."

" We will cease to speak of them, then," replied
the artist, with a friendlier smile than his last one,
" and I will leave you to feel whether it is not better
to be a true woman than a lady.   Do you really think,
Miss Hepzibah, that any lady of your family has
ever done a more heroic thing since this house was
built, than you are performing in it to-day?   Never;
and if the Pyncheons had always acted so nobly, I
doubt whether an old wizard Maule's anathema, of
which you told me once, would have had much weight
with Providence against them."

" Ah!—no, no!" said Hepzibah, not displeased at
this allusion to the sombre dignity of an inherited
curse.   " If old Maule's ghost, or a descendant of
his, could see me behind the counter to-day, he would
call it the fulfilment of his worst wishes.   But I thank
you for your kindness, Mr. Holgrave, and will do my
utmost to be a good shopkeeper."

" Pray do," said Holgrave, " and let me have the
pleasure of being your first customer.   I am about
taking a walk to the sea-shore before going to my
rooms, where I misuse Heaven's blessed sunshine
by tracing out human features through its agency.
A few of those biscuits, dipt in sea-water, will be
just what I need for breakfast.   What is the price
of half-a-dozen?"

" Let me be a lady a moment longer," replied
Hepzibah, with a manner of antique stateliness, to
which a melancholy smile lent a kind of grace.   She
put the biscuits into his hand, but rejected the com-
pensation.   " A Pyncheon must not, at all events,
under her forefathers' roof, receive money for a
morsel of bread, from her only friend!"

Holgrave took his departure, leaving her, for the
moment, with spirits not quite so much depressed.
Soon, however, they had subsided nearly to their
former dead level.   With a beating heart, she listened
to the footsteps of early passengers, which now began
to be frequent along the street.   Once or twice they
seemed to linger; these strangers, or neighbours,

as the case might be, were looking at the display of toys and pretty commodities in Hepzibah's shop-window. She was doubly tortured; in part, with a sense of overwhelming shame, that strange and unloving eyes should have the privilege of gazing, and partly because the idea occurred to her, with ridiculous importunity, that the window was not arranged so skilfully, nor nearly to so much advantage, as it might have been. It seemed as if the whole fortune or failure of her shop might depend on the display of a different set of articles, or substituting a fairer apple for one which appeared to be specked. So she made the change, and straightway fancied that everything was spoiled by it; not recognizing that it was the nervousness of the juncture, and her own native squeamishness, as an old maid, that wrought all the seeming mischief.

Anon, there was an encounter, just at the door-step, betwixt two labouring men, as their rough voices denoted them to be. After some slight talk about their own affairs, one of them chanced to notice the shop-window, and directed the other's attention to it.

"See here!" cried he; "what do you think of this? Trade seems to be looking up in Pyncheon-street!"

"Well, well, this is a sight, to be sure!" exclaimed the other. "In the old Pyncheon-house, and underneath the Pyncheon-elm! Who would have thought it? Old Maid Pyncheon is setting up a cent-shop!"

"Will she make it go, think you, Dixey?" said his friend. "I don't call it a very good stand. There's another shop just round the corner."

"Make it go!" cried Dixey, with a most contemptuous expression, as if the very idea were impossible to be conceived. "Not a bit of it! Why, her face—I've seen it, for I dug her garden for her one year—her face is enough to frighten the Old Nick himself, if he had ever so great a mind to trade with her. People can't stand it, I tell you! She scowls dreadfully, reason or none, out of pure ugliness of temper!"

"Well, that's not so much matter," remarked the other man. "These sour-tempered folks are most handy at business, and know pretty well what they are about. But, as you say, I don't think she'll do much. This business of keeping cent-shops is over-done, like all other kinds of trade, handicraft, and bodily labour. I know it, to my cost! My wife kept a cent-shop three months, and lost five dollars on her outlay!"

"Poor business!" responded Dixey, in a tone as if he were shaking his head,—"poor business!"

For some reason or other, not very easy to analyze, there had hardly been so bitter a pang, in all her previous misery about the matter, as what thrilled Hepzibah's heart, on overhearing the above conversa-tion. The testimony in regard to her scowl was frightfully important; it seemed to hold up her image, wholly relieved from the false light of her self-parti-alities, and so hideous that she dared not look at it. She was absurdly hurt, moreover, by the slight and idle effect that her setting-up shop—an event of such breathless interest to herself—appeared to have upon the public, of which these two men were the nearest representatives. A glance; a passing word or two; a coarse laugh; and she was doubtless forgotten, be-fore they turned the corner! They cared nothing for her dignity, and just as little for her degradation. Then, also, the augury of ill-success, uttered from the sure wisdom of experience, fell upon her half-dead hope like a clod into a grave. The man's wife had already tried the same experiment, and failed! How could the born lady—the recluse of half a lifetime, utterly unpractised in the world, at sixty years of age—how could she ever dream of succeeding, when the hard, vulgar, keen, busy, hackneyed New Eng-land woman, had lost five dollars on her little outlay! Success presented itself as an impossibility, and the hope of it as a wild hallucination.

Some malevolent spirit, doing his utmost to drive
Hepzibah mad, unrolled before her imagination a
kind of panorama, representing the great thoroughfare of a city, all astir with customers.   So many and
so magnificent shops as there were !   Groceries, toy-
shops, dry-goods stores, with their immense panes of
plate-glass, their gorgeous fixtures, their vast and
complete assortments of merchandise, in which
fortunes had been invested; and those noble mirrors
at the further end of each establishment, doubling all
this wealth by a brightly-burnished vista of unrealities !   On one side of the street this splendid
bazaar, with a multitude of perfumed and glossy
salesmen, smirking, smiling, bowing, and measuring
out the goods.   On the other, the dusty old House
of the Seven Gables, with the antiquated shop-window
under its projecting storey, and Hepzibah herself, in
a gown of rusty black silk, behind the counter, scowling at the world as it went by !   This mighty contrast
thrust itself forward, as a fair expression of the odds
against which she was to begin her struggle for a
subsistence.   Success?   Preposterous !   She would
never think of it again !   The house might just as
well be buried in an eternal fog, while all the other
houses had the sunshine on them ; for not a foot
would ever cross the threshold, nor a hand so much
as try the door !

But, at this instant, the shop-bell, right over her
head, tinkled as if it were bewitched.   The old gentlewoman's heart seemed to be attached to the same
steel spring, for it went through a series of sharp
jerks, in unison with the sound.   The door was
thrust open, although no human form was perceptible on the other side of the half-window.   Hepzibah,
nevertheless, stood at a gaze, with her hands clasped,
looking very much as if she had summoned up an
evil spirit, and were afraid, yet resolved, to hazard
the encounter.

" Heaven help me !" she groaned mentally.   " Now
is my hour of need !"

The door, which moved with difficulty on its creaking and rusty hinges, being forced quite open, a square and sturdy little urchin became apparent, with cheeks as red as an apple. He was clad rather shabbily (but as it seemed, more owing to his mother's carelessness than his father's poverty), in a blue apron, very wide and short trousers, shoes somewhat out at the toes, and a chip-hat, with the frizzles of his curly hair sticking through the crevices. A book and a small slate under his arm indicated that he was on his way to school. He stared at Hepzibah a moment, as an elder customer than himself would have been likely enough to do, not knowing what to make of the tragic attitude and queer scowl wherewith she regarded him.

" Well, child," said she, taking heart at sight of a personage so little formidable,—" well, my child, what did you wish for?"

" That Jim Crow, there, in the window," answered the urchin, holding out a cent, and pointing to the gingerbread figure that had attracted his notice, as he loitered along to school; " the one that has not a broken foot."

So Hepzibah put forth her lank arm, and taking the effigy from the shop-window, delivered it to her first customer.

" No matter for the money," said she, giving him a little push towards the door; for her old gentility was contumaciously squeamish at sight of the copper coin, and, besides, it seemed such pitiful meanness to take the child's pocket-money in exchange for a bit of stale ginger-bread. " No matter for the cent. You are welcome to Jim Crow."

The child, staring with round eyes, at this instance of liberality, wholly unprecedented in his large experience of cent-shops, took the man of gingerbread, and quitted the premises. No sooner had he reached the sidewalk (little cannibal that he was!) than Jim Crow's head was in his mouth. As he had not been careful to shut the door, Hepzibah was at the pains of closing it after him, with a pettish ejaculation or two about the troublesomeness of young people, and particularly of small boys. She had just placed another representative of the renowned Jim Crow at the window, when again the shop-bell tinkled clamorously, and again the door being thrust open, with its characteristic jerk and jar, disclosed the same sturdy little urchin who, precisely two minutes ago, had made his exit. The crumbs and discoloration of the cannibal feast, as yet hardly consummated, were exceedingly visible about his mouth.

" What is it now, child?" asked the maiden lady, rather impatiently; " did you come back to shut the door?"

" No," answered the urchin, pointing to the figure that had just been put up; " I want that other Jim Crow."

" Well, here it is for you," said Hepzibah, reaching it down; but, recognizing that this pertinacious customer would not quit her on any other terms, so long as she had a gingerbread figure in her shop, she partly drew back her extended hand,—" Where is the cent?"

The little boy had the cent ready, but like a true-born Yankee would have preferred the better bargain to the worse. Looking somewhat chagrined, he put the coin into Hepzibah's hand, and departed, sending the second Jim Crow in quest of the former one. The new shopkeeper dropped the first solid result of her commercial enterprise into the till. It was done. The sordid stain of that copper coin could never be washed away from her palm. The little school-boy, aided by the impish figure of the negro dancer, had wrought an irreparable ruin. The structure of ancient aristocracy had been demolished by him, even as if his childish gripe had torn down the seven-gabled mansion! Now let Hepzibah turn the old Pyncheon portraits with their faces to the wall; and take the map of her eastern territory to kindle the kitchen fire, and blow up the flame with the empty breath of

her ancestral traditions ! What had she to do with
ancestry? Nothing : no more than with posterity !
No lady now, but simply Hepzibah Pyncheon, a
forlorn old maid, and keeper of a cent-shop !

Nevertheless, even while she paraded these ideas
somewhat ostentatiously through her mind, it is altogether surprising what a calmness had come over her.
The anxiety and misgivings which had tormented
her, whether asleep or in melancholy day-dreams,
ever since her project began to take an aspect of
solidity, had now vanished quite away. She felt the
novelty of her position, indeed, but no longer with
disturbance or affright. Now and then there came
a thrill of almost youthful enjoyment. It was the
invigorating breath of a fresh outward atmosphere,
after the long torpor and monotonous seclusion of
her life. So wholesome is effort ! So miraculous the
strength that we do not know of ! The healthiest
glow that Hepzibah had known for years had come
now, in the dreaded crisis, when, for the first time,
she had put forth her hand to help herself. The
little circlet of the school-boy's copper coin—dim and
lustreless though it was, with the small services which
it had been doing here and there about the world—had
proved a talisman, fragrant with good, and deserving
to be set in gold and worn next her heart. It was as
potent, and perhaps endowed with the same kind of
efficacy, as a galvanic ring ! Hepzibah, at all events,
was indebted to its subtle operation, both in body
and spirit ; so much the more, as it inspired her with
energy to get some breakfast, at which, still the
better to keep up her courage, she allowed herself an
extra spoonful in her infusion of black tea.

Her introductory day of shop-keeping did not run
on, however, without many and serious interruptions
of this mode of cheerful vigour. As a general rule,
Providence seldom vouchsafes to mortals any more
than just that degree of encouragement which suffices
to keep them at a reasonably full exertion of their
powers. In the case of our old gentlewoman, after

the excitement of new effort had subsided, the despondency of her whole life threatened ever and anon
to return. It was like the heavy mass of clouds which
we may often see obscuring the sky, and making a
gray twilight everywhere, until, towards nightfall, it
yields temporarily to a glimpse of sunshine. But,
always, the envious cloud strives to gather again
across the streak of celestial azure.

Customers came in, as the forenoon advanced, but
rather slowly; in some cases too, it must be owned,
with little satisfaction either to themselves or Miss
Hepzibah; nor, on the whole, with an aggregate of
very rich emolument to the till. A little girl, sent by
her mother to match a skein of cotton thread of a
peculiar hue, took one that the near-sighted old lady
pronounced extremely like, but soon came running
back, with a blunt and cross message, that it would
not do, and besides, was very rotten! Then there
was a pale, care-wrinkled woman, not old but
haggard, and already with streaks of gray among her
hair, like silver ribbons; one of those women, naturally delicate, whom you at once recognize as worn to
death by a brute—probably a drunken brute—of a
husband, and at least nine children. She wanted a
few pounds of flour, and offered the money, which
the decayed gentlewoman silently rejected, and gave
the poor soul better measure than if she had taken it.
Shortly afterwards, a man in a blue cotton frock,
much soiled, came in and bought a pipe, filling the
whole shop, meanwhile, with the hot odour of strong
drink, not only exhaled in the torrid atmosphere of
his breath, but oozing out of his entire system, like
an inflammable gas. It was impressed on Hepzibah's
mind that this was the husband of the care-wrinkled
woman. He asked for a paper of tobacco; and as
she had neglected to provide herself with the article,
her brutal customer dashed down his newly-bought
pipe, and left the shop muttering unintelligible words,
which had the tone and bitterness of a curse. Here-

upon Hepzibah threw up her eyes, unintentionally scowling in the face of Providence !

No less than five persons, during the forenoon, inquired for ginger-beer, or root-beer, or any drink of a similar brewage, and, obtaining nothing of the kind, went off in an exceedingly bad humour. Three of them left the door open, and the other two pulled it so spitefully in going out that the little bell played the very deuce with Hepzibah's nerves. A round, bustling, fire-ruddy housewife of the neighbourhood burst breathless into the shop, fiercely demanding yeast; and when the poor gentlewoman, with her cold shyness of manner, gave her hot customer to understand that she did not keep the article, this very capable housewife took upon herself to administer a regular rebuke.

" A cent-shop, and no yeast !" quoth she; " that will never do ! Who ever heard of such a thing ? Your loaf will never rise, no more than mine will to-day. You had better shut up shop at once."

" Well," said Hepzibah, heaving a deep sigh, " perhaps I had !"

Several times, moreover, besides the above instance, her ladylike sensibilities were seriously infringed upon by the familiar, if not rude tone, with which people addressed her. They evidently considered themselves not merely her equals, but her patrons and superiors. Now, Hepzibah had unconsciously flattered herself with the idea that there would be a gleam or halo, of some kind or other, about her person, which would insure an obeisance to her sterling gentility, or, at least a tacit recognition of it. On the other hand, nothing tortured her more intolerably than when this recognition was too prominently expressed. To one or two rather officious offers of sympathy, her responses were little short of acrimonious; and, we regret to say, Hepzibah was thrown into a positively unchristian state of mind, by the suspicion that one of her customers was drawn to the shop, not by any

real need of the article which she pretended to seek,
but by a wicked wish to stare at her. The vulgar
creature was determined to see for herself what sort
of a figure a mildewed piece of aristocracy, after wast-
ing all the bloom, and much of the decline of her life,
apart from the world, would cut behind a counter.
In this particular case, however mechanical and
innocuous it might be at other times, Hepzibah's
contortion of brow served her in good stead.

" I never was so frightened in my life!" said the
curious customer, in describing the incident to one of
her acquaintances. "She's a real old vixen, take
my word for it! She says little, to be sure; but if
you could only see the mischief in her eye!"

On the whole, therefore, her new experience led our
decayed gentlewoman to very disagreeable conclusions as to the temper and manners of what she
termed the lower classes, whom heretofore she had
looked down upon with a gentle and pitying complais-
ance, as herself occupying a sphere of unquestionable
superiority. But, unfortunately, she had likewise to
struggle against a bitter emotion of a directly opposite
kind : a sentiment of virulence, we mean, towards
the idle aristocracy to which it had so recently been
her pride to belong. When a lady, in a delicate and
costly summer garb, with a floating veil and grace-
fully-swaying gown, and, altogether, an ethereal
lightness that made you look at her beautifully-
slippered feet, to see whether she trod on the dust or
floated in the air,—when such a vision happened to
pass through this retired street, leaving it tenderly
and delusively fragrant with her passage, as if a
bouquet of tea-roses had been borne along,—then,
again, it is to be feared, old Hepzibah's scowl could
no longer vindicate itself entirely on the plea of near-
sightedness.

" For what end," thought she, giving vent to that
feeling of hostility which is the only real abasement
of the poor, in presence of the rich,—" for what good
end, in the wisdom of Providence, does that woman

live? Must the whole world toil, that the palms of her hands may be kept white and delicate?"

Then, ashamed and penitent, she hid her face.

"May God forgive me!" said she.

Doubtless, God did forgive her. But, taking the inward and outward history of the first half-day into consideration, Hepzibah began to fear that the shop would prove her ruin in a moral and religious point of view, without contributing very essentially towards even her temporal welfare.

IV

A DAY BEHIND THE COUNTER

TOWARDS noon, Hepzibah saw an elderly gentleman, large and portly, and of remarkably dignified demeanour, passing slowly along, on the opposite side of the white and dusty street. On coming within the shadow of the Pyncheon-elm, he stopt, and (taking off his hat, meanwhile, to wipe the perspiration from his brow) seemed to scrutinize, with especial interest, the dilapidated and rusty-visaged House of the Seven Gables. He himself, in a very different style, was as well worth looking at as the house. No better model need be sought, nor could have been found, of a very high order of respectability, which, by some indescribable magic, not merely expressed itself in his looks and gestures, but even governed the fashion of his garments, and rendered them all proper and essential to the man. Without appearing to differ, in any tangible way, from other people's clothes, there was yet a wide and rich gravity about them, that must have been a characteristic of the wearer, since it could not be defined as pertaining either to the cut or material. His gold-headed cane,

too,—a serviceable staff of dark, polished wood,—
had similar traits, and had it chosen to take a walk
by itself, would have been recognized anywhere as a
tolerably adequate representative of its master. This
character—which showed itself so strikingly in everything about him, and the effect of which we seek to
convey to the reader—went no deeper than his station,
habits of life, and external circumstances. One perceived him to be a personage of mark, influence, and
authority; and especially, you could feel just as
certain that he was opulent as if he had exhibited his
bank account, or as if you had seen him touching the
twigs of the Pyncheon-elm, and, Midas-like, trans-
muting them to gold.

In his youth he had probably been considered a
handsome man; at his present age, his brow was too
heavy, his temples too bare, his remaining hair too
gray, his eye too cold, his lips too closely compressed,
to bear any relation to mere personal beauty. He
would have made a good and massive portrait; better
now, perhaps, than at any previous period of his life,
although his look might grow positively harsh, in the
process of being fixed upon the canvas. The artist
would have found it desirable to study his face, and
prove its capacity for varied expression; to darken
it with a frown—to kindle it up with a smile.

While the elderly gentleman stood looking at the
Pyncheon-house, both the frown and the smile passed
successively over his countenance. His eye rested
on the shop-window, and, putting up a pair of gold-
bowed spectacles, which he held in his hand, he
minutely surveyed Hepzibah's little arrangement of
toys and commodities. At first it seemed not to please
him,—nay, to cause him exceeding displeasure,—and
yet, the very next moment, he smiled. While the
latter expression was yet on his lips, he caught a
glimpse of Hepzibah, who had involuntarily bent forward to the window; and then the smile changed from
acrid and disagreeable to the sunniest complacency
and benevolence. He bowed, with a happy mixture

of dignity and courteous kindliness, and pursued his way.

"There he is!" said Hepzibah to herself, gulping down a very bitter emotion, and, since she could not rid herself of it, trying to drive it back into her heart. "What does he think of it, I wonder? Does it please him? Ah!—he is looking back!"

The gentleman had paused in the street, and turned himself half about, with his eyes fixed on the shop-window. In fact, he wheeled wholly round, and commenced a step or two, as if designing to enter the shop; but, as it chanced, his purpose was anticipated by Hepzibah's first customer, the little cannibal of Jim Crow, who, staring up at the window, was irresistibly attracted by an elephant of gingerbread. What a grand appetite had this small urchin!—two Jim Crows immediately after breakfast!—and now an elephant, as a preliminary whet before dinner! By the time this latter purchase was completed, the elderly gentleman had resumed his way, and turned the street corner.

"Take it as you like, Cousin Jaffrey!" muttered the maiden lady, as she drew back, after cautiously thrusting out her head, and looking up and down the street. "Take it as you like! You have seen my little shop-window! Well!—What have you to say? —is not the Pyncheon-house my own, while I'm alive?"

After this incident, Hepzibah retreated to the back parlour, where she at first caught up a half-finished stocking, and began knitting at it with nervous and irregular jerks; but quickly finding herself at odds with the stitches, she threw it aside, and walked hurriedly about the room. At length, she paused before the portrait of the stern old Puritan, her ancestor, and the founder of the house. In one sense, this picture had almost faded into the canvas, and hidden itself behind the duskiness of age; in another, she could not but fancy that it had been growing more prominent, and strikingly expressive, ever since her

earliest familiarity with it, as a child. For, while
the physical outline and substance were darkening
away from the beholder's eye, the bold, hard, and,
at the same time, indirect character of the man,
seemed to be brought out in a kind of spiritual relief.
Such an effect may occasionally be observed in pictures of antique date. They acquire a look which an
artist (if he have anything like the complacency of
artists now-a-days) would never dream of presenting
to a patron as his own characteristic expression, but
which, nevertheless, we at once recognize as reflect-
ing the unlovely truth of a human soul. In such
cases, the painter's deep conception of his subject's
inward traits has wrought itself into the essence of
the picture, and is seen after the superficial colouring
has been rubbed off by time.

While gazing at the portrait, Hepzibah trembled
under its eye. Her hereditary reverence made her
afraid to judge the character of the original so harshly
as a perception of the truth compelled her to do. But
still she gazed, because the face of the picture enabled
her—at least, she fancied so—to read more accurately, and to a greater depth, the face which she had
just seen in the street.

" This is the very man !" murmured she to herself.
" Let Jaffrey Pyncheon smile as he will, there is that
look beneath ! Put on him a skull-cap, and a band,
and a black cloak, and a Bible in one hand and a
sword in the other,—then let Jaffrey smile as he
might,—nobody would doubt that it was the old
Pyncheon come again ! He has proved himself the
very man to build up a new house ! Perhaps, too,
to draw down a new curse !"

Thus did Hepzibah bewilder herself with these fantasies of the old time. She had dwelt too much alone,
—too long in the Pyncheon-house,—until her very
brain was impregnated with the dry rot of its timbers.
She needed a walk along the noon-day street, to keep
her sane.

By the spell of contrast, another portrait rose up

before her, painted with more daring flattery than any
artist would have ventured upon, but yet so delicately
touched that the likeness remained perfect.   Malbone's miniature, though from the same original, was
far inferior to Hepzibah's air-drawn picture, at which
affection and sorrowful remembrance wrought together.   Soft, mildly, and cheerfully contemplative,
with full, red lips, just on the verge of a smile,
which the eyes seemed to herald by a gentle kindling-
up of their orbs !   Feminine traits, moulded insepar-
ably with those of the other sex !   The miniature,
likewise, had this last peculiarity ; so that you inevitably thought of the original as resembling his mother,
and she, a lovely and lovable woman, with perhaps
some beautiful infirmity of character, that made it
all the pleasanter to know, and easier to love her.

"Yes," thought Hepzibah, with grief of which it
was only the more tolerable portion that welled up
from her heart to her eyelids, "they persecuted his
mother in him !   He never was a Pyncheon !"

But here the shop-bell rang ; it was like a sound
from a remote distance—so far had Hepzibah descended into the sepulchral depths of her reminiscences.   On entering the shop, she found an old man
there, a humble resident of Pyncheon-street, and
whom, for a great many years past, she had suffered
to be a kind of familiar of the house.   He was an
immemorial personage, who seemed always to have
had a white head and wrinkles, and never to have
possessed but a single tooth, and that a half-decayed
one, in the front of the upper jaw.   Well advanced
as Hepzibah was, she could not remember when Uncle
Venner, as the neighbourhood called him, had not
gone up and down the street, stooping a little and
drawing his feet heavily over the gravel or pavement.
But still there was something tough and vigorous
about him, that not only kept him in daily breath,
but enabled him to fill a place which would else have
been vacant in the apparently crowded world.   To go
of errands, with his slow and shuffling gait, which

made you doubt how he ever was to arrive anywhere; to saw a small household's foot or two of firewood, or knock to pieces an old barrel, or split up a pine board, for kindling-stuff; in summer, to dig the few yards of garden ground appertaining to a low-rented tenement, and share the produce of his labour at the halves; in winter, to shovel away the snow from the side-walk, or open paths to the wood-shed, or along the clothes-line; such were some of the essential offices which Uncle Venner performed among at least a score families. Within that circle, he claimed the same sort of privilege, and probably felt as much warmth of interest, as a clergyman does in the range of his parishioners. Not that he laid claim to the tithe pig; but, as an analogous mode of reverence, he went his rounds, every morning, to gather up the crumbs of the table and overflowings of the dinner-pot, as food for a pig of his own.

In his younger days—for, after all, there was a dim tradition that he had been, not young, but younger— Uncle Venner was commonly regarded as rather deficient, than otherwise, in his wits. In truth, he had virtually pleaded guilty to the charge, by scarcely aiming at such success as other men seek, and by taking only that humble and modest part, in the intercourse of life, which belongs to the alleged deficiency. But, now, in his extreme old age,—whether it were that his long and hard experience had actually brightened him, or that his decaying judgment rendered him less capable of fairly measuring himself,—the venerable man made pretensions to no little wisdom, and really enjoyed the credit of it. There was likewise, at times, a vein of something like poetry in him; it was the moss or wall-flower of his mind in its small dilapidation, and gave a charm to what might have been vulgar and common-place in his earlier and middle life. Hepzibah had a regard for him, because his name was ancient in the town, and had formerly been respectable. It was a still better reason for awarding him a species of familiar reverence, that

Uncle Venner was himself the most ancient existence, whether of man or thing, in Pyncheon-street, except the House of the Seven Gables, and perhaps the elm that overshadowed it.

The patriarch now presented himself before Hepzibah, clad in an old blue coat, which had a fashionable air, and must have accrued to him from the cast-off wardrobe of some dashing clerk. As for his trousers, they were of tow-cloth, very short in the legs, and bagging down strangely in the rear, but yet having a suitableness to his figure which his other garment entirely lacked. His hat had relation to no other part of his dress, and but very little to the head that wore it. Thus Uncle Venner was a miscellaneous old gentleman, partly himself, but, in good measure, somebody else; patched together, too, of different epochs; an epitome of times and fashions.

" So you have really begun trade," said he, " really begun trade! Well, I'm glad to see it. Young people should never live idle in the world, nor old ones neither, unless when the rheumatize gets hold of them. It has given me warning already; and in two or three years longer, I shall think of putting aside business, and retiring to my farm. That's yonder —the great brick house, you know—the workhouse, most folks call it; but I mean to do my work first, and go there to be idle and enjoy myself. And I'm glad to see you beginning to do your work, Miss Hepzibah !"

" Thank you, Uncle Venner," said Hepzibah, smiling; for she always felt kindly towards the simple and talkative old man. Had he been an old woman, she might probably have repelled the freedom which she now took in good part. " It is time for me to begin work, indeed ! Or, to speak the truth, I have just begun, when I ought to be giving it up."

" O, never say that, Miss Hepzibah," answered the old man. " You are a young woman yet. Why, I hardly thought myself younger than I am now, it seems so little while ago since I used to see you play-

ing about the door of the old house, quite a small
child! Oftener, though, you used to be sitting at the
threshold, and looking gravely into the street; for
you had always a grave kind of way with you,—a
grown-up air, when you were only the height of my
knee. It seems as if I saw you now; and your grandfather, with his red cloak and his white wig, and his
cocked hat, and his cane, coming out of the house,
and stepping so grandly up the street! Those old
gentlemen that grew up before the Revolution used
to put on grand airs. In my young days, the great
man of the town was commonly called King; and his
wife, not Queen to be sure, but Lady. Now-a-days,
a man would not dare to be called King; and if he
feels himself a little above common folks, he only
stoops so much the lower to them. I met my cousin,
the judge, ten minutes ago; and, in my old tow-cloth
trousers, as you see, the judge raised his hat to me,
I do believe! At any rate, the judge bowed and
smiled!"

"Yes," said Hepzibah, with something bitter stealing unawares into her tone; "my cousin Jaffrey is
thought to have a very pleasant smile!"

"And so he has!" replied Uncle Venner. "And
that's rather remarkable in a Pyncheon; for, begging
your pardon, Miss Hepzibah, they never had the
name of being an easy and agreeable set of folks.
There was no getting close to them. But now,
Miss Hepzibah, if an old man may be bold to ask,
why don't Judge Pyncheon, with his great means,
step forward, and tell his cousin to shut up her
little shop at once? It's for your credit to be doing
something; but it's not for the judge's credit to let
you!"

"We won't talk of this, if you please, Uncle Venner," said Hepzibah, coldly. "I ought to say, however, that if I choose to earn bread for myself, it is
not Judge Pyncheon's fault. Neither will he deserve
the blame," added she, more kindly, remembering
Uncle Venner's privileges of age and humble familiar-

ity, "if I should, by-and-by, find it convenient to retire with you to your farm."

"And it's no bad place, neither, that farm of mine!" cried the old man, cheerily, as if there were something positively delightful in the prospect. "No bad place is the great brick farm-house, especially for them that will find a good many old cronies there, as will be my case. I quite long to be among them, sometimes, of the winter evenings; for it is but dull business for a lonesome, elderly man like me, to be nodding by the hour together, with no company but his air-tight stove. Summer or winter, there's a great deal to be said in favour of my farm! And, take it in the autumn, what can be pleasanter than to spend a whole day on the sunny side of a barn or a wood-pile, chatting with somebody as old as one's self; or perhaps idling away the time with a natural born simpleton, who knows how to be idle, because even our busy Yankees never have found out how to put him to any use? Upon my word, Miss Hepzibah, I doubt whether I've ever been so comfortable as I mean to be at my farm, which most folks call the workhouse. But you,—you're a young woman yet, —you never need go there? Something still better will turn up for you. I'm sure of it!"

Hepzibah fancied that there was something peculiar in her venerable friend's look and tone; insomuch, that she gazed into his face with considerable earnestness, endeavouring to discover what secret meaning, if any, might be lurking there. Individuals whose affairs have reached an utterly desperate crisis almost invariably keep themselves alive with hopes, so much the more airily magnificent, as they have the less of solid matter within their grasp, whereof to mould any judicious and moderate expectation of good. Thus, all the while Hepzibah was perfecting the scheme of her little shop, she had cherished an unacknowledged idea that some harlequin trick of fortune would intervene in her favour. For example, an uncle—who had sailed for India fifty years before, and never been heard of since—might yet return, and adopt her to be the comfort of his very extreme and decrepit age, and adorn her with pearls, diamonds, and oriental shawls and turbans, and make her the ultimate heiress of his unreckonable riches.   Or the member of parliament, now at the head of the English branch of the family,—with which the elder stock, on this side of the Atlantic, had held little or no intercourse for the last two centuries,—this eminent gentleman might invite Hepzibah to quit the ruinous House of the Seven Gables, and come over to dwell with her kindred at Pyncheon Hall.   But, for reasons the most imperative, she could not yield to his request.   It was more probable, therefore, that the descendants of a Pyncheon who had emigrated to Virginia, in some past generation, and became a great planter there,—hearing of Hepzibah's destitution, and impelled by the splendid generosity of character with which their Virginian mixture must have enriched the New England blood,—would send her a remittance of a thousand dollars, with a hint of repeating the favour annually.   Or—and surely anything so undeniably just could not be beyond the limits of reasonable anticipation—the great claim to the heritage of Waldo County might finally be decided in favour of the Pyncheons; so that, instead of keeping a cent-shop, Hepzibah would build a palace, and look down from its highest tower on hill, dale, forest, field, and town, as her own share of the ancestral territory.

These were some of the fantasies which she had long dreamed about; and, aided by these, Uncle Venner's casual attempt at encouragement kindled a strange festal glory in the poor, bare, melancholy chambers of her brain, as if that inner world were suddenly lighted up with gas.   But either he knew nothing of her castles in the air—as how should he? —or else her earnest scowl disturbed his recollection, as it might a more courageous man's.   Instead of pursuing any weightier topic, Uncle Venner was

pleased to favour Hepzibah with some sage counsel
in her shop-keeping capacity.

" Give no credit ! "—these were some of his golden
maxims,—" Never take paper-money !   Look well to
your change !   Ring the silver on the four-pound
weight !   Shove back all English halfpence and base
copper tokens, such as are very plenty about town !
At your leisure hours, knit children's woollen socks
and mittens !   Brew your own yeast, and make your
own ginger-beer ! "

And while Hepzibah was doing her utmost to
digest the hard little pellets of his already uttered
wisdom, he gave vent to his final, and what he
declared to be his all-important, advice, as follows :—

" Put on a bright face for your customers, and smile
pleasantly as you hand them what they ask for !   A
stale article, if you dip it in a good, warm, sunny
smile, will go off better than a fresh one that you've
scowled upon."

To this last apothegm poor Hepzibah responded
with a sigh so deep and heavy that it almost rustled
Uncle Venner quite away, like a withered leaf,—as
he was,—before an autumnal gale.   Recovering himself, however, he bent forward, and, with a good deal
of feeling in his ancient visage, beckoned her nearer
to him.

" When do you expect him home ? " whispered he.

" Whom do you mean ? " asked Hepzibah, turning
pale.

" Ah ! you don't love to talk about it," said Uncle
Venner.   " Well, well ! we'll say no more, though
there's word of it, all over town.   I remember him,
Miss Hepzibah, before he could run alone ! "

During the remainder of the day, poor Hepzibah
acquitted herself even less creditably, as a shopkeeper, than in her earlier efforts.   She appeared to
be walking in a dream ; or, more truly, the vivid life
and reality assumed by her emotions made all outward
occurrences unsubstantial, like the teasing phantasms
of a half-conscious slumber.   She still responded,

mechanically, to the frequent summons of the shop-bell, and, at the demand of her customers, went prying with vague eyes about the shop, proffering them one article after another, and thrusting aside—perversely as most of them supposed—the identical thing they asked for.   There is sad confusion, indeed, when the spirit thus flits away into the past, or into the more awful future, or, in any manner, steps across the spaceless boundary betwixt its own region and the actual world; where the body remains to guide itself, as best it may, with little more than the mechanism of animal life.   It is like death, without death's quiet privilege,—its freedom from mortal care.   Worst of all, when the actual duties are comprised in such petty details as now vexed the brooding soul of the old gentlewoman.   As the animosity of fate would have it, there was a great influx of custom, in the course of the afternoon.   Hepzibah blundered to and fro about her small place of business, committing the most unheard of errors : now stringing up twelve, and now seven tallow-candles, instead of ten to the pound; selling ginger for Scotch snuff, pins for needles, and needles for pins; misreckoning her change, sometimes to the public detriment, and much oftener to her own; and thus she went on, doing her utmost to bring chaos back again, until, at the close of the day's labour, to her inexplicable astonishment, she found the money-drawer almost destitute of coin. After all her painful traffic, the whole proceeds were perhaps half-a-dozen coppers, and a questionable ninepence, which, ultimately, proved to be copper likewise.

At this price, or at whatever price, she rejoiced that the day had reached its end.   Never before had she had such a sense of the intolerable length of time that creeps between dawn and sunset, and of the miserable irksomeness of having aught to do, and of the better wisdom that it would be, to lie down at once, in sullen resignation, and let life, and its toils and vexations, trample over one's prostrate body, as they may !

Hepzibah's final operation was with the little devourer
of Jim Crow and the elephant, who now proposed to
eat a camel. In her bewilderment she offered him first
a wooden dragoon, and next a handful of marbles;
neither of which being adapted to his else omnivorous
appetite, she hastily held out her whole remaining
stock of natural history in gingerbread, and huddled
the small customer out of the shop. She then muffled
the bell in an unfinished stocking, and put up the
oaken bar across the door.

During the latter process an omnibus came to a
standstill under the branches of the elm-tree. Hepzibah's heart was in her mouth. Remote and dusky,
and with no sunshine on all the intervening space,
was that region of the past, whence her only guest
might be expected to arrive ! Was she to meet him
now?

Somebody, at all events, was passing from the
furthest interior of the omnibus towards its entrance.
A gentleman alighted; but it was only to offer his
hand to a young girl, whose slender figure nowise
needed such assistance, now lightly descended the
steps, and made an airy little jump from the final one
to the sidewalk. She rewarded her cavalier with a
smile, the cheery glow of which was seen reflected on
his own face as he re-entered the vehicle. The girl
then turned towards the House of the Seven Gables,
to the door of which, meanwhile,—not the shop-door
but the antique portal,—the omnibus-man had carried
a light trunk and band-box. First giving a sharp
rap of the old iron knocker, he left his passenger and
her luggage at the door-step, and departed.

" Who can it be?" thought Hepzibah, who had
been screwing her visual organs into the acutest focus
of which they were capable. " The girl must have
mistaken the house !"

She stole swiftly into the hall, and, herself invisible,
gazed through the dusky side-lights of the portal at
the young, blooming, and very cheerful face, which
presented itself for admittance into the gloomy old

mansion. It was a face to which almost any door would have opened of its own accord.

The young girl, so fresh, so unconventional, and yet so orderly and obedient to common rules, as you at once recognized her to be, was widely in contrast, at that moment, with everything about her. The sordid and ugly luxuriance of gigantic weeds that grew in the angle of the house, and the heavy projection that overshadowed her, and the time-worn framework of the door,—none of these things belonged to her sphere. But, even as a ray of sunshine, fall into what dismal place it may, instantaneously creates for itself a propriety in being there, so did it seem altogether fit that the girl should be standing at the threshold. It was no less evidently proper that the door should swing open to admit her. The maiden lady, herself, sternly inhospitable in her first purposes, soon began to feel that the door ought to be shoved back, and the rusty key be turned in the reluctant lock.

" Can it be Phœbe?" questioned she within herself. " It must be little Phœbe ; for it can be nobody else, —and there is a look of her father about her too ! But what does she want here? and how like a country cousin, to come down upon a poor body in this way, without so much as a day's notice, or asking whether she would be welcome ! Well ; she must have a night's lodging, I suppose, and to-morrow the child shall go back to her mother !"

Phœbe, it must be understood, was that one little off-shoot of the Pyncheon race to whom we have already referred, as a native of a rural part of New England, where the old fashions and feelings of relationship are still partially kept up. In her own circle, it was regarded as by no means improper for kinsfolk to visit one another, without invitation, or preliminary and ceremonious warning. Yet, in consideration of Miss Hepzibah's recluse way of life, a letter had actually been written and despatched, conveying information of Phœbe's projected visit. This

epistle, for three or four days past, had been in the
pocket of the penny-postman, who, happening to have
no other business in Pyncheon-street, had not yet
made it convenient to call at the House of the Seven
Gables.

"No!—she can stay only one night," said Hepzibah, unbolting the door. "If Clifford were to find
her here, it might disturb him !"

V

MAY AND NOVEMBER

PHŒBE PYNCHEON slept, on the night of her arrival,
in a chamber that looked down on the garden of the
old house. It fronted towards the east, so that at
a very seasonable hour a glow of crimson light came
flooding through the window, and bathed the dingy
ceiling and paper-hangings in its own hue. There
were curtains to Phœbe's bed ; a dark, antique canopy
and ponderous festoons, of a stuff which had been
rich, and even magnificent, in its time ; but which now
brooded over the girl like a cloud, making a night
in that one corner, while elsewhere it was beginning
to be day. The morning light, however, soon stole
into the aperture at the foot of the bed, betwixt those
faded curtains. Finding the new guest there,—with
a bloom on her cheeks like the morning's own, and a
gentle stir of departing slumber in her limbs, as when
an early breeze moves the foliage,—the dawn kissed
her brow. It was the caress which a dewy maiden—
such as the Dawn is, immortally—gives to her sleep-
ing sister, partly from the impulse of irresistible
fondness, and partly as a pretty hint that it is time
now to unclose her eyes.

At the touch of those lips of light, Phœbe quietly

awoke, and, for a moment, did not recognize where
she was, nor how those heavy curtains chanced to be
festooned around her. Nothing, indeed, was absolutely
plain to her, except that it was now early morning,
and that, whatever might happen next, it was proper,
first of all, to get up and say her prayers. She was
the more inclined to devotion, from the grim aspect
of the chamber and its furniture, especially the tall,
stiff chairs; one of which stood close by her bedside,
and looked as if some old-fashioned personage had
been sitting there all night, and had vanished only
just in season to escape discovery.

When Phœbe was quite dressed, she peeped out of
the window, and saw a rose-bush in the garden.
Being a very tall one, and of luxurious growth, it
had been propped up against the side of the house,
and was literally covered with a rare and very beautiful species of white rose. A large portion of them,
as the girl afterwards discovered, had blight or mildew at their hearts; but, viewed at a fair distance,
the whole rose-bush looked as if it had been brought
from Eden that very summer, together with the
mould in which it grew. The truth was, nevertheless, that it had been planted by Alice Pyncheon,—
she was Phœbe's great-great-grand-aunt,—in soil
which, reckoning only its cultivation as a garden-
plat, was now unctuous with nearly two hundred
years of vegetable decay. Growing as they did, however, out of the old earth, the flowers still sent a
fresh and sweet incense up to their Creator; nor could
it have been the less pure and acceptable, because
Phœbe's young breath mingled with it, as the fragrance floated past the window. Hastening down the
creaking and carpetless staircase, she found her way
into the garden, gathered some of the most perfect of
the roses, and brought them to her chamber.

Little Phœbe was one of those persons who
possess, as their exclusive patrimony, the gift of
practical arrangement. It is a kind of natural magic
that enables these favoured ones to bring out the

hidden capabilities of things around them; and particularly to give a look of comfort and habitableness to any place which, for however brief a period, may happen to be their home. A wild hut of underbush, tossed together by wayfarers through the primitive forest, would acquire the home aspect by one night's lodging of such a woman, and would retain it long after her quiet figure had disappeared into the surrounding shade. No less a portion of such homely witchcraft was requisite to reclaim, as it were, Phœbe's waste, cheerless, and dusky chamber, which had been untenanted so long—except by spiders, and mice, rats, and ghosts—that it was all overgrown with the desolation which watches to obliterate every trace of man's happier hours. What was precisely Phœbe's process, we find it impossible to say. She appeared to have no preliminary design, but gave a touch here, and another there; brought some articles of furniture to light, and dragged others into the shadow; looped up or let down a window-curtain; and, in the course of half-an-hour, had fully succeeded in throwing a kindly and hospitable smile over the apartment. No longer ago than the night before, it had resembled nothing so much as the old maid's heart; for there was neither sunshine nor household-fire in one nor the other, and, save for ghosts and ghostly reminiscences, not a guest, for many years gone-by, had entered the heart or the chamber.

There was still another peculiarity of this inscrutable charm. The bed-chamber, no doubt, was a chamber of very great and varied experience, as a scene of human life; the joy of bridal nights had throbbed itself away here; new immortals had first drawn earthly breath here; and here old people had died. But—whether it were the white roses, or whatever the subtile influence might be—a person of delicate instinct would have known, at once, that it was now a maiden's bed-chamber, and had been purified of all former evil and sorrow by her sweet breath and happy thoughts. Her dreams of the past night, being such cheerful ones, had exorcised the gloom, and now haunted the chamber in its stead.

After arranging matters to her satisfaction, Phœbe emerged from her chamber, with a purpose to descend again into the garden. Besides the rose-bush, she had observed several other species of flowers, growing there in a wilderness of neglect, and obstructing one another's development (as is often the parallel case in human society) by their uneducated entanglement and confusion. At the head of the stairs, however, she met Hepzibah, who, it being still early, invited her into a room which she would probably have called her boudoir, had her education embraced any such French phrase. It was strewn about with a few old books, and a work-basket, and a dusty writing-desk; and had, on one side, a large, black article of furniture, of very strange appearance, which the old gentlewoman told Phœbe was a harpsichord. It looked more like a coffin than anything else, and, indeed,—not having been played upon, or opened, for years,—there must have been a vast deal of dead music in it, stifled for want of air. Human finger was hardly known to have touched its chords since the days of Alice Pyncheon, who had learned the sweet accomplishment of melody in Europe.

Hepzibah bade her young guest sit down, and, herself taking a chair near by, looked as earnestly at Phœbe's trim little figure, as if she expected to see right into its springs and motive secrets.

"Cousin Phœbe," said she, at last, "I really can't see my way clear to keep you with me."

These words, however, had not the inhospitable bluntness with which they may strike the reader; for the two relatives, in a talk before bedtime, had arrived at a certain degree of mutual understanding. Hepzibah knew enough to enable her to appreciate the circumstances (resulting from the second marriage of the girl's mother) which made it desirable for Phœbe to establish herself in another home. Nor did she misinterpret Phœbe's character, and the genial activity pervading it,—one of the most valuable traits of the true New England woman,—which had impelled her forth, as might be said, to seek her fortune, but with a self-respecting purpose to confer as much benefit as she could anywise receive. As one of her nearest kindred, she had naturally betaken herself to Hepzibah, with no idea of forcing herself on her cousin's protection, but only for a visit of a week or two, which might be indefinitely extended, should it prove for the happiness of both.

To Hepzibah's blunt observation, therefore, Phœbe replied, as frankly, and more cheerfully—

"Dear cousin, I cannot tell how it will be," said she. "But I really think we may suit one another much better than you suppose."

"You are a nice girl,—I see it plainly," continued Hepzibah; "and it is not any question as to that point which makes me hesitate. But, Phœbe, this house of mine is but a melancholy place for a young person to be in. It lets in the wind and rain, and the snow, too, in the garret and upper chambers, in winter-time; but it never lets in the sunshine! And as for myself, you see what I am,—a dismal and lonesome old woman (for I begin to call myself old, Phœbe), whose temper, I am afraid, is none of the best, and whose spirits are as bad as can be. I cannot make your life pleasant, Cousin Phœbe, neither can I so much as give you bread to eat."

"You will find me a cheerful little body," answered Phœbe, smiling, and yet with a kind of gentle dignity; "and I mean to earn my bread. You know I have not been brought up a Pyncheon. A girl learns many things in a New England village."

"Ah! Phœbe," said Hepzibah, sighing, "your knowledge would do but little for you here! And then it is a wretched thought, that you should fling away your young days in a place like this. Those cheeks would not be so rosy, after a month or two Look at my face!"—and, indeed, the contrast was very striking,—"you see how pale I am! It is my

idea that the dust and continual decay of these old
houses are unwholesome for the lungs."

"There is the garden,—the flowers to be taken
care of," observed Phœbe. "I should keep myself
healthy with exercise in the open air."

"And, after all, child," exclaimed Hepzibah, suddenly rising, as if to dismiss the subject, "it is not
for me to say who shall be a guest or inhabitant of
the old Pyncheon-house. Its master is coming."

"Do you mean Judge Pyncheon?" asked Phœbe,
in surprise.

"Judge Pyncheon!" answered her cousin, angrily.
"He will hardly cross the threshold while I live!
No, no! But, Phœbe, you shall see the face of him
I speak of."

She went in quest of the miniature already described, and returned with it in her hand. Giving
it to Phœbe, she watched her features narrowly, and
with a certain jealousy as to the mode in which the
girl would show herself affected by the picture.

"How do you like the face?" asked Hepzibah.

"It is handsome!—it is very beautiful!" said
Phœbe, admiringly. "It is as sweet a face as a
man's can be, or ought to be. It has something of
a child's expression,—and yet not childish,—only,
one feels so very kindly towards him! He ought
never to suffer anything. One would bear much for
the sake of sparing him toil or sorrow. Who is it,
Cousin Hepzibah?"

"Did you never hear," whispered her cousin,
bending towards her, "of Clifford Pyncheon?"

"Never! I thought there were no Pyncheons
left, except yourself and our cousin Jaffrey,"
answered Phœbe. "And yet I seem to have heard
the name of Clifford Pyncheon. Yes!—from my
father, or my mother; but has he not been a long
while dead?"

"Well, well, child, perhaps he has!" said Hepzibah, with a sad, hollow laugh; "but, in old houses
like this, you know, dead people are very apt to come

back again! We shall see. And, Cousin Phœbe,
since, after all that I have said, your courage does
not fail you, we will not part so soon. You are welcome, my child, for the present, to such a home as
your kinswoman can offer you."

With this measured, but not exactly cold assurance of a hospitable purpose, Hepzibah kissed her
cheek.

They now went below stairs, where Phœbe—not
so much assuming the office as attracting it to herself, by the magnetism of innate fitness—took the
most active part in preparing breakfast. The mistress of the house, meanwhile, as is usual with
persons of her stiff and unmalleable cast, stood mostly
aside; willing to lend her aid, yet conscious that her
natural inaptitude would be likely to impede the business in hand. Phœbe, and the fire that boiled the
tea-kettle, were equally bright, cheerful, and efficient,
in their respective offices. Hepzibah gazed forth
from her habitual sluggishness, the necessary result
of long solitude, as from another sphere. She could
not help being interested, however, and even amused,
at the readiness with which her new inmate adapted
herself to the circumstances, and brought the house,
moreover, and all its rusty old appliances, into a
suitableness for her purposes. Whatever she did, too,
was done without conscious effort, and with frequent
outbreaks of song, which were exceedingly pleasant
to the ear. This natural tunefulness made Phœbe
seem like a bird in a shadowy tree; or conveyed the
idea that the stream of life warbled through her heart
as a brook sometimes warbles through a pleasant
little dell. It betokened the cheeriness of an active
temperament, finding joy in its activity, and, therefore, rendering it beautiful; it was a New England
trait,—the stern old stuff of Puritanism, with a gold
thread in the web.

Hepzibah brought out some old silver spoons, with
the family crest upon them, and a China tea-set,
painted over with grotesque figures of man, bird, and

beast, in as grotesque a landscape. These pictured people were odd humorists, in a world of their own, —a world of vivid brilliancy, so far as colour went, and still unfaded, although the tea-pot and small cups were as ancient as the custom itself of tea-drinking.

" Your great-great-great-great-grandmother had these cups, when she was married," said Hepzibah to Phœbe. " She was a Davenport, of a good family. They were almost the first tea-cups ever seen in the colony; and if one of them were to be broken my heart would break with it. But it is nonsense to speak so about a brittle tea-cup, when I remember what my heart has gone through, without breaking."

The cups—not having been used, perhaps, since Hepzibah's youth—had contracted no small burden of dust, which Phœbe washed away with so much care and delicacy as to satisfy even the proprietor of this invaluable china.

" What a nice little housewife you are !" exclaimed the latter smiling, and, at the same time frowning so prodigiously that the smile was sunshine under a thunder-cloud. " Do you do other things as well? Are you as good at your book as you are at washing tea-cups?"

" Not quite, I am afraid," said Phœbe, laughing at the form of Hepzibah's question. " But I was schoolmistress for the little children of our district, last summer, and might have been so still."

" Ah ! 'tis all very well !" observed the maiden lady, drawing herself up.—" But these things must have come to you with your mother's blood. I never knew a Pyncheon that had any turn for them."

It is very queer, but not the less true, that people are generally quite as vain, or even more so, of their deficiencies, than of their available gifts; as was Hepzibah of this native inapplicability, so to speak, of the Pyncheons, to any useful purpose. She regarded it as an hereditary trait; and so, perhaps, it was, but, unfortunately, a morbid one, such as is often generated in families that remain long above the surface of society.

Before they left the breakfast-table, the shop-bell rang sharply, and Hepzibah set down the remnant of her final cup of tea, with a look of sallow despair that was truly piteous to behold. In cases of distasteful occupation, the second day is generally worse than the first; we return to the rack with all the soreness of the preceding torture in our limbs. At all events, Hepzibah had fully satisfied herself of the impossibility of ever becoming wonted to this peevishly obstreperous little bell. Ring as often as it might, the sound always smote upon her nervous system rudely and suddenly. And especially now, while, with her crested tea-spoons and antique china, she was flattering herself with ideas of gentility, she felt an unspeakable disinclination to confront a customer.

"Do not trouble yourself, dear cousin!" cried Phœbe, starting lightly up. "I am shopkeeper to-day."

"You, child!" exclaimed Hepzibah. "What can a little country-girl know of such matters?"

"O, I have done all the shopping for the family, at our village store," said Phœbe. "And I have had a table at a fancy fair, and made better sales than anybody. These things are not to be learnt; they depend upon a knack, that comes, I suppose," added she, smiling, "with one's mother's blood. You shall see that I am as nice a little saleswoman as I am a housewife!"

The old gentlewoman stole behind Phœbe, and peeped from the passage-way into the shop, to note how she would manage her undertaking. It was a case of some intricacy. A very ancient woman, in a white short gown, and a green petticoat with a string of gold beads about her neck, and what looked like a night-cap on her head, had brought a quantity of yarn to barter for the commodities of the shop. She was probably the very last person in town who still kept the time-honoured spinning-wheel in constant

revolution. It was worth while to hear the croaking
and hollow tones of the old lady, and the pleasant
voice of Phœbe, mingling in one twisted thread of
talk; and still better, to contrast their figures,—so
light and bloomy—so decrepit and dusky,—with only
the counter betwixt them, in one sense, but more than
threescore years, in another. As for the bargain, it
was wrinkled slyness and craft pitted against native
truth and sagacity.

" Was not that well done?" asked Phœbe, laughing, when the customer was gone.

" Nicely done, indeed, child !" answered Hepzibah.
" I could not have gone through with it nearly so
well. As you say, it must be a knack that belongs to
you on the mother's side."

It is a very genuine admiration, that with which
persons too shy or too awkward to take a due part in
the bustling world regard the real actors in life's
stirring scenes; so genuine, in fact, that the former
are usually fain to make it palatable to their self-love,
by assuming that these active and forcible qualities
are incompatible with others, which they choose to
deem higher and more important. Thus, Hepzibah
was well content to acknowledge Phœbe's vastly
superior gifts as a shopkeeper; she listened, with
compliant ear, to her suggestion of various methods
whereby the influx of trade might be increased, and
rendered profitable, without a hazardous outlay of
capital. She consented that the village maiden
should manufacture yeast, both liquid and in cakes;
and should brew a certain kind of beer, nectareous to
the palate, and of rare stomachic virtues; and, moreover, should bake and exhibit for sale some little
spice-cakes, which whosoever tasted would longingly
desire to taste again. All such proofs of a ready
mind, and skilful handiwork, were highly acceptable
to the aristocratic hucksteress, so long as she could
murmur to herself, with a grim smile, and a half-
natural sigh, and a sentiment of mixed wonder, pity,
and growing affection—

" What a nice little body she is ! If she could only be a lady, too !—but that's impossible ! Phœbe is no Pyncheon. She takes everything from her mother."

As to Phœbe's not being a lady, or whether she were a lady or no, it was a point, perhaps, difficult to decide, but which could hardly have come up for judgment at all, in any fair and healthy mind. Out of New England, it would be impossible to meet with a person combining so many ladylike attributes with so many others that form no necessary (if compatible) part of the character. She shocked no canon of taste : she was admirably in keeping with herself, and never jarred against surrounding circumstances. Her figure, to be sure,—so small as to be almost childlike, and so elastic that motion seemed as easy or easier to it than rest,—would hardly have suited one's idea of a countess. Neither did her face—with the brown ringlets on either side, and the slightly piquant nose, and the wholesome bloom, and the clear shade of tan, and the half a dozen freckles, friendly remembrancers of the April sun and breeze—precisely give us a right to call her beautiful. But there was both lustre and depth in her eyes. She was very pretty, as graceful as a bird, and graceful much in the same way; as pleasant about the house as a gleam of sunshine falling on the floor through a shadow of twinkling leaves, or as a ray of firelight that dances on the wall, while evening is drawing nigh. Instead of discussing her claim to rank among ladies, it would be preferable to regard Phœbe as the example of feminine grace and availability combined, in a state of society, if there were any such, where ladies did not exist. There it should be woman's office to move in the midst of practical affairs, and to gild them all, the very homeliest,—were it even the scouring of pots and kettles,—with an atmosphere of loveliness and joy.

Such was the sphere of Phœbe. To find the born and educated lady, on the other hand, we need look no further than Hepzibah, our forlorn old maid, in her rustling and rusty silks, with her deeply-cherished and ridiculous consciousness of long descent, her shadowy claims to princely territory, and, in the way of accomplishment, her recollections, it may be, of having formerly thrummed on a harpsichord, and walked a minuet, and worked an antique tapestry-stitch on her sampler. It was a fair parallel between new Plebeianism and old Gentility.

It really seemed as if the battered visage of the House of the Seven Gables, black and heavy-browed as it still certainly looked, must have shown a kind of cheerfulness glimmering through its dusky windows, as Phœbe passed to and fro in the interior. Otherwise it is impossible to explain how the people of the neighbourhood so soon became aware of the girl's presence. There was a great run of custom, setting steadily in, from about ten o'clock until towards noon,—relaxing, somewhat, at dinner-time, but recommencing in the afternoon, and, finally, dying away half-an-hour or so before the long day's sunset. One of the staunchest patrons was little Ned Wiggins, the devourer of Jim Crow and the elephant, who to-day had signalized his omnivorous prowess by swallowing two dromedaries and a locomotive. Phœbe laughed, as she summed up her aggregate of sales, upon the slate, while Hepzibah, first drawing on a pair of silk gloves, reckoned over the sordid accumulation of copper coin, not without silver intermixed, that had jingled into the till.

" We must renew our stock, Cousin Hepzibah !" cried the little saleswoman. " The gingerbread figures are all gone, and so are those Dutch wooden milkmaids, and most of our other playthings. There has been constant inquiry for cheap raisins, and a great cry for whistles, and trumpets, and Jew's-harps ; and at least a dozen little boys have asked for molasses-candy. And we must contrive to get a peck of russet apples, late in the season as it is. But dear cousin, what an enormous heap of copper ! Positively a copper mountain !"

"Well done! well done! well done!" quoth Uncle Venner, who had taken occasion to shuffle in and out of the shop several times in the course of the day. "Here's a girl that will never end her days at my farm! Bless my eyes, what a brisk little soul!"

"Yes, Phœbe is a nice girl," said Hepzibah, with a scowl of austere approbation. "But, Uncle Venner, you have known the family a great many years. Can you tell me whether there ever was a Pyncheon whom she takes after?"

"I don't believe there ever was," answered the venerable man. "At any rate, it never was my luck to see her like among them, nor, for that matter, anywhere else. I've seen a great deal of the world, not only in people's kitchens and back-yards, but at the street-corners, and on the wharves, and in other places where my business calls me; and I'm free to say, Miss Hepzibah, that I never knew a human creature do her work so much like one of God's angels as this child Phœbe does!"

Uncle Venner's eulogium, if it appear rather too high-strained for the purpose and occasion, had, nevertheless, a sense in it which was both subtle and true. There was a spiritual quality in Phœbe's activity. The life of the long and busy day—spent in occupations that might so easily have taken a squalid and ugly aspect—had been made pleasant, and even lovely, by the spontaneous grace with which these homely duties seemed to bloom out of her character; so that labour, while she dealt with it, had the easy and flexible charm of play. Angels do not toil, but let their good works grow out of them; and so did Phœbe.

The two relatives—the young maid and the old one—found time, before nightfall, in the intervals of trade, to make rapid advances towards affection and confidence. A recluse, like Hepzibah, usually displays remarkable frankness, and at least temporary affability, on being absolutely cornered, and brought to the point of personal intercourse; like the angel whom Jacob wrestled with, she is ready to bless you, when once overcome.

The old gentlewoman took a dreary and proud satisfaction in leading Phœbe from room to room of the house, and recounting the traditions with which, as we may say, the walls were lugubriously frescoed. She showed the indentations made by the lieutenant-governor's sword-hilt in the door-panels of the apartment where old Colonel Pyncheon, a dead host, had received his affrighted visitors with an awful frown. The dusky terror of that frown, Hepzibah observed, was thought to be lingering ever since in the passage way. She bade Phœbe step into one of the tall chairs, and inspect the ancient map of the Pyncheon territory at the eastward. In a tract of land on which she laid her finger, there existed a silver mine, the locality of which was precisely pointed out in some memoranda of Colonel Pyncheon himself, but only to be made known when the family claim should be recognized by government. Thus it was for the interest of all New England that the Pyncheons should have justice done them. She told, too, how that there was undoubtedly an immense treasure of English guineas hidden somewhere about the house, or in the cellar, or possibly in the garden.

" If you should happen to find it, Phœbe," said Hepzibah, glancing aside at her with a grim yet kindly smile, " we will tie up the shop-bell for good and all."

" Yes, my dear cousin," answered Phœbe; " but, in the meantime, I hear somebody ringing it !"

When the customer was gone, Hepzibah talked rather vaguely, and at great length, about a certain Alice Pyncheon, who had been exceedingly beautiful and accomplished in her lifetime, a hundred years ago. The fragrance of her rich and delightful character still lingered about the place where she had lived, as a dried rosebud scents the drawer where it has withered and perished. This lovely Alice had met with some great and mysterious calamity, and had grown thin and white, and gradually faded out of the world. But, even now, she was supposed to haunt the House of the Seven Gables, and a great many times,—especially when one of the Pyncheons was to die—she had been heard playing sadly and beautifully on the harpsichord. One of these tunes, just as it had sounded from her spiritual touch, had been written down by an amateur of music; it was so exquisitely mournful that nobody, to this day, could bear to hear it played, unless when a great sorrow had made them know the still profounder sweetness of it.

"Was it the same harpsichord that you showed me?" inquired Phœbe.

"The very same," said Hepzibah. "It was Alice Pyncheon's harpsichord. When I was learning music, my father would never let me open it. So, as I could only play on my teacher's instrument, I have forgotten all my music long ago."

Leaving these antique themes, the old lady began to talk about the daguerreotypist, whom, as he seemed to be a well-meaning and orderly young man, and in narrow circumstances, she had permitted to take up his residence in one of the seven gables. But on seeing more of Mr. Holgrave, she hardly knew what to make of him. He had the strangest companions imaginable; men with long beards, and dressed in linen blouses, and other such new-fangled and ill-fitting garments; reformers, temperance lecturers, and all manner of cross-looking philanthropists; community-men, and come-outers, as Hepzibah believed, who acknowledged no law, and ate no solid food, but lived on the scent of other people's cookery, and turned up their noses at the fare. As for the daguerreotypist, she had read a paragraph in a penny paper, the other day, accusing him of making a speech full of wild and disorganizing matter, at a meeting of his banditti-like associates. For her own part, she had reason to believe that he practised animal magnetism, and, if such things were in fashion

now-a-days, should be apt to suspect him of studying
the Black Art, up there in his lonesome chamber.

"But, dear cousin," said Phœbe, "if the young
man is so dangerous, why do you let him stay? If
he does nothing worse, he may set the house on
fire!"

"Why, sometimes," answered Hepzibah, "I have
seriously made it a question, whether I ought not to
send him away. But, with all his oddities, he is a
quiet kind of a person, and has such a way of taking
hold of one's mind, that, without exactly liking him
(for I don't know enough of the young man), I should
be sorry to lose sight of him entirely. A woman
clings to slight acquaintances, when she lives so much
alone as I do."

"But if Mr. Holgrave is a lawless person!"
remonstrated Phœbe, a part of whose essence it was
to keep within the limits of law.

"O!" said Hepzibah, carelessly,—for, formal as
she was, still, in her life's experience, she had
gnashed her teeth against human law,—"I suppose
he has a law of his own!"

VI

MAULE'S WELL

AFTER an early tea, the little country girl strayed
into the garden. The enclosure had formerly been
very extensive, but was now contracted within small
compass, and hemmed about, partly by high wooden
fences, and partly by the out-buildings of houses that
stood on another street. In its centre was a grass-
plat, surrounding a ruinous little structure, which
showed just enough of its original design to indicate

that it had once been a summer-house. A hop-vine, springing from last year's root, was beginning to clamber over it, but would be long in covering the roof with its green mantle. Three of the seven gables either fronted or looked sideways, with a dark solemnity of aspect, down into the garden.

The black rich soil had fed itself with the decay of a long period of time; such as fallen leaves, the petals of flowers, and the stalks and seed-vessels of vagrant and lawless plants, more useful after their death than ever while flaunting in the sun. The evil of these departed years would naturally have sprung up again, in such rank weeds (symbolic of the transmitted vices of society) as are always prone to root themselves about human dwellings. Phœbe saw, however, that their growth must have been checked by a degree of careful labour, bestowed daily and systematically on the garden. The white double rose-bush had evidently been propped up anew against the house, since the commencement of the season; and a pear-tree and three damson-trees, which, except a row of currant-bushes, constituted the only varieties of fruit, bore marks of the recent amputation of several superfluous or defective limbs. There were also a few species of antique and hereditary flowers, in no very flourishing condition, but scrupulously weeded; as if some person, either out of love or curiosity, had been anxious to bring them to such perfection as they were capable of attaining. The remainder of the garden presented a well-selected assortment of esculent vegetables, in a praiseworthy state of advancement. Summer squashes, almost in their golden blossom; cucumbers, now evincing a tendency to spread away from the main stock, and ramble far and wide; two or three rows of string-beans, and as many more that were about to festoon themselves on poles; tomatoes, occupying a site so sheltered and sunny, that the plants were already gigantic, and promised an early and abundant harvest.

Phœbe wondered whose care and toil it could have been that had planted these vegetables, and kept the soil so clean and orderly. Not, surely, her cousin Hepzibah's, who had no taste nor spirits for the lady-like employment of cultivating flowers, and— with her recluse habits, and tendency to shelter herself within the dismal shadow of the house—would hardly have come forth, under the speck of open sky, to weed and hoe among the fraternity of beans and squashes.

It being her first day of complete estrangement from rural objects, Phœbe found an unexpected charm in this little nook of grass, and foliage, and aristocratic flowers, and plebeian vegetables. The eye of Heaven seemed to look down into it pleasantly, and with a peculiar smile, as if glad to perceive that nature, elsewhere overwhelmed, and driven out of the dusty town, had here been able to retain a breathing-place. The spot acquired a somewhat wilder grace, and yet a very gentle one, from the fact that a pair of robins had built their nest in the pear-tree, and were making themselves exceedingly busy and happy in the dark intricacy of its boughs. Bees, too,—strange to say,—had thought it worth their while to come hither, possibly from the range of hives beside some farm-house, miles away. How many aërial voyages might they have made, in quest of honey, or honey-laden, betwixt dawn and sunset! Yet, late as it now was, there still arose a pleasant hum out of one or two of the squash-blossoms, in the depths of which these bees were plying their golden labour. There was one other object in the garden which nature might fairly claim as her inalienable property, in spite of whatever man could do to render it his own. This was a fountain, set round with a rim of old mossy stones, and paved, in its bed, with what appeared to be a sort of Mosaic work of variously coloured pebbles. The play and slight agitation of the water, in its upward gush, wrought magically with these variegated pebbles, and made a

continually shifting apparition of quaint figures,
vanishing too suddenly to be definable. Thence,
swelling over the rim of moss-grown stones, the
water stole away under the fence, through what we
regret to call a gutter rather than a channel.

Nor must we forget to mention a hen-coop of very
reverend antiquity that stood in the further corner of
the garden, not a great way from the fountain. It
now contained only Chanticleer, his two wives, and a
solitary chicken. All of them were pure specimens
of a breed which had been transmitted down as an
heir-loom in the Pyncheon family, and were said,
while in their prime, to have attained almost the size
of turkeys, and, on the score of delicate flesh, to be
fit for a prince's table. In proof of the authenticity
of this legendary renown, Hepzibah could have
exhibited the shell of a great egg, which an ostrich
need hardly have been ashamed of. Be that as it
might, the hens were now scarcely larger than
pigeons, and had a queer, rusty, withered aspect,
and a gouty kind of movement, and a sleepy and
melancholy tone throughout all the variations of
their clucking and cackling. It was evident that the
race had degenerated, like many a noble race besides, in consequence of too strict a watchfulness to
keep it pure. These feathered people had existed
too long in their distinct variety; a fact of which the
present representatives, judging by their lugubrious
deportment, seemed to be aware. They kept themselves alive, unquestionably, and laid now and then
an egg, and hatched a chicken, not for any pleasure
of their own, but that the world might not absolutely
lose what had once been so admirable a breed of
fowls. The distinguishing mark of the hens was a
crest of lamentably scanty growth, in these latter
days, but so oddly and wickedly analogous to Hepzibah's turban, that Phœbe—to the poignant distress
of her conscience, but inevitably—was led to fancy
a general resemblance betwixt these forlorn bipeds
and her respectable relative.

The girl ran into the house to get some crumbs of
bread, cold potatoes, and other scraps as were suit-
able to the accommodating appetite of fowls.
Returning, she gave a peculiar call, which they
seemed to recognize. The chicken crept through the
pales of the coop, and ran, with some show of live-
liness, to her feet; while Chanticleer and the ladies of
his household regarded her with queer, sidelong
glances, and then croaked one to another, as if communicating their sage opinions of her character. So
wise, as well as antique, was their aspect, as to give
colour to the idea, not merely that they were the
descendants of a time-honoured race, but that they
had existed, in their individual capacity, ever since
the House of the Seven Gables was founded, and
were somehow mixed up with its destiny. They
were a species of tutelary sprite, or Banshee; although winged and feathered differently from most
other guardian angels.

" Here, you odd little chicken!" said Phœbe;
" here are some nice crumbs for you!"

The chicken hereupon, though almost as venerable
in appearance as its mother,—possessing, indeed, the
whole antiquity of its progenitors, in miniature—
mustered vivacity enough to flutter upward and
alight on Phœbe's shoulder.

" That little fowl pays you a high compliment!"
said a voice behind Phœbe.

Turning quickly, she was surprised at sight of a
young man, who had found access into the garden
by a door opening out of another gable than that
whence she had emerged. He held a hoe in his
hand, and, while Phœbe was gone in quest of the
crumbs, had begun to busy himself with drawing up
fresh earth about the roots of the tomatoes.

" The chicken really treats you like an old acquaintance," continued he, in a quiet way, while a
smile made his face pleasanter than Phœbe at first
fancied it. " Those venerable personages in the
coop, too, seem very affably disposed. You are

lucky to be in their good graces so soon! They have known me much longer, but never honour me with any familiarity, though hardly a day passes without my bringing them food. Miss Hepzibah, I suppose, will interweave the fact with her other traditions, and set it down that the fowls know you to be a Pyncheon!"

"The secret is," said Phœbe, smiling, "that I have learned how to talk with hens and chickens."

"Ah! but these hens," answered the young man, —"these hens of aristocratic lineage would scorn to understand the vulgar language of a barn-yard fowl. I prefer to think,—and so would Miss Hepzibah,— that they recognize the family tone. For you are a Pyncheon?"

"My name is Phœbe Pyncheon," said the girl, with a manner of some reserve; for she was aware that her new acquaintance could be no other than the daguerreotypist, of whose lawless propensities the old maid had given her a disagreeable idea. "I did not know that my cousin Hepzibah's garden was under another person's care."

"Yes," said Holgrave, "I dig, and hoe, and weed, in this black old earth, for the sake of refreshing myself with what little nature and simplicity may be left in it, after men have so long sown and reaped here. I turn up the earth by way of pastime. My sober occupation, so far as I have any, is with a lighter material. In short, I make pictures out of sunshine; and, not to be too much dazzled with my own trade, I have prevailed with Miss Hepzibah to let me lodge in one of those dusky gables. It is like a bandage over one's eyes to come into it. But would you like to see a specimen of my productions?"

"A daguerreotype likeness, do you mean?" asked Phœbe, with less reserve; for, in spite of prejudice, her own youthfulness sprang forward to meet his. "I don't much like pictures of that sort—they are so hard and stern; besides dodging away from the eye, and trying to escape altogether. They are conscious of looking very unamiable, I suppose, and therefore hate to be seen."

" If you would permit me," said the artist, looking at Phœbe, " I should like to try whether the daguerreotype can bring out disagreeable traits on a perfectly amiable face. But there certainly is truth in what you have said. Most of my likenesses do look unamiable; but the very sufficient reason, I fancy, is because the originals are so. There is a wonderful insight in heaven's broad and simple sunshine. While we give it credit only for depicting the merest surface, it actually brings out the secret character with a truth that no painter would ever venture upon, even could he detect it. There is, at least, no flattery in my humble line of art. Now, here is a likeness which I have taken over and over again, and still with no better result. Yet the original wears, to common eyes, a very different expression. It would gratify me to have your judgment on this character."

He exhibited a daguerreotype miniature, in a morocco case. Phœbe merely glanced at it, and gave it back.

" I know the face," she replied, " for its stern eye has been following me about all day. It is my Puritan ancestor, who hangs yonder in the parlour. To be sure, you have found some way of copying the portrait without its black velvet cap and gray beard, and have given him a modern coat and satin cravat, instead of his cloak and band. I don't think him improved by your alterations."

" You would have seen other differences had you looked a little longer," said Holgrave, laughing, yet apparently much struck. " I can assure you that this is a modern face, and one which you will very probably meet. Now, the remarkable point is, that the original wears, to the world's eye, —and, for aught I know, to his most intimate friends,—an exceedingly pleasant countenance, indicative of benevolence, openness of heart, sunny good-humour, and other praiseworthy qualities of that cast. The sun, as you see, tells quite another story, and will not be coaxed out of it, after half-a-dozen patient attempts on my part. Here we have the man, sly, subtle, hard, imperious, and, withal, cold as ice. Look at that eye! Would you like to be at its mercy? At that mouth! Could it ever smile? And yet, if you could only see the benign smile of the original! It is so much the more unfortunate, as he is a public character of some eminence, and the likeness was intended to be engraved."

"Well, I don't wish to see it any more," observed Phœbe, turning away her eyes. "It is certainly very like the old portrait. But my cousin Hepzibah has another picture,—a miniature. If the original is still in the world, I think he might defy the sun to make him look stern and hard."

"You have seen that picture, then!" exclaimed the artist, with an expression of much interest. "I never did, but have a great curiosity to do so. And you judge favourably of the face?"

"There never was a sweeter one," said Phœbe. "It is almost too soft and gentle for a man's."

"Is there nothing wild in the eye?" continued Holgrave, so earnestly, that it embarrassed Phœbe, as did also the quiet freedom with which he presumed on their so recent acquaintance. "Is there nothing dark or sinister, anywhere? Could you not conceive the original to have been guilty of a great crime?"

"It is nonsense," said Phœbe, a little impatiently, "for us to talk about a picture which you have never seen. You mistake it for some other. A crime, indeed! Since you are a friend of my cousin Hepzibah's, you should ask her to show you the picture."

"It will suit my purpose still better to see the original," replied the daguerreotypist coolly. "As to his character, we need not discuss its points; they have already been settled by a competent tribunal, or one which called itself competent. But stay! Do not go yet, if you please! I have a proposition to make you.''

Phœbe was on the point of retreating, but turned back, with some hesitation; for she did not exactly comprehend his manner, although, on better observation, its feature seemed rather to be lack of ceremony than any approach to offensive rudeness. There was an odd kind of authority, too, in what he now proceeded to say, rather as if the garden were his own than a place to which he was admitted merely by Hepzibah's courtesy.

'' If agreeable to you,'' he observed, '' it would give me pleasure to turn over these flowers, and those ancient and respectable fowls, to your care. Coming fresh from country air and occupations, you will soon feel the need of some such out-of-door employment. My own sphere does not so much lie among flowers. You can trim and tend them, therefore, as you please; and I will ask only the least trifle of a blossom, now and then, in exchange for all the good, honest kitchen-vegetables with which I propose to enrich Miss Hepzibah's table. So we will be fellow-labourers, somewhat on the community system.''

Silently, and rather surprised at her own compliance, Phœbe accordingly betook herself to weeding a flower-bed, but busied herself still more with cogitations respecting this young man, with whom she so unexpectedly found herself on terms approaching to familiarity. She did not altogether like him. His character perplexed the little country-girl, as it might a more practised observer; for, while the tone of his conversation had generally been playful, the impression left on her mind was that of gravity, and, except as his youth modified it, almost sternness. She rebelled, as it were, against a certain magnetic element in the artist's nature, which he exercised towards her, possibly without being conscious of it.

After a little while the twilight, deepened by the shadows of the fruit-trees, and the surrounding buildings, threw an obscurity over the garden.

"There," said Holgrave, "it is time to give over work! That last stroke of the hoe has cut off a bean-stalk. Good night, Miss Phœbe Pyncheon! Any bright day, if you will put one of those rose-buds in your hair, and come to my rooms in Central-street, I will seize the purest ray of sunshine, and make a picture of the flower and its wearer."

He retired towards his own solitary gable, but turned his head on reaching the door, and called to Phœbe, with a tone which certainly had laughter in it, yet which seemed to be more than half in earnest.

"Be careful not to drink at Maule's well!" said he. "Neither drink nor bathe your face in it!"

"Maule's well!" answered Phœbe. "Is that it with the rim of mossy stones? I have no thought of drinking there—but why not?"

"O," rejoined the daguerreotypist, "because, like an old lady's cup of tea, it is water bewitched!"

He vanished; and Phœbe, lingering a moment, saw a glimmering light, and then the steady beam of a lamp, in a chamber of the gable. On returning into Hepzibah's department of the house, she found the low-studded parlour so dim and dusky that her eyes could not penetrate the interior. She was indistinctly aware, however, that the gaunt figure of the old gentlewoman was sitting in one of the straight-backed chairs, a little withdrawn from the window, the faint gleam of which showed the blanched pale-ness of her cheek, turned sideway towards a corner.

"Shall I light a lamp, Cousin Hepzibah?" she asked.

"Do, if you please, my dear child," answered Hepzibah. "But put it on the table in the corner of the passage. My eyes are weak; and I can seldom bear the lamp-light on them."

What an instrument is the human voice! How wonderfully responsive to every emotion of the human soul! In Hepzibah's tone, at that moment, there was a certain rich depth and moisture, as if the words, common-place as they were, had been steeped in the warmth of her heart. Again, while lighting the lamp in the kitchen, Phœbe fancied that her cousin spoke to her.

"In a moment, cousin!" answered the girl. "These matches just glimmer, and go out."

But, instead of a response from Hepzibah, she seemed to hear the murmur of an unknown voice. It was strangely indistinct, however, and less like articulate words than an unshaped sound, such as would be the utterance of feeling and sympathy, rather than of the intellect. So vague was it, that its impression or echo in Phœbe's mind was that of unreality. She concluded that she must have mistaken some other sound for that of the human voice; or else that it was altogether in her fancy.

She set the lighted lamp in the passage, and again entered the parlour. Hepzibah's form, though its sable outline mingled with the dusk, was now less imperfectly visible. In the remoter parts of the room, however, its walls being so ill adapted to reflect light, there was nearly the same obscurity as before.

"Cousin," said Phœbe, "did you speak to me just now?"

"No, child!" replied Hepzibah.

Fewer words than before, but with the same mysterious music in them! Mellow, melancholy, yet not mournful, the tone seemed to gush up out of the deep well of Hepzibah's heart, all steeped in its profoundest emotion. There was a tremor in it, too, that—as all strong feeling is electric—partly communicated itself to Phœbe. The girl sat silently for a moment. But soon, her senses being very acute, she became conscious of an irregular respiration in an obscure corner of the room. Her physical organization, moreover, being at once delicate and healthy, gave her a perception, operating with almost the effect of a spiritual medium, that somebody was near at hand.

"My dear cousin," asked she, overcoming an

indefinable reluctance, "is there not some one in the room with us?"

"Phœbe, my dear little girl," said Hepzibah, after a moment's pause, "you were up betimes, and have been busy all day. Pray go to bed; for I am sure you must need rest. I will sit in the parlour a while and collect my thoughts. It has been my custom for more years, child, than you have lived!"

While thus dismissing her, the maiden lady stept forward, kissed Phœbe, and pressed her to her heart, which beat against the girl's bosom with a strong, high, and tumultuous swell. How came there to be so much love in this desolate old heart, that it could afford to well over thus abundantly?

"Good-night, cousin," said Phœbe, strangely affected by Hepzibah's manner. "If you begin to love me, I am glad!"

She retired to her chamber, but did not soon fall asleep, nor then very profoundly. At some uncertain period in the depths of night, and, as it were, through the thin veil of a dream, she was conscious of a footstep mounting the stairs, heavily, but not with force and decision. The voice of Hepzibah, with a hush through it, was going up along with the footsteps; and, again, responsive to her cousin's voice, Phœbe heard that vague strange murmur, which might be likened to an indistinct shadow of human utterance.

VII

THE GUEST

WHEN Phœbe awoke—which she did with the early twittering of the conjugal couple of robins in the pear-tree,—she heard movements below stairs, and, hastening down, found Hepzibah already in the kitchen. She stood by a window, holding a book in close contiguity to her nose, as if with the hope of gaining an olfactory acquaintance with its contents, since her imperfect vision made it not very easy to read them. If any volume could have manifested its essential wisdom in the mode suggested, it would certainly have been the one now in Hepzibah's hand; and the kitchen, in such an event, would forthwith have steamed with the fragrance of venison, turkeys, capons, larded partridges, puddings, cakes, and Christmas-pies, in all manner of elaborate mixture and concoction. It was a cookery book, full of innumerable old fashions of English dishes, and illustrated with engravings, which represented the arrangements of the table at such banquets as it might have befitted a nobleman to give, in the great hall of his castle. And, amid these rich and potent devices of the culinary art (not one of which, probably, had been tested, within the memory of any man's grand-father), poor Hepzibah was seeking for some nimble little titbit, which, with what skill she had, and such materials as were at hand, she might toss up for breakfast.

Soon, with a deep sigh, she put aside the savoury volume, and inquired of Phœbe whether old Speckle, as she called one of the hens, had laid an egg the preceding day. Phœbe ran to see, but returned without the expected treasure in her hand. At that instant, however, the blast of a fishdealer's conch was heard, announcing his approach along the street. With energetic raps at the shop-window, Hepzibah summoned the man in, and made purchase of what he warranted as the finest mackerel in his cart, and as fat a one as ever he felt with his finger so early in the season. Requesting Phœbe to roast some coffee,—which she casually observed was the real Mocha, and so long kept that each of the small berries ought to be worth its weight in gold,—the maiden lady heaped fuel into the vast receptacle of the ancient fireplace in such quantity as soon to drive the lingering dusk out of the kitchen. The country-girl, willing to give her utmost assistance, proposed to make an Indian cake, after her mother's peculiar method, of easy manufacture, and which she could vouch for as possessing a richness, and, if rightly prepared, a delicacy, unequalled by any other mode of breakfast-cake. Hepzibah gladly assenting, the kitchen was soon the scene of savoury preparation. Perchance, amid their proper element of smoke, which eddied forth from the ill-constructed chimney, the ghosts of departed cook-maids looked wonder-ingly on, or peeped down the great breadth of the flue, despising the simplicity of the projected meal, yet ineffectually pining to thrust their shadowy hands into each inchoate dish. The half-starved rats, at any rate, stole visibly out of their hiding-places, and sat on their hind-legs, snuffing the fumy atmosphere, and wistfully awaiting an opportunity to nibble.

Hepzibah had no natural turn for cookery, and, to say the truth, had fairly incurred her present meagre-ness, by often choosing to go without her dinner rather than be attendant on the rotation of the spit, or ebullition of the pot. Her zeal over the fire, therefore, was quite an heroic test of sentiment. It was touching, and positively worthy of tears (if Phœbe, the only spectator, except the rats and ghosts aforesaid, had not been better employed than in shed-ding them), to see her rake out a bed of fresh and glowing coals, and proceed to broil the mackerel. Her usually pale cheeks were all a-blaze with heat and hurry. She watched the fish with as much tender care and minuteness of attention as if,—we know not how to express it otherwise,—as if her own heart were on the gridiron, and her immortal happiness were involved in its being done precisely to a turn !

Life within doors has few pleasanter prospects than a neatly-arranged and well-provisioned breakfast-table. We come to it freshly, in the dewy youth of the day, and when our spiritual and sensual elements are in better accord than at a later period ; so that the material delights of the morning meal are capable of being fully enjoyed, without any very grievous reproaches, whether gastric or conscientious, for yielding even a trifle overmuch to the animal department of our nature. The thoughts, too, that run around the ring of familiar guests, have a piquancy and mirthfulness, and oftentimes a vivid truth, which more rarely find their way into the elaborate intercourse of dinner. Hepzibah's small and ancient table, supported on its slender and graceful legs, and covered with a cloth of the richest damask, looked worthy to be the scene and centre of one of the cheerfullest of parties. The vapour of the broiled fish arose like incense from the shrine of a barbarian idol, while the fragrance of the Mocha might have gratified the nostrils of a tutelary Lar, or whatever power has scope over a modern breakfast-table. Phœbe's Indian cakes were the sweetest offering of all,—in their hue befitting the rustic altars of the innocent and golden age,—or, so brightly yellow were they, resembling some of the bread which was changed to glistening gold, when Midas tried to eat it. The butter must not be forgotten,—butter which Phœbe herself had churned, in her own rural home, and brought it to her cousin as a propitiatory gift— smelling of clover-blossoms, and diffusing the charm of pastoral scenery through the dark-panelled parlour. All this, with the quaint gorgeousness of the old China cups and saucers, and the crested spoons, and a silver cream-jug (Hepzibah's only other article of plate, and shaped like the rudest porringer), set out a board at which the stateliest of old Colonel Pyncheon's guests need not have scorned to take his place. But the Puritan's face scowled down out of the picture, as if nothing on the table pleased his appetite.

By way of contributing what grace she could, Phœbe gathered some roses and a few other flowers, possessing either scent or beauty, and arranged them in a glass pitcher, which, having long ago lost its

handle, was so much the fitter for a flower-vase. The
early sunshine—as fresh as that which peeped into
Eve's bower, while she and Adam sat at breakfast
there—came twinkling through the branches of the
pear-tree, and fell quite across the table. All was
now ready. There were chairs and plates for three.
A chair and plate for Hepzibah,—the same for
Phœbe,—but what other guest did her cousin look
for?

Throughout this preparation, there had been a
constant tremor in Hepzibah's frame; an agitation
so powerful that Phœbe could see the quivering of
her gaunt shadow, as thrown by the fire-light on the
kitchen wall, or by the sunshine on the parlour floor.
Its manifestations were so various, and agreed so
little with one another, that the girl knew not what
to make of it. Sometimes it seemed an ecstasy of
delight and happiness. At such moments, Hepzibah
would fling out her arms, and enfold Phœbe in them,
and kiss her cheek as tenderly as ever her mother
had; she appeared to do so by an inevitable impulse,
and as if her bosom were oppressed with tenderness,
of which she must needs pour out a little, in order to
gain breathing-room. The next moment, without
any visible cause for the change, her unwonted joy
shrank back, appalled as it were, and clothed itself in
mourning; or it ran and hid itself, so to speak, in
the dungeon of her heart, where it had long lain
chained, while a cold, spectral sorrow took the place
of the imprisoned joy, that was afraid to be enfranchised—a sorrow as black as that was bright.
She often broke into a little, nervous, hysteric laugh,
more touching than any tears could be; and forthwith, as if to try which was the most touching, a
gust of tears would follow; or perhaps the laughter
and tears came both at once, and surrounded our
poor Hepzibah, in a moral sense, with a kind of
pale, dim rainbow. Towards Phœbe, as we have
said, she was affectionate,—far tenderer than ever
before, in their brief acquaintance, except for that

one kiss on the preceding night,—yet with a continually recurring pettishness and irritability. She would speak sharply to her; then, throwing aside all the starched reserve of her ordinary manner, ask pardon, and the next instant renew the just-forgiven injury.

At last, when their mutual labour was all finished, she took Phœbe's hand in her own trembling one.

" Bear with me, my dear child," she cried; " for truly my heart is full to the brim! Bear with me; for I love you, Phœbe, though I speak so roughly! Think nothing of it, dearest child! By-and-bye, I shall be kind, and only kind!"

" My dearest cousin, cannot you tell me what has happened?" asked Phœbe, with a sunny and tearful sympathy. " What is it that moves you so?"

" Hush! hush! He is coming!" whispered Hepzibah, hastily wiping her eyes. " Let him see you first, Phœbe; for you are young and rosy, and cannot help letting a smile break out, whether or no. He always liked bright faces! And mine is old, now, and the tears are hardly dry on it. He never could abide tears. There; draw the curtain a little, so that the shadow may fall across his side of the table! But let there be a good deal of sunshine, too; for he never was fond of gloom, as some people are. He has had but little sunshine in his life,—poor Clifford,—and, oh, what a black shadow! Poor, poor Clifford!"

Thus murmuring, in an under tone, as if speaking rather to her own heart than to Phœbe, the old gentlewoman stepped on tiptoe about the room, making such arrangements as suggested themselves at the crisis.

Meanwhile, there was a step in the passage-way, above stairs. Phœbe recognized it as the same which had passed upward, as through her dream, in the night-time. The approaching guest, whoever it might be, appeared to pause at the head of the staircase; he paused twice or thrice in the descent; he paused again at the foot. Each time the delay seemed to be without purpose, but rather from a forgetfulness of the purpose which had set him in motion, or as if the person's feet came involuntarily to a stand-still, because the motive power was too feeble to sustain his progress. Finally, he made a long pause at the threshold of the parlour. He took hold of the knob of the door; then loosened his grasp, without opening it. Hepzibah, her hands convulsively clasped, stood gazing at the entrance.

"Dear Cousin Hepzibah, pray don't look so!" said Phœbe, trembling; for her cousin's emotion, and this mysteriously reluctant stop, made her feel as if a ghost were coming into the room. "You really frighten me! Is something awful going to happen?"

"Hush!" whispered Hepzibah. "Be cheerful! whatever may happen, be nothing but cheerful!"

The final pause at the threshold proved so long, that Hepzibah, unable to endure the suspense, rushed forward, threw open the door, and led in the stranger by the hand. At the first glance, Phœbe saw an elderly personage, in an old-fashioned dressing-gown of faded damask, and wearing his gray, or almost white hair, of an unusual length. It quite overshadowed his forehead, except when he thrust it back, and stared vaguely about the room. After a very brief inspection of his face, it was easy to conceive that his footstep must necessarily be such an one as that which, slowly, and with as indefinite an aim as a child's first journey across a floor, had just brought him hitherward. Yet there were no tokens that his physical strength might not have sufficed for a free and determined gait. It was the spirit of the man that could not walk. The expression of his countenance—while, notwithstanding, it had the light of reason in it—seemed to waver, and glimmer, and nearly to die away, and feebly to recover itself again. It was like a flame which we see twinkling among half-extinguished embers; we gaze at it more intently than if it were a positive blaze, gushing vividly upward,—more intently, but with a certain impatience, as if it ought either to kindle itself into satisfactory splendour, or be at once extinguished.

For an instant after entering the room, the guest stood still, retaining Hepzibah's hand, instinctively, as a child does that of the grown person who guides it. He saw Phœbe, however, and caught an illumination from her youthful and pleasant aspect, which, indeed, threw a cheerfulness about the parlour, like the circle of reflected brilliancy around the glass vase of flowers that was standing in the sunshine. He made a salutation, or, to speak nearer the truth, an ill-defined, abortive attempt at courtesy. Imperfect as it was, however, it conveyed an idea, or, at least, gave a hint, of indescribable grace, such as no practised art of external manners could have attained. It was too slight to seize upon, at the instant; yet, as recollected afterwards, seemed to transfigure the whole man.

"Dear Clifford," said Hepzibah, in the tone with which one soothes a wayward infant, "this is our cousin Phœbe,—little Phœbe Puncheon,—Arthur's only child, you know. She has come from the country to stay with us a while; for our old house has grown to be very lonely now."

"Phœbe?—Phœbe Puncheon?—Phœbe?" repeated the guest, with a strange, sluggish, ill-defined utterance. "Arthur's child! Ah, I forget! No matter! She is very welcome!"

"Come, dear Clifford, take this chair," said Hepzibah, leading him to his place. "Pray, Phœbe, lower the curtain a very little more. Now let us begin breakfast."

The guest seated himself in the place assigned him, and looked strangely around. He was evidently trying to grapple with the present scene, and bring it home to his mind with a more satisfactory distinctness. He desired to be certain, at least, that he was here, in the low-studded, cross-beamed, oaken-panelled parlour, and not in some other spot, which had stereotyped itself into his senses. But the effort was too great to be sustained with more than a fragmentary success. Continually, as we may express it, he faded away out of his place; or, in other words, his mind and consciousness took their departure, leaving his wasted, gray, and melancholy figure,—a substantial emptiness, a material ghost,—to occupy his seat at table. Again, after a blank moment, there would be a flickering taper-gleam in his eye-balls. It betokened that his spiritual part had returned, and was doing its best to kindle the heart's household fire, and light up intellectual lamps in the dark and ruinous mansion, where it was doomed to be a forlorn inhabitant.

At one of these moments, of less torpid, yet still imperfect animation, Phœbe became convinced of what she had at first rejected as too extravagant and startling an idea. She saw that the person before her must have been the original of the beautiful miniature in her cousin Hepzibah's possession. Indeed, with a feminine eye for costume, she had at once identified the damask dressing-gown, which enveloped him, as the same in figure, material, and fashion, with that so elaborately represented in the picture. This old, faded garment, with all its pristine brilliancy extinct, seemed, in some indescribable way, to translate the wearer's untold misfortune, and make it perceptible to the beholder's eye. It was the better to be discerned, by this exterior type, how worn and old were the soul's more immediate garments; that form and countenance, the beauty and grace of which had almost transcended the skill of the most exquisite of artists. It could the more adequately be known that the soul of the man must have suffered some miserable wrong, from its earthly experience. There he seemed to sit, with a dim veil of decay and ruin betwixt him and the world, but through which, at flitting intervals, might be caught the same expression, so refined, so softly imaginative, which Malbone—venturing a happy touch, with suspended breath—had imparted to the miniature! There had been something so innately characteristic in this look, that all the dusky years, and the burthen of unfit calamity which had fallen upon him, did not suffice utterly to destroy it.

Hepzibah had now poured out a cup of deliciously fragrant coffee, and presented it to her guest. As his eyes met hers, he seemed bewildered and disquieted.

" Is this you, Hepzibah?" he murmured, sadly; then, more apart, and perhaps unconscious that he was overheard, " How changed! how changed! And is she angry with me? Why does she bend her brow so?"

Poor Hepzibah! It was that wretched scowl, which time, and her near-sightedness, and the fret of inward discomfort, had rendered so habitual that any vehemence of mood invariably evoked it. But, at the indistinct manner of his words, her whole face grew tender, and even lovely, with sorrowful affection;— the harshness of her features disappeared, as it were, behind the warm and misty glow.

" Angry!" she repeated; " angry with you, Clifford!"

Her tone, as she uttered the exclamation, had a plaintive and really exquisite melody thrilling through it, yet without subduing a certain something which an obtuse auditor might still have mistaken for asperity. It was as if some transcendent musician should draw a soul-thrilling sweetness out of a cracked instrument, which makes its physical imperfection heard in the midst of ethereal harmony,—so deep was the sensibility that found an organ in Hepzibah's voice!

" There is nothing but love, here, Clifford," she added,—" nothing but love! You are at home!"

The guest responded to her tone by a smile, which did not half light up his face. Feeble as it was, however, and gone in a moment, it had a charm of wonderful beauty. It was followed by a coarser expression; or one that had the effect of coarseness on the fine mould and outline of his countenance because there was nothing intellectual to temper it. It was a look of appetite. He ate food with what might almost be termed voracity; and seemed to forget himself, Hepzibah, the young girl, and everything else around him, in the sensual enjoyment which the bountifully spread table afforded. In his natural system, though high-wrought and delicately refined, a sensibility to the delights of the palate was probably inherent. It would have been kept in check, however, and even converted into an accomplishment, and one of the thousand modes of intellectual culture, had his more ethereal characteristics retained their vigour. But, as it existed now, the effect was painful, and made Phœbe droop her eyes.

In a little while the guest became sensible of the fragrance of the yet untasted coffee. He quaffed it eagerly. The subtle essence acted on him like a charmed draught, and caused the opaque substance of his animal being to grow transparent, or, at least, translucent; so that a spiritual gleam was transmitted through it, with a clearer lustre than hitherto.

" More, more !" he cried, with nervous haste in his utterance, as if anxious to retain his grasp of what sought to escape him. " This is what I need ! Give me more !"

Under this delicate and powerful influence, he sat more erect, and looked out from his eyes with a glance that took note of what it rested on. It was not so much that his expression grew more intellectual; this, though it had its share, was not the most peculiar effect. Neither was what we call the moral nature so forcibly awakened as to present itself in remarkable prominence. But a certain fine temper of being was now—not brought out in full relief, but changeably and imperfectly betrayed—of which it was the function to deal with all beautiful and enjoyable things. In a character where it should exist as the chief attribute, it would bestow on its possessor an exquisite taste, and an enviable susceptibility of happiness. Beauty would be his life; his aspirations would all tend toward it; and, allowing his frame and physical organs to be in consonance, his own developments would likewise be beautiful. Such a man should have nothing to do with sorrow; nothing with strife; nothing with the marytrdom which, in an infinite variety of shapes, awaits those who have the heart, and will, and conscience, to fight a battle with the world. To these heroic tempers, such martyrdom is the richest meed in the world's gift. To the individual before us, it could only be a grief, intense in due proportion with the severity of the infliction. He had no right to be a martyr; and, beholding him so fit to be happy, and so feeble for all other purposes, a generous, strong, and noble spirit would, methinks, have been ready to sacrifice what little enjoyment it might have planned for itself, —it would have flung down the hopes, so paltry in its regard,—if thereby the wintry blasts of our rude sphere might come tempered to such a man.

Not to speak it harshly or scornfully, it seemed Clifford's nature to be a Sybarite. It was perceptible, even there, in the dark old parlour, in the inevitable polarity with which his eyes were attracted towards the quivering play of sunbeams through the shadowy foliage. It was seen in his appreciating notice of the vase of flowers, the scent of which he inhaled with a zest almost peculiar to a physical organization so refined that spiritual ingredients are moulded in with it It was betrayed in the unconscious smile with which he regarded Phœbe, whose fresh and maidenly figure was both sunshine and flowers,—their essence, in a prettier and more agreeable mode of manifestation. Not less evident was this love and necessity for the Beautiful, in the instinctive caution with which, even so soon, his eyes turned away from his hostess, and wandered to any quarter rather than come back. It was Hepzibah's misfortune,—not Clifford's fault. How could he,—so yellow as she was, so wrinkled, so sad of mien, with that odd uncouthness of a turban on her head, and that most perverse of scowls contorting her brow,—how could he love to gaze at her? But, did he owe her no affection for so much as she had silently given? He owed her nothing. A nature like Clifford's can contract no debts of that kind. It is,—we say it without censure, nor in diminution of the claim which it indefeasibly possesses on beings of another mould,— it is always selfish in its essence; and we must give it leave to be so, and heap up our heroic and disinterested love upon it so much the more, without a recompense. Poor Hepzibah knew this truth, or, at least, acted on the instinct of it. So long estranged from what was lovely, as Clifford had been, she rejoiced,—rejoiced, though with a present sigh, and a secret purpose to shed tears in her own chamber,— that he had brighter objects now before his eyes than her age and uncomely features. They never possessed a charm; and if they had, the canker of her grief for him would long since have destroyed it.

The guest leaned back in his chair. Mingled in his countenance with a dreamy delight, there was a troubled look of effort and unrest. He was seeking to make himself more fully sensible of the scene around him; or, perhaps, dreading it to be a dream, or a play of imagination, was vexing the fair moment with a struggle for some added brilliancy and more durable illusion.

" How pleasant !—How delightful !" he murmured, but not as if addressing any one. " Will it last? How balmy the atmosphere, through that open window! An open window! How beautiful that play of sunshine! Those flowers, how very fragrant! That young girl's face, how cheerful, how blooming !—a flower with the dew on it, and sunbeams in the dew drops! Ah! this must be all a dream! A dream! A dream! But it has quite hidden the four stone walls!"

Then his face darkened, as if the shadow of a cavern or a dungeon had come over it; there was no more light in its expression than might have come through the iron grates of a prison window,—still lessening, too, as if he were sinking further into the depths. Phœbe (being of that quickness and activity of temperament that she seldom long refrained from taking a part, and generally a good one, in what was going forward) now felt herself moved to address the stranger.

"Here is a new kind of rose, which I found this morning, in the garden," said she, choosing a small crimson one from among the flowers in the vase. "There will be but five or six on the bush, this season. This is the most perfect of them all; not a speck of blight or mildew in it. And how sweet it is!—sweet like no other rose! One can never forget that scent!"

"Ah!—let me see!—let me hold it!" cried the guest, eagerly seizing the flower, which, by the spell peculiar to remembered odours, brought innumerable associations along with the fragrance that it exhaled. "Thank you! This has done me good. I remember how I used to prize this flower—long ago, I suppose, very long ago!—or was it only yesterday? It makes me feel young again! Am I young? Either this remembrance is singularly distinct, or this consciousness strangely dim! But how kind of the fair young girl! Thank you! Thank you!"

The favourable excitement derived from this little crimson rose afforded Clifford the brightest moment which he enjoyed at the breakfast-table. It might have lasted longer, but that his eyes happened, soon afterwards, to rest on the face of the old Puritan, who, out of his dingy frame and lustreless canvas, was looking down on the scene like a ghost, and a most ill-tempered and ungenial one. The guest made an impatient gesture of the hand, and addressed Hepzibah with what might easily be recognized as the licensed irritability of a petted member of the family.

"Hepzibah!—Hepzibah!" cried he, with no little force and distinctness,—"why do you keep that odious picture on the wall? Yes, yes!—that is precisely your taste! I have told you a thousand times, that it was the evil genius of the house!—my evil genius particularly! Take it down, at once!"

"Dear Clifford," said Hepzibah, sadly, "you know it cannot be!"

"Then, at all events," continued he, still speaking with some energy, "pray cover it with a crimson curtain, broad enough to hang in folds, and with a golden border and tassels. I cannot bear it! It must not stare me in the face!"

"Yes, dear Clifford, the picture shall be covered," said Hepzibah, soothingly. "There is a crimson curtain in a trunk above stairs,—a little faded and moth-eaten, I'm afraid,—but Phœbe and I will do wonders with it."

"This very day, remember!" said he; and then added, in a low, self-communing voice,—"Why should we live in this dismal house at all? Why not go to the south of France?—to Italy?—Paris, Naples, Venice, Rome? Hepzibah will say, we have not the means. A droll idea, that!"

He smiled to himself, and threw a glance of fine sarcastic meaning towards Hepzibah.

But the several moods of feeling, faintly as they were marked, through which he had passed, occurring in so brief an interval of time, had evidently wearied the stranger. He was probably accustomed to a sad monotony of life, not so much flowing in a stream, however sluggish, as stagnating in a pool around his feet. A slumberous veil diffused itself over his countenance, and had an effect, morally speaking, on its naturally delicate and elegant outline, like that which a brooding mist, with no sunshine in it, throws over the features of a landscape. He appeared to become grosser,—almost cloddish. If aught of interest or beauty—even ruined beauty—had heretofore been visible in this man, the beholder might now begin to doubt it, and to accuse his own imagination of deluding him with whatever grace had flickered over that visage, and whatever exquisite lustre had gleamed in those filmy eyes.

Before he had quite sunken away, however, the sharp and peevish tinkle of the shop-bell made itself audible. Striking most disagreeably on Clifford's auditory organs and the characteristic sensibility of his nerves, it caused him to start upright out of his chair.

"Good Heavens, Hepzibah! what horrible disturbance have we now in the house?" cried he, wreaking his resentful impatience—as a matter of course, and a custom of old—on the one person in the world that loved him. "I have never heard such a hateful clamour! Why do you permit it? In the name of all dissonance, what can it be?"

It was very remarkable into what prominent relief —even as if a dim picture should leap suddenly from its canvas—Clifford's character was thrown, by this apparently trifling annoyance. The secret was, that an individual of his temper can always be pricked more acutely through his sense of the beautiful and harmonious than through his heart. It is even possible—for similar cases have often happened— that if Clifford, in his foregoing life, had enjoyed the means of cultivating his taste to its utmost perfectibility, that subtle attribute might before this period, have completely eaten out or filed away his affections. Shall we venture to pronounce, therefore, that his long and black calamity may not have had a redeeming drop of mercy at the bottom?

"Dear Clifford, I wish I could keep the sound from your ears," said Hepzibah, patiently, but reddening with a painful suffusion of shame. "It is very disagreeable even to me. But, do you know, Clifford, I have something to tell you? This ugly noise,— pray run, Phœbe, and see who is there! this naughty little tinkle is nothing but our shop-bell!"

"Shop-bell!" repeated Clifford, with a bewildered stare.

"Yes, our shop-bell," said Hepzibah, a certain

natural dignity, mingled with deep emotion, now asserting itself in her manner. "For you must know, dearest Clifford, that we are very poor. And there was no other resource, but either to accept assistance from a hand that I would push aside (and so would you!) were it to offer bread when we were dying for it—no help, save from him, or else to earn our subsistence with my own hands! Alone, I might have been content to starve. But you were to be given back to me! Do you think then, dear Clifford," added she, with a wretched smile, "that I have brought an irretrievable disgrace on the old house, by opening a little shop in the front gable? Our great-great-grandfather did the same, when there was far less need! Are you ashamed of me?"

"Shame! Disgrace! Do you speak these words to me, Hepzibah?" said Clifford,—not angrily, however; for when a man's spirit has been thoroughly crushed, he may be peevish at small offences, but never resentful of great ones. So he spoke with only a grieved emotion. "It was not kind to say so, Hepzibah! What shame can befall me, now?"

And then the unnerved man—he that had been born for enjoyment, but had met a doom so very wretched—burst into a woman's passion of tears. It was but of brief continuance, however; soon leaving him in a quiescent, and, to judge by his countenance, not an uncomfortable state. From this mood, too, he partially rallied for an instant, and looked at Hepzibah with a smile, the keen half-derisory purport of which was a puzzle to her.

"Are we so very poor, Hepzibah?" said he.

Finally, his chair being deep and softly cushioned, Clifford fell asleep. Hearing the more regular rise and fall of his breath—(which, however, even then, instead of being strong and full, had a feeble kind of tremor, corresponding with the lack of vigour in his character) — hearing these tokens of settled slumber, Hepzibah seized the opportunity to peruse his face more attentively than she had yet dared to

do. Her heart melted away in tears; her profoundest spirit sent forth a moaning voice, low, gentle, but
inexpressibly sad. In this depth of grief and pity,
she felt that there was no irreverence in gazing at his
altered, aged, ruined face. But no sooner was she
a little relieved than her conscience smote her for
gazing curiously at him, now that he was so changed;
and, turning hastily away, Hepzibah let down the
curtain over the sunny window, and left Clifford to
slumber there.

VIII

THE PYNCHEON OF TO-DAY

PHŒBE, on entering the shop, beheld there the
already familiar face of the little devourer—if we can
reckon his mighty deeds aright—of Jim Crow, the
elephant, the camel, the dromedaries, and the locomotive. Having expended his private fortune, on
the two preceding days, in the purchase of the above
unheard-of luxuries, the young gentleman's present
errand was on the part of his mother, in quest of
three eggs and half a pound of raisins. These articles
Phœbe accordingly supplied, and, as a mark of
gratitude for his previous patronage, and a slight
superadded morsel after breakfast, put likewise into
his hand a whale! The great fish, reversing his experience with the prophet of Nineveh, immediately
began his progress down the same red pathway of
fate whither so varied a caravan had preceded him.
This remarkable urchin, in truth, was the very
emblem of old Father Time, both in respect of his
all-devouring appetite for men and things, and because he, as well as Time, after engulfing thus much
of creation, looked almost as youthful as if he had
been just that moment made.

After partly closing the door, the child turned back, and mumbled something to Phœbe, which, as the whale was but half disposed of, she could not perfectly understand.

"What did you say, my little fellow?" asked she.

"Mother wants to know," repeated Ned Higgins, more distinctly, "how Old Maid Pyncheon's brother does? Folks say he has got home."

"My cousin Hepzibah's brother!" exclaimed Phœbe, surprised at this sudden explanation of the relationship between Hepzibah and her guest. "Her brother! And where can he have been?"

The little boy only put his thumb to his broad snub-nose, with that look of shrewdness which a child, spending much of his time in the street, so soon learns to throw over his features, however unintelligent in themselves. Then, as Phœbe continued to gaze at him, without answering his mother's message, he took his departure.

As the child went down the steps, a gentleman ascended them, and made his entrance into the shop. It was the portly, and, had it possessed the advantage of a little more height, would have been the stately figure of a man considerably in the decline of life, dressed in a black suit of some thin stuff, resembling broadcloth as closely as possible. A gold-headed cane, of rare oriental wood, added materially to the high respectability of his aspect, as did also a white neckcloth of the utmost snowy purity, and the conscientious polish of his boots. His dark, square countenance, with its almost shaggy depth of eyebrows, was naturally impressive, and would, perhaps, have been rather stern, had not the gentleman considerately taken upon himself to mitigate the harsh effect by a look of exceeding good-humour and benevolence. Owing, however, to a somewhat massive accumulation of animal substance about the lower region of his face, the look was, perhaps, unctuous, rather than spiritual, and had, so to speak, a kind of fleshly effulgence, not altogether so satisfactory as he doubtless intended it to be. A susceptible observer, at any rate, might have regarded it as affording very little evidence of the genuine benignity of soul, whereof it purported to be the outward reflection. And if the observer chanced to be ill-natured, as well as acute and susceptible, he would probably suspect that the smile on the gentleman's face was a good deal akin to the shine on his boots, and that each must have cost him and his boot-black, respectively, a good deal of hard labour to bring out and preserve them.

As the stranger entered the little shop, where the projection of the second storey and the thick foliage of the elm-tree, as well as the commodities at the window, created a sort of gray medium, his smile grew as intense as if he had set his heart on counteracting the whole gloom of the atmosphere (besides any moral gloom pertaining to Hepzibah and her inmates) by the unassisted light of his countenance. On perceiving a young rose-bud of a girl, instead of the gaunt presence of the old maid, a look of surprise was manifest. He at first knit his brows; then smiled with more unctuous benignity than ever.

" Ah, I see how it is ! " said he, in a deep voice,— a voice which had it come from the throat of an uncultivated man, would have been gruff, but by dint of careful training, was now sufficiently agreeable,— " I was not aware that Miss Hepzibah Pyncheon had commenced business under such favourable auspices. You are her assistant, I suppose?"

" I certainly am," answered Phœbe, and added, with a little air of ladylike assumption (for civil as the gentleman was, he evidently took her to be a young person serving for wages), " I am a cousin of Miss Hepzibah, on a visit to her."

" Her cousin?—and from the country? Pray pardon me, then," said the gentleman, bowing and smiling, as Phœbe never had been bowed to nor smiled on before; " in that case, we must be better acquainted; for, unless I am sadly mistaken, you

are my own little kinswoman likewise! Let me see,
—Mary?—Dolly?—Phœbe?—yes, Phœbe is the
name! Is it possible that you are Phœbe Pyncheon,
only child of my dear cousin and classmate, Arthur?
Ah, I see your father now, about your mouth. Yes,
yes! we must be better acquainted! I am your
kinsman, my dear. Surely you must have heard of
Judge Pyncheon?"

As Phœbe curtsied in reply, the judge bent forward,
with the pardonable and even praiseworthy purpose
—considering the nearness of blood, and the difference of age—of bestowing on his young relative a
kiss of acknowledged kindred and natural affection.
Unfortunately (without design, or only with such
instinctive design as gives no account of itself to
the intellect), Phœbe, just at the critical moment,
drew back; so that her highly respectable kinsman,
with his body bent over the counter, and his lips
protruded, was betrayed into the rather absurd pre-
dicament of kissing the empty air. It was a modern
parallel to the case of Ixion embracing a cloud, and
was so much the more ridiculous, as the judge prided
himself on eschewing all airy matter, and never mis-
taking a shadow for a substance. The truth was,—
and it is Phœbe's only excuse,—that although Judge
Pyncheon's glowing benignity might not be absolutely
unpleasant to the feminine beholder, with the width
of a street, or even an ordinary-sized room, inter-
posed between, yet it became quite too intense, when
this dark, full-fed physiognomy (so roughly bearded,
too, that no razor could ever make it smooth) sought
to bring itself into actual contact with the object of
its regards. The man, the sex, somehow or other,
was entirely too prominent in the judge's demonstra-
tions of that sort. Phœbe's eyes sank, and without
knowing why, she felt herself blushing deeply under
his look. Yet she had been kissed before, and without any particular squeamishness, by perhaps half-
a-dozen different cousins, younger as well as older,
than this dark-browed, grisly-bearded, white-neck-

clothed, and unctuously-benevolent judge! Then
why not by him?

On raising her eyes, Phœbe was startled by the
change in Judge Pyncheon's face. It was quite as
striking, allowing for the difference of scale, as that
betwixt a landscape under a broad sunshine and just
before a thunder-storm; not that it had the passionate intensity of the latter aspect, but was cold, hard,
immitigable, like a day-long brooding cloud.

" Dear me! what is to be done now?" thought
the country-girl to herself. " He looks as if there
were nothing softer in him than a rock, nor milder
than the east wind! I meant no harm! Since he is
really my cousin, I would have let him kiss me, if I
could!"

Then, all at once, it struck Phœbe that this very
Judge Pyncheon was the original of the miniature
which the daguerreotypist had shown her in the
garden, and that the hard, stern, relentless look, now
on his face, was the same that the sun had so inflexibly persisted in bringing out. Was it, therefore, no
momentary mood, but, however skilfully concealed,
the settled temper of his life? And not merely so,
but was it hereditary in him, and transmitted down
as a precious heirloom, from that bearded ancestor,
in whose picture both the expression, and, to a
singular degree, the features, of the modern judge
were shown as by a kind of prophecy? A deeper
philosopher than Phœbe might have found something
very terrible in this idea. It implied that the weaknesses and defects, the bad passions, the mean tendencies, and the moral diseases, which lead to crime,
are handed down from one generation to another,
by a far surer process of transmission than human
law has been able to establish, in respect to the
riches and honours which it seeks to entail upon
posterity.

But, as it happened, scarcely had Phœbe's eyes
rested again on the judge's countenance, than all its
ugly sternness vanished; and she found herself quite

overpowered by the sultry, dog-day heat, as it were, of benevolence, which this excellent man diffused out of his great heart into the surrounding atmosphere; —very much like a serpent, which, as a preliminary to fascination, is said to fill the air with his peculiar odour.

" I like that, Cousin Phœbe !" cried he, with an emphatic nod of approbation. " I like it much, my little cousin ! You are a good child, and know how to take care of yourself. A young girl—especially if she be a very pretty one—can never be too chary of her lips."

" Indeed, sir," said Phœbe, trying to laugh the matter off, " I did not mean to be unkind."

Nevertheless, whether or no it were entirely owing to the inauspicious commencement of their acquaintance, she still acted under a certain reserve, which was by no means customary to her frank and genial nature. The fantasy would not quit her, that the original Puritan, of whom she had heard so many sombre traditions,—the progenitor of the whole race of New England Pyncheons, the founder of the House of the Seven Gables, and who had died so strangely in it,—had now stept into the shop. In these days of off-hand equipment, the matter was easily enough arranged. On his arrival from the other world, he had merely found it necessary to spend a quarter of an hour at a barber's, who had trimmed down the Puritan's full beard into a pair of grizzled whiskers; then, patronizing a ready-made clothing establishment, he had exchanged his velvet doublet and sable cloak, with the richly-worked band under his chin, for a white collar and cravat, coat, vest, and pantaloons; and lastly, putting aside his steel-hilted broadsword, to take up a gold-headed cane, the Colonel Pyncheon, of two centuries ago, steps forward as the judge, of the passing moment !

Of course, Phœbe was far too sensible a girl to entertain this idea in any other way than as matter for a smile. Possibly, also, could the two personages have stood together before her eye, many points of difference would have been perceptible, and perhaps only a general resemblance. The long lapse of intervening years, in a climate so unlike that which had fostered the ancestral Englishman, must inevitably have wrought important changes in the physical system of his descendant. The judge's volume of muscle could hardly be the same as the colonel's; there was undoubtedly less beef in him. Though looked upon as a weighty man, among his contemporaries, in respect of animal substance, and as favoured with a remarkable degree of fundamental development, well adapting him for the judicial bench, we conceive that the modern Judge Pyncheon, if weighed in the same balance with his ancestor, would have required at least an old-fashioned fifty-six to keep the scale in equilibrio. Then the judge's face had lost the ruddy English hue, that showed its warmth through all the duskiness of the colonel's weather-beaten cheek, and had taken a sallow shade, the established complexion of his countrymen. If we mistake not, moreover, a certain quality of nervousness had become more or less manifest, even in so solid a specimen of Puritan descent as the gentleman now under discussion. As one of its effects, it bestowed on his countenance a quicker mobility than the old Englishman's had possessed, and keener vivacity, but at the expense of a sturdier something, on which these acute endowments seemed to act like dissolving acids. This process, for aught we know, may belong to the great system of human progress, which, with every ascending footstep, as it diminishes the necessity for animal force, may be destined gradually to spiritualize us, by refining away our grosser attributes of body. If so, Judge Pyncheon could endure a century or two more of such refinement, as well as most other men.

The similarity, intellectual and moral, between the judge and his ancestor, appears to have been at least as strong as the resemblance of mien and feature would afford reason to anticipate. In old Colonel Pyncheon's funeral discourse, the clergyman absolutely canonized his deceased parishioner, and opening, as it were, a vista through the roof of the church, and thence through the firmament above, showed him seated, harp in hand, among the crowned choristers of the spiritual world. On his tombstone, too, the record is highly eulogistic; nor does history, so far as he holds a place upon its page, assail the consistency and uprightness of his character. So, also, as regards the Judge Pyncheon of to-day, neither clergyman, nor legal critic, nor inscriber of tomb-stones, nor historian of general or local politics, would venture a word against this eminent person's sincerity as a Christian, or respectability as a man, or integrity as a judge, or courage and faithfulness as the often tried representative of his political party. But, besides these cold, formal, and empty words of the chisel that inscribes, the voice that speaks, and the pen that writes, for the public eye and for distant time, —and which inevitably lose much of their truth and freedom by the fatal consciousness of so doing,— there were traditions about the ancestor, and private diurnal gossip about the judge, remarkably accordant in their testimony. It is often instructive to take the woman's, the private and domestic view of a public man; nor can anything be more curious than the vast discrepancy between portraits intended for engraving, and the pencil-sketches that pass from hand to hand, behind the original's back.

For example, tradition affirmed that the Puritan had been greedy of wealth; the judge, too, with all the show of liberal expenditure, was said to be as close-fisted as if his gripe were of iron. The ancestor had clothed himself in a grim assumption of kindliness, a rough heartiness of word and manner, which most people took to be the genuine warmth of nature, making its way through the thick and inflexible hide of a manly character. His descendant, in compliance with the requirements of a nicer age, had etherealized

this rude benevolence into that broad benignity of
smile, wherewith he shone like a noon-day sun along
the streets, or glowed like a household fire in the
drawing-rooms of his private acquaintance.   The
Puritan,—if not belied by some singular stories, murmured, even at this day, under the narrator's breath,
—had fallen into certain transgressions to which men
of his great animal development, whatever their faith
or principles, must continue liable, until they put off
impurity, along with the gross earthly substance that
involves it.   We must not stain our page with any
contemporary scandal, to a similar purport, that may
have been whispered against the judge.   The Puritan,
again, an autocrat in his own household, had worn
out three wives, and, merely by the remorseless
weight and hardness of his character in the conjugal
relation, had sent them, one after another, broken-
hearted to their graves.   Here, the parallel in some
sort fails.   The judge had wedded but a single wife,
and lost her in the third or fourth year of their
marriage.   There was a fable, however,—for such
we choose to consider it, though, not impossibly,
typical of Judge Pyncheon's marital deportment,—
that the lady got her death-blow in the honey-moon,
and never smiled again, because her husband compelled her to serve him with coffee every morning at
his bedside, in token of fealty to her liege-lord and
master.

But it is too fruitful a subject, this of hereditary
resemblances,—the frequent recurrence of which, in
a direct line, is truly unaccountable, when we consider how large an accumulation of ancestry lies behind every man, at the distance of one or two centuries.   We shall only add, therefore, that the Puritan
—so, at least, says chimney-corner tradition, which
often preserves traits of character with marvellous
fidelity—was bold, imperious, relentless, crafty; laying his purposes deep, and following them out with
an inveteracy of pursuit that knew neither rest nor
conscience; trampling on the weak, and, when

essential to his ends, doing his utmost to beat down the strong. Whether the judge in any degree resembled him, the further progress of our narrative may show.

Scarcely any of the items in the above-drawn parallel occurred to Phœbe, whose country birth and residence, in truth, had left her pitifully ignorant of most of the family traditions, which lingered, like cobwebs and incrustations of smoke, about the rooms and chimney-corners of the House of the Seven Gables. Yet there was a circumstance, very trifling in itself, which impressed her with an odd degree of horror. She had heard of the anathema flung by Maule, the executed wizard, against Colonel Pyncheon and his posterity,—that God would give them blood to drink,—and likewise of the popular notion, that this miraculous blood might now and then be heard gurgling in their throats. The latter scandal, —as became a person of sense, and, more especially, a member of the Pyncheon family,—Phœbe had set down for the absurdity which it unquestionably was. But ancient superstitions, after being steeped in human hearts, and embodied in human breath, and passing from lip to ear, in manifold repetition, through a series of generations, become imbued with an effect of homely truth. The smoke of the domestic hearth has scented them, through and through. By long transmission among household facts, they grow to look like them, and have such a familiar way of making themselves at home, that their influence is usually greater than we suspect. Thus it happened, that when Phœbe heard a certain noise in Judge Pyncheon's throat,—rather habitual with him, not altogether voluntary, yet indicative of nothing, unless it were a slight bronchial complaint, or, as some people hinted, an apoplectic symptom,—when the girl heard this queer and awkward ingurgitation (which the writer never did hear, and therefore cannot describe), she, very foolishly, started, and clasped her hands.

Of course, it was exceedingly ridiculous in Phœbe to be discomposed by such a trifle, and still more unpardonable to show her discomposure to the individual most concerned in it. But the incident chimed in so oddly with her previous fancies about the colonel and the judge, that, for the moment, it seemed quite to mingle their identity.

"What is the matter with you, young woman?" said Judge Pyncheon, giving her one of his harsh looks. "Are you afraid of anything?"

"O, nothing, sir,—nothing in the world!" answered Phœbe, with a little laugh of vexation at herself. "But perhaps you wish to speak with my cousin Hepzibah. Shall I call her?"

"Stay a moment, if you please," said the judge, again beaming sunshine out of his face. "You seem to be a little nervous this morning. The town air, Cousin Phœbe, does not agree with your good, wholesome country habits. Or, has anything happened to disturb you? anything remarkable in Cousin Hepzibah's family?—An arrival, eh? I thought so! No wonder you are out of sorts, my little cousin. To be an inmate with such a guest may well startle an innocent young girl!"

"You quite puzzle me, sir," replied Phœbe, gazing inquiringly at the judge. "There is no frightful guest in the house, but only a poor, gentle, child-like man, whom I believe to be Cousin Hepzibah's brother. I am afraid (but you, sir, will know better than I) that he is not quite in his sound senses; but so mild and quiet he seems to be, that a mother might trust her baby with him; and I think he would play with the baby, as if he were only a few years older than itself. He startle me!—O, no indeed!"

"I rejoice to hear so favourable and so ingenuous an account of my cousin Clifford," said the benevolent judge. "Many years ago, when we were boys and young men together, I had a great affection for him, and still feel a tender interest in all his concerns. You say, Cousin Phœbe, he appears to be weak-minded. Heaven grant him at least enough of intellect to repent of his past sins!"

"Nobody, I fancy," observed Phœbe, "can have fewer to repent of."

"And is it possible, my dear," rejoined the judge, with a commiserating look, "that you have never heard of Clifford Pyncheon?—that you know nothing of his history? Well, it is all right; and your mother has shown a very proper regard for the good name of the family with which she connected herself. Believe the best you can of this unfortunate person, and hope the best! It is a rule which Christians should always follow, in their judgments of one another; and especially is it right and wise among near relatives, whose characters have necessarily a degree of mutual dependence. But is Clifford in the parlour? I will just step in and see."

"Perhaps, sir, I had better call my cousin Hepzibah," said Phœbe; hardly knowing, however, whether she ought to obstruct the entrance of so affectionate a kinsman into the private regions of the house. "Her brother seemed to be just falling asleep, after breakfast; and I am sure she would not like him to be disturbed. Pray, sir, let me give her notice!"

But the judge showed a singular determination to enter unannounced; and as Phœbe, with the vivacity of a person whose movements unconsciously answer to her thoughts, had stepped towards the door, he used little or no ceremony in putting her aside.

"No, no, Miss Phœbe!" said Judge Pyncheon, in a voice as deep as a thunder-growl, and with a frown as black as the cloud whence it issues. "Stay you here! I know the house, and know my cousin Hepzibah, and know her brother Clifford likewise!—nor need my little country cousin put herself to the trouble of announcing me!"—in these latter words, by-the-by, there were symptoms of a change from his sudden harshness into his previous benignity of manner.—"I am at home here, Phœbe, you must recollect, and

you are the stranger. I will just step in, therefore,
and see for myself how Clifford is, and assure him
and Hepzibah of my kindly feelings and best wishes.
It is right, at this juncture, that they should both hear
from my own lips how much I desire to serve them.
Ha! there is Hepzibah herself!"

Such was the case. The vibrations of the judge's
voice had reached the old gentlewoman in the parlour,
where she sat, with face averted, waiting on her
brother's slumber. She now issued forth, as would
appear, to defend the entrance, looking, we must
needs say, amazingly like the dragon which, in fairy
tales, is wont to be the guardian over an enchanted
beauty. The habitual scowl of her brow was, undeniably, too fierce, at this moment, to pass itself off
on the innocent score of near-sightedness; and it
was bent on Judge Pyncheon in a way that seemed
to confound, if not alarm him, so inadequately had
he estimated the moral force of a deeply-grounded
antipathy. She made a repelling gesture with her
hand, and stood, a perfect picture of prohibition, at
full length, in the dark frame of the doorway. But
we must betray Hepzibah's secret, and confess that
the native timorousness of her character even now
developed itself, in a quick tremour, which, to her
own perception, set each of her joints at variance with
its fellows.

Possibly, the judge was aware how little true hardihood lay behind Hepzibah's formidable front. At
any rate, being a gentleman of steady nerves, he soon
recovered himself, and failed not to approach his
cousin with outstretched hand; adopting the sensible
precaution, however, to cover his advance with a
smile, so broad and sultry, that, had it been only half
as warm as it looked, a trellis of grapes might at once
have turned purple under its summer-like exposure.
It may have been his purpose, indeed, to melt poor
Hepzibah on the spot, as if she were a figure of
yellow wax.

"Hepzibah, my beloved cousin, I am rejoiced!"

exclaimed the judge, most emphatically. "Now, at length, you have something to live for. Yes, and all of us, let me say, your friends and kindred, have more to live for than we had yesterday. I have lost no time in hastening to offer any assistance in my power towards making Clifford comfortable. He belongs to us all. I know how much he requires,—how much he used to require,—with his delicate taste, and his love of the beautiful. Anything in my house, —pictures, books, wine, luxuries of the table,—he may command them all! It would afford me most heart-felt gratification to see him! Shall I step in, this moment?"

"No," replied Hepzibah, her voice quivering too painfully to allow of many words. "He cannot see visitors!"

"A visitor, my dear cousin!—do you call me so?" cried the judge, whose sensibility, it seems, was hurt by the coldness of the phrase. "Nay, then, let me be Clifford's host, and your own likewise. Come at once to my house. The country air, and all the conveniences—I may say luxuries—that I have gathered about me, will do wonders for him. And you and I, dear Hepzibah, will consult together, and watch together, and labour together, to make our dear Clifford happy. Come! why should we make more words about what is both a duty and a pleasure, on my part? Come to me at once!"

On hearing these so hospitable offers, and such generous recognition of the claims of kindred, Phœbe felt very much in the mood of running up to Judge Pyncheon, and giving him, of her own accord, the kiss from which she had so recently shrunk away. It was quite otherwise with Hepzibah; the judge's smile seemed to òperate on her acerbity of heart like sunshine upon vinegar, making it ten times sourer than ever.

"Clifford," said she,—still too agitated to utter more than an abrupt sentence,—" Clifford has a home here!"

" May Heaven forgive you, Hepzibah," said Judge Pyncheon,—reverently lifting his eyes towards that high court of equity to which he appealed,—" if you suffer any ancient prejudice or animosity to weigh with you in this matter! I stand here, with an open heart, willing and anxious to receive yourself and Clifford into it. Do not refuse my good offices,—my earnest propositions for your welfare! They are such, in all respects, as it behoves your nearest kinsman to make. It will be a heavy responsibility, cousin, if you confine your brother to this dismal house and stifled air, when the delightful freedom of my country-seat is at his command."

" It would never suit Clifford," said Hepzibah, as briefly as before.

" Woman!" broke forth the judge, giving way to his resentment, " what is the meaning of all this? Have you other resources? Nay, I suspected as much! Take care, Hepzibah, take care! Clifford is on the brink of as black a ruin as ever befell him yet! But why do I talk with you, woman as you are? Make way!—I must see Clifford!"

Hepzibah spread out her gaunt figure across the door, and seemed really to increase in bulk; looking the more terrible also, because there was so much terror and agitation in her heart. But Judge Pyncheon's evident purpose of forcing a passage was interrupted by a voice from the inner room; a weak, tremulous, wailing voice, indicating helpless alarm, with no more energy for self-defence than belongs to a frightened infant.

" Hepzibah, Hepzibah!" cried the voice; " go down on your knees to him! Kiss his feet! Entreat him not to come in! Oh, let him have mercy on me! Mercy!—mercy!"

For the instant it appeared doubtful whether it were not the judge's resolute purpose to set Hepzibah aside, and step across the threshold into the parlour whence issued that broken and miserable murmur of entreaty. It was not pity that restrained him, for, at the first

sound of the enfeebled voice, a red fire kindled in his
eyes, and he made a quick pace forward, with something inexpressibly fierce and grim darkening forth,
as it were, out of the whole man.   To know Judge
Pyncheon, was to see him at that moment.   After
such a revelation, let him smile with what sultriness
he would, he could much sooner turn grapes purple,
or pumpkins yellow, than melt the iron-branded impression out of the beholder's memory.   And it
rendered his aspect not the less, but more frightful,
that it seemed not to express wrath or hatred, but a
certain hot fellness of purpose, which annihilated
everything but itself.

Yet, after all, are we not slandering an excellent
and amiable man?   Look at the judge now!   He is
apparently conscious of having erred, in too energetic-
ally pressing his deeds of loving-kindness on persons
unable to appreciate them.   He will await their better
mood, and hold himself as ready to assist them then
as at this moment.   As he draws back from the door,
an all-comprehensive benignity blazes from his visage,
indicating that he gathers Hepzibah, little Phœbe,
and the invisible Clifford, all three, together with the
whole world besides, into his immense heart, and
gives them a warm bath in its flood of affection.

"You do me great wrong, dear cousin Hepzibah!"
said he, first kindly offering her his hand, and then
drawing on his glove preparatory to departure.
"Very great wrong!   But I forgive it, and will study
to make you think better of me.   Of course, our poor
Clifford being in so unhappy a state of mind, I cannot
think of urging an interview at present.   But I shall
watch over his welfare, as if he were my own beloved
brother; nor do I at all despair, my dear cousin, of
constraining both him and you to acknowledge your
injustice.   When that shall happen, I desire no other
revenge than your acceptance of the best offices in my
power to do you."

With a bow to Hepzibah, and a degree of
paternal benevolence in his parting nod to Phœbe,

the judge left the shop, and went smiling along the
street. As is customary with the rich, when they aim
at the honours of a republic, he apologized, as it were,
to the people, for his wealth, prosperity, and elevated
station, by a free and hearty manner towards those
who knew him; putting off the more of his dignity,
in due proportion with humbleness of the man whom
he saluted, and thereby proving a haughty consciousness of his advantages as irrefragably as if he had
marched forth preceded by a troop of lackeys to clear
the way. On this particular forenoon, so excessive
was the warmth of Judge Pyncheon's kindly aspect,
that (such, at least, was the rumour about town) an
extra passage of the water-carts was found essential,
in order to lay the dust occasioned by so much extra
sunshine !

No sooner had he disappeared than Hepzibah grew
deadly white, and, staggering towards Phœbe, let her
head fall on the young girl's shoulder.

"O, Phœbe !" murmured she, "that man has been
the horror of my life ! Shall I never, never have the
courage—will my voice never cease from trembling
long enough to let me tell him what he is?"

"Is he so very wicked?" asked Phœbe. "Yet his
offers were surely kind !"

"Do not speak of them—he has a heart of iron !"
rejoined Hepzibah. "Go, now, and talk to Clifford !
Amuse and keep him quiet ! It would disturb him
wretchedly to see me so agitated as I am. There,
go, dear child, and I will try to look after the shop."

Phœbe went, accordingly, but perplexed herself
meanwhile with queries as to the purport of the scene
which she had just witnessed, and also, whether
judges, clergymen, and other characters of that
eminent stamp and respectability, could really, in any
single instance, be otherwise than just and upright
men. A doubt of this nature has a most disturbing
influence, and, if shown to be a fact, comes with fearful and startling effect, on minds of the trim, orderly,
and limit-loving class, in which we find our little

country-girl.   Dispositions more boldly speculative
may derive a stern enjoyment from the discovery,
since there must be evil in the world, that a high man
is as likely to grasp his share of it as a low one.   A
wider scope of view, and a deeper insight, may see
rank, dignity, and station, all proved illusory, so far
as regards their claim to human reverence, and yet
not feel as if the universe were thereby tumbled headlong into chaos.   But Phœbe, in order to keep the
universe in its old place, was fain to smother, in some
degree, her own intuitions as to Judge Pyncheon's
character.   And as for her cousin's testimony in dis-
paragement of it, she concluded that Hepzibah's judgment was embittered by one of those family feuds,
which render hatred the more deadly, by the dead and
corrupted love that they intermingle with its native
poison.

IX

CLIFFORD AND PHŒBE

TRULY was there something high, generous, and
noble, in the native composition of our poor old Hepzibah ! Or else—and it was quite as probably the case
—she had been enriched by poverty, developed by
sorrow, elevated by the strong and solitary affection
of her life, and thus endowed with heroism, which
never could have characterized her in what are called
happier circumstances.   Through dreary years, Hepzibah had looked forward—for the most part despair-
ingly, never with any confidence of hope, but always
with the feeling that it was her brightest possibility—
to the very position in which she now found herself.
In her own behalf she had asked nothing of Providence, but the opportunity of devoting herself to this

brother, whom she had so loved—so admired for what
he was, or might have been—and to whom she had
kept her faith, alone of all the world, wholly, un-
falteringly, at every instant, and throughout life.
And here, in his late decline, the lost one had come
back out of his long and strange misfortune, and was
thrown on her sympathy, as it seemed, not merely for
the bread of his physical existence, but for everything
that should keep him morally alive. She had responded to the call. She had come forward—our
poor, gaunt Hepzibah, in her rusty silks, with her
rigid joints, and the sad perversity of her scowl—ready
to do her utmost; and with affection enough, if that
were all, to do a hundred times as much! There
could be few more tearful sights—and Heaven forgive
us, if a smile insist on mingling with our conception
of it!—few sights with truer pathos in them, than
Hepzibah presented, on that first afternoon.

How patiently did she endeavour to wrap Clifford
up in her great, warm love, and make it all the
world to him, so that he should retain no torturing
sense of the coldness and dreariness without! Her
little efforts to amuse him! How pitiful, yet magnanimous, they were!

Remembering his early love of poetry and fiction,
she unlocked a book-case, and took down several
books that had been excellent reading in their day.
There was a volume of Pope, with the Rape of the
Lock in it, and another of the Tatler, and an odd one
of Dryden's Miscellanies, all with tarnished gilding
on their covers, and thoughts of tarnished brilliancy
inside. They had no success with Clifford. These,
and all such writers of society, whose new works glow
like the rich texture of a just-woven carpet, must be
content to relinquish their charm, for every reader,
after an age or two, and could hardly be supposed to
retain any portion of it for a mind that had utterly lost
its estimate of modes and manners. Hepzibah then
took up Rasselas, and began to read of the Happy
Valley, with a vague idea that some secret of a con-

tented life had there been elaborated, which might at least serve Clifford and herself for this one day. But the Happy Valley had a cloud over it. Hepzibah troubled her auditor, moreover, by innumerable sins of emphasis, which he seemed to detect, without any reference to the meaning; nor, in fact, did he appear to take much note of the sense of what she read, but evidently felt the tedium of the lecture, without harvesting its profit. His sister's voice, too, naturally harsh, had, in the course of her sorrowful lifetime, contracted a kind of croak, which, when it once gets into the human throat, is as ineradicable as sin. In both sexes, occasionally, this lifelong croak, accompanying each word of joy or sorrow, is one of the symptoms of a settled melancholy; and wherever it occurs, the whole history of misfortune is conveyed in its slightest accent. The effect is as if the voice had been dyed black; or—if we must use a more moderate simile—this miserable croak, running through all the variations of the voice, is like a black silken thread, on which the crystal beads of speech are strung, and whence they take their hue. Such voices have put on mourning for dead hopes; and they ought to die and be buried along with them !

Discerning that Clifford was not gladdened by her efforts, Hepzibah searched about the house for the means of more exhilarating pastime. At one time her eyes chanced to rest on Alice Pyncheon's harpsichord. It was a moment of great peril; for—despite the traditionary awe that had gathered over this instrument of music, and the dirges which spiritual fingers were said to play on it,—the devoted sister had solemn thoughts of thrumming on its chords for Clifford's benefit, and accompanying the performance with her voice. Poor Clifford ! Poor Hepzibah ! Poor harpsichord ! All three would have been miserable together. By some good agency,—possibly, by the unrecognized interposition of the long-buried Alice herself,—the threatening calamity was averted.

But the worst of all,—the hardest stroke of fate for

Hepzibah to endure, and perhaps for Clifford too,—was his invincible distaste for her appearance. Her features, never the most agreeable, and now harsh with age and grief, and resentment against the world for his sake ; her dress, and especially her turban ; the queer and quaint manners which had unconsciously grown upon her in solitude ; such being the poor gentlewoman's outward characteristics, it is no great marvel, although the mournfullest of pities, that the instinctive lover of the Beautiful was fain to turn away his eyes. There was no help for it. It would be the latest impulse to die within him. In his last extremity, the expiring breath stealing faintly through Clifford's lips, he would doubtless press Hepzibah's hand, in fervent recognition of all her lavished love, and close his eyes,—but not so much to die, as to be constrained to look no longer on her face ! Poor Hepzibah ! She took counsel with herself what might be done, and thought of putting ribbons on her turban ; but, by the instant rush of several guardian angels, was withheld from an experiment that could hardly have proved less fatal to the beloved object of her anxiety.

To be brief, besides Hepzibah's disadvantages of person, there was an uncouthness pervading all her deeds ; a clumsy something, that could but ill adapt itself for use, and not at all for ornament. She was a grief to Clifford, and she knew it. In this extremity, the antiquated virgin turned to Phœbe. No grovelling jealousy was in her heart. Had it pleased Heaven to crown the heroic fidelity of her life by making her personally the medium of Clifford's happiness, it would have rewarded her for all the past, by a joy with no bright tints, indeed, but deep and true, and worth a thousand gayer ecstasies. This could not be. She therefore turned to Phœbe, and resigned the task into the young girl's hands. The latter took it up, cheerfully, as she did everything, but with no sense of a mission to perform, and succeeding all the better for that same simplicity.

By the involuntary effect of a genial temperament, Phœbe soon grew to be absolutely essential to the daily comfort, if not the daily life, of her two forlorn companions. The grime and sordidness of the House of the Seven Gables seemed to have vanished, since her appearance there; the gnawing tooth of the dry-rot was stayed, among the old timbers of its skeleton-frame; the dust had ceased to settle down so densely, from the antique ceilings, upon the floors and furniture of the rooms below; or, at any rate, there was a little housewife, as light-footed as the breeze that sweeps a garden walk, gliding hither and thither, to brush it all away. The shadows of gloomy events, that haunted the else lonely and desolate apartments; the heavy, breathless scent which death had left in more than one of the bed-chambers, ever since his visits of long ago;—these were less powerful than the purifying influence scattered throughout the atmosphere of the household by the presence of one youthful, fresh, and thoroughly wholesome heart. There was no morbidness in Phœbe; if there had been, the old Pyncheon-house was the very locality to ripen it into incurable disease. But now her spirit resembled, in its potency, a minute quantity of ottar of rose in one of Hepzibah's huge, iron-bound trunks, diffusing its fragrance through the various articles of linen and wrought-lace, kerchiefs, caps, stockings, folded dresses, gloves, and whatever else was treasured there. As every article in the great trunk was the sweeter for the rose-scent, so did all the thoughts and emotions of Hepzibah and Clifford, sombre as they might seem, acquire a subtle attribute of happiness from Phœbe's intermixture with them. Her activity of body, intellect, and heart, impelled her continually to perform the ordinary little toils that offered themselves around her, and to think the thought proper for the moment, and to sympathize,—now with the twittering gaiety of the robins in the pear-tree, and now to such a depth as she could with Hepzibah's dark anxiety, or the vague moan of her brother. This facile adaptation was at once the symptom of perfect health, and its best preservative.

A nature like Phœbe's has invariably its due influence, but is seldom regarded with due honour. Its spiritual force, however, may be partially estimated by the fact of her having found a place for herself, amid circumstances so stern as those which surrounded the mistress of the house; and also by the effect which she produced on a character of so much more mass than her own. For the gaunt, bony frame and limbs of Hepzibah, as compared with the tiny lightsomeness of Phœbe's figure, were perhaps in some fit proportion with the normal weight and substance, respectively, of the woman and the girl.

To the guest,—to Hepzibah's brother,—or cousin Clifford, as Phœbe now began to call him,—she was especially necessary. Not that he could ever be said to converse with her, or often manifest, in any other very definite mode, his sense of a charm in her society. But, if she were a long while absent, he became pettish and nervously restless, pacing the room to and fro, with the uncertainty that characterized all his movements; or else would sit broodingly in his great chair, resting his head on his hands, and evincing life only by an electric sparkle of ill-humour, whenever Hepzibah endeavoured to arouse him. Phœbe's presence, and the contiguity of her fresh life on his blighted one, was usually all that he required. Indeed, such was the native gush and play of her spirit, that she was seldom perfectly quiet and undemonstrative, any more than a fountain ever ceases to dimple and warble with its flow. She possessed the gift of song, and that, too, so naturally, that you would as little think of inquiring whence she had caught it, or what master had taught her, as of asking the same questions about a bird, in whose small strain of music we recognize the voice of the Creator as distinctly as in the loudest accents of his thunder. So long as Phœbe sang she might stray at her own will about the house. Clif-

ford was content, whether the sweet, airy homeliness
of her tones came down from the upper chambers, or
along the passage-way from the shop, or was sprinkled
through the foliage of the pear-tree, inward from the
garden, with the twinkling sunbeams. He would sit
quietly, with a gentle pleasure gleaming over his face,
brighter now, and now a little dimmer, as the song
happened to float near him, or was more remotely
heard. It pleased him best, however, when she sat
on a low footstool at his knee.

It is perhaps remarkable, considering her temperament, that Phœbe oftener choose a strain of pathos
than of gaiety. But the young and happy are not ill
pleased to temper their life with a transparent shadow.
The deepest pathos of Phœbe's voice and song, moreover, came sifted through the golden texture of a
cheery spirit, and was somehow so interfused with the
quality thence acquired, that one's heart felt all the
lighter for having wept at it. Broad mirth, in the
sacred presence of dark misfortune, would have jarred
harshly and irreverently with the solemn symphony
that rolled its undertone through Hepzibah's and her
brother's life. Therefore, it was well that Phœbe so
often chose sad themes, and not amiss that they
ceased to be so sad while she was singing them.

Becoming habituated to her companionship, Clifford
readily showed how capable of imbibing pleasant tints
and gleams of cheerful light from all quarters his
nature must originally have been. He grew youthful
while she sat by him. A beauty—not precisely real,
even in its utmost manifestation, and which a painter
would have watched long to seize and fix upon his
canvas, and, after all, in vain—beauty, nevertheless,
that was not a mere dream, would sometimes play
upon and illuminate his face. It did more than to
illuminate; it transfigured him with an expression
that could only be interpreted as the glow of an exquisite and happy spirit. That gray hair, and those
furrows—with their record of infinite sorrow, so
deeply written across his brow, and so compressed,

as with a futile effort to crowd in all the tale, that the
whole inscription was made illegible—these for the
moment vanished.   An eye, at once tender and acute,
might have beheld in the man some shadow of what
he was meant to be.   Anon, as age came stealing,
like a sad twilight, back over his figure, you would
have felt tempted to hold an argument with Destiny,
and affirm, that either this being should not have
been made mortal, or mortal existence should have
been tempered to his qualities.   There seemed no
necessity for his having drawn breath at all—the
world never wanted him—but, as he had breathed, it
ought always to have been the balmiest of summer
air.   The same perplexity will invariably haunt us
with regard to natures that tend to feed exclusively
upon the Beautiful, let their earthly fate be as lenient
as it may.

Phœbe, it is probable, had but a very imperfect
comprehension of the character over which she had
thrown so beneficent a spell.   Nor was it necessary.
The fire upon the hearth can gladden a whole semi-
circle of faces round about it, but need not know the
individuality of one among them all.   Indeed, there
was something too fine and delicate in Clifford's traits
to be perfectly appreciated by one whose sphere lay
so much in the Actual as Phœbe's did.   For Clifford,
however, the reality, and simplicity, and thorough
homeliness of the girl's nature, were as powerful a
charm as any that she possessed.   Beauty, it is true,
and beauty almost perfect in its own style, was indis-
pensable.   Had Phœbe been coarse in feature, shaped
clumsily, of harsh voice, and uncouthly mannered, she
might have been rich with all good gifts, beneath this
unfortunate exterior, and still, so long as she wore
the guise of a woman, she would have shocked Clifford, and depressed him by her lack of beauty.   But
nothing more beautiful—nothing prettier, at least—
was ever made than Phœbe.   And, therefore, to this
man—whose whole poor and impalpable enjoyment of
existence, heretofore, and until both his heart and

fancy died within him, had been a dream—whose images of women had more and more lost their warmth and substance, and been frozen, like the pictures of secluded artists, into the chillest ideality—to him, this little figure of the cheeriest household life was just what he required to bring him back into the breathing world. Persons who have wandered, or been expelled, out of the common track of things, even were it for a better system, desire nothing so much as to be led back. They shiver in their loneliness, be it on a mountain-top or in a dungeon. Now, Phœbe's presence made a home about her—that very sphere which the outcast, the prisoner, the potentate —the wretch beneath mankind, the wretch aside from it, or the wretch above it—instinctively pines after—a home! She was real! Holding her hand, you felt something; a tender something; a substance, and a warm one; and so long as you should feel its grasp, soft as it was, you might be certain that your place was good in the whole sympathetic chain of human nature. The world was no longer a delusion.

By looking a little further in this direction, we might suggest an explanation of an often-suggested mystery. Why are poets so apt to choose their mates, not for any similarity of poetic endowment, but for qualities which might make the happiness of the rudest handicraftsmen as well as that of the ideal craftsmen of the spirit? Because, probably, at his highest elevation, the poet needs no human intercourse; but he finds it dreary to descend, and be a stranger.

There was something very beautiful in the relation that grew up between this pair, so closely and constantly linked together, yet with such a waste of gloomy and mysterious years from his birth-day to hers. On Clifford's part, it was the feeling of a man naturally endowed with the liveliest sensibility to feminine influence, but who had never quaffed the cup of passionate love, and knew that it was now too late. He knew it, with the instinctive delicacy that

had survived his intellectual decay.   Thus, his sentiment for Phœbe, without being paternal, was not less
chaste than if she had been his daughter.   He was a
man, it is true, and recognized her as a woman.   She
was his only representative of womankind.   He took
unfailing note of every charm that appertained to her
sex, and saw the ripeness of her lips, and the virginal
development of her bosom.   All her little womanly
ways, budding out of her, like blossoms on a young
fruit-tree, had their effect on him, and sometimes
caused his very heart to tingle with the keenest thrills
of pleasure.   At such moments—for the effect was
seldom more than momentary—the half-torpid man
would be full of harmonious life, just as a long-silent
harp is full of sound when the musician's fingers
sweep across it.   But, after all, it seemed rather a
perception, or a sympathy, than a sentiment belonging to himself as an individual.   He read Phœbe, as
he would a sweet and simple story; he listened to
her, as if she were a verse of household poetry,
which God, in requital of his bleak and dismal lot,
had permitted some angel, that most pitied him, to
warble through the house.   She was not an actual
fact for him, but the interpretation of all that he had
lacked on earth, brought warmly home to his conception; so that this mere symbol, or lifelike picture,
had almost the comfort of reality.

But we strive in vain to put the idea into words.
No adequate expression of the beauty and profound
pathos with which it impresses us is unattainable.
This being, made only for happiness, and heretofore
so miserably failing to be happy—his tendencies so
hideously thwarted, that, some unknown time ago,
the delicate springs of his character, never morally
or intellectually strong, had given way, and he was
now imbecile—this poor, forlorn voyager from the
Islands of the Blest, in a frail bark, on a tempest-
uous sea, had been flung, by the last mountain-wave
of his shipwreck, into a quiet harbour.   There, as
he lay more than half lifeless on the strand, the

fragrance of an earthly rose-bud had come to his nostrils, and, as odours will, had summoned up reminiscences or visions of all the living and breathing beauty amid which he should have had his home. With his native susceptibility of happy influences, he inhales the slight, ethereal rapture into his soul, and expires!

And how did Phœbe regard Clifford? The girl's was not one of those natures which are most attracted by what is strange and exceptional in human character. The path which would best have suited her was the well-worn track of ordinary life; the companions in whom she would most have delighted were such as one encounters at every turn. The mystery which enveloped Clifford, so far as it affected her at all, was an annoyance, rather than the piquant charm which many women might have found in it. Still her native kindliness was brought strongly into play, not by what was darkly picturesque in his situation, nor so much even, by the finer grace of his character, as by the simple appeal of a heart so forlorn as his to one so full of genuine sympathy as hers. She gave him an affectionate regard, because he needed so much love, and seemed to have received so little. With a ready tact, the result of ever-active and wholesome sensibility, she discerned what was good for him and did it. Whatever was morbid in his mind and experience she ignored; and thereby kept their intercourse healthy, by the incautious, but, as it were, heaven-directed freedom of her whole conduct. The sick in mind and, perhaps, in body, are rendered more darkly and hopelessly so, by the manifold reflection of their disease, mirrored back from all quarters, in the deportment of those about them; they are compelled to inhale the poison of their own breath, in infinite repetition. But Phœbe afforded her poor patient a supply of purer air. She impregnated it, too, not with a wild-flower scent—for wildness was no trait of hers—but with the perfume of garden-roses,

pinks, and other blossoms of much sweetness, which
nature and man have consented together in making
grow, from summer to summer, and from century
to century. Such a flower was Phœbe, in her relation with Clifford, and such the delight that he
inhaled from her.

Yet, it must be said, her petals sometimes drooped
a little, in consequence of the heavy atmosphere
about her. She grew more thoughtful than heretofore. Looking aside at Clifford's face, and seeing
the dim, unsatisfactory elegance and the intellect
almost quenched, she would try to inquire what had
been his life. Was he always thus? Had this veil
been over him from his birth?—this veil, under
which far more of his spirit was hidden than revealed,
and through which he so imperfectly discerned the
actual world,—or was its gray texture woven of
some dark calamity? Phœbe loved no riddles, and
would have been glad to escape the perplexity of
this one. Nevertheless, there was so far a good
result of her meditations on Clifford's character,
that, when her involuntary conjectures, together with
the tendency of every strange circumstance to tell its
own story, had gradually taught her the fact, it had
no terrible effect upon her. Let the world have done
him what vast wrong it might, she knew cousin
Clifford too well,—or fancied so,—ever to shudder
at the touch of his thin delicate fingers.

Within a few days after the appearance of this
remarkable inmate, the routine of life had established itself with a good deal of uniformity in the
old house of our narrative. In the morning, very
shortly after breakfast, it was Clifford's custom to
fall asleep in his chair; nor, unless accidentally
disturbed, would he emerge from a dense cloud of
slumber, or the thinner mists that flitted to and fro,
until well towards noon-day. These hours of drowsy
head were the season of the old gentlewoman's
attendance on her brother, while Phœbe took charge
of the shop; an arrangement which the public

speedily understood, and evinced their decided pre-
ference of the younger shopwoman by the multiplicity of their calls during her administration of
affairs.   Dinner over, Hepzibah took her knitting-
work,—a long stocking of gray yarn, for her
brother's winter wear,—and with a sigh, and a
scowl of affectionate farewell to Clifford, and a
gesture enjoining watchfulness on Phœbe, went to
take her seat behind the counter.   It was now the
young girl's turn to be the nurse,—the guardian,
the playmate,—or whatever is the fitter phrase,—of
the gray-haired man.

X

THE PYNCHEON-GARDEN

CLIFFORD, except for Phœbe's more active instiga-
tion, would ordinarily have yielded to the torpor
which had crept through all his modes of being, and
which sluggishly counselled him to sit in his morning chair till eventide.   But the girl seldom failed
to propose a removal to the garden, where Uncle
Venner and the daguerreotypist had made such
repairs on the roof of the ruinous arbour, or summer-
house, that it was now a sufficient shelter from sunshine and casual showers.   The hop-vine, too, had
begun to grow luxuriantly over the sides of the little
edifice, and made an interior of verdant seclusion,
with innumerable peeps and glimpses into the wilder
solitude of the garden.

Here, sometimes, in this green play-place of
flickering light, Phœbe read to Clifford.   Her acquaintance, the artist, who appeared to have a literary turn, had supplied her with works of fiction, in
pamphlet-form, and a few volumes of poetry, in alto-

gether a different style and taste from those which
Hepzibah selected for his amusement. Small thanks
were due to the books, however, if the girl's read-
ings were in any degree more successful than her
elderly cousin's. Phœbe's voice had always a pretty
music in it, and could either enliven Clifford by its
sparkle and gaiety of tone, or soothe him by a continued flow of pebbly and brook-like cadences. But
the fictions—in which the country-girl, unused to
works of that nature, often became deeply absorbed
—interested her strange auditor very little, or not at
all. Pictures of life, scenes of passion or sentiment,
wit, humour, and pathos, were all thrown away, or
worse than thrown away, on Clifford; either because
he lacked an experience by which to test their truth,
or because his own griefs were a touch-stone of
reality that few feigned emotions could withstand.
When Phœbe broke into a peal of merry laughter
at what she read, he would now and then laugh for
sympathy, but often respond with a troubled, ques-
tioning look. If a tear—a maiden's sunshiny tear,
over imaginary woe—dropped upon some melancholy
page, Clifford either took it as a token of actual
calamity, or else grew peevish, and angrily motioned
her to close the volume. And wisely too! Is not
the world sad enough, in genuine earnest, without
making a pastime of mock-sorrows?

With poetry it was rather better. He delighted
in the swell and subsidence of the rhythm, and the
happily-recurring rhyme. Nor was Clifford incapable of feeling the sentiment of poetry,—not, perhaps, where it was highest or deepest, but where it
was most flitting and ethereal. It was impossible
to foretell in what exquisite verse the awakening
spell might lurk; but, on raising her eyes from the
page to Clifford's face, Phœbe would be made aware,
by the light breaking through it, that a more delicate
intelligence than her own had caught a lambent flame
from what she read. One glow of this kind, however, was often the precursor of gloom for many

hours afterward; because, when the glow left him, he seemed conscious of a missing sense and power, and groped about for them, as if a blind man should go seeking his lost eyesight.

It pleased him more, and was better for his inward welfare, that Phœbe should talk, and make passing occurrences vivid to his mind by her accompanying description and remarks. The life of the garden offered topics enough for such discourse as suited Clifford best. He never failed to inquire what flowers had bloomed since yesterday. His feeling for flowers was very exquisite, and seemed not so much a taste as an emotion; he was fond of sitting with one in his hand, intently observing it, and looking from its petals into Phœbe's face, as if the garden-flower were the sister of the household-maiden. Not merely was there a delight in the flower's perfume, or pleasure in its beautiful form, and the delicacy or brightness of its hue; but Clifford's enjoyment was accompanied with a perception of life, character, and individuality, that made him love these blossoms of the garden, as if they were endowed with sentiment and intelligence. This affection and sympathy for flowers is almost exclusively a woman's trait. Men, if endowed with it by nature, soon lose, forget, and learn to despise it, in their contact with coarser things than flowers. Clifford, too, had long forgotten it, but found it again now, as he slowly revived from the chill torpor of his life.

It is wonderful how many pleasant incidents continually came to pass in that secluded garden-spot, when once Phœbe had set herself to look for them. She had seen or heard a bee there, on the first day of her acquaintance with the place. And often—almost continually, indeed—since then, the bees kept coming thither, heaven knows why, or by what pertinacious desire for far-fetched sweets, when, no doubt, there were broad clover fields, and all kinds of garden growth, much nearer home than this.

Thither the bees came, however, and plunged into
the squash-blossoms, as if there were no other
squash-vines within a long day's flight, or as if the
soil of Hepzibah's garden gave its productions just
the very quality which these laborious little wizards
wanted, in order to impart the Hymettus odour to
their whole hive of New England honey. When
Clifford heard their sunny, buzzing murmur in the
heart of the great yellow blossoms, he looked about
him with a joyful sense of warmth, the blue sky, and
green grass, and of God's free air in the whole
height from earth to heaven. After all, there need
be no question why the bees came to that one green
nook in the dusty town. God sent them thither to
gladden our poor Clifford. They brought the rich
summer with them, in requital of a little honey.

When the bean-vines began to flower on the poles,
there was one particular variety which bore a vivid
scarlet blossom. The daguerreotypist had found
these beans in a garret, over one of the seven gables,
treasured up in an old chest of drawers, by some
horticultural Pyncheon of days gone by, who, doubtless, meant to sow them the next summer, but was
himself first sown in Death's garden-ground. By
way of testing whether there was still a living germ
in such ancient seeds, Holgrave had planted some
of them; and the result of his experiment was a
splendid row of bean-vines, clambering, early, to the
full height of the poles, and arraying them, from top
to bottom, in a spiral profusion of red blossoms.
And, ever since the unfolding of the first bud, a
multitude of humming-birds had been attracted
thither. At times, it seemed as if for every one of
the hundred blossoms there was one of these tiniest
fowls of the air; a thumb's bigness of burnished
plumage hovering and vibrating about the bean-poles.
It was with indescribable interest, and even more than
childish delight, that Clifford watched the humming-
birds. He used to thrust his head softly out of the
arbour, to see them the better; all the while, too,

motioning Phœbe to be quiet, and snatching glimpses of the smile upon her face, so as to heap his enjoyment up the higher with her sympathy. He had not merely grown young ;—he was a child again.

Hepzibah, whenever she happened to witness one of these fits of miniature enthusiasm, would shake her head, with a strange mingling of the mother and sister, and of pleasure and sadness in her aspect. She said that it had always been thus with Clifford, when the humming-birds came,—always, from his babyhood,—and that his delight in them had been one of the earliest tokens by which he showed his love for beautiful things. And it was a wonderful coincidence, the good lady thought, that the artist should have planted these scarlet-flowering beans—which the humming-birds sought far and wide, and which had not grown in the Pyncheon-garden before for forty years—on the very summer of Clifford's return.

Then would the tears stand in poor Hepzibah's eyes, or overflow them with a too abundant gush, so that she was fain to betake herself into some corner, lest Clifford should espy her agitation. Indeed, all the enjoyments of this period were provocative of tears. Coming so late as it did, it was a kind of Indian summer, with a mist in its balmiest sunshine, and decay and death in its gaudiest delight. The more Clifford seemed to taste the happiness of a child, the sadder was the difference to be recognized. With a mysterious and terrible Past, which had annihilated his memory, and a blank Future before him, he had only this visionary and impalpable Now, which, if you once look closely at it, is nothing. He himself, as was perceptible by many symptoms, lay darkly behind his pleasure, and knew it to be a baby-play, which he was to toy and trifle with, instead of thoroughly believing. Clifford saw, it may be, in the mirror of his deeper consciousness, that he was an example and representative of that great class of people whom an inexplicable Providence is continually putting at cross-purposes with the world; breaking what seems its own promise in their nature; with-holding their proper food, and setting poison before them for a banquet;—and thus, when it might so easily, as one would think, have been adjusted other-wise, making their existence a strangeness, a solitude, and torment. All his life long he had been learning how to be wretched, as one learns a foreign tongue; and now, with the lesson thoroughly at heart, he could with difficulty comprehend his little airy happiness. Frequently, there was a dim shadow of doubt in his eyes. "Take my hand, Phœbe," he would say, "and pinch it hard with your little fingers! Give me a rose, that I may press its thorns, and prove myself awake, by the sharp touch of pain!" Evidently, he desired this prick of a trifling anguish, in order to assure himself, by that quality which he best knew to be real, that the garden, and the seven weather-beaten gables, and Hepzibah's scowl and Phœbe's smile, were real likewise. Without this signet in his flesh, he could have attributed no more substance to them than to the empty confusion of imaginary scenes with which he had fed his spirit, until even that poor sustenance was exhausted.

The author needs great faith in his reader's sympathy; else he must hesitate to give details so minute, and incidents apparently so trifling, as are essential to make up the idea of this garden-life. It was the Eden of a thunder-smitten Adam, who had fled for refuge thither out of the same dreary and perilous wilderness into which the original Adam was expelled.

One of the available means of amusement, of which Phœbe made the most, in Clifford's behalf, was that feathered society, the hens, a breed of whom, as we have already said, was an immemorial heirloom in the Pyncheon family. In compliance with a whim of Clifford, as it troubled him to see them in confine-ment, they had been set at liberty, and now roamed at will about the garden; doing some little mischief, but hindered from escape by buildings, on three sides, and the difficult peaks of a wooden fence on the other. They spent much of their abundant leisure on the margin of Maule's well, which was haunted by a kind of snail, evidently a titbit to their palates; and the brackish water itself, however nauseous to the rest of the world, was so greatly esteemed by these fowls, that they might be seen tasting, turning up their heads, and smacking their bills, with precisely the air of wine-bibbers round a probationary cask. Their generally quiet, yet often brisk and constantly diversified talk, one to another, or sometimes in soliloquy, —as they scratched worms out of the rich, black soil, or pecked at such plants as suited their taste,—had such a domestic tone, that it was almost a wonder why you could not establish a regular interchange of ideas about household matters, human and gallinaceous. All hens are well worth studying, for the piquancy and rich variety of their manners; but by no possibility can there have been other fowls of such odd appearance and deportment as these ancestral ones. They probably embodied the traditionary peculiarities of their whole line of progenitors, derived through an unbroken succession of eggs; or else, this individual Chanticleer and his two wives had grown to be humorists, and a little crack-brained withal, on account of their solitary way of life, and out of sympathy for Hepzibah, their lady-patroness.

Queerly, indeed, they looked ! Chanticleer himself, though stalking on two stilt-like legs, with the dignity of interminable descent in all his gestures, was hardly bigger than an ordinary partridge; his two wives were about the size of quails; and as for the one chicken, it looked small enough to be still in the egg, and, at the same time, sufficiently old, withered, wizened, and experienced, to have been the founder of the antiquated race. Instead of being the youngest of the family, it rather seemed to have aggregated into itself the ages, not only of these living specimens of the breed, but of all its forefathers and foremothers, whose united excellences and oddities were squeezed

into its little body. Its mother evidently regarded
it as the one chicken of the world, and as necessary,
in fact, to the world's continuance, or, at any rate,
to the equilibrium of the present system of affairs,
whether in church or state. No lesser sense of the
infant fowl's importance could have justified, even
in a mother's eyes, the perseverance with which she
watched over its safety, ruffling her small person to
twice its proper size, and flying in everybody's face
that so much as looked towards her hopeful progeny.
No lower estimate could have vindicated the indefatigable zeal with which she scratched, and her unscru-
pulousness in digging up the choicest flower or vegetable, for the sake of the fat earth-worm at its root.
Her nervous cluck, when the chicken happened to be
hidden in the long grass or under the squash-leaves;
her gentle croak of satisfaction, while sure of it
beneath her wing; her note of ill-concealed fear and
obstreperous defiance, when she saw her arch-enemy,
a neighbour's cat, on the top of the high fence;—one
or other of these sounds was to be heard at almost
every moment of the day. By degrees, the observer
came to feel nearly as much interest in this chicken
of illustrious race as the mother-hen did.

Phœbe, after getting well acquainted with the old
hen, was sometimes permitted to take the chicken
in her hand, which was quite capable of grasping its
cubic inch or two of body. While she curiously examined its hereditary marks—the peculiar speckle of
its plumage, the funny tuft on its head, and a knob
on each of its legs—the little biped, as she insisted,
kept giving her a sagacious wink. The daguerreotypist once whispered her that these marks betokened
the oddities of the Pyncheon family, and that the
chicken itself was a symbol of the life of the old
house, embodying its interpretation, likewise, although an unintelligible one, as such clues generally
are. It was a feathered riddle; a mystery hatched
out of an egg, and just as mysterious as if the egg
had been addle!

The second of Chanticleer's two wives, ever since Phœbe's arrival, had been in a state of heavy despondency, caused, as it afterwards appeared, by her inability to lay an egg. One day, however, by her self-important gait, the side-way turn of her head, and the cock of her eye, as she pried into one and another nook of the garden,—croaking to herself, all the while, with inexpressible complacency,—it was made evident that this identical hen, much as mankind undervalued her, carried something about her person, the worth of which was not to be estimated either in gold or precious stones. Shortly after, there was a prodigious cackling and gratulation of Chanticleer and all his family, including the wizened chicken, who appeared to understand the matter quite as well as did his sire, his mother, or his aunt. That afternon Phœbe found a diminutive egg,—not in the regular nest—it was far too precious to be trusted there,—but cunningly hidden under the currant-bushes on some dry stalks of last year's grass. Hepzibah, on learning the fact, took possession of the egg, and appropriated it to Clifford's breakfast, on account of a certain delicacy of flavour, for which, as she affirmed, these eggs had always been famous. Thus unscrupulously did the old gentlewoman sacrifice the continuance, perhaps, of an ancient feathered race, with no better end than to supply her brother with a dainty that hardly filled the bowl of a tea-spoon! It must have been in reference to this outrage that Chanticleer, the next day, accompanied by the bereaved mother of the egg, took his post in front of Phœbe and Clifford, and delivered himself of a harangue that might have proved as long as his own pedigree, but for a fit of merriment on Phœbe's part. Hereupon, the offended fowl stalked away on his long stilts, and utterly withdrew his notice from Phœbe and the rest of human nature, until she made her peace with an offering of spice-cake, which, next to snails, was the delicacy most in favour with his aristocratic taste.

We linger too long, no doubt, beside this paltry rivulet of life that flowed through the garden of the Pyncheon-house. But we deem it pardonable to record these mean incidents, and poor delights, because they proved so greatly to Clifford's benefit. They had the earth-smell in them, and contributed to give him health and substance. Some of his occupations wrought less desirably upon him. He had a singular propensity, for example, to hang over Maule's well, and look at the constantly shifting phantasmagoria of figures produced by the agitation of the water over the mosaic work of coloured pebbles at the bottom. He said that faces looked upward to him there,—beautiful faces, arrayed in bewitching smiles,—each momentary face so fair and rosy, and every smile so sunny, that he felt wronged at its departure, until the same flitting witchcraft made a new one. But sometimes he would suddenly cry out, "The dark face gazes at me!" and be miserable the whole day afterwards. Phœbe, when she hung over the fountain by Clifford's side, could see nothing of all this,—neither the beauty nor the ugliness,—but only the coloured pebbles, looking as if the gush of the water shook and disarranged them. And the dark face that so troubled Clifford, was no more than the shadow thrown from a branch of one of the damson-trees, and breaking the inner light of Maule's well. The truth was, however, that his fancy—reviving faster than his will and judgment, and always stronger than they—created shapes of loveliness that were symbolic of his native character, and now and then a stern and dreadful shape, that typified his fate.

On Sundays, after Phœbe had been at church—for the girl had a church-going conscience, and would hardly have been at ease had she missed either prayer, singing, sermon, or benediction—after church-time, therefore, there was, ordinarily, a sober little festival in the garden. In addition to Clifford, Hepzibah, and Phœbe, two guests made up the company. One was the artist, Holgrave, who, in spite of his consociation with reformers, and his other queer and questionable traits, continued to hold an elevated place in Hepzibah's regard. The other, we are almost ashamed to say, was the venerable Uncle Venner, in a clean shirt, and a broadcloth coat, more respectable than his ordinary wear, inasmuch as it was neatly patched on each elbow, and might be called an entire garment, except for a slight inequality in the length of its skirts. Clifford, on several occasions, had seemed to enjoy the old man's intercourse, for the sake of his mellow, cheerful vein, which was like the sweet flavour of a frost-bitten apple, such as one picks up under the tree in December. A man at the very lowest point of the social scale was easier and more agreeable for the fallen gentleman to encounter than a person at any of the intermediate degrees; and, moreover, as Clifford's young manhood had been lost, he was fond of feeling himself comparatively youthful, now, in apposition with the patriarchal age of Uncle Venner. In fact, it was sometimes observable that Clifford half wilfully hid from himself the consciousness of being stricken in years, and cherished visions of an earthly future still before him; visions, however, too indistinctly drawn to be followed by disappointment—though, doubtless, by depression—when any casual incident or recollection made him sensible of the withered leaf.

So this oddly-composed little social party used to assemble under the ruinous arbour. Hepzibah—stately as ever, at heart, and yielding not an inch of her old gentility, but resting upon it so much the more, as justifying a princess-like condescension—exhibited a not ungraceful hospitality. She talked kindly to the vagrant artist, and took sage counsel —lady as she was—with the wood-sawyer, the messenger of everybody's petty errands, the patched philosopher. And Uncle Venner, who had studied the world at street-corners, and at other posts equally well adapted for just observation, was as ready to give out his wisdom as a town-pump to give water,

" Miss Hepzibah, ma'am," said he once, after they had all been cheerful together, " I really enjoy these quiet little meetings, of a Sabbath afternoon. They are very much like what I expect to have, after I retire to my farm!"

" Uncle Venner," observed Clifford, in a drowsy, inward tone, " is always talking about his farm. But I have a better scheme for him by-and-by. We shall see!"

" Ah, Mr. Clifford Pyncheon!" said the man of patches, " you may scheme for me as much as you please; but I'm not going to give up this one scheme of my own, even if I never bring it really to pass. It does seem to me that men make a wonderful mistake in trying to heap up property upon property. If I had done so, I should feel as if Providence was not bound to take care of me; and, at all events, the city wouldn't be! I'm one of those people who think that infinity is big enough for us all,—and eternity long enough!"

" Why, so they are, Uncle Venner," remarked Phœbe, after a pause; for she had been trying to fathom the profundity and appositeness of this concluding apothegm. " But for this short life of ours, one would like a house and a moderate garden-spot of one's own."

" It appears to me," said the daguerreotypist, smiling, " that Uncle Venner has the principles of Fourier at the bottom of his wisdom; only they have not quite so much distinctness in his mind, as in that of the systematizing Frenchman."

" Come, Phœbe," said Hepzibah, " it is time to bring the currants."

And then, while the yellow richness of the declining sunshine still fell into the open space of the garden, Phœbe brought out a loaf of bread, and a china-bowl of currants, freshly gathered from the bushes, and crushed with sugar. These, with water—but not from the fountain of ill omen, close at hand—constituted all the entertainment. Meanwhile, Holgrave took some pains to establish an intercourse with Clifford, actuated, it might seem, entirely by an impulse of kindliness, in order that the present hour might be cheerfuller than most which the poor recluse had spent, or was destined yet to spend. Nevertheless, in the artist's deep, thoughtful, all-observant eyes, there was, now and then, an expression, not sinister, but questionable; as if he had some other interest in the scene than a stranger, a youthful and unconnected adventurer, might be supposed to have. With great mobility of outward mood, however, he applied himself to the task of enlivening the party; and with so much success, that even dark-hued Hepzibah threw off one tint of melancholy, and made what shift she could with the remaining portion. Phœbe said to herself,—" How pleasant he can be !" As for Uncle Venner, as a mark of friendship and approbation, he readily consented to afford the young man his countenance in the way of his profession— not metaphorically, be it understood, but literally, by allowing a daguerreotype of his face, so familiar to the town, to be exhibited at the entrance of Holgrave's studio.

Clifford, as the company partook of their little banquet, grew to be the gayest of them all. Either it was one of those up-quivering flashes of the spirit, to which minds in an abnormal state are liable, or else the artist had subtly touched some chord that made musical vibration. Indeed, what with the pleasant summer evening, and the sympathy of this little circle of not unkindly souls, it was perhaps natural that a character so susceptible as Clifford's should become animated, and show itself readily responsive to what was said around him. But he gave out his own thoughts likewise, with an airy and fanciful glow; so that they glistened, at it were, through the arbour, and made their escape among the interstices of the foliage. He had been as cheerful, no doubt, while alone with Phœbe, but never with such tokens of acute, although partial intelligence.

But, as the sunlight left the peaks of the seven gables, so did the excitement fade out of Clifford's eyes. He gazed vaguely and mournfully about him, as if he missed something precious, and missed it the more drearily for not knowing precisely what it was.

"I want my happiness!" at last he murmured, hoarsely and indistinctly, hardly shaping out the words. "Many, many years have I waited for it! It is late! It is late! I want my happiness!"

Alas, poor Clifford! You are old, and worn with troubles that ought never to have befallen you. You are partly crazy, and partly imbecile; a ruin, a failure, as almost everybody is—though some in less degree, or less perceptibly than their fellows. Fate has no happiness in store for you; unless your quiet home in the old family residence with the faithful Hepzibah, and your long summer afternoons with Phœbe, and these Sabbath festivals with Uncle Venner and the daguerreotypist, deserve to be called happiness! Why not? If not the thing itself, it is marvellously like it, and the more so for that ethereal and intangible quality which causes it all to vanish at too close an introspection. Take it, therefore, while you may! Murmur not,—question not,—but make the most of it!

XI

THE ARCHED WINDOW

FROM the inertness, or what we may term the vegetative character of his ordinary mood, Clifford would perhaps have been content to spend one day after another, interminably—or, at least, throughout the summer-time—in just the kind of life described in the preceding pages. Fancying, however, that

it might be for his benefit occasionally to diversify
the scene, Phœbe sometimes suggested that he should
look out upon the life of the street. For this purpose, they used to mount the staircase together, to
the second storey of the house, where, at the termin-
ation of a wide entry, there was an arched window
of uncommonly large dimensions, shaded by a pair
of curtains. It opened above the porch, where there
had formerly been a balcony, the balustrade of which
had long since gone to decay, and been removed.
At this arched window, throwing it open, but keeping
himself in comparative obscurity by means of the
curtain, Clifford had an opportunity of witnessing
such a portion of the great world's movement as
might be supposed to roll through one of the retired
streets of a not very populous city. But he and
Phœbe made a sight as well worth seeing as any
that the city could exhibit. The pale, gray, childish,
aged, melancholy, yet often simply cheerful, and
sometimes delicately intelligent aspect of Clifford,
peering from behind the faded crimson of the curtain
—watching the monotony of every-day occurrences
with a kind of inconsequential interest and earnestness, and, at every petty throb of his sensibility,
turning for sympathy to the eyes of the bright young
girl !

If once he were fairly seated at the window, even
Pyncheon-street would hardly be so dull and lonely
but that, somewhere or other along its extent, Clifford
might discover matter to occupy his eye, and titillate,
if not engross, his observation. Things familiar to
the youngest child that had begun its out-look at
existence seemed strange to him. A cab; an omnibus, with its populous interior, dropping here and
there a passenger, and picking up another, and thus
typifying that vast rolling vehicle, the world, the
end of whose journey is everywhere and nowhere;—
these objects he followed eagerly with his eyes, but
forgot them before the dust raised by the horses and
wheels had settled along their track. As regarded

novelties (among which cabs and omnibuses were to
be reckoned) his mind appeared to have lost its proper
gripe and retentiveness. Twice or thrice, for example, during the sunny hours of the day, a water-
cart went along by the Pyncheon-house, leaving a
broad wake of moistened earth, instead of the white
dust that had risen at a lady's lightest footfall; it
was like a summer shower, which the city authorities
had caught and tamed, and compelled it into the
commonest routine of their convenience. With the
water-cart Clifford could never grow familiar; it
always affected him with just the same surprise as
at first. His mind took an apparently sharp impression from it, but lost the recollection of this per-
ambulatory shower, before its next reappearance, as
completely as did the street itself, along which the
heat so quickly strewed white dust again. It was
the same with the railroad. Clifford could hear the
obstreperous howl of the steam-devil, and, by leaning a little way from the arched window, could catch
a glimpse of the trains of cars, flashing a brief transit
across the extremity of the street. The idea of
terrible energy thus forced upon him was new at
every recurrence, and seemed to affect him as disagreeably, and with almost as much surprise, the
hundredth time as the first.

Nothing gives a sadder sense of decay than this
loss or suspension of the power to deal with unaccustomed things, and to keep up with the swiftness of
the passing moment. It can merely be a suspended
animation; for, were the power actually to perish,
there would be little use of immortality. We are less
than ghosts, for the time being, whenever this calamity befalls us.

Clifford was indeed the most inveterate of conser-
vatives. All the antique fashions of the street were
dear to him; even such as were characterized by a
rudeness that would naturally have annoyed his fastidious senses. He loved the old rumbling and jolting
carts, the former track of which he still found in his

long-buried remembrance, as the observer of to-day finds the wheel-tracks of ancient vehicles in Hercula-neum. The butcher's cart, with its snowy canopy, was an acceptable object; so was the fish-cart, heralded by its horn; so, likewise, was the country-man's cart of vegetables, plodding from door to door, with long pauses of the patient horse, while his owner drove a trade in turnips, carrots, summer-squashes, string-beans, green peas, and new pota-toes, with half the housewives of the neighbourhood. The baker's cart, with the harsh music of its bells, had a pleasant effect on Clifford, because, as few things else did, it jingled the very dissonance of yore. One afternoon, a scissor-grinder chanced to set his wheel a-going under the Pyncheon-elm, and just in front of the arched window. Children came running with their mothers' scissors, or the carving-knife, or the paternal razor, or anything else that lacked an edge (except, indeed, poor Clifford's wits), that the grinder might apply the article to his magic wheel, and give it back as good as new. Round went the busily-revolving machinery, kept in motion by the scissor-grinder's foot, and wore away the hard steel against the hard stone, whence issued an intense and spiteful prolongation of a hiss, as fierce as those emitted by Satan and his compeers in Pandemonium though squeezed into smaller compass. It was an ugly, little venomous serpent of a noise, as ever did petty violence to human ears. But Clifford listened with rapturous delight. The sound, however dis-agreeable, had very brisk life in it, and, together with the circle of curious children watching the revolu-tions of the wheel, appeared to give him a more vivid sense of active, bustling, and sunshiny existence, than he had attained in almost any other way. Nevertheless, its charm lay chiefly in the past; for the scissor-grinder's wheel had hissed in his childish ears.

He sometimes made doleful complaint that there were no stage-coaches, now-a-days. And he asked,

in an injured tone, what had become of all those old
square-top chaises, with wings sticking out on either
side, that used to be drawn by a plough-horse, and
driven by a farmer's wife and daughter, peddling
whortleberries and blackberries about the town.
Their disappearance made him doubt, he said,
whether the berries had not left off growing in the
broad pastures, and along the shady country lanes.

But anything that appealed to the sense of beauty,
in however humble a way, did not require to be re-
commended by these old associations. This was
observable when one of those Italian boys (who are
rather a modern feature of our streets) came
along with his barrel-organ, and stopped under the
wide and cool shadows of the elm. With his quick
professional eye, he took note of the two faces watching him from the arched window, and, opening his
instrument, began to scatter its melodies abroad.
He had a monkey on his shoulder, dressed in a Highland plaid; and, to complete the sum of splendid
attractions wherewith he presented himself to the
public, there was a company of little figures, whose
sphere and habitation was in the mahogany case of
his organ, and whose principle of life was the music,
which the Italian made it his business to grind out.
In all their variety of occupation,—the cobbler, the
blacksmith, the soldier, the lady with her fan, the
toper with his bottle, the milk-maid sitting by her
cow,—this fortunate little society might truly be said
to enjoy a harmonious existence, and to make life
literally a dance. The Italian turned a crank; and,
behold! every one of these small individuals started
into the most curious vivacity. The cobbler wrought
upon a shoe; the blacksmith hammered his iron;
the soldier waved his glittering blade; the lady raised
a tiny breeze with her fan; the jolly toper swigged
lustily at his bottle: the scholar opened his book,
with eager thirst for knowledge, and turned his head
to and fro along the page; the milk-maid energetic-
ally drained her cow; and a miser counted gold into

his strong box; all at the same turning of a crank. Yes; and, moved by the self-same impulse, a lover saluted his mistress on her lips! Possibly, some cynic, at once merry and bitter, had desired to signify, in this pantomimic scene, that we mortals, whatever our business or amusement — however serious, however trifling—all dance to one identical tune, and, in spite of our ridiculous activity, bring nothing finally to pass. For the most remarkable aspect of the affair was, that, at the cessation of the music, everybody was petrified, at once, from the most extravagant life into a dead torpor. Neither was the cobbler's shoe finished, nor the blacksmith's iron shaped out; nor was there a drop less of brandy in the toper's bottle, nor a drop more of milk in the milkmaid's pail, nor one additional coin in the miser's strong box, nor was the scholar a page deeper in his book. All were precisely in the same condition as before they made themselves so ridiculous by their haste to toil, to enjoy, to accumulate gold, and to become wise. Saddest of all, moreover, the lover was none the happier for the maiden's granted kiss! But, rather than swallow this last too acrid ingredient, we reject the whole moral of the show!

The monkey, meanwhile, with a thick tail curling out into preposterous prolixity from beneath his tartans, took his station at the Italian's feet. He turned a wrinkled and abominable little visage to every passer-by, and to the circle of children that soon gathered round, and to Hepzibah's shop-door, and upward to the arched window, whence Phœbe and Clifford were looking down. Every moment, also, he took off his Highland-bonnet, and performed a bow and scrape. Sometimes, moreover, he made personal application to individuals, holding out his small black palm, and otherwise plainly signifying his excessive desire for whatever filthy lucre might happen to be in anybody's pocket. The mean and low, yet strangely man-like expression of his wilted countenance; the prying and crafty glance, that showed him ready to gripe at every miserable advantage; his enormous tail (too enormous to be decently concealed under his gabardine), and the deviltry of nature which it betokened;—take this monkey just as he was, in short, and you could desire no better image of the Mammon of copper-coin, symbolizing the grossest form of the love of money. Neither was there any possibility of satisfying the covetous little devil. Phœbe threw down a whole handful of cents, which he picked up with joyless eagerness, handed them over to the Italian for safe-keeping, and immediately recommenced a series of pantomimic petitions for more.

Doubtless, more than one New Englander—or, let him be of what country he might, it is as likely to be the case—passed by, and threw a look at the monkey, and went on, without imagining how nearly his own moral condition was here exemplified. Clifford, however, was a being of another order. He had taken childish delight in the music, and smiled, too, at the figures which it set in motion. But, after looking a while at the long-tailed imp, he was so shocked by his horrible ugliness, spiritual as well as physical, that he actually began to shed tears; a weakness which men of merely delicate endowments, and destitute of the fiercer, deeper, and more tragic power of laughter, can hardly avoid, when the worst and meanest aspect of life happens to be presented to them.

Pyncheon-street was sometimes enlivened by spectacles of more imposing pretensions than the above, and which brought the multitude along with them. With a shivering repugnance at the idea of personal contact with the world, a powerful impulse still seized on Clifford, whenever the rush and roar of the human tide grew strongly audible to him. This was made evident, one day, when a political procession, with hundreds of flaunting banners, and drums, fifes, clarions, and cymbals, reverberating between the rows of buildings, marched all through town, and trailed its length of trampling footsteps, and most infrequent uproar, past the ordinarily quiet House of the Seven Gables. As a mere object of sight, nothing is more deficient in picturesque features than a procession, seen in its passage through narrow streets. The spectator feels it to be fool's play, when he can distinguish the tedious common-place of each man's visage, with the perspiration and weary self-importance on it, and the very cut of his pantaloons, and the stiffness or laxity of his shirt-collar, and the dust on the back of his black coat. In order to become majestic, it should be viewed from some vantage-point, as it rolls its slow and long array through the centre of a wide plain, or the stateliest public square of a city; for then, by its remoteness, it melts all the petty personalities, of which it is made up, into one broad mass of existence—one great life—one collected body of mankind, with a vast homogeneous spirit animating it. But, on the other hand, if an impressible person, standing alone over the brink of one of these processions, should behold it, not in its atoms, but in its aggregate—as a mighty river of life, massive in its tide, and black with mystery, and, out of its depths, calling to the kindred depths within him—then the contiguity would add to the effect. It might so fascinate him that he would hardly be restrained from plunging into the surging stream of human sympathies.

So it proved with Clifford. He shuddered; he grew pale; he threw an appealing look at Hepzibah and Phœbe, who were with him at the window. They comprehended nothing of his emotions, and supposed him merely disturbed by the unaccustomed tumult. At last, with tremulous limbs, he started up, set his foot on the window-sill, and, in an instant more, would have been in the unguarded balcony. As it was, the whole procession might have seen him, a wild, haggard figure, his gray locks floating in the wind that waved their banners; a lonely being, estranged from his race, but now feeling himself man

again, by virtue of the irrepressible instinct that possessed him. Had Clifford attained the balcony, he
would probably have leaped into the street; but
whether impelled by the species of terror that sometimes urges its victim over the very precipice which
he shrinks from, or by a natural magnetism, tending towards the great centre of humanity, it were not
easy to decide. Both impulses might have wrought
on him at once.

But his companions, affrighted by his gesture—
which was that of a man hurried away in spite of
himself—seized Clifford's garment and held him back.
Hepzibah shrieked. Phœbe, to whom all extravagance was a horror, burst into sobs and tears.

"Clifford, Clifford! are you crazy?" cried his
sister.

"I hardly know, Hepzibah!" said Clifford, drawing a long breath. "Fear nothing—it is over now
—but had I taken that plunge, and survived it, methinks it would have made me another man!"

Possibly, in some sense, Clifford may have been
right. He needed a shock; or perhaps he required
to take a deep, deep plunge into the ocean of human
life, and to sink down and be covered by its profound-
ness, and then to emerge, sobered, invigorated,
restored to the world and to himself. Perhaps,
again, he required nothing less than the great final
remedy—death!

A similar yearning to renew the broken links of
brotherhood with his kind sometimes showed itself in
a milder form; and once it was made beautiful by
the religion that lay even deeper than itself. In the
incident now to be sketched, there was a touching
recognition on Clifford's part of God's care and love
towards him, towards this poor forsaken man, who,
if any mortal could, might have been pardoned for
regarding himself as thrown aside, forgotten, and
left to be the sport of some fiend, whose playfulness
was an ecstasy of mischief.

It was the Sabbath morning; one of those bright,

calm Sabbaths, with its own hallowed atmosphere, when Heaven seems to diffuse itself over the earth's face in a solemn smile, no less sweet than solemn. On such a Sabbath morn, were we pure enough to be its medium, we should be conscious of the earth's natural worship ascending through our frames, on whatever spot of ground we stood. The church-bells, with various tones, but all in harmony, were calling out, and responding to one another—"It is the Sabbath!—The Sabbath!—Yea; the Sabbath!" —and over the whole city the bells scattered the blessed sounds, now slowly, now with livelier joy, now one bell alone, now all the bells together, crying earnestly—"It is the Sabbath!" and flinging their accents afar off, to melt into the air, and pervade it with the holy word. The air, with God's sweetest and tenderest sunshine in it, was meet for mankind to breathe into their hearts, and send it forth again as the utterance of prayer.

Clifford sat at the window, with Hepzibah, watching the neighbours as they stepped into the street. All of them, however unspiritual on other days, were transfigured by the Sabbath influence; so that their very garments—whether it were an old man's decent coat, well brushed for the thousandth time, or a little boy's first sack and trousers, finished yesterday by his mother's needle—had somewhat of the quality of ascension-robes. Forth, likewise, from the portal of the old house, stepped Phœbe, putting up her small green sunshade, and throwing upward a glance and smile of parting kindness to the faces at the arched window. In her aspect there was a familiar gladness, and a holiness that you could play with, and yet reverence it as much as ever. She was like a prayer, offered up in the homeliest beauty of one's mother-tongue. Fresh was Phœbe, moreover, and airy and sweet in her apparel; as if nothing that she wore— neither her gown, nor her small straw bonnet, nor her little kerchief, any more than her snowy stockings—had ever been put on before; or, if worn, were all the fresher for it, and with a fragrance as if they had lain among the rose-buds.

The girl waved her hand to Hepzibah and Clifford, and went up the street; a religion in herself, warm, simple, true, with a substance that could walk on earth, and a spirit that was capable of heaven.

" Hepzibah," asked Clifford, after watching Phœbe to the corner, " do you never go to church?"

" No, Clifford !" she replied, " not these many, many years !"

" Were I to be there," he rejoined, " it seems to me that I could pray once more, when so many human souls were praying all around me !"

She looked into Clifford's face, and beheld there a soft, natural effusion; for his heart gushed out, as it were, and ran over at his eyes, in delightful reverence for God, and kindly affection for his human brethren. The emotion communicated itself to Hepzibah. She yearned to take him by the hand, and go and kneel down, they two together,—both so long separate from the world, and, as she now recognized, scarcely friends with Him above,—to kneel down among the people, and be reconciled to God and man at once.

" Dear brother," said she, earnestly, " let us go ! We belong nowhere. We have not a foot of space in any church to kneel upon; but let us go to some place of worship, even if we stand in the broad aisle. Poor and forsaken as we are, some pew-door will be opened to us !"

So Hepzibah and her brother made themselves ready,—as ready as they could, in the best of their old-fashioned garments, which had hung on pegs, or been laid away in trunks, so long that the dampness and mouldy smell of the past was on them,— made themselves ready in their faded bettermost, to go to church. They descended the staircase together,—gaunt, sallow Hepzibah, and pale, emaciated, age-stricken Clifford ! They pulled open the front door, and stepped across the threshold, and felt, both of them, as if they were standing in the presence of the whole world, and with mankind's great and terrible eye on them alone. The eye of their Father seemed to be withdrawn, and gave them no encouragement. The warm sunny air of the street made them shiver. Their hearts quaked within them, at the idea of taking one step further.

" It cannot be, Hepzibah !—it is too late," said Clifford, with deep sadness. " We are ghosts ! We have no right among human beings,—no right anywhere, but in this old house, which has a curse on it, and which therefore we are doomed to haunt ! And, besides," he continued, with a fastidious sensibility, inalienably characteristic of the man, " it would not be fit nor beautiful to go ! It is an ugly thought, that I should be frightful to my fellow-beings, and that children would cling to their mother's gowns, at sight of me !"

They shrank back into the dusky passage-way, and closed the door. But, going up the staircase again, they found the whole interior of the house tenfold more dismal, and the air closer and heavier, for the glimpse and breath of freedom which they had just snatched. They could not flee; their jailer had but left the door ajar in mockery, and stood behind it, to watch them stealing out. At the threshold, they felt his pitiless gripe upon them. For what other dungeon is so dark as one's own heart ! What jailer so inexorable as one's self !

But it would be no fair picture of Clifford's state of mind, were we to represent him as continually or prevailingly wretched. On the contrary, there was no other man in the city, we are bold to affirm, of so much as half his years, who enjoyed so many lightsome and griefless moments as himself. He had no burthen of care upon him; there were none of those questions and contingencies with the future to be settled which wear away all other lives, and render them not worth having, by the very process of providing for their support. In this respect he was a child —a child for the whole term of his existence, be it

long or short. Indeed, his life seemed to be standing still at a period little in advance of childhood, and
to cluster all his reminiscences about that epoch;
just as, after the torpor of a heavy blow, the sufferer's
reviving consciousness goes back to a moment considerably behind the accident that stupefied him. He
sometimes told Phœbe and Hepzibah his dreams, in
which he invariably played the part of a child or a
very young man. So vivid were they in his relation
of them, that he once held a dispute with his sister
as to the particular figure or print of a chintz morn-
ing-dress, which he had seen their mother wear, in
the dream of the preceding night. Hepzibah, piqu-
ing herself on a woman's accuracy in such matters,
held it to be slightly different from what Clifford
described; but, producing the very gown from an
old trunk, it proved to be identical with his remembrance of it. Had Clifford, every time that he
emerged out of dreams so life-like, undergone the torture of transformation from a boy into an old and
broken man, the daily recurrence of the shock would
have been too much to bear. It would have caused
an acute agony to thrill, from the morning twilight,
all the day through, until bedtime; and even then
would have mingled a dull, inscrutable pain, and
pallid hue of misfortune, with the visionary bloom
and adolescence of his slumber. But the nightly
moonshine interwove itself with the morning mist,
and enveloped him as in a robe, which he hugged
about his person, and seldom let realities pierce
through; he was not often quite awake, but slept
open-eyed, and perhaps fancied himself most dreaming then.

Thus, lingering always so near his childhood, he
had sympathies with children, and kept his heart the
fresher thereby, like a reservoir into which rivulets
were pouring, not far from the fountain-head.
Though prevented, by a subtle sense of propriety,
from desiring to associate with them, he loved few
things better than to look out of the arched window,

and see a little girl driving her hoop along the side-walk, or schoolboys at a game of ball. Their voices, also, were very pleasant to him, heard at a distance, all swarming and intermingling together, as flies do in a sunny room.

Clifford would, doubtless, have been glad to share their sports. One afternoon he was seized with an irresistible desire to blow soap-bubbles; an amuse-ment, as Hepzibah told Phœbe apart, that had been a favourite one with her brother when they were both children. Behold him, therefore, at the arched window, with an earthen pipe in his mouth! Behold him, with his gray hair, and a wan, unreal smile over his countenance, where still hovered a beautiful grace, which his worst enemy must have acknow-ledged to be spiritual and immortal since it had sur-vived so long! Behold him scattering airy spheres abroad, from the window into the street! Little impalpable worlds were those soap-bubbles, with the big world depicted, in hues bright as imagination, on the nothing of their surface. It was curious to see how the passers-by regarded these brilliant fantasies, as they came floating down, and made the dull atmos-phere imaginative about them. Some stopped to gaze, and, perhaps, carried a pleasant recollection of the bubbles onward as far as the street corner; some looked angrily upward, as if poor Clifford wronged them, by setting an image of beauty afloat so near their dusty pathway. A great many put out their fingers or their walking-sticks, to touch withal; and were perversely gratified, no doubt, when the bubble, with all its pictured earth and sky scene, vanished as if it had never been.

At length, just as an elderly gentleman of very dignified presence happened to be passing, a large bubble sailed majestically down, and burst right against his nose! He looked up,—at first with a stern, keen glance, which penetrated at once into the obscurity behind the arched window,—then with a smile, which might be conceived as diffusing a dog-

day sultriness for the space of several yards about
him.

" Aha, Cousin Clifford !" cried Judge Pyncheon.
" What ! still blowing soap-bubbles ?"

The tone seemed as if meant to be kind and sooth-
ing, but yet had a bitterness of sarcasm in it. As for
Clifford, an absolute palsy of fear came over him.
Apart from any definite cause of dread which his past
experience might have given him, he felt that native
and original horror of the excellent judge which is
proper to a weak, delicate, and apprehensive character, in the presence of massive strength. Strength
is incomprehensible by weakness, and therefore the
more terrible. There is no greater bugbear than a
strong-willed relative, in the circle of his own connections.

XII

THE DAGUERREOTYPIST

It must not be supposed that the life of a personage naturally so active as Phœbe could be wholly confined within the precincts of the old Pyncheon-house.
Clifford's demands upon her time were usually satisfied, in those long days, considerably earlier than
sunset. Quiet as his daily existence seemed, it nevertheless drained all the resources by which he lived.
It was not physical exercise that overwearied him ;
for—except that he sometimes wrought a little with a
hoe, or paced the garden walk, or, in rainy weather,
traversed a large unoccupied room—it was his tendency to remain only too quiescent, as regarded any
toil of the limbs and muscles. But, either there was
a smouldering fire within him that consumed his
vital energy, or the monotony that would have
dragged itself with benumbing effect over a mind

differently situated, was no monotony to Clifford. Possibly, he was in a state of second growth and recovery, and was constantly assimilating nutriment for his spirit and intellect from sights, sounds, and events, which passed as a perfect void to persons more practised with the world. As all is activity and vicissitude to the new mind of a child, so might it be, likewise, to a mind that had undergone a kind of new creation, after its long-suspended life.

Be the cause what it might, Clifford commonly retired to rest thoroughly exhausted, while the sunbeams were still melting through his window-curtains, or were thrown with late lustre on the chamber wall. And while he thus slept early, as other children do, and dreamed of childhood, Phœbe was free to follow her own tastes for the remainder of the day and evening.

This was a freedom essential to the health even of a character so little susceptible of morbid influences as that of Phœbe. The old house, as we have already said, had both the dry-rot and the damp-rot in its walls ; it was not good to breathe no other atmosphere than that. Hepzibah, though she had her valuable and redeeming traits, had grown to be a kind of lunatic, by imprisoning herself so long in one place, with no other company than a single series of ideas, and but one affection, and one bitter sense of wrong. Clifford, the reader may perhaps imagine, was too inert to operate morally on his fellow-creatures, however intimate and exclusive their relations with him. But the sympathy or magnetism among human beings is more subtle and universal than we think ; it exists, indeed, among different classes of organized life, and vibrates from one to another. A flower, for instance, as Phœbe herself observed, always began to droop sooner in Clifford's hand, or Hepzibah's, than in her own : and by the same law, converting her whole daily life into a flower-fragrance for these two sickly spirits, the blooming girl must inevitably droop and fade much sooner than if worn on a younger and happier breast. Unless she had now and then indulged her brisk impulses, and breathed rural air in a suburban walk, or ocean breezes along the shore—had occasionally obeyed the impulse of nature, in New England girls, by attending a metaphysical or philosophical lecture, or viewing a seven-mile panorama, or listening to a concert—had gone shopping about the city, ransacking entire depôts of splendid merchandise, and bringing home a ribbon—had employed, likewise, a little time to read the Bible in her chamber, and had stolen a little more to think of her mother and her native place—unless for such moral medicines as the above we should soon have beheld our poor Phœbe grow thin, and put on a bleached, unwholesome aspect, and assume strange, shy ways, prophetic of old maidenhood and a cheerless future.

Even as it was, a change grew visible; a change partly to be regretted, although whatever charm it infringed upon was repaired by another, perhaps more precious. She was not so constantly gay, but had her moods of thought, which Clifford, on the whole, liked better than her former phase of unmingled cheerfulness; because now she understood him better and more delicately, and sometimes even interpreted him to himself. Her eyes looked larger, and darker, and deeper; so deep, at some silent moments, that they seemed like Artesian wells, down, down, into the infinite. She was less girlish than when we first beheld her alighting from the omnibus; less girlish, but more a woman.

The only youthful mind with which Phœbe had an opportunity of frequent intercourse was that of the daguerreotypist. Inevitably by the pressure of the seclusion about them, they had been brought into habits of some familiarity. Had they met under different circumstances, neither of these young persons would have been likely to bestow much thought upon the other; unless, indeed, their extreme dissimilarity should have proved a principle of mutual attraction. Both, it is true, were characters proper to New

England life, and possessing a common ground, therefore, in their more external developments; but as unlike, in their respective interiors, as if their native climes had been at world-wide distance. During the early part of their acquaintance, Phœbe had held back rather more than was customary with her frank and simple manners from Holgrave's not very marked advances. Nor was she yet satisfied that she knew him well, although they almost daily met and talked together, in a kind, friendly, and what seemed to be a familiar way.

The artist, in a desultory manner, had imparted to Phœbe something of his history. Young as he was, and had his career terminated at the point already attained, there had been enough of incident to fill, very creditably, an autobiographic volume. A romance on the plan of Gil Blas, adapted to American society and manners, would cease to be a romance. The experience of many individuals among us, who think it hardly worth the telling, would equal the vicissitudes of the Spaniard's earlier life; while their ultimate success, or the point whither they tend, may be incomparably higher than any that a novelist would imagine for his hero. Holgrave, as he told Phœbe, somewhat proudly, could not boast of his origin, unless as being exceedingly humble, nor of his education, except that it had been the scantiest possible, and obtained by a few winter-months' attendance at a district school. Left early to his own guidance, he had begun to be self-dependent while yet a boy; and it was a condition aptly suited to his natural force of will. Though now but twenty-two years old (lacking some months, which are years in such a life), he had already been, first, a country schoolmaster; next, a salesman in a country store; and, either at the same time or afterwards, the political editor of a country newspaper. He had subsequently travelled New England and the Middle States, as a pedler, in the employment of a Connecticut manufactory of cologne-water and other essences. In an

episodical way, he had studied and practised den-
tistry, and with very flattering success, especially in
many of the factory-towns along our inland streams.
As a supernumerary official, of some kind or other,
aboard a packet-ship, he had visited Europe, and
found means, before his return, to see Italy, and
part of France and Germany. At a later period he
had spent some months in a community of Fourier-
ists. Still more recently, he had been a public
lecturer on Mesmerism, for which science (as he
assured Phœbe, and, indeed, satisfactorily proved,
by putting Chanticleer, who happened to be scratch-
ing near by, to sleep) he had very remarkable endowments.

His present phase, as a daguerreotypist, was of no
more importance in his own view, nor likely to be
more permanent, than any of the preceding ones.
It had been taken up with the careless alacrity of an
adventurer, who had his bread to earn. It would be
thrown aside as carelessly, whenever he should
choose to earn his bread by some other equally digres-
sive means. But what was most remarkable, and
perhaps, showed a more than common poise in the
young man, was the fact, that, amid all these personal
vicissitudes, he had never lost his identity. Homeless as he had been—continually changing his where-
about, and, therefore, responsible neither to public
opinion nor to individuals—putting off one exterior,
and snatching up another, to be soon shifted for a
third—he had never violated the innermost man, but
had carried his conscience along with him. It was
impossible to know Holgrave, without recognizing
this to be the fact. Hepzibah had seen it. Phœbe
soon saw it, likewise, and gave him the sort of confidence which such a certainty inspires. She was
startled, however, and sometimes repelled--not by
any doubt of his integrity to whatever law he acknowledged—but by a sense that his law differed from
her own. He made her uneasy, and seemed to un-
settle everything around her, by his lack of reverence

for what was fixed, unless, at a moment's warning, it could establish its right to hold its ground.

Then, moreover, she scarcely thought him affectionate in his nature. He was too calm and cool an observer. Phœbe felt his eye, often; his heart, seldom, or never. He took a certain kind of interest in Hepzibah and her brother, and Phœbe herself. He studied them attentively, and allowed no slightest circumstance of their individualities to escape him. He was ready to do them whatever good he might; but, after all, he never exactly made common cause with them, nor gave any reliable evidence that he loved them better, in proportion as he knew them more. In his relations with them, he seemed to be in quest of mental food, not heart-sustenance. Phœbe could not conceive what interested him so much in her friends and herself, intellectually, since he cared nothing for them, or, comparatively, so little, as objects of human affection.

Always, in his interviews with Phœbe, the artist made especial inquiry as to the welfare of Clifford, whom, except at the Sunday festival, he seldom saw.

" Does he still seem happy?" he asked one day.

" As happy as a child," answered Phœbe; " but —like a child, too—very easily disturbed."

" How disturbed?" inquired Holgrave. " By things without, or by thoughts within?"

" I cannot see his thoughts! How should I?" replied Phœbe with simple piquancy. " Very often, his humour changes without any reason that can be guessed at, just as a cloud comes over the sun. Latterly, since I have begun to know him better, I feel it to be not quite right to look closely into his moods. He has had such a great sorrow, that his heart is made all solemn and sacred by it. When he is cheerful—when the sun shines into his mind—then I venture to peep in, just as far as the light reaches, but no further. It is holy ground where the shadow falls!"

"How prettily you express this sentiment!" said the artist. "I can understand the feeling, without possessing it. Had I your opportunities, no scruples would prevent me from fathoming Clifford to the full depth of my plummet-line."

"How strange that you should wish it!" remarked Phœbe, involuntarily. "What is Cousin Clifford to you?"

"O, nothing—of course, nothing!" answered Holgrave, with a smile. "Only this is such an odd and incomprehensible world! The more I look at it, the more it puzzles me; and I begin to suspect that a man's bewilderment is the measure of his wisdom. Men, and women, and children, too, are such strange creatures, that one never can be certain that he really knows them; nor ever guess what they have been, from what he sees them to be now. Judge Pyncheon! Clifford! What a complex riddle—a complexity of complexities—do they present! It requires intuitive sympathy, like a young girl's, to solve it. A mere observer, like myself (who never have any intuitions, and am, at best, only subtle and acute), is pretty certain to go astray."

The artist now turned the conversation to themes less dark than that which they had touched upon. Phœbe and he were young together; nor had Holgrave, in his premature experience of life, wasted entirely that beautiful spirit of youth, which, gushing forth from one small heart and fancy, may diffuse itself over the universe, making it all as bright as on the first day of creation. Man's own youth is the world's youth; at least, he feels as if it were, and imagines that the earth's granite substance is something not yet hardened, and which he can mould into whatever shape he likes. So it was with Holgrave. He could talk sagely about the world's old age, but never actually believed what he said; he was a young man still, and therefore looked upon the world —that gray-bearded and wrinkled profligate, decrepit, without being venerable—as a tender stripling, cap-

able of being improved into all that it ought to be,
but scarcely yet had shown the remotest promise of
becoming. He had that sense, or inward prophecy
—which a young man had better never have been
born than not to have, and a mature man had better
die at once than utterly to relinquish—that we are not
doomed to creep on for ever in the old, bad way, but
that, this very now, there are the harbingers abroad
of a golden era, to be accomplished in his own lifetime. It seemed to Holgrave—as doubtless it has
seemed to the hopeful of every century, since the
epoch of Adam's grandchildren—that in this age,
more than ever before, the moss-grown and rotten
Past is to be torn down, and lifeless institutions to
be thrust out of the way, and their dead corpses
buried, and everything to begin anew.

As to the main point—may we never live to doubt
it !—as to the better centuries that are coming, the
artist was surely right. His error lay in supposing
that this age, more than any past or future one, is
destined to see the tattered garments of Antiquity
exchanged for a new suit, instead of gradually renew-
ing themselves by patchwork; in applying his own
little life-span as the measure of an interminable
achievement; and, more than all, in fancying that
it mattered anything to the great end in view, whether
he himself should contend for it or against it. Yet
it was well for him to think so. This enthusiasm,
infusing itself through the calmness of his character,
and thus taking an aspect of settled thought and
wisdom, would serve to keep his youth pure, and
make his aspirations high. And when, with the
years settling down more weightily upon him, his
early faith should be modified by inevitable experience, it would be with no harsh and sudden revolution of his sentiments. He would still have faith in
man's brightening destiny, and perhaps love him all
the better, as he should recognize his helplessness
in his own behalf; and the haughty faith, with which
he began life, would be well bartered for a far

humbler one, at its close, in discerning that man's best-directed effort accomplishes a kind of dream, while God is the sole worker of realities.

Holgrave had read very little, and that little in passing through the thoroughfare of life, where the mystic language of his books was necessarily mixed up with the babble of the multitude, so that both one and the other were apt to lose any sense that might have been properly their own. He considered himself a thinker, and was certainly of a thoughtful turn, but, with his own path to discover, had perhaps hardly yet reached the point where an educated man begins to think. The true value of his character lay in that deep consciousness of inward strength, which made all his past vicissitudes seem merely like a change of garments; in that enthusiasm, so quiet that he scarcely knew of its existence, but which gave a warmth to everything that he laid his hand on; in that personal ambition, hidden from his own as well as other eyes—among his more generous impulses, but in which lurked a certain efficacy, that might solidify him from a theorist into the champion of some practicable cause. Altogether, in his culture and want of culture,—in his crude, wild, and misty philosophy, and the practical experience that counteracted some of its tendencies; in his magnanimous zeal for man's welfare, and his recklessness of whatever the ages had established in man's behalf; in his faith, and in his infidelity; in what he had, and in what he lacked,—the artist might fitly enough stand forth as the representative of many compeers in his native land.

His career it would be difficult to prefigure. There appeared to be qualities in Holgrave, such as, in a country where everything is free to the hand that can grasp it, could hardly fail to put some of the world's prizes within his reach. But these matters are delightfully uncertain. At almost every step in life, we meet with young men of just about Holgrave's age, for whom we anticipate wonderful things, but of whom, even after much and careful inquiry, we never happen to hear another word. The effervescence of youth and passion, and the fresh gloss of the intellect and imagination, endow them with a false brilliancy, which makes fools of themselves and other people. Like certain chintzes, calicoes, and ginghams, they show finely in their first newness, but cannot stand the sun and rain, and assume a very sober aspect after washing-day.

But our business is with Holgrave as we find him on this particular afternoon, and in the arbour of the Pyncheon-garden. In that point of view, it was a pleasant sight to behold this young man, with so much faith in himself, and so fair an appearance of admirable powers—so little harmed, too, by the many tests that had tried his metal—it was pleasant to see him in his kindly intercourse with Phœbe. Her thought had scarcely done him justice, when it pronounced him cold; or, if so, he had grown warmer now. Without such purpose on her part, and unconsciously on his, she made the House of the Seven Gables like a home to him, and the garden a familiar precinct. With the insight on which he prided himself, he fancied that he could look through Phœbe, and all around her, and could read her off like a page of a child's story-book. But these transparent natures are often deceptive in their depth; these pebbles at the bottom of the fountain are further from us than we think. Thus the artist, whatever he might judge of Phœbe's capacity, was beguiled, by some silent charm of hers, to talk freely of what he dreamed of doing in the world. He poured himself out as to another self. Very possibly, he forgot Phœbe while he talked to her, and was moved only by the inevitable tendency of thought, when rendered sympathetic by enthusiasm and emotion, to flow into the first safe reservoir which it finds. But, had you peeped at them through the chinks of the garden-fence, the young man's earnestness and heightened colour might have led you to suppose that he was making love to the young girl!

At length, something was said by Holgrave that made it apposite for Phœbe to inquire what had first brought him acquainted with her cousin Hepzibah, and why he now chose to lodge in the desolate old Pyncheon-house. Without directly answering her, he turned from the Future, which had heretofore been the theme of his discourse, and began to speak of the influences of the Past. One subject, indeed, is but the reverberation of the other.

" Shall we never, never get rid of this Past?" cried he, keeping up the earnest tone of his preceding conversation.—" It lies upon the Present like a giant's dead body! In fact, the case is just as if a young giant were compelled to waste all his strength in carrying about the corpse of the old giant, his grandfather, who died a long while ago, and only needs to be decently buried. Just think a moment, and it will startle you to see what slaves we are to bygone times, —to Death, if we give the matter the right word!"

" But I do not see it," observed Phœbe.

" For example, then," continued Holgrave; " a dead man, if he happen to have made a will, disposes of wealth no longer his own; or, if he die intestate, it is distributed in accordance with the notions of men much longer dead than he. A dead man sits on all our judgment-seats; and living judges do but search out and repeat his decisions. We read in dead men's books! We laugh at dead men's jokes, and cry at dead men's pathos! We are sick of dead men's diseases, physical and moral, and die of the same remedies with which dead doctors killed their patients! We worship the living Deity according to dead men's forms and creeds! Whatever we seek to do, of our own free motion, a dead man's icy hand obstructs us! Turn our eyes to what point we may, a dead man's white, immitigable face encounters them, and freezes our very heart! And we must be dead ourselves, before we can begin to have our

proper influence on our own world, which will then
be no longer our world, but the world of another
generation, with which we shall have no shadow of
a right to interfere. I ought to have said, too, that
we live in dead men's houses; as, for instance, in this
of the seven gables!"

" And why not," said Phœbe, " so long as we can
be comfortable in them?"

" But we shall live to see the day, I trust," went
on the artist, " when no man shall build his house for
posterity. Why should he? He might just as
reasonably order a durable suit of clothes—leather, or
gutta percha, or whatever else lasts longest—so that
his great-grandchildren should have the benefit of
them, and cut precisely the same figure in the world
that he himself does. If each generation were
allowed and expected to build its own houses, that
single change, comparatively unimportant in itself,
would imply almost every reform which society is
now suffering for. I doubt whether even our public
edifices—our capitols, state-houses, court-houses,
city-halls, and churches—ought to be built of such
permanent materials as stone or brick. It were better
that they should crumble to ruin, once in twenty
years, or thereabouts, as a hint to the people to
examine into and reform the institutions which they
symbolize."

" How you hate everything old!" said Phœbe, in
dismay. " It makes me dizzy to think of such a
shifting world!"

" I certainly love nothing mouldy," answered Holgrave. " Now, this old Pyncheon-house! Is it a
wholesome place to live in, with its black shingles,
and the green moss that shows how damp they are?
—its dark, low-studded rooms?—its grime and
sordidness, which are the crystallization on its walls
of the human breath, that has been drawn and
exhaled here, in discontent and anguish? The house
ought to be purified with fire,—purified till only its
ashes remain!"

" Then why do you live in it?" asked Phœbe, a little piqued.

" Oh, I am pursuing my studies here ; not in books, however," replied Holgrave. " The house, in my view, is expressive of that odious and abominable Past, with all its bad influences, against which I have just been declaiming. I dwell in it for a while, that I may know the better how to hate it. By-the-by, did you ever hear the story of Maule, the wizard, and what happened between him and your immeasurably great-grandfather?"

" Yes, indeed !" said Phœbe; " I heard it long ago, from my father, and two or three times from my cousin Hepzibah, in the month that I have been here. She seems to think that all the calamities of the Pyncheons began from that quarrel with the wizard, as you call him. And you, Mr. Holgrave, look as if you thought so too ! How singular, that you should believe what is so very absurd, when you reject many things that are a great deal worthier of credit !"

" I do believe it," said the artist, seriously; " not as a superstition, however, but as proved by unquestionable facts, and as exemplifying a theory. Now see ;—under those seven gables, at which we now look up—and which old Colonel Pyncheon meant to be the house of his descendants, in prosperity and happiness, down to an epoch far beyond the present— under that roof, through a portion of three centuries, there has been perpetual remorse of conscience, a constantly defeated hope, strife amongst kindred, various misery, a strange form of death, dark suspicion, unspeakable disgrace; all, or most of which calamity, I have the means of tracing to the old Puritan's inordinate desire to plant and endow a family. To plant a family ! This idea is at the bottom of most of the wrong and mischief which men do. The truth is, that, once in every half century, at longest, a family should be merged into the great, obscure mass of humanity, and forget all about its ancestors. Human blood, in order to keep its freshness, should run in hidden streams, as the water of an aqueduct is conveyed in subterranean pipes. In the family existence of these Pyncheons, for instance—forgive me, Phœbe; but I cannot think of you as one of them—in their brief New England pedigree, there has been time enough to infect them all with one kind of lunacy or another!"

"You speak very unceremoniously of my kindred," said Phœbe, debating with herself whether she ought to take offence.

"I speak true thoughts to a true mind!" answered Holgrave, with a vehemence which Phœbe had not before witnessed in him. "The truth is as I say! Furthermore, the original perpetrator and father of this mischief appears to have perpetuated himself, and still walks the streets—at least, his very image, in mind and body—with the fairest prospect of transmitting to posterity as rich and as wretched an inheritance as he has received! Do you remember the daguerreotype, and its resemblance to the old portrait?"

"How strangely in earnest you are!" exclaimed Phœbe, looking at him with surprise and perplexity: half alarmed, and partly inclined to laugh. "You talk of the lunacy of the Pyncheons—is it contagious?"

"I understand you!" said the artist, colouring and laughing. "I believe I am a little mad. This subject has taken hold of my mind with the strangest tenacity of clutch, since I have lodged in yonder old gable. As one method of throwing it off, I have put an incident of the Pyncheon family history, with which I happen to be acquainted, into the form of a legend, and mean to publish it in a magazine."

"Do you write for the magazines?" inquired Phœbe.

"Is it possible you did not know it?" cried Holgrave.—"Well, such is literary fame! Yes, Miss Phœbe Pyncheon, among the multitude of my mar-

vellous gifts, I have that of writing stories; and my
name has figured, I can assure you, on the covers of
Graham and Godey, making as respectable an appearance, for aught I could see, as any of the canonized
bead-roll with which it was associated. In the
humorous line, I am thought to have a very pretty
way with me; and as for pathos, I am as provocative
of tears as an onion. But shall I read you my
story?"

"Yes, if it is not very long," said Phœbe,—and
added, laughingly,—"nor very dull."

As this latter point was one which the daguerreotypist could not decide for himself, he forthwith produced his roll of manuscript, and, while the late
sunbeams gilded the seven gables, began to read.

XIII

ALICE PYNCHEON

THERE was a message brought one day, from the
worshipful Gervayse Pyncheon to young Matthew
Maule, the carpenter, desiring his immediate presence at the House of the Seven Gables.

"And what does your master want with me?" said
the carpenter to Mr. Pyncheon's black servant.
"Does the house need any repair? Well it may, by
this time; and no blame to my father who built it,
neither! I was reading the old Colonel's tombstone
no longer ago than last Sabbath; and reckoning from
that date, the house has stood seven-and-thirty years.
No wonder if there should be a job to do on the
roof."

"Don't know what massa wants," answered
Scipio. "The house is a berry good house, and old
Colonel Pyncheon think so too, I reckon;—else why

the old man haunt it so, and frighten a poor niggar as he does?"

"Well, well, friend Scipio; let your master know that I'm coming," said the carpenter with a laugh. "For a fair, workmanlike job, he'll find me his man. And so the house is haunted, is it? It will take a tighter workman than I am to keep the spirits out of the seven gables. Even if the Colonel would be quit," he added, muttering to himself, "my old grandfather, the wizard, will be pretty sure to stick to the Pyncheons, as long as their walls hold together."

"What's that you mutter to yourself, Matthew Maule?" asked Scipio. "And what for do you look so black at me?"

"No matter, darkey!" said the carpenter. "Do you think nobody is to look black but yourself? Go, tell your master I'm coming; and if you happen to see Mistress Alice, his daughter, give Matthew Maule's humble respects to her. She has brought a fair face from Italy,—fair, and gentle, and proud,—has that same Alice Pyncheon!"

"He talk of Mistress Alice!" cried Scipio, as he returned from his errand. "The low carpenter-man! He no business so much as to look at her a great way off!"

This young Matthew Maule, the carpenter, it must be observed, was a person little understood, and not very generally liked, in the town where he resided; not that anything could be alleged against his integrity, or his skill and diligence in the handicraft which he exercised. The aversion (as it might justly be called) with which many persons regarded him, was partly the result of his own character and deportment, and partly an inheritance.

He was the grandson of a former Matthew Maule, one of the early settlers of the town, and who had been a famous and terrible wizard in his day. This old reprobate was one of the sufferers when Cotton Mather, and his brother ministers, and the learned judges, and other wise men, and Sir William Phipps, the sagacious governor, made such laudable efforts to weaken the great enemy of souls, by sending a multitude of his adherents up the rocky pathway of Gallows Hill. Since those days, no doubt, it had grown to be suspected, that, in consequence of an unfortunate overdoing of a work praiseworthy in itself, the proceedings against the witches had proved far less acceptable to the Beneficent Father than to that very Arch Enemy whom they were intended to distress and utterly overwhelm. It is not the less certain, however, that awe and terror brooded over the memories of those who died for this horrible crime of witchcraft. Their graves, in the crevices of the rocks, were supposed to be incapable of retaining the occupants who had been so hastily thrust into them. Old Matthew Maule, especially, was known to have as little hesitation or difficulty in rising out of his grave as an ordinary man in getting out of bed, and was as often seen at midnight as living people at noonday. This pestilent wizard (in whom his just punishment seemed to have wrought no manner of amends) had an inveterate habit of haunting a certain mansion, styled the House of the Seven Gables, against the owner of which he pretended to hold an unsettled claim for ground-rent. The ghost, it appears—with the pertinacity which was one of his distinguishing characteristics while alive—insisted that he was the rightful proprietor of the site upon which the house stood. His terms were, that either the aforesaid ground-rent, from the day when the cellar began to be dug, should be paid down, or the mansion itself given up; else he, the ghostly creditor, would have his finger in all the affairs of the Pyncheons, and make everything go wrong with them, though it should be a thousand years after his death. It was a wild story, perhaps, but seemed not altogether so incredible, to those who could remember what an inflexibly obstinate old fellow this wizard Maule had been.

Now, the wizard's grandson, the young Matthew Maule of our story, was popularly supposed to have inherited some of his ancestor's questionable traits. It is wonderful how many absurdities were promulgated in reference to the young man. He was fabled, for example, to have a strange power of getting into people's dreams, and regulating matters there according to his own fancy, pretty much like the stage-manager of a theatre. There was a great deal of talk among the neighbours, particularly the petticoated ones, about what they called the witchcraft of Maule's eye. Some said that he could look into people's minds; others, that by the marvellous power of this eye, he could draw people into his own mind, or send them, if he pleased, to do errands to his grandfather, in the spiritual world; others, again, that it was what is termed an Evil Eye, and possessed the valuable faculty of blighting corn, and drying children into mummies with the heart-burn. But, after all, what worked most to the young carpenter's disadvantage was, first, the reserve and sternness of his natural disposition, and next, the fact of his not being a church-communicant, and the suspicion of his holding heretical tenets in matters of religion and polity.

After receiving Mr. Pyncheon's message, the carpenter merely tarried to finish a small job, which he happened to have in hand, and then took his way towards the House of the Seven Gables. This noted edifice, though its style might be getting a little out of fashion, was still as respectable a family residence as that of any gentleman in town. The present owner, Gervayse Pyncheon, was said to have contracted a dislike to the house, in consequence of a shock to his sensibility, in early childhood, from the sudden death of his grandfather. In the very act of running to climb Colonel Pyncheon's knee, the boy had discovered the old Puritan to be a corpse! On arriving at manhood, Mr. Pyncheon had visited England, where he married a lady of fortune, and had subsequently spent many years, partly in the mother country, and partly in various cities on the continent of Europe. During this period, the family mansion had been consigned to the charge of a kinsman, who was allowed to make it his home, for the time being, in consideration of keeping the premises in thorough repair. So faithfully had this contract been fulfilled, that now, as the carpenter approached the house, his practised eye could detect nothing to criticize in its condition. The peaks of the seven gables rose up sharply; the shingled roof looked thoroughly water-tight; and the glittering plaster-work entirely covered the exterior walls, and sparkled in the October sun, as if it had been new only a week ago.

The house had that pleasant aspect of life which is like the cheery expression of comfortable activity in the human countenance. You could see, at once, that there was the stir of a large family within it. A huge load of oak-wood was passing through the gate-way, towards the out-buildings in the rear; the fat cook—or probably it might be the housekeeper—stood at the side-door, bargaining for some turkeys and poultry, which a countryman had brought for sale. Now and then, a maid-servant, neatly dressed, and now the shining sable face of a slave, might be seen bustling across the windows, in the lower part of the house. At an open window of a room in the second storey, hanging over some pots of beautiful and delicate flowers—exotics, but which had never known a more genial sunshine than that of the New England autumn—was the figure of a young lady, an exotic, like the flowers, and beautiful and delicate as they. Her presence imparted an indescribable grace and faint witchery to the whole edifice. In other respects, it was a substantial, jolly-looking mansion, and seemed fit to be the residence of a patri-arch, who might establish his own head-quarters in the front gable, and assign one of the remainder to each of his six children; while the great chimney in the centre should symbolize the old fellow's hospitable heart, which kept them all warm, and made a great whole of the seven smaller ones.

There was a vertical sun-dial on the front gable; and as the carpenter passed beneath it, he looked up and noted the hour.

"Three o'clock!" said he to himself. "My father told me that dial was put up only an hour before the old Colonel's death. How truly it has kept time these seven-and-thirty years past! The shadow creeps and creeps, and is always looking over the shoulder of the sunshine!"

It might have befitted a craftsman, like Matthew Maule, on being sent for to a gentleman's house, to go to the back-door, where servants and work-people were usually admitted; or at least to the side-entrance, where the better class of tradesmen made application. But the carpenter had a great deal of pride and stiffness in his nature; and, at this moment, moreover, his heart was bitter with the sense of hereditary wrong, because he considered the great Pyncheon-house to be standing on soil which should have been his own. On this very site, beside a spring of delicious water, his grandfather had felled the pine-trees and built a cottage, in which children had been born to him; and it was only from a dead man's stiffened fingers that Colonel Pyncheon had wrested away the title-deeds. So young Maule went straight to the principal entrance, beneath a portal of carved oak, and gave such a peal of the iron knocker that you would have imagined the stern old wizard himself to be standing on the threshold.

Black Scipio answered the summons, in a pro-digious hurry; but showed the whites of his eyes, in amazement, on beholding only the carpenter.

"Lord-a-mercy! what a great man he be, this carpenter fellow!" mumbled Scipio, down in his throat. "Anybody think he beat on the door with his biggest hammer!"

"Here I am!" said Maule, sternly. "Show me the way to your master's parlour!"

As he stepped into the house, a note of sweet and melancholy music thrilled and vibrated along the passage way, proceeding from one of the rooms above stairs. It was the harpsichord which Alice Pyncheon had brought with her from beyond the sea. The fair Alice bestowed most of her maiden leisure between flowers and music, although the former were apt to droop, and the melodies were often sad. She was of foreign education, and could not take kindly to the New England modes of life, in which nothing beautiful had ever been developed.

As Mr. Pyncheon had been impatiently awaiting Maule's arrival, black Scipio, of course, lost no time in ushering the carpenter into his master's presence. The room in which this gentleman sat was a parlour of moderate size, looking out upon the garden of the house, and having its windows partly shadowed by the foliage of fruit-trees. It was Mr. Pyncheon's peculiar apartment, and was provided with furniture in an elegant and costly style, principally from Paris; the floor (which was unusual, at that day) being covered with a carpet, so skilfully and richly wrought, that it seemed to glow as with living flowers. In one corner stood a marble woman, to whom her own beauty was the sole and sufficient garment. Some pictures—that looked old, and had a mellow tinge diffused through all their artful splendour—hung on the walls. Near the fireplace was a large and very beautiful cabinet of ebony, inlaid with ivory; a piece of antique furniture which Mr. Pyncheon had bought in Venice, and which he used as the treasure-place for medals, ancient coins, and whatever small and valuable curiosities he had picked up on his travels. Through all this variety of decoration, however, the room showed its original characteristics; its low stud, its cross-beam, its chimney-piece, with the old-fashioned Dutch tiles; so that it was the emblem of a mind industriously stored with foreign ideas, and elaborated into artificial refinement, but neither larger, nor, in its proper self, more elegant, than before.

There were two objects that appeared rather out of place in this very handsomely furnished room. One was a large map, or surveyor's plan, of a tract of land, which looked as if it had been drawn a good many years ago, and was now dingy with smoke, and soiled here and there with the touch of fingers. The other was a portrait of a stern old man, in a Puritan garb, painted roughly, but with a bold effect, and a remarkably strong expression of character.

At a small table, before a fire of English sea-coal, sat Mr. Pyncheon, sipping coffee, which had grown to be a very favourite beverage with him in France. He was a middle-aged and really handsome man, with a wig flowing down upon his shoulders; his coat was of blue velvet, with lace on the borders and at the button-holes; and the fire-light glistened on the spacious breadth of his waistcoat, which was flowered all over with gold. On the entrance of Scipio, ushering in the carpenter, Mr. Pyncheon turned partly round, but resumed his former position, and proceeded deliberately to finish his cup of coffee, without immediate notice of the guest whom he had summoned to his presence. It was not that he intended any rudeness, or improper neglect—which, indeed, he would have blushed to be guilty of—but it never occurred to him that a person in Maule's station had a claim on his courtesy, or would trouble himself about it, one way or the other.

The carpenter, however, stepped at once to the hearth, and turned himself about, so as to look Mr. Pyncheon in the face.

"You sent for me," said he. "Be pleased to explain your business, that I may go back to my own affairs."

"Ah! excuse me," said Mr. Pyncheon, quietly. "I did not mean to tax your time without a recompense. Your name, I think, is Maule—Thomas or Matthew Maule—a son or grandson of the builder of this house?"

" Matthew Maule," replied the carpenter, " son of him who built the house,—grandson of the rightful proprietor of the soil."

"I know the dispute to which you allude," observed Mr. Pyncheon, with undisturbed equanimity. " I am well aware that my grandfather was compelled to resort to a suit at law, in order to establish his claim to the foundation-site of this edifice. We will not, if you please, renew the discussion. The matter was settled at the time, and by the competent authorities,—equitably, it is to be presumed,—and, at all events, irrevocably. Yet, singularly enough, there is an incidental reference to this very subject in what I am now about to say to you. And this same inveterate grudge—excuse me, I mean no offence—this irritability, which you have just shown, is not entirely aside from the matter."

" If you can find anything for your purpose, Mr. Pyncheon," said the carpenter, " in a man's natural resentment for the wrongs done to his blood, you are welcome to it!"

" I take you at your word, Goodman Maule," said the owner of the seven gables, with a smile, " and will proceed to suggest a mode in which your hereditary resentments—justifiable, or otherwise—may have had a bearing on my affairs. You have heard, I suppose, that the Pyncheon family, ever since my grandfather's days, have been prosecuting a still unsettled claim to a very large extent of territory at the eastward?"

" Often," replied Maule—and it is said that a smile came over his face—" very often, from my father!"

" This claim," continued Mr. Pyncheon, after pausing a moment, as if to consider what the carpenter's smile might mean, " appeared to be on the very verge of a settlement and full allowance, at the period of my grandfather's decease. It was well

known, to those in his confidence, that he anticipated
neither difficulty nor delay. Now, Colonel Pyncheon,
I need hardly say, was a practical man, well acquainted
with public and private business, and not at all the
person to cherish ill-founded hopes, or to attempt the
following out of an impracticable scheme. It is
obvious to conclude, therefore, that he had grounds,
not apparent to his heirs, for his confident anticipation of success in the matter of this eastern claim.
In a word I believe—and my legal advisers coincide
in the belief, which, moreover, is authorized, to a
certain extent, by the family traditions—that my
grandfather was in possession of some deed, or other
document, essential to this claim, but which has since
disappeared."

"Very likely," said Matthew Maule—and again,
it is said, there was a dark smile on his face—"but
what can a poor carpenter have to do with the grand
affairs of the Pyncheon family?"

"Perhaps nothing," returned Mr. Pyncheon:
"possibly much!"

Here ensued a great many words between Matthew
Maule and the proprietor of the seven gables, on the
subject which the latter had thus broached. It seems
(although Mr. Pyncheon had some hesitation in
referring to stories so exceedingly absurd in their
aspect) that the popular belief pointed to some
mysterious connection and dependence, existing between the family of the Maules and these vast, unreal-
ized possessions of the Pyncheons. It was an ordinary saying, that the old wizard, hanged though he
was, had obtained the best end of the bargain, in his
contest with Colonel Pyncheon; inasmuch as he had
got possession of the great eastern claim, in exchange for an acre or two of garden-ground. A very
aged woman, recently dead, had often used the meta-
phorical expression, in her fire-side talk, that miles
and miles of the Pyncheon lands had been shovelled
into Maule's grave; which, by-the-by, was but a
very shallow nook, between two rocks, near the sum-

mit of Gallows Hill. Again, when the lawyers were making inquiry for the missing document, it was a by-word, that it would never be found, unless in the wizard's skeleton hand. So much weight had the shrewd lawyers assigned to these fables, that—(but Mr. Pyncheon did not see fit to inform the carpenter of the fact)—they had secretly caused the wizard's grave to be searched. Nothing was discovered, however, except that, unaccountably, the right hand of the skeleton was gone.

Now, what was unquestionably important, a portion of these popular rumours could be traced, though rather doubtfully and indistinctly, to chance words and obscure hints of the executed wizard's son, and the father of this present Matthew Maule. And here Mr. Pyncheon could bring an item of his own personal evidence into play. Though but a child at the time, he either remembered or fancied that Matthew's father had had some job to perform, on the day before, or possibly the very morning of the Colonel's decease, in the private room where he and the carpenter were at this moment talking. Certain papers belonging to Colonel Pyncheon, as his grandson distinctly recollected, had been spread out on the table.

Matthew Maule understood the insinuated suspicion.

" My father," he said, but still there was that dark smile, making a riddle of his countenance, " my father was an honester man than the bloody old Colonel ! Not to get his rights back again would he have carried off one of those papers !"

" I shall not bandy words with you," observed the foreign-bred Mr. Pyncheon, with haughty composure. " Nor will it become me to resent any rudeness towards either my grandfather or myself. A gentleman, before seeking intercourse with a person of your station and habits, will first consider whether the urgency of the end may compensate for the disagreeableness of the means. It does so, in the present instance.''

He then renewed the conversation, and made great pecuniary offers to the carpenter, in case the latter should give information leading to the discovery of the lost document, and the consequent success of the eastern claim. For a long time Matthew Maule is said to have turned a cold ear to these propositions. At last, however, with a strange kind of laugh, he inquired whether Mr. Pyncheon would make over to him the old wizard's homestead-ground, together with the House of the Seven Gables, now standing on it, in requital of the documentary evidence so urgently required.

The wild chimney-corner legend (which, without copying all its extravagances, my narrative essentially follows) here gives an account of some very strange behaviour on the part of Colonel Pyncheon's portrait. This picture, it must be understood, was supposed to be so intimately connected with the fate of the house, and so magically built into its walls, that, if once it should be removed, that very instant the whole edifice would come thundering down in a heap of dusty ruin. All through the foregoing conversation between Mr. Pyncheon and the carpenter, the portrait had been frowning, clenching its fist, and giving many such proofs of excessive discomposure, but without attracting the notice of either of the two colloquists. And, finally, at Matthew Maule's audacious suggestion of a transfer of the seven-gabled structure, the ghostly portrait is averred to have lost all patience, and to have shown itself on the point of descending bodily from its frame. But such incredible incidents are merely to be mentioned aside.

'' Give up this house !'' exclaimed Mr. Pyncheon, in amazement at the proposal. '' Were I to do so, my grandfather would not rest quiet in his grave !''

'' He never has, if all stories are true,'' remarked

the carpenter, composedly. "But that matter concerns his grandson more than it does Matthew
Maule. I have no other terms to propose."

Impossible as he at first thought it to comply with
Maule's conditions, still, on a second glance, Mr.
Pyncheon was of opinion that they might at least be
made matter of discussion. He himself had no personal attachment for the house, nor any pleasant
associations connected with his childish residence in
it. On the contrary, after seven-and-thirty years,
the presence of his dead grandfather seemed still to
pervade it, as on that morning when the affrighted
boy had beheld him, with so ghastly an aspect,
stiffening in his chair. His long abode in foreign
parts, moreover, and familiarity with many of the
castles and ancestral halls of England, and the
marble palaces of Italy, had caused him to look con-
temptuously at the House of the Seven Gables,
whether in point of splendour or convenience. It
was a mansion exceedingly inadequate to the style
of living which it would be incumbent on Mr.
Pyncheon to support, after realizing his territorial
rights. His steward might deign to occupy it, but
never, certainly, the great landed proprietor himself. In the event of success, indeed, it was his purpose to return to England; nor, to say the truth,
would he recently have quitted that more congenial
home, had not his own fortune, as well as his
deceased wife's, begun to give symptoms of exhaus-
tion. The eastern claim once fairly settled, and put
upon the firm basis of actual possession, Mr. Pyncheon's property—to be measured by miles, not acres
—would be worth an earldom, and would reasonably
entitle him to solicit, or enable him to purchase, that
elevated dignity from the British monarch. Lord
Pyncheon!—or the Earl of Waldo!—how could such
a magnate be expected to contract his grandeur
within the pitiful compass of seven shingled gables?

In short, on an enlarged view of the business, the
carpenter's terms appeared so ridiculously easy, that

Mr. Pyncheon could scarcely forbear laughing in his face. He was quite ashamed, after the foregoing reflections, to propose any diminution of so moderate a recompense for the immense service to be rendered.

"I consent to your proposition, Maule," cried he. "Put me in possession of the document essential to establish my rights, and the House of the Seven Gables is your own!"

According to some versions of the story, a regular contract to the above effect was drawn up by a lawyer, and signed and sealed in the presence of witnesses. Others say that Matthew Maule was contented with a private written agreement, in which Mr. Pyncheon pledged his honour and integrity to the fulfilment of the terms concluded upon. The gentleman then ordered wine, which he and the carpenter drank together, in confirmation of their bargain. During the whole preceding discussion and subsequent formalities, the old Puritan's portrait seems to have persisted in its shadowy gestures of disapproval; but without effect, except that, as Mr. Pyncheon set down the emptied glass, he thought he beheld his grandfather frown.

"This sherry is too potent a wine for me; it has affected my brain already," he observed, after a somewhat startled look at the picture. "On returning to Europe, I shall confine myself to the more delicate vintages of Italy and France, the best of which will not bear transportation."

"My Lord Pyncheon may drink what wine he will, and wherever he pleases," replied the carpenter, as if he had been privy to Mr. Pyncheon's projects. "But first, sir, if you desire tidings of this lost document, I must crave the favour of a little talk with your fair daughter Alice."

"You are mad, Maule!" exclaimed Mr. Pyncheon, haughtily; and now, at last, there was anger mixed up with his pride. "What can my daughter have to do with a business like this?"

Indeed, at this new demand on the carpenter's

part, the proprietor of the seven gables was even
more thunder-struck than at the cool proposition to
surrender his house.   There was, at least, an assign-
able motive for the first stipulation; there appeared
to be none whatever for the last.   Nevertheless,
Matthew Maule sturdily insisted on the young lady
being summoned, and even gave her father to understand, in a mysterious kind of explanation—which
made the matter considerably darker than it looked
before—that the only chance of acquiring the requisite knowledge was through the clear, crystal
medium of a pure and virgin intelligence like that of
the fair Alice.   Not to encumber our story with Mr.
Pyncheon's scruples, whether of conscience, pride, or
fatherly affection, he at length ordered his daughter
to be called.   He well knew that she was in her
chamber, and engaged in no occupation that could
not readily be laid aside; for, as it happened, ever
since Alice's name had been spoken, both her father
and the carpenter had heard the sad and sweet
music of her harpsichord, and the airier melancholy
of her accompanying voice.

So Alice Pyncheon was summoned, and appeared.
A portrait of this young lady, painted by a Venetian
artist, and left by her father in England, is said to
have fallen into the hands of the present Duke of
Devonshire, and to be now preserved at Chatsworth,
not on account of any associations with the original,
but for its value as a picture, and the high character
of beauty in the countenance.   If ever there was a
lady born, and set apart from the world's vulgar
mass by a certain gentle and cold stateliness, it was
this very Alice Pyncheon.   Yet there was the
womanly mixture in her; the tenderness, or, at least,
the tender capabilities.   For the sake of that redeeming quality, a man of generous nature would have
forgiven all her pride, and have been content almost
to lie down in her path, and let Alice set her slender
foot upon his heart.   All that he would have required
was simply the acknowledgment that he was indeed

a man, and a fellow-being, moulded of the same elements as she.

As Alice came into the room her eyes fell upon the carpenter, who was standing near its centre, clad in a green woollen jacket, a pair of loose breeches, open at the knees, and with a long pocket for his rule, the end of which protruded; it was as proper a mark of the artisan's calling, as Mr. Pyncheon's full-dress sword of that gentleman's aristocratic pretensions. A glow of artistic approval brightened over Alice Pyncheon's face; she was struck with admiration—which she made no attempt to conceal—of the remarkable comeliness, strength, and energy, of Maule's figure. But that admiring glance (which most other men, perhaps, would have cherished as a sweet recollection, all through life) the carpenter never forgave. It must have been the devil himself that made Maule so subtile in his perception.

"Does the girl look at me as if I were a brute beast?" thought he, setting his teeth. "She shall know whether I have a human spirit; and the worse for her, if it prove stronger than her own!"

"My father, you sent for me," said Alice, in her sweet and harp-like voice. "But, if you have business with this young man, pray let me go again. You know I do not love this room, in spite of that Claude, with which you try to bring back sunny recollections."

"Stay a moment, young lady, if you please!" said Matthew Maule. "My business with your father is over. With yourself, it is now to begin!"

Alice looked towards her father, in surprise and inquiry.

"Yes, Alice," said Mr. Pyncheon, with some disturbance and confusion. "This young man—his name is Matthew Maule—professes, so far as I can understand him, to be able to discover, through your means, a certain paper or parchment, which was missing long before your birth. The importance of the document in question renders it advisable to neglect no possible, even if improbable, method of regaining it. You will therefore oblige me, my dear Alice, by answering this person's inquiries, and complying with his lawful and reasonable requests, so far as they may appear to have the aforesaid object in view. As I shall remain in the room, you need apprehend no rude nor unbecoming deportment, on the young man's part; and, at your slightest wish, of course, the investigation, or whatever we may call it, shall immediately be broken off."

"Mistress Alice Pyncheon," remarked Matthew Maule, with the utmost deference, but yet a half-hidden sarcasm in his look and tone, "will no doubt feel herself quite safe in her father's presence, and under his all-sufficient protection."

"I certainly shall entertain no manner of apprehension, with my father at hand," said Alice, with maidenly dignity. "Neither do I conceive that a lady, while true to herself, can have aught to fear, from whomsoever or in any circumstances!"

Poor Alice! By what unhappy impulse did she thus put herself at once on terms of defiance against a strength which she could not estimate?

"Then, Mistress Alice," said Matthew Maule, handing a chair—gracefully enough for a craftsman —"will it please you only to sit down, and do me the favour (though altogether beyond a poor carpenter's deserts) to fix your eyes on mine!"

Alice complied. She was very proud. Setting aside all advantages of rank, this fair girl deemed herself conscious of a power—combined of beauty, high, unsullied purity, and the preservative force of womanhood—that could make her sphere impenetrable, unless betrayed by treachery within. She instinctively knew, it may be, that some sinister or evil potency was now striving to pass her barriers; nor would she decline the contest. So Alice put woman's might against man's might; a match not often equal on the part of woman.

Her father, meanwhile, had turned away, and seemed absorbed in the contemplation of a landscape by Claude, where a shadowy and sun-streaked vista penetrated so remotely into an ancient wood, that it would have been no wonder if his fancy had lost itself in the picture's bewildering depths. But, in truth, the picture was no more to him, at that moment, than the blank wall against which it hung. His mind was haunted with the many and strange tales which he had heard, attributing mysterious if not supernatural endowments to these Maules, as well as the grandson, here present, as his two immediate ancestors. Mr. Pyncheon's long residence abroad, and intercourse with men of wit and fashion —courtiers, worldlings, and free-thinkers—had done much towards obliterating the grim Puritan superstitions, which no man of New England birth, at that early period, could entirely escape. But, on the other hand, had not a whole community believed Maule's grandfather to be a wizard? Had not the crime been proved? Had not the wizard died for it? Had he not bequeathed a legacy of hatred against the Pyncheons to this only grandson, who, as it now appeared, was now about to exercise a subtle influence over the daughter of his enemy's house? Might not this influence be the same that was called witchcraft?

Turning half around, he caught a glimpse of Maule's figure in the looking-glass. At some paces from Alice, with his arms uplifted in the air, the carpenter made a gesture, as if directing downward a slow, ponderous, and invisible weight upon the maiden.

" Stay, Maule !" exclaimed Mr. Pyncheon, stepping forward. " I forbid your proceeding further !"

" Pray, my dear father, do not interrupt the young man," said Alice, without changing her position. " His efforts, I assure you, will prove very harmless."

Again Mr. Pyncheon turned his eyes towards the

Claude. It was then his daughter's will, in opposition to his own, that the experiment should be fairly tried. Henceforth, therefore, he did but consent, not urge it. And was it not for her sake, far more than his own, that he desired its success? That lost parchment once restored, the beautiful Alice Pyncheon, with the rich dowry which he could then bestow, might wed an English duke, or a German reigning-prince, instead of some New England clergyman or lawyer! At the thought, the ambitious father almost consented, in his heart, that, if the devil's power were needed to the accomplishment of this great object, Maule might evoke him. Alice's own purity would be her safeguard.

With his mind full of imaginary magnificence, Mr. Pyncheon heard a half-uttered exclamation from his daughter. It was very faint and low; so indistinct that there seemed but half a will to shape out the words, and too undefined a purport to be intelligible. Yet it was a call for help!—his conscience never doubted it;—and little more than a whisper to his ear, it was a dismal shriek, and long re-echoed so, in the region round his heart! But, this time, the father did not turn.

After a further interval, Maule spoke.

"Behold your daughter!" said he.

Mr. Pyncheon came hastily forward. The carpenter was standing erect in front of Alice's chair, and pointing his finger towards the maiden with an expression of triumphant power, the limits of which could not be defined, as, indeed, its scope stretched vaguely towards the unseen and the infinite. Alice sat in an attitude of profound repose, with the long brown lashes drooping over her eyes.

"There she is!" said the carpenter. "Speak to her!"

"Alice! My daughter!" exclaimed Mr. Pyncheon. "My own Alice!"

She did not stir.

"Louder!" said Maule, smiling.

"Alice! awake!" cried her father. "It troubles me to see you thus! Awake!"

He spoke loudly, with terror in his voice, and close to that delicate ear, which had always been so sensitive to every discord. But the sound evidently reached her not. It is indescribable what a sense of remote, dim, unattainable distance, betwixt himself and Alice, was impressed on the father by this impossibility of reaching her with his voice.

"Best touch her!" said Matthew Maule. "Shake the girl, and roughly too! My hands are hardened with too much use of axe, saw, and plane,—else I might help you!"

Mr. Pyncheon took her hand, and pressed it with the earnestness of startled emotion. He kissed her, with so great a heart-throb in the kiss, that he thought she must needs feel it. Then, in a gust of anger at her insensibility, he shook her maiden form with a violence which, the next moment, it affrighted him to remember. He withdrew his encircling arms, and Alice—whose figure, though flexible, had been wholly impassive—relapsed into the same attitude as before these attempts to arouse her. Maule having shifted his position, her face was turned towards him, slightly, but with what seemed to be a reference of her very slumber to his guidance.

Then it was a strange sight to behold how the man of conventionalities shook the powder out of his periwig; how the reserved and stately gentleman forgot his dignity; how the gold-embroidered waistcoat flickered and glistened in the fire-light, with the convulsion of rage, terror, and sorrow, in the human heart that was beating under it.

"Villain!" cried Mr. Pyncheon, shaking his clenched fist at Maule. "You and the fiend together have robbed me of my daughter! Give her back, spawn of the old wizard, or you shall climb Gallows Hill in your grandfather's footsteps!"

"Softly, Mr. Pyncheon!" said the carpenter, with scornful composure. "Softly, an' it please your

worship, else you will spoil those lace ruffles at your
wrists! Is it my crime if you have sold your daughter for the mere hope of getting a sheet of yellow
parchment into your clutch? There sits Mistress
Alice, quietly asleep! Now let Matthew Maule try
whether she be as proud as the carpenter found her
a while since."

He spoke, and Alice responded with a soft, sub-
dued, inward acquiescence, and a bending of her
form towards him, like the flame of a torch when
it indicates a gentle draft of air. He beckoned with
his hand, and rising from her chair—blindly but undoubtingly, as tending to her sure and inevitable
centre—the proud Alice approached him. He waved
her back, and retreating, Alice sank again into her
seat.

" She is mine!" said Matthew Maule. " Mine,
by the right of the strongest spirit!"

In the further progress of the legend there is a
long, grotesque, and occasionally awe-striking
account of the carpenter's incantations (if so they
are to be called) with a view of discovering the lost
document. It appears to have been his object to con-
vert the mind of Alice into a kind of telescopic medium,
through which Mr. Pyncheon and himself might
obtain a glimpse into the spiritual world. He succeeded accordingly, in holding an imperfect sort of
intercourse, at one remove, with the departed personages, in whose custody the so much valued secret
had been carried beyond the precincts of earth.
During her trance, Alice described three figures as
being present to her spiritualized perception. One
was an aged, dignified, stern-looking gentleman,
clad as for a solemn festival, in grave and costly
attire, but with a great blood-stain on his richly-
wrought band; the second, an aged man, meanly
dressed, with a dark and malign countenance, and
a broken halter about his neck; the third, a person
not so advanced in life as the former two, but beyond the middle age, wearing a coarse woollen tunic

and leather breeches, and with a carpenter's rule
sticking out of his side pocket.   These three visionary characters possessed a mutual knowledge of the
missing document.   One of them, in truth—it was
he with the blood-stain on his band—seemed, unless
his gestures were misunderstood, to hold the parchments in his immediate keeping but was prevented,
by his two partners in the mystery, from disburthen-
ing himself of the trust.   Finally, when he showed
a purpose of shouting forth the secret, loudly enough
to be heard from his own sphere into that of mortals,
his companions struggled with him, and pressed
their hands over his mouth; and forthwith—whether
that he were choked by it, or that the secret itself
was of a crimson hue—there was a fresh flow of
blood upon his band.   Upon this, the two meanly-
dressed figures mocked and jeered at the much-
abashed old dignitary, and pointed their fingers at
the stain.

At this juncture, Maule turned to Mr. Pyncheon.
" It will never be allowed," said he.   " The custody of this secret, that would so enrich his heirs,
makes part of your grandfather's retribution.   He
must choke with it until it is no longer of any value.
And keep you the House of the Seven Gables!   It
is too dearly-bought an inheritance, and too heavy
with the curse upon it, to be shifted yet awhile from
the Colonel's posterity!"

Mr. Pyncheon tried to speak, but—what with fear
and passion—could make only a gurgling murmur
in his throat.   The carpenter smiled.

" Aha, worshipful sir!—so you have old Maule's
blood to drink!" said he, jeeringly.

" Fiend in man's shape! why dost thou keep
dominion over my child!" cried Mr. Pyncheon,
when his choked utterance could make way.   " Give
me back my daughter! Then go thy ways; and may
we never meet again!"

" Your daughter!" said Matthew Maule.   " Why,
she is fairly mine! Nevertheless, not to be too hard

with fair Mistress Alice, I will leave her in your keeping; but I do not warrant you that she shall never have occasion to remember Maule, the carpenter.''

He waved his hands with an upward motion; and after a few repetitions of similar gestures, the beautiful Alice Pyncheon awoke from her strange trance. She awoke without the slightest recollection of her visionary experience; but as one losing herself in a momentary reverie, and returning to the consciousness of actual life, in almost as brief an interval as the down-sinking flame of the hearth could quiver again up the chimney. On recognizing Matthew Maule, she assumed an air of somewhat cold but gentle dignity; the rather, as there was a certain peculiar smile on the carpenter's visage, that stirred the native pride of the fair Alice. So ended, for that time, the quest for the lost title-deed of the Pyncheon territory at the eastward; nor, though often subsequently renewed, has it ever yet befallen a Pyncheon to set his eye upon that parchment.

But, alas for the beautiful, the gentle, yet too haughty Alice! A power that she little dreamed of had laid its grasp upon her maiden soul. A will, most unlike her own, constrained her to do its grotesque and fantastic bidding. Her father, as it proved, had martyred his poor child to an inordinate desire for measuring his land by miles instead of acres. And, therefore, while Alice Pyncheon lived she was Maule's slave, in a bondage more humiliating a thousand-fold than that which binds its chain around the body. Seated by his humble fireside, Maule had but to wave his hand; and wherever the proud lady chanced to be—whether in her chamber, or entertaining her father's stately guests, or worshipping at church—whatever her place or occupation, her spirit passed from beneath her own control, and bowed itself to Maule. "Alice, laugh!"—the carpenter, beside his hearth, would say; or perhaps intensely will it, without a spoken word. And even were it prayer-time, or at a funeral, Alice must break into wild laughter. " Alice, be sad !"—and at the instant down would come her tears, quenching all the mirth of those around her like sudden rain upon a bonfire. " Alice, dance !"—and dance she would, not in such court-like measures as she had learned abroad, but some high-paced jig, or hop-skip riga-doon, befitting the brisk lasses at a rustic merry-making. It seemed to be Maule's impulse not to ruin Alice, nor to visit her with any black or gigan-tic mischief, which would have crowned her sorrows with the grace of tragedy, but to wreak a low, un-generous scorn upon her. Thus all the dignity of life was lost. She felt herself too much abased, and longed to change natures with some worm !

One evening, at a bridal-party—(but not her own ; for, so lost from self-control, she would have deemed it sin to marry)—poor Alice was beckoned forth by her unseen despot, and constrained, in her gossamer white dress and satin slippers, to hasten along the street to the mean dwelling of a labouring-man. There was laughter and good cheer within ; for Matthew Maule, that night, was to wed the labourer's daugh-ter, and had summoned proud Alice Pyncheon to wait upon his bride. And so she did ; and when the twain were one, Alice awoke out of her enchanted sleep. Yet, no longer proud—humbly, and with a smile all steeped in sadness—she kissed Maule's wife, and went her way. It was an inclement night ; the south-east wind drove the mingled snow and rain into her thinly-sheltered bosom ; her satin slippers were wet through and through, as she trod the muddy side-walks. The next day, a cold ; soon, a settled cough ; anon, a hectic cheek, a wasted form, that sat beside the harpsichord, and filled the house with music ! Music, in which a strain of the heavenly choristers was echoed ! O, joy ! For Alice had borne her last humiliation ! O, greater joy ! For Alice was penitent of her one earthly sin, and proud no more !

The Pyncheons made a great funeral for Alice.
The kith and kin were there, and the whole respectability of the town besides. But, last in the procession, came Matthew Maule, gnashing his teeth,
as if he would have bitten his own heart in twain—
the darkest and wofullest man that ever walked
behind a corpse! He meant to humble Alice—not to
kill her; but he had taken a woman's delicate soul
into his rude gripe, to play with—and she was dead!

XIV

PHŒBE'S GOOD-BYE

HOLGRAVE, plunging into his tale with the energy
and absorption natural to a young author, had given
a good deal of action to the parts capable of being
developed and exemplified in that manner. He now
observed that a certain remarkable drowsiness
(wholly unlike that with which the reader possibly
feels himself affected) had been flung over the senses
of his auditress. It was the effect, unquestionably,
of the mystic gesticulations by which he had sought
to bring bodily before Phœbe's perception the figure
of the mesmerizing carpenter. With the lids drooping over her eyes—now lifted for an instant, and
drawn down again, as with leaden weights—she
leaned slightly towards him, and seemed almost to
regulate her breath by his. Holgrave gazed at her,
as he rolled up his manuscript, and recognized an
incipient stage of that curious psychological condition, which, as he had himself told Phœbe, he possessed more than an ordinary faculty of producing.
A veil was beginning to be muffled about her, in
which she could behold only him, and live only in
his thoughts and emotions. His glance, as he fast-

ened it on the young girl, grew involuntarily more concentrated; in his attitude there was the consciousness of power, investing his hardly mature figure with a dignity that did not belong to its physical manifestation. It was evident that with but one wave of his hand, and a corresponding effort of his will, he could complete his mastery over Phœbe's yet free and virgin spirit: he could establish an influence over this good, pure, and simple child, as dangerous, and perhaps as disastrous, as that which the carpenter of his legend had acquired and exercised over the ill-fated Alice.

To a disposition like Holgrave's, at once speculative and active, there is no temptation so great as the opportunity of acquiring empire over the human spirit; nor any idea more seductive to a young man than to become the arbiter of a young girl's destiny. Let us, therefore—whatever his defects of nature and education, and in spite of his scorn for creeds and institutions—concede to the daguerreotypist the rare and high quality of reverence for another's individuality. Let us allow him integrity, also, for ever after to be confided in; since he forbade himself to twine that one link more which might have rendered his spell over Phœbe indissoluble.

He made a slight gesture upward with his hand.

" You really mortify me, my dear Miss Phœbe ! " he exclaimed, smiling half-sarcastically at her. " My poor story, it is but too evident, will never do for Godey or Graham ! Only think of your falling asleep at what I hoped the newspaper critics would pronounce a most brilliant, powerful, imaginative, pathetic, and original winding up ! Well, the manuscript must serve to light lamps with;—if indeed, being so imbued with my gentle dulness, it is any longer capable of flame ! "

" Me asleep ! How can you say so ? " answered Phœbe, as unconscious of the crisis through which she had passed as an infant of the precipice to the verge of which it has rolled. " No, no ! I consider

myself as having been very attentive; and, though
I don't remember the incidents quite distinctly, yet
I have an impression of a vast deal of trouble and
calamity—so, no doubt, the story will prove exceedingly attractive."

By this time, the sun had gone down, and was
tinting the clouds towards the zenith with those
bright hues which are not seen there until some
time after sunset, and when the horizon has quite
lost its richer brilliancy. The moon, too, which had
long been climbing overhead, and unobtrusively melting its disk into the azure—like an ambitious dema-
gogue, who hides his aspiring purpose by assuming the prevalent hue of popular sentiment—now
began to shine out, broad and oval, in its middle
pathway. These silvery beams were already powerful enough to change the character of the lingering
daylight. They softened and embellished the aspect
of the old house; although the shadows fell deeper
into the angles of its many gables, and lay brooding
under the projecting storey, and within the half-open
door. With the lapse of every moment, the garden
grew more picturesque; the fruit-trees, shrubbery,
and flower-bushes, had a dark obscurity among them.
The commonplace characteristics—which, at noontide, it seemed to have taken a century of sordid life
to accumulate—were now transfigured by a charm of
romance. A hundred mysterious years were whis-
pering among the leaves, whenever the slight sea-
breeze found its way thither and stirred them.
Through the foliage that roofed the little summer-
house, the moonlight flickered to and fro, and fell
silvery white on the dark floor, the table and the
circular bench, with a continual shift and play,
according as the chinks and wayward crevices among
the twigs admitted or shut out the glimmer.

So sweetly cool was the atmosphere, after all the
feverish day, that the summer eve might be fancied
as sprinkling dews and liquid moonlight, with a dash
of icy temper in them, out of a silver vase. Here

and there, a few drops of this freshness were scattered on a human heart, and gave it youth again, and sympathy with the eternal joy of nature. The artist chanced to be one on whom the reviving influence fell. It made him feel—what he sometimes almost forgot, thrust so early as he had been into the rude struggle of man with man—how youthful he still was.

" It seems to me," he observed, " that I never watched the coming of so beautiful an eve, and never felt anything so very much like happiness as at this moment. After all, what a good world we live in ! How good and beautiful ! How young it is, too, with nothing really rotten or ageworn in it ! This old house, for example, which sometimes has positively oppressed my breath with its smell of decaying timber ! And this garden, where the black mould always clings to my spade as if I were a sexton, delving in a grave-yard ! Could I keep the feeling that now possesses me, the garden would every day be virgin soil, with the earth's first freshness in the flavour of its beans and squashes; and the house !— it would be like a bower in Eden, blossoming with the earliest roses that God ever made. Moonlight, and the sentiment in man's heart responsive to it, are the greatest of renovators and reformers. And all other reform and renovation, I suppose, will prove to be no better than moonshine !"

" I have been happier than I am now; at least, much gayer," said Phœbe, thoughtfully. " Yet I am sensible of a great charm in this brightening moonlight; and I love to watch how the day, tired as it is, lags away reluctantly, and hates to be called yesterday so soon. I never cared much about moonlight before. What is there, I wonder, so beautiful in it to-night?"

" And you have never felt it before?" inquired the artist, looking earnestly at the girl, through the twilight.

" Never," answered Phœbe; " and life does not

look the same, now that I have felt it so. It seems
as if I had looked at everything hitherto in broad
daylight, or else in the ruddy light of a cheerful fire,
glimmering and dancing through a room. Ah, poor
me!" she added, with a half-melancholy laugh, "I
shall never be so merry as before I knew Cousin
Hepzibah and poor Cousin Clifford. I have grown
a great deal older in this little time. Older, and I
hope wiser, and—not exactly sadder—but certainly,
with not half so much lightness in my spirits! I
have given them my sunshine, and have been glad
to give it; but, of course, I cannot both give and
keep it. They are welcome, notwithstanding!"

"You have lost nothing, Phœbe, worth keeping,
nor which it was possible to keep," said Holgrave,
after a pause. "Our first youth is of no value; for
we are never conscious of it, until after it is gone.
But sometimes—always, I suspect, unless one is
exceedingly unfortunate—there comes a sense of
second youth, gushing out of the heart's joy at being
in love; or, possibly, it may come to crown some
other grand festival in life, if any other such there
be. This bemoaning of one's self (as you do now)
over the first, careless, shallow gaiety of youth
departed, and this profound happiness at youth re-
gained—so much deeper and richer than that we lost
—are essential to the soul's development. In some
cases, the two states come almost simultaneously,
and mingle the sadness and the rapture in one
mysterious emotion."

"I hardly think I understand you," said Phœbe.

"No wonder," replied Holgrave, smiling; "for
I have told you a secret which I hardly began to
know, before I found myself giving it utterance.
Remember it, however; and when the truth becomes
clear to you, then think of this moonlight scene!"

"It is entirely moonlight now, except only a little
flush of faint crimson, upward from the west, between those buildings," remarked Phœbe. "I must
go in. Cousin Hepzibah is not quick at figures, and

will give herself a headache over the day's accounts, unless I help her."

But Holgrave detained her a little longer.

"Miss Hepzibah tells me," observed he, "that you return to the country, in a few days."

"Yes, but only for a little while," answered Phœbe; "for I look upon this as my present home. I go to make a few arrangements, and to take a more deliberate leave of my mother and friends. It is pleasant to live where one is much desired, and very useful; and I think I may have the satisfaction of feeling myself so, here."

"You surely may, and more than you imagine," said the artist. "Whatever health, comfort and natural life, exist in the house, are embodied in your person. These blessings came along with you, and will vanish when you leave the threshold. Miss Hepzibah, by secluding herself from society, has lost all true relation with it, and is, in fact, dead; although she galvanizes herself into a semblance of life, and stands behind the counter, afflicting the world with a greatly-to-be-deprecated scowl. Your poor cousin Clifford is another dead and long-buried person, on whom the governor and council have wrought a necromantic miracle. I should not wonder if he were to crumble away, some morning after you are gone, and nothing be seen of him more, except a heap of dust. Miss Hepzibah, at any rate, will lose what little flexibility she has. They both exist by you."

"I should be very sorry to think so," answered Phœbe, gravely. "But it is true that my small abilities were precisely what they needed; and I have a real interest in their welfare—an odd kind of motherly sentiment—which I wish you would not laugh at! And let me tell you frankly, Mr. Holgrave, I am sometimes puzzled to know whether you wish them well or ill."

"Undoubtedly," said the daguerreotypist, "I do feel an interest in this antiquated, poverty-stricken old

maiden-lady, and this degraded and shattered gentleman—this abortive lover of the beautiful. A kindly
interest, too, helpless old children that they are! But
you have no conception what a different kind of
heart mine is from your own. It is not my impulse,
as regards these two individuals, either to help or
hinder; but to look on, to analyze, to explain matters
to myself, and to comprehend the drama which, for
almost two hundred years, has been dragging its
slow length over the ground where you and I now
tread. If permitted to witness the close, I doubt not
to derive a moral satisfaction from it, go matters
how they may. There is a conviction within me
that the end draws nigh. But though Providence
sent you hither to help, and sends me only as a privileged and meet spectator, I pledge myself to lend
these unfortunate beings whatever aid I can."

" I wish you would speak more plainly," cried
Phœbe, perplexed and displeased; " and above all
that you would feel more like a Christian and a
human being! How is it possible to see people in
distress, without desiring, more than anything else,
to help and comfort them? You talk as if this old
house were a theatre; and you seem to look at Hepzibah's and Clifford's misfortunes, and those of
generations before them, as a tragedy, such as I
have seen acted in the hall of a country hotel, only
the present one appears to be played exclusively for
your amusement. I do not like this. The play costs
the performers too much, and the audience is too
cold-hearted."

" You are severe," said Holgrave, compelled to
recognize a degree of truth in this piquant sketch of
his own mood.

" And then," continued Phœbe, " what can you
mean by your conviction, which you tell me of, that
the end is drawing near? Do you know of any new
trouble hanging over my poor relatives? If so, tell
me at once, and I will not leave them!"

" Forgive me, Phœbe! said the daguerreotypist,

holding out his hand, to which the girl was constrained to yield her own. " I am somewhat of a mystic, it must be confessed. The tendency is in my blood, together with the faculty of mesmerism, which might have brought me to Gallows Hill, in the good old times of witchcraft. Believe me, if I were really aware of any secret, the disclosure of which would benefit your friends—who are my own friends, likewise—you should learn it before we part. But I have no such knowledge."

" You hold something back !" said Phœbe.

" Nothing—no secrets but my own," answered Holgrave. " I can perceive, indeed, that Judge Pyncheon still keeps his eye on Clifford, in whose ruin he had so large a share. His motives and intentions, however, are a mystery to me. He is a determined and relentless man, with the genuine character of an inquisitor; and had he any object to gain by putting Clifford to the rack, I verily believe that he would wrench his joints from their sockets, in order to accomplish it. But so wealthy and eminent as he is—so powerful in his own strength and in the support of society on all sides—what can Judge Pyncheon have to hope or fear from the imbecile, branded, half-torpid Clifford?"

" Yet," urged Phœbe, " you did speak as if misfortune were impending !"

" O, that was because I am morbid !" replied the artist. " My mind has a twist aside, like almost everybody's mind, except your own. Moreover, it is so strange to find myself an inmate of this old Pyncheon-house, and sitting in this old garden—(hark, how Maule's well is murmuring !)—that, were it only for this one circumstance, I cannot help fancying that Destiny is arranging its fifth act for a catastrophe."

" There !" cried Phœbe, with renewed vexation; for she was by nature as hostile to mystery as the sunshine to a dark corner. " You puzzle me more than ever !"

" Then let us part friends !" said Holgrave, pressing her hand. " Or, if not friends, let us part before you entirely hate me. You, who love everybody else in the world !"

"Good-bye, then," said Phœbe, frankly. " I do not mean to be angry a great while, and should be sorry to have you think so. There has Cousin Hepzibah been standing in the shadow of the door-way, this quarter of an hour past ! She thinks I stay too long in the damp garden. So, good-night, and good-bye !"

On the second morning thereafter, Phœbe might have been seen, in her straw bonnet, with a shawl on one arm and a little carpet-bag on the other, bidding adieu to Hepzibah and Cousin Clifford. She was to take a seat in the next train of cars, which would transport her to within half-a-dozen miles of her country village.

The tears were in Phœbe's eyes; a smile, dewy with affectionate regret, was glimmering around her pleasant mouth. She wondered how it came to pass, that her life of a few weeks, here, in this heavy-hearted old mansion, had taken such hold of her, and so melted into her associations, as now to seem a more important centre-point of remembrance than all which had gone before. How had Hepzibah—grim, silent, and irresponsive to her overflow of cordial sentiment—contrived to win so much love? And Clifford—in his abortive decay, with the mystery of fearful crime upon him, and the close prison-atmosphere yet lurking in his breath—how had he transformed himself into the simplest child, whom Phœbe felt bound to watch over, and be, as it were, the providence of his unconsidered hours ! Everything, at that instant of farewell, stood out prominently to her view. Look where she would, lay her hand on what she might, the object responded to her consciousness, as if a moist human heart were in it.

She peeped from the window into the garden, and felt herself more regretful at leaving this spot of black earth, vitiated with such an age-long growth of weeds, than joyful at the idea of again scenting her pine-forests and fresh clover-fields. She called Chanticleer, his two wives, and the venerable chicken, and threw them some crumbs of bread from the breakfast-table. These being hastily gobbled up, the chicken spread its wings, and alighted close by Phœbe on the window-sill, where it looked gravely into her face and vented its emotions in a croak. Phœbe bade it be a good old chicken during her absence, and promised to bring it a little bag of buckwheat.

"Ah, Phœbe!" remarked Hepzibah, "you do not smile so naturally as when you came to us! Then the smile chose to shine out; now, you choose it should. It is well that you are going back, for a little while, into your native air. There has been too much weight on your spirits. The house is too gloomy and lonesome; the shop is full of vexations; and as for me, I have no faculty of making things look brighter than they are. Dear Clifford has been your only comfort!"

"Come hither, Phœbe," suddenly cried her cousin Clifford, who had said very little all the morning. "Close!—closer!—and look me in the face!"

Phœbe put one of her small hands on each elbow of his chair, and leaned her face towards him, so that he might peruse it as carefully as he would. It is probable that the latent emotions of this parting hour had revived, in some degree, his bedimmed and enfeebled faculties. At any rate, Phœbe soon felt that, if not the profound insight of a seer, yet a more than feminine delicacy of appreciation was making her heart the subject of its regard. A moment before, she had known nothing which she would have sought to hide. Now, as if something were hinted to her own consciousness through the medium of another's perception, she was fain to let her eyelids droop beneath Clifford's gaze. A blush, too—the redder, because she strove hard to keep it down—ascended higher, in a tide of fitful progress, until even her brow was all suffused with it.

" It is enough, Phœbe," said Clifford, with a melancholy smile. " When I first saw you, you were the prettiest little maiden in the world; and now you have deepened into beauty! Girlhood has passed into womanhood; the bud is a bloom! Go, now!—I feel lonelier than I did."

Phœbe took leave of the desolate couple, and passed through the shop, twinkling her eyelids to shake off a dewdrop; for—considering how brief her absence was to be, and therefore the folly of being cast down about it—she would not so far acknowledge her tears as to dry them with her handkerchief. On the door-step, she met the little urchin whose marvellous feats of gastronomy have been recorded in the earlier pages of our narrative. She took from the window some specimen or other of natural history—her eyes being too dim with moisture to inform her accurately whether it was a rabbit or a hippopotamus—put it into the child's hand, as a parting gift, and went her way. Old Uncle Venner was just coming out of his door, with a wood-horse and saw on his shoulder; and trudging along the street, he scrupled not to keep company with Phœbe, so far as their paths lay together; nor, in spite of his patched coat and rusty beaver, and the curious fashion of his tow-cloth trousers, could she find it in her heart to outwalk him.

" We shall miss you next Sabbath afternoon," observed the street philosopher. " It is unaccountable how little while it takes some folks to grow just as natural to a man as his own breath; and, begging your pardon, Miss Phœbe (though there can be no offence in an old man's saying it), that's just what you've grown to me! My years have been a great many, and your life is but just beginning; and yet, you are somehow as familiar to me as if I had found you at my mother's door, and you had blossomed, like a running vine, all along my pathway since.

Come back soon, or I shall be gone to my farm; for I begin to find these wood-sawing jobs a little too tough for my back-ache."

"Very soon, Uncle Venner," said Phœbe.

"And let it be all the sooner, Phœbe, for the sake of those poor souls yonder," continued her companion. "They can never do without you now,— never, Phœbe, never!—no more than if one of God's angels had been living with them, and making their dismal house pleasant and comfortable! Don't it seem to you they'd be in a sad case, if, some pleasant summer morning like this, the angel should spread his wings, and fly to the place he came from? Well, just so they feel, now that you are going home by the railroad! They can't bear it, Miss Phœbe; so be sure to come back!"

"I am no angel, Uncle Venner," said Phœbe, smiling, as she offered him her hand at the street-corner. "But I suppose people never feel so much like angels as when they are doing what little good they may. So I shall certainly come back!"

Thus parted the old man and the rosy girl; and Phœbe took the wings of the morning, and was soon flitting almost as rapidly away as if endowed with the aërial locomotion of the angels to whom Uncle Venner had so graciously compared her.

XV

THE SCOWL AND SMILE

SEVERAL days passed over the seven gables, heavily and drearily enough. In fact (not to attribute the whole gloom of sky and earth to the one inauspicious circumstance of Phœbe's departure) an easterly storm had set in, and indefatigably applied itself to the task of making the black roof and walls of the old house look more cheerless than ever before. Yet was the outside not half so cheerless as the interior. Poor Clifford was cut off, at once, from all his scanty resources of enjoyment. Phœbe was not there; nor did the sunshine fall upon the floor. The garden, with its muddy walks, and the chill, dripping foliage of its summer-house, was an image to be shuddered at. Nothing flourished in the cold, moist, pitiless atmosphere, drifting with the brackish scud of sea-breezes, except the moss along the joints of the shingle-roof, and the great bunch of weeds, that had lately been suffering from drought, in the angle between the two front gables.

As for Hepzibah, she seemed not merely possessed with the east wind, but to be, in her very person, only another phase of this gray and sullen spell of weather; the east wind itself, grim and disconsolate, in a rusty black silk gown, and with a turban of cloud-wreaths on its head. The custom of the shop fell off, because a story had got abroad that she soured her small beer and other damageable commodities, by scowling on them. It is, perhaps, true that the public had something reasonably to complain of in her deportment; but towards Clifford she was neither ill-tempered nor unkind, nor felt less warmth of heart than always, had it been possible to make it reach him. The inutility of her best efforts, however, palsied the poor old gentlewoman. She could do little else than sit silently in a corner of the room, when the wet pear-tree branches, sweeping across the small windows, created a noon-day dusk, which Hepzibah unconsciously darkened with her woe-begone aspect. It was no fault of Hepzibah's. Everything—even the old chairs and tables, that had known what weather was for three or four such life-times as her own—looked as damp and chill as if the present were their worst experience. The picture of the Puritan colonel shivered on the wall. The house itself shivered, from every attic of its seven gables, down to the great kitchen fireplace, which served all the better as an emblem of the mansion's heart, because, though built for warmth, it was now so comfortless and empty.

Hepzibah attempted to enliven matters by a fire in the parlour. But the storm-demon kept watch above, and, whenever a flame was kindled, drove the smoke back again, choking the chimney's sooty throat with its own breath. Nevertheless, during four days of this miserable storm, Clifford wrapt himself in an old cloak, and occupied his customary chair. On the morning of the fifth, when summoned to breakfast, he responded only by a broken-hearted murmur, expressive of a determination not to leave his bed. His sister made no attempt to change his purpose. In fact, entirely as she loved him, Hepzibah could hardly have borne any longer the wretched duty—so impracticable by her few and rigid faculties —of seeking pastime for a still sensitive, but ruined mind, critical and fastidious, without force or volition. It was, at least, something short of positive despair, that, to-day, she might sit shivering alone, and not suffer continually a new grief, and unreasonable pang of remorse, at every fitful sigh of her fellow-sufferer.

But Clifford, it seemed, though he did not make his appearance below stairs, had, after all, bestirred himself in quest of amusement. In the course of the forenoon, Hepzibah heard a note of music, which (there being no other tuneful contrivance in the House of the Seven Gables) she knew must proceed from Alice Pyncheon's harpsichord. She was aware that Clifford, in his youth, had possessed a cultivated taste for music, and a considerable degree of skill in its practice. It was difficult, however, to conceive of his retaining an accomplishment to which daily exercise is so essential, in the measure indicated by the sweet, airy, and delicate, though most melancholy strain, that now stole upon her ear. Nor was it less marvellous that the long-silent instrument should be capable of so much melody. Hepzibah involuntarily thought of the ghostly harmonies, prelusive of death in the family, which were attributed to the agency of the legendary Alice. But it was, perhaps, proof of the agency of other than spiritual fingers, that, after a few touches, the chords seemed to snap asunder with their own vibrations, and the music ceased.

But a harsher sound succeeded to the mysterious notes; nor was the easterly day fated to pass without an event sufficient in itself to poison, for Hepzibah and Clifford, the balmiest air that ever brought the humming-birds along with it. The final echoes of Alice Pyncheon's performance (or Clifford's, if his we must consider it) were driven away by no less vulgar a dissonance than the ringing of the shop-bell. A foot was heard scraping itself on the threshold, and thence somewhat ponderously stepping on the floor. Hepzibah delayed a moment, while muffling herself in a faded shawl, which had been her defensive armour in a forty years' warfare against the east wind. A characteristic sound, however—neither a cough nor a hem, but a kind of rumbling and reverberating spasm in somebody's capacious depth of chest—impelled her to hurry forward, with that aspect of fierce faint-heartedness so common to women in cases of perilous emergency. Few of her sex, on such occasions, have ever looked so terrible as our poor scowling Hepzibah. But the visitor quietly closed the shop-door behind him, stood up his umbrella against the counter, and turned a visage of composed benignity, to meet the alarm and anger which his appearance had excited.

Hepzibah's presentiment had not deceived her. It was no other than Judge Pyncheon, who, after in vain trying the front door, had now effected his entrance into the shop.

"How do you do, Cousin Hepzibah?—and how does this most inclement weather affect our poor Clifford?" began the judge; and wonderful it seemed, indeed, that the easterly storm was not put to shame, or, at any rate, a little mollified, by the genial benevolence of his smile. " I could not rest without calling to ask, once more, whether I can in any manner promote his comfort, or your own."

" You can do nothing," said Hepzibah, controlling her agitation as well as she could. " I devote myself to Clifford. He has every comfort which his situation admits of."

" But, allow me to suggest, dear cousin," rejoined the judge, " you err—in all affection and kindness, no doubt, and with the very best intentions—but you do err, nevertheless, in keeping your brother so secluded. Why insulate him thus from all sympathy and kindness? Clifford, alas! has had too much of solitude. Now let him try society—the society, that is to say, of kindred and old friends. Let me, for instance, but see Clifford; and I will answer for the good effect of the interview."

" You cannot see him," answered Hepzibah. " Clifford has kept his bed since yesterday."

" What! How! Is he ill?" exclaimed Judge Pyncheon, starting with what seemed to be angry alarm; for the very frown of the old Puritan darkened through the room as he spoke. " Nay, then, I must and will see him! What if he should die?"

" He is in no danger of death," said Hepzibah,— and added, with bitterness that she could repress no longer, " none;—unless he should be persecuted to death, now, by the same man who long ago attempted it!"

" Cousin Hepzibah," said the judge, with an impressive earnestness of manner, which grew even to tearful pathos, as he proceeded, " is it possible that you do not perceive how unjust, how unkind, how unchristian, is this constant, this long-continued bitterness against me, for a part which I was constrained by duty and conscience, by the force of law, and at my own peril, to act? What did I do, in detriment to Clifford, which it was possible to leave undone? How could you, his sister,—if, for your never-ending sorrow, as it has been for mine, you had known what I did,—have shown greater tenderness? And do you think, cousin, that it has cost me no pang?—that it has left no anguish in my bosom, from that day to this, amidst all the prosperity with which Heaven has blessed me?—or that I do not now rejoice, when it is deemed consistent with the dues of public justice and the welfare of society that this dear kinsman, this early friend, this nature so delicately and beautifully constituted,—so unfortunate, let us pronounce him, and forbear to say, so guilty,—that our own Clifford, in fine, should be given back to life and its possibilities of enjoyment? Ah, you little know me, Cousin Hepzibah! You little know this heart! It now throbs at the thought of meeting him! There lives not the human being (except yourself,—and you not more than I) who has shed so many tears for Clifford's calamity! You behold some of them now. There is none who would so delight to promote his happiness! Try me, Hepzibah!—try me, cousin!—try the man whom you have treated as your enemy and Clifford's! Try Jaffrey Pyncheon, and you shall find him true, to the heart's core!'

"In the name of Heaven," cried Hepzibah, provoked only to intenser indignation by this out-gush of the inestimable tenderness of a stern nature,— "in God's name, whom you insult, and whose power I could almost question, since He hears you utter so many false words, without palsying your tongue,— give over, I beseech you, this loathsome pretence of affection for your victim! You hate him! Say so like a man! You cherish, at this moment, some black purpose against him in your heart! Speak it out at once!—or, if you hope so to promote it better, hide it till you can triumph in its success! But never speak again of your love for my poor brother! I cannot bear it! It will drive me beyond a woman's decency! It will drive me mad! Forbear! Not another word! It will make me spurn you!"

For once, Hepzibah's wrath had given her courage. She had spoken. But, after all, was this unconquerable distrust of Judge Pyncheon's integrity, and this utter denial, apparently, of his claim to stand in the ring of human sympathies,—were they founded in any just perception of his character, or merely the offspring of a woman's unreasonable prejudice, deduced from nothing?

The judge, beyond all question, was a man of eminent respectability. The church acknowledged it; the state acknowledged it. It was denied by nobody. In all the very extensive sphere of those who knew him, whether in his public or private capacities, there was not an individual—except Hepzibah, and some lawless mystic, like the daguerreotypist, and, possibly, a few political opponents—who would have dreamed of seriously disputing his claim to a high and honourable place in the world's regard. Nor (we must do him the further justice to say) did Judge Pyncheon himself, probably, entertain many or frequent doubts, that his enviable reputation accorded with his deserts. His conscience, therefore, usually considered the surest witness to a man's integrity,—his conscience, unless it might be for the little space of five minutes in the twenty-four hours, or, now and then, some black day in the whole year's circle,—his conscience bore an accordant testimony with the world's laudatory voice. And yet, strong as this evidence may seem to be, we should hesitate to peril our own conscience on the assertion, that the judge and the consenting world were right, and that poor Hepzibah, with her solitary prejudice, was wrong. Hidden from mankind,—forgotten by himself, or buried so deeply under a sculptured and ornamental pile of ostentatious deeds that his daily life could take no note of it,—there may have lurked some evil and unsightly thing. Nay, we could almost

venture to say, further, that a daily guilt might have
been acted by him, continually renewed, and reddening forth afresh, like the miraculous blood-stain of a
murder, without his necessarily and at every moment
being aware of it.

Men of strong minds, great force of character, and
a hard texture of the sensibilities, are very capable
of falling into mistakes of this kind.   They are ordinarily men to whom forms are of paramount importance.   Their field of action lies among the external
phenomena of life.   They possess vast ability in
grasping, and arranging, and appropriating to themselves, the big, heavy, solid unrealities, such as gold,
landed estate, offices of trust and emolument, and
public honours.   With these materials, and with
deeds of goodly aspect, done in the public eye, an
individual of this class builds up, as it were, a tall
and stately edifice, which, in the view of other people,
and ultimately in his own view, is no other than the
man's character, or the man himself.   Behold, therefore, a palace !   Its splendid halls, and suites of
spacious apartments, are floored with the mosaic-
work of costly marbles ; its windows, the whole
height of each room, admit the sunshine through the
most transparent of plate-glass ; its high cornices are
gilded, and its ceilings gorgeously painted ; and a
lofty dome—through which, from the central pavement, you may gaze up to the sky, as with no
obstructing medium between—surmounts the whole.
With what fairer and nobler emblem could any man
desire to shadow forth his character?   Ah ! but in
some low and obscure nook,—some narrow closet
on the ground-floor, shut, locked, and bolted, and the
key flung away,—or beneath the marble pavement,
in a stagnant water-puddle, with the richest pattern of
mosaic-work above,—may lie a corpse, half-decayed,
and still decaying, and diffusing its death-scent all
through the palace !   The inhabitant will not be conscious of it, for it has long been his daily breath !
Neither will the visitors, for they smell only the rich

odours which the master sedulously scatters through
the palace, and the incense which they bring, and delight to burn before him! Now and then, perchance,
comes in a seer, before whose sadly-gifted eye the
whole structure melts into thin air, leaving only the
hidden nook, the bolted closet, with the cobwebs
festooned over its forgotten door, or the deadly hole
under the pavement, and the decaying corpse within.
Here, then, we are to seek the true emblem of the
man's character, and of the deed that gives whatever
reality it possesses to his life. And, beneath the show
of a marble palace, that pool of stagnant water, foul
with many impurities, and, perhaps, tinged with
blood,—that secret abomination, above which, possibly, he may say his prayers, without remembering
it,—is this man's miserable soul!

To apply this train of remark somewhat more
closely to Judge Pyncheon. We might say (without
in the least imputing crime to a personage of his
eminent respectability) that there was enough of
splendid rubbish in his life to cover up and paralyze
a more active and subtile conscience than the judge
was ever troubled with. The purity of his judicial
character, while on the bench; the faithfulness of his
public service in subsequent capacities; his devoted-
ness to his party, and the rigid consistency with which
he had adhered to its principles, or, at all events, kept
pace with its organized movements; his remarkable
zeal as president of a Bible society; his unimpeach-
able integrity as treasurer of a widow's and orphan's
fund; his benefits to horticulture, by producing two
much-esteemed varieties of the pear, and to agricul-
ture, through the agency of the famous Pyncheon-
bull; the cleanliness of his moral deportment, for a
great many years past; the severity with which he
had frowned upon, and finally cast off, an expensive
and dissipated son, delaying forgiveness until within
the final quarter of an hour of the young man's life;
his prayers at morning and eventide, and graces at
meal-time; his efforts in furtherance of the temperance

cause; his confining himself, since the last attack of
the gout, to five diurnal glasses of old sherry wine;
the snowy whiteness of his linen, the polish of his
boots, the handsomeness of his gold-headed cane, the
square and roomy fashion of his coat, and the fineness
of its material, and, in general, the studied propriety
of his dress and equipment; the scrupulousness with
which he paid public notice in the street, by a bow,
a lifting of the hat, a nod, or a motion of the hand,
to all and sundry his acquaintances, rich or poor;
the smile of broad benevolence wherewith he made it
a point to gladden the whole world;—what room
could possibly be found for darker traits, in a portrait
made up of lineaments like these? This proper face
was what he beheld in the looking-glass. This
admirably arranged life was what he was conscious
of, in the progress of every day. Then, might not he
claim to be its result and sum, and say to himself and
the community—" Behold Judge Pyncheon there!"

And, allowing that many, many years ago, in his
early and reckless youth, he had committed some one
wrong act—or, that, even now, the inevitable force
of circumstances should occasionally make him do
one questionable deed, among a thousand praiseworthy, or at least blameless ones—would you char-
acterize the judge by that one necessary deed, and that
half-forgotten act, and let it overshadow the fair
aspect of a lifetime? What is there so ponderous in
evil, that a thumb's bigness of it should outweigh the
mass of things not evil which were heaped into the
other scale! This scale and balance system is a
favourite one with people of Judge Pyncheon's
brotherhood. A hard, cold man, thus unfortunately
situated, seldom or never looking inward, and reso-
lutely taking his idea of himself from what purports
to be his image as reflected in the mirror of public
opnion, can scarcely arrive at true self-knowledge,
except through loss of property and reputation. Sick-
ness will not always help him to it; not always the
death-hour!

But our affair now is with Judge Pyncheon as he stood confronting the fierce outbreak of Hepzibah's wrath. Without premeditation, to her own surprise, and even terror, she had given vent, for once, to the inveteracy of her resentment, cherished against this kinsman for thirty years.

Thus far the judge's countenance had expressed mild forbearance—grave and almost gentle deprecation of his cousin's unbecoming violence—free and Christian-like forgiveness of the wrong inflicted by her words. But when those words were irrevocably spoken, his look assumed sternness, the sense of power, and immitigable resolve; and this with so natural and imperceptible a change, that it seemed as if the iron man had stood there from the first, and the meek man not at all. The effect was as when the light vapoury clouds, with their soft colouring, suddenly vanish from the stony brow of a precipitous mountain, and leave there the frown which you at once feel to be eternal. Hepzibah almost adopted the insane belief that it was her old Puritan ancestor, and not the modern judge, on whom she had just been wreaking the bitterness of her heart. Never did a man show stronger proof of the lineage attributed to him than Judge Pyncheon at this crisis, by his unmistakable resemblance to the picture in the inner room.

"Cousin Hepzibah," said he, very calmly, "it is time to have done with this."

"With all my heart!" answered she. "Then why do you persecute us any longer? Leave poor Clifford and me in peace. Neither of us desires anything better!"

"It is my purpose to see Clifford before I leave this house," continued the judge. "Do not act like a mad-woman, Hepzibah! I am his only friend, and an all-powerful one. Has it never occurred to you— are you so blind as not to have seen—that, without not merely my consent, but my efforts, my representations, the exertion of my whole influence, political, official, personal, Clifford would never have been what you call free? Did you think his release a triumph over me? Not so, my good cousin; not so, by any means! The furthest possible from that! No; but it was the accomplishment of a purpose long entertained on my part. I set him free!"

"You!" answered Hepzibah. "I never will believe it! He owed his dungeon to you—his freedom to God's providence!"

"I set him free!" re-affirmed Judge Pyncheon, with the calmest composure. "And I come hither now to decide whether he shall retain his freedom. It will depend upon himself. For this purpose I must see him."

"Never!—it would drive him mad!" exclaimed Hepzibah, but with an irresoluteness sufficiently perceptible to the keen eye of the judge; for, without the slightest faith in his good intentions, she knew not whether there was most to dread in yielding or resistance. "And why should you wish to see this wretched, broken man, who retains hardly a fraction of his intellect, and will hide even that from an eye which has no love in it?"

"He shall see love enough in mine, if that be all!" said the judge, with well-grounded confidence in the benignity of his aspect. "But, Cousin Hepzibah, you confess a great deal, and very much to the purpose. Now, listen, and I will frankly explain my reasons for insisting on this interview. At the death, thirty years since, of our Uncle Jaffrey, it was found—I know not whether the circumstance ever attracted much of your attention, among the sadder interests that clustered round that event—but it was found that his visible estate, of every kind, fell far short of any estimate ever made of it. He was supposed to be immensely rich. Nobody doubted that he stood among the weightiest men of his day. It was one of his eccentricities, however—and not altogether a folly, neither— to conceal the amount of his property by making distant and foreign investments, perhaps under other names than his own, and by various means, familiar enough to capitalists, but unnecessary here to be specified. By Uncle Jaffrey's last will and testament, as you are aware, his entire property was bequeathed to me, with the single exception of a life interest to yourself in this old family mansion, and the strip of patrimonial estate remaining attached to it."

"And do you seek to deprive us of that?" asked Hepzibah, unable to restrain her bitter contempt. "Is this your price for ceasing to persecute poor Clifford?"

"Certainly not, my dear cousin!" answered the judge, smiling benevolently. "On the contrary, as you must do me the justice to own, I have constantly expressed my readiness to double or treble your resources, whenever you should make up your mind to accept any kindness of that nature at the hands of your kinsman. No, no! But here lies the gist of the matter. Of my uncle's unquestionably great estate, as I have said, not the half,—no, not one-third, as I am fully convinced—was apparent after his death. Now, I have the best possible reasons for believing that your brother Clifford can give me a clue to the recovery of the remainder."

"Clifford!—Clifford know of any hidden wealth? —Clifford have it in his power to make you rich?" cried the old gentlewoman, affected with a sense of something like ridicule, at the idea. "Impossible! You deceive yourself! It is really a thing to laugh at!"

"It is as certain as that I stand here!" said Judge Pyncheon, striking his gold-headed cane on the floor, and at the same time stamping his foot, as if to express his conviction the more forcibly by the whole emphasis of his substantial person. "Clifford told me so himself!"

"No, no!" exclaimed Hepzibah, incredulously. "You are dreaming, Cousin Jaffrey!"

"I do not belong to the dreaming class of men,"

said the judge, quietly. " Some months before my
uncle's death, Clifford boasted to me of the possession of the secret of incalculable wealth. His purpose was to taunt me, and excite my curiosity. I
know it well. But, from a pretty distinct recollection of the particulars of our conversation, I am
thoroughly convinced that there was truth in what
he said. Clifford, at this moment, if he chooses—
and choose he must !—can inform me where to find
the schedule, the documents, the evidences, in whatever shape they exist, of the vast amount of Uncle
Jaffrey's missing property. He has the secret. His
boast was no idle word. It had a directness, an
emphasis, a particularity, that showed a back-bone
of solid meaning within the mystery of his expression."

" But what could have been Clifford's object,"
asked Hepzibah, " in concealing it so long?"

" It was one of the bad impulses of our fallen
nature," replied the judge, turning up his eyes.
" He looked upon me as his enemy. He considered
me as the cause of his overwhelming disgrace, his
imminent peril of death, his irretrievable ruin. There
was no great probability, therefore, of his volunteer-
ing information, out of his dungeon, that should
elevate me still higher on the ladder of prosperity.
But the moment has now come when he must give up
his secret."

"And what if he should refuse?" inquired Hepzibah. " Or—as I steadfastly believe—what if he has
no knowledge of this wealth?"

" My dear cousin," said Judge Pyncheon, with a
quietude which he had the power of making more
formidable than any violence, " since your brother's
return I have taken the precaution (a highly proper
one in the near kinsman and natural guardian of an
individual so situated) to have his deportment and
habit constantly and carefully overlooked. Your
neighbours have been eye-witnesses to whatever has
passed in the garden. The butcher, the baker, the

fishmonger, some of the customers of your shop, and many a prying old woman, have told me several of the secrets of your interior. A still larger circle—I myself, among the rest—can testify to his extravagancies at the arched window. Thousands beheld him, a week or two ago, on the point of flinging himself thence into the street. From all this testimony I am led to apprehend—reluctantly and with deep grief—that Clifford's misfortunes have so affected his intellect, never very strong, that he cannot safely remain at large. The alternative, you must be aware—and its adoption will depend entirely on the decision which I am now about to make—the alternative is his confinement, probably for the remainder of his life, in a public asylum for persons in his unfortunate state of mind."

"You cannot mean it!" shrieked Hepzibah.

"Should my cousin Clifford," continued Judge Pyncheon, wholly undisturbed, "from mere malice, and hatred of one whose interests ought naturally to be dear to him,—a mode of passion that, as often as any other, indicates mental disease,—should he refuse me the information so important to myself, and which he assuredly possesses, I shall consider it the one needed jot of evidence to satisfy my mind of his insanity. And, once sure of the course pointed out by conscience, you know me too well, Cousin Hepzibah, to entertain a doubt that I shall pursue it."

"O, Jaffrey—Cousin Jaffrey!" cried Hepzibah, mournfully, not passionately, "it is you that are diseased in mind, not Clifford! You have forgotten that a woman was your mother!—that you have had sisters, brothers, children of your own!—or that there ever was affection between man and man, or pity from one man to another, in this miserable world! Else how could you have dreamed of this? You are not young, Cousin Jaffrey!—no, nor middle-aged,—but already an old man! The hair is white upon your head! How many years have you to live?

Are you not rich enough for that little time? Shall you be hungry? Shall you lack clothes, or a roof to shelter you, between this point and the grave? No! but with the half of what you now possess, you could revel in costly food and wines, and build a house twice as splendid as you now inhabit, and make a far greater show to the world,—and yet leave riches to your only son to make him bless the hour of your death! Then, why should you do this cruel, cruel thing!—so mad a thing that I know not whether to call it wicked! Alas, Cousin Jaffrey, this hard and grasping spirit has run in our blood these two hundred years! You are but doing over again, in another shape, what your ancestor before you did, and sending down to your posterity the curse inherited from him!"

"Talk sense, Hepzibah, for Heaven's sake!" exclaimed the judge, with the impatience natural to a reasonable man on hearing anything so utterly absurd as the above, in a discussion about matters of business. "I have told you my determination. I am not apt to change. Clifford must give up his secret, or take the consequences. And let him decide quickly; for I have several affairs to attend to this morning, and an important dinner engagement with some political friends."

"Clifford has no secret!" answered Hepzibah. "And God will not let you do the thing you meditate."

"We shall see," said the unmoved judge. "Meanwhile, choose whether you will summon Clifford, and allow this business to be amicably settled by an interview between two kinsmen, or drive me to harsher measures, which I should be most happy to feel myself justified in avoiding. The responsibility is altogether on your part."

"You are stronger than I," said Hepzibah, after a brief consideration; "and you have no pity in your strength! Clifford is not now insane; but the interview which you insist upon may go far to make him so. Nevertheless, knowing you as I do, I believe it to be my best course to allow you to judge for yourself as to the improbability of his possessing any valuable secret. I will call Clifford. Be merciful in your dealings with him!—be far more merciful than your heart bids you be!—for God is looking at you, Jaffrey Pyncheon!"

The judge followed his cousin from the shop, where the foregoing conversation had passed, into the parlour, and flung himself heavily into the great ancestral chair. Many a former Pyncheon had found repose in its capacious arms:—rosy children, after their sports; young men, dreamy with love; grown men, weary with cares; old men, burthened with winters;—they had mused, and slumbered, and departed to a yet profounder sleep. It had been a long tradition, though a doubtful one, that this was the very chair, seated in which, the earliest of the judge's New England forefathers—he whose picture still hung upon the wall—had given a dead man's silent and stern reception to the throng of distinguished guests. From that hour of evil omen, until the present, it may be,—though we know not the secret of his heart,—but it may be that no wearier and sadder man had ever sunk into the chair than this same Judge Pyncheon, whom we have just beheld so immitigably hard and resolute. Surely, it must have been at no slight cost that he had thus fortified his soul with iron. Such calmness is a mightier effort than the violence of weaker men. And there was yet a heavy task for him to do. Was it a little matter,—a trifle to be prepared for in a single moment, and to be rested from in another moment—that he must now, after thirty years, encounter a kinsman risen from a living tomb, and wrench a secret from him, or else consign him to a living tomb again?

" Did you speak?" asked Hepzibah, looking in from the threshold of the parlour; for she imagined that the judge had uttered some sound which she

was anxious to interpret as a relenting impulse.
"I thought you called me back."

"No, no!" gruffly answered Judge Pyncheon,
with a harsh frown, while his brow grew almost a
black purple, in the shadow of the room. "Why
should I call you back? Time flies! Bid Clifford
come to me!"

The judge had taken his watch from his vest-
pocket, and now held it in his hand, measuring the
interval which was to ensue before the appearance
of Clifford.

XVI

CLIFFORD'S CHAMBER

NEVER had the old house appeared so dismal to
poor Hepzibah as when she departed on that
wretched errand. There was a strange aspect in it.
As she strode along the foot-worn passages, and
opened one crazy door after another, and ascended
the creaking staircase, she gazed wistfully and fear-
fully around. It would have been no marvel, to her
excited mind, if, behind or beside her, there had
been the rustle of dead people's garments, or pale
visages awaiting her on the landing-place above.
Her nerves were set all ajar by the scene of passion
and terror through which she had just struggled.
Her colloquy with Judge Pyncheon, who so perfectly
represented the person and attributes of the founder
of the family, had called back the dreary past. It
weighed upon her heart. Whatever she had heard,
from legendary aunts and grandmothers, concern-
ing the good or evil fortunes of the Pyncheons,—
stories which had heretofore been kept warm in her
remembrance by the chimney-corner glow that was
associated with them,—now recurred to her, sombre,

ghastly, cold, like most passages of family history, when brooded over in melancholy mood. The whole seemed little else but a series of calamity, reproducing itself in successive generations, with one general hue, and varying in little, save the outline. But Hepzibah now felt as if the judge, and Clifford, and herself,—they three together,—were on the point of adding another incident to the annals of the house, with a bolder relief of wrong and sorrow, which would cause it to stand out from all the rest. Thus it is that the grief of the passing moment takes upon itself an individuality, and a character of climax, which it is destined to lose, after a while, and to fade into the dark gray tissue common to the grave or glad events of many years ago. It is but for a moment, comparatively, that anything looks strange or startling;—a truth that has the bitter and the sweet in it.

But Hepzibah could not rid herself of the sense of something unprecedented at that instant passing, and soon to be accomplished. Her nerves were in a shake. Instinctively she paused before the arched window, and looked out upon the street, in order to seize its permanent objects with her mental grasp, and thus to steady herself from the reel and vibration which affected her more immediate sphere. It brought her up, as we may say, with a kind of shock, when she beheld everything under the same appearance as the day before, and numberless preceding days, except for the difference between sunshine and storm. Her eyes travelled along the street, from door-step to door-step, noting the wet side-walks, with here and there a puddle in hollows that had been imperceptible until filled with water. She screwed her dim optics to their acutest point, in the hope of making out, with greater distinctness, a certain window, where she half saw, half guessed, that a tailor's seamstress was sitting at her work. Hepzibah flung herself upon that unknown woman's companionship, even thus far off. Then she was

attracted by a chaise rapidly passing, and watched
its moist and glistening top, and its splashing wheels,
until it had turned the corner, and refused to carry
any further her idly-trifling, because appalled and
overburthened, mind.   When the vehicle had disappeared, she allowed herself still another loitering
moment; for the patched figure of good Uncle Venner
was now visible, coming slowly from the head of the
street downward, with a rheumatic limp, because the
east wind had got into his joints.   Hepzibah wished
that he would pass yet more slowly, and befriend her
shivering solitude a little longer.   Anything that
would take her out of the grievous present, and
interpose human beings betwixt herself and what
was nearest to her,—whatever would defer, for an
instant, the inevitable errand on which she was
bound,— all such impediments were welcome.   Next
to the lightest heart, the heaviest is apt to be most
playful.

Hepzibah had little hardihood for her own proper
pain, and far less for what she must inflict on Clifford.   Of so slight a nature, and so shattered by his
previous calamities, it could not well be short of
utter ruin to bring him face to face with the hard,
relentless man, who had been his evil destiny through
life.   Even had there been no bitter recollections,
nor any hostile interest now at stake between them,
the mere natural repugnance of the more sensitive
system to the massive, weighty, and unimpressible
one, must, in itself, have been disastrous to the
former.   It would be like flinging a porcelain vase,
with already a crack in it, against a granite column.
Never before had Hepzibah so adequately estimated
the powerful character of her cousin Jaffrey,—
powerful by intellect, energy of will, the long habit
of acting among men, and, as she believed, by his
unscrupulous pursuit of selfish ends through evil
means.   It did but increase the difficulty, that Judge
Pyncheon was under a delusion as to the secret which
he supposed Clifford to possess.   Men of his strength

of purpose and customary sagacity, if they chance to adopt a mistaken opinion in practical matters, so wedge it and fasten it among things known to be true, that to wrench it out of their minds is hardly less difficult than pulling up an oak. Thus, as the judge required an impossibility of Clifford, the latter, as he could not perform it, must needs perish. For what, in the grasp of a man like this, was to become of Clifford's soft, poetic nature, that never should have had a task more stubborn than to set a life of beautiful enjoyment to the flow and rhythm of musical cadences? Indeed, what had become of it already? Broken! Blighted! All but annihilated! Soon to be wholly so!

For a moment, the thought crossed Hepzibah's mind, whether Clifford might not really have such knowledge of their deceased uncle's vanished estate as the judge imputed to him. She remembered some vague intimations, on her brother's part, which—if the supposition were not essentially preposterous—might have been so interpreted. There had been schemes of travel and residence abroad, day-dreams of brilliant life at home, and splendid castles in the air, which it would have required boundless wealth to build and realize. Had this wealth been in her power, how gladly would Hepzibah have bestowed it all upon her iron-hearted kinsman, to buy for Clifford the freedom and seclusion of the desolate old house! But she believed that her brother's schemes were as destitute of actual substance and purpose as a child's pictures of its future life, while sitting in a little chair by its mother's knee. Clifford had none but shadowy gold at his command; and it was not the stuff to satisfy Judge Pyncheon!

Was there no help in their extremity? It seemed strange that there should be none, with a city round about her. It would be so easy to throw up the window, and send forth a shriek, at the strange agony of which everybody would come hastening to the rescue, well understanding it to be the cry of a human

soul, at some dreadful crisis! But how wild, how
almost laughable the fatality,—and yet how continually it comes to pass, thought Hepzibah, in this
dull delirium of a world,—that whosoever, and with
however kindly a purpose, should come to help, they
would be sure to help the strongest side! Might and
wrong combined, like iron magnetized, are endowed
with irresistible attraction. There would be Judge
Pyncheon—a person eminent in the public view, of
high station and great wealth, a philanthropist, a
member of congress and of the church, and intimately
associated with whatever else bestows good name,
—so imposing, in these advantageous lights, that
Hepzibah herself could hardly help shrinking from
her own conclusions as to his hollow integrity. The
judge on one side! And who on the other? The
guilty Clifford! Once a by-word! Now, an
indistinctly-remembered ignominy!

Nevertheless, in spite of this perception that the
judge would draw all human aid to his own behalf,
Hepzibah was so unaccustomed to act for herself,
that the least word of counsel would have swayed
her to any mode of action. Little Phœbe Pyncheon
would at once have lighted up the whole scene, if
not by any available suggestion, yet simply by the
warm vivacity of her character. The idea of the
artist occurred to Hepzibah. Young and unknown,
mere vagrant adventurer as he was, she had been
conscious of a force in Holgrave which might well
adapt him to be the champion of a crisis. With this
thought in her mind, she unbolted a door, cobwebbed
and long disused, but which had served as a former
medium of communication between her own part of
the house and the gable where the wandering daguerreotypist had now established his temporary home.
He was not there. A book, face downward, on the
table, a roll of manuscript, a half-written sheet, a
newspaper, some tools of his present occupation, and
several rejected daguerreotypes, conveyed an impression as if he were close at hand. But at this

period of the day, as Hepzibah might have anticipated, the artist was at his public rooms. With an
impulse of idle curiosity that flickered among her
heavy thoughts, she looked at one of the daguerreotypes, and beheld Judge Pyncheon frowning at her!
Fate stared her in the face. She turned back from
her fruitless quest, with a heart-sinking sense of
disappointment. In all her years of seclusion, she
had never felt, as now, what it was to be alone. It
seemed as if the house stood in a desert, or by some
spell was made invisible to those who dwelt around,
or passed beside it; so that any mode of misfortune,
miserable accident, or crime, might happen in it,
without the possibility of aid. In her grief and
wounded pride, Hepzibah had spent her life in divesting herself of friends;—she had wilfully cast off the
support which God has ordained His creatures to need
from one another;—and it was now her punishment,
that Clifford and herself would fall the easier victims
to their kindred enemy.

Returning to the arched window, she lifted her
eyes—scowling, poor, dim-sighted Hepzibah, in the
face of heaven!—and strove hard to send up a prayer
through the dense gray pavement of clouds. Those
mists had gathered, as if to symbolize a great, brooding mass of human trouble, doubt, confusion, and
chill indifference, between earth and the better
regions. Her faith was too weak, the prayer too
heavy to be thus uplifted. It fell back a lump of
lead upon her heart. It smote her with the wretched
conviction, that Providence intermeddled not in these
petty wrongs of one individual to his fellow, nor had
any balm for these little agonies of a solitary soul;
but shed its justice and its mercy, in a broad, sun-
like sweep, over half the universe at once. Its vast-
ness made it nothing. But Hepzibah did not see
that, just as there comes a warm sunbeam into every
cottage window, so comes a love-beam of God's care
and pity, for every separate need.

At last, finding no other pretext for deferring the

torture that she was to inflict on Clifford—her reluctance to which was the true cause of her loitering at
the window, her search for the artist, and even her
abortive prayer—dreading, also, to hear the stern
voice of Judge Pyncheon from below stairs, chiding
her delay—she crept slowly, a pale, grief-stricken
figure, a dismal shape of woman, with almost torpid
limbs, slowly to her brother's door and knocked!

There was no reply!

And how should there have been? Her hand,
tremulous with the shrinking purpose which directed
it, had smitten so feebly against the door, that the
sound could hardly have gone inward. She knocked
again. Still no response! Nor was it to be wondered at. She had struck with the entire force of
her heart's vibration, communicating, by some subtle
magnetism, her own terror to the summons. Clifford
would turn his face to the pillow, and cover his
head beneath the bed-clothes, like a startled child
at midnight. She knocked a third time three regular
strokes, gentle, but perfectly distinct, and with meaning in them; for, modulate it with what cautious art
we will, the hand cannot help playing some tune of
what we feel upon the senseless wood.

Clifford returned no answer.

" Clifford! dear brother!" said Hepzibah. " Shall
I come in?"

A silence.

Two or three times, and more, Hepzibah repeated
his name without result; till thinking her brother's
sleep unwontedly profound, she undid the door, and
entering, found the chamber vacant. How could he
have come forth, and when, without her knowledge?
Was it possible that, in spite of the stormy day, and
worn out with the irksomeness within doors, he had
betaken himself to his customary haunt in the
garden, and was now shivering under the cheerless
shelter of the summer-house? She hastily threw up
a window, thrust forth her turbaned head and the
half of her gaunt figure, and searched the whole

garden through, as completely as her dim vision
would allow.　She could see the interior of the summer-house, and its circular seat kept moist by the
droppings of the roof.　It had no occupant.　Clifford
was not thereabouts, unless indeed he had crept for
concealment—(as for a moment Hepzibah fancied
might be the case)—into a great wet mass of tangled
and broad-leaved shadow, where the squash-vines
were clambering tumultuously upon an old wooden
frame-work, set casually aslant against the fence.
This could not be, however; he was not there; for
while Hepzibah was looking, a strange grimalkin
stole forth from the very spot, and picked his way
across the garden.　Twice he paused to snuff the air,
and then anew directed his course to the parlour-
window.　Whether it was only on account of the
stealthy prying manner common to the race, or that
this cat seemed to have more than ordinary mischief
in his thoughts, the old gentlewoman, in spite of
her much perplexity, felt an impulse to drive the
animal away, and accordingly flung down a window-
stick.　The cat stared up at her, like a detected thief
or murderer, and the next instant took to flight.　No
other living creature was visible in the garden.
Chanticleer and his family had either not left their
roost, disheartened by the interminable rain, or had
done the next wisest thing, by seasonably returning
to it.　Hepzibah closed the window.

But where was Clifford?　Could it be, that, aware
of the presence of his Evil Destiny, he had crept
silently down the staircase, while the judge and
Hepzibah stood talking in the shop, and had softly
undone the fastenings of the outer door, and made
his escape into the street?　With that thought, she
seemed to behold his gray, wrinkled, yet childlike
aspect, in the old-fashioned garments which he wore
about the house; a figure such as one sometimes
imagines himself to be, with the world's eye upon
him, in a troubled dream.　This figure of her
wretched brother would go wandering through the

city, attracting all eyes, and everybody's wonder and
repugnance, like a ghost, the more to be shuddered
at because visible at noontide. To incur the ridicule
of the younger crowd, that knew him not—the
harsher scorn and indignation of a few old men,
who might recall his once familiar features! To be
the sport of boys, who, when old enough to run
about the streets, have no more reverence for what
is beautiful and holy, nor pity for what is sad—no
more sense of sacred misery, sanctifying the human
shape in which it embodies itself—than if Satan were
the father of them all! Goaded by their taunts, their
loud shrill cries, and cruel laughter—insulted by the
filth of the public ways, which they would fling upon
him—or, as it might well be, distracted by the mere
strangeness of his situation, though nobody should
afflict him with so much as a thoughtless word—
what wonder if Clifford were to break into some wild
extravagance, which was certain to be interpreted
as lunacy? Thus Judge Pyncheon's fiendish scheme
would be ready accomplished to his hands!

Then Hepzibah reflected that the town was almost
completely water-girdled. The wharves stretched
out towards the centre of the harbour, and, in this
inclement weather, were deserted by the ordinary
throng of merchants, labourers, and seafaring men;
each wharf a solitude, with the vessels moored stem
and stern, along its misty length. Should her
brother's aimless footsteps stray thitherward, and he
but bend one moment over the deep, black tide,
would he not bethink himself that here was the sure
refuge within his reach, and that, with a single step,
or the slightest overbalance of his body, he might be
for ever beyond his kinsman's gripe? O, the temptation! To make of his ponderous sorrow a security!
To sink, with its leaden weight upon him, and never
rise again!

The horror of this last conception was too much
for Hepzibah. Even Jaffrey Pyncheon must help her

now! She hastened down the staircase, shrieking as she went.

"Clifford is gone!" she cried. "I cannot find my brother! Help, Jaffrey Pyncheon! Some harm will happen to him!"

She threw open the parlour door. But, what with the shade of branches across the windows, and the smoke-blackened ceiling, and the dark oak-panelling of the walls, there was hardly so much daylight in the room that Hepzibah's imperfect sight could accurately distinguish the judge's figure. She was certain, however, that she saw him sitting in the ancestral arm-chair, near the centre of the floor, with his face somewhat averted, and looking towards a window. So firm and quiet is the nervous system of such men as Judge Pyncheon, that he had perhaps stirred not more than once since her departure, but, in the hard composure of his temperament, retained the position into which accident had thrown him.

"I tell you, Jaffrey," cried Hepzibah, impatiently, as she turned from the parlour-door to search other rooms, "my brother is not in the chamber! You must help me seek him!"

But Judge Pyncheon was not the man to let himself be startled from an easy-chair with haste ill-befitting either the dignity of his character or his broad personal basis, by the alarm of an hysteric woman. Yet considering his own interest in the matter, he might have bestirred himself with a little more alacrity.

"Do you hear me, Jaffrey Pyncheon?" screamed Hepzibah, as she again approached the parlour-door, after an ineffectual search elsewhere. "Clifford is gone!"

At this instant, on the threshold of the parlour, emerging from within, appeared Clifford himself! His face was preternaturally pale; so deadly white, indeed, that, through all the glimmering indistinctness of the passage-way, Hepzibah could discern his

features, as if a light fell on them alone. Their vivid
and wild expression seemed likewise sufficient to
illuminate them; it was an expression of scorn and
mockery, coinciding with the emotions indicated by
his gesture. As Clifford stood on the threshold,
partly turning back, he pointed his finger within the
parlour, and shook it slowly, as though he would
have summoned, not Hepzibah alone, but the whole
world, to gaze at some object inconceivably ridiculous.
This action, so ill-timed and extravagant—accompanied, too, with a look that showed more like joy
than any other kind of excitement—compelled Hepzibah to dread that her stern kinsman's ominous visit
had driven her poor brother to absolute insanity. Nor
could she otherwise account for the judge's quiescent
mood than by supposing him craftily on the watch,
while Clifford developed these symptoms of a distracted mind.

" Be quiet, Clifford!" whispered his sister, raising
her hand, to impress caution. " O, for Heaven's
sake, be quiet!"

" Let him be quiet! What can he do better?"
answered Clifford, with a still wider gesture, pointing to the room which he had just quitted. " As
for us, Hepzibah, we can dance now!—we can
sing, laugh, play, do what we will! The weight
is gone, Hepzibah! it is gone off this weary old
world; and we may be as light-hearted as little Phœbe
herself!"

And, in accordance with these words, he began to
laugh, still pointing his finger at the object, invisible
to Hepzibah, within the parlour. She was seized
with a sudden intuition of some horrible thing. She
thrust herself past Clifford, and disappeared into the
room; but almost immediately returned, with a cry
choking in her throat. Gazing at her brother, with
an affrighted glance of inquiry, she beheld him all
in a tremor and a quake, from head to foot, while
amid these commoted elements of passion or alarm,
still flickered his gusty mirth.

" My God! what is to become of us?" gasped Hepzibah.

" Come!" said Clifford, in a tone of brief decision, most unlike what was usual with him. " We stay here too long! Let us leave the old house to our cousin Jaffrey! He will take good care of it!"

Hepzibah now noticed that Clifford had on a cloak —a garment of long ago—in which he had constantly muffled himself during these days of easterly storm. He beckoned with his hand, and intimated, so far as she could comprehend him, his purpose that they should go together from the house. There are chaotic, blind, or drunken moments, in the lives of persons who lack real force of character—moments of test, in which courage would most assert itself— but where these individuals, if left to themselves, stagger aimlessly along, or follow implicitly whatever guidance may befall them, even if it be a child's. No matter how preposterous or insane, a purpose is a god-send to them. Hepzibah had reached this point. Unaccustomed to action or responsibility— full of horror at what she had seen, and afraid to inquire, almost to imagine, how it had come to pass —affrighted at the fatality which seemed to pursue her brother—stupefied by the dim, thick, stifling atmosphere of dread, which filled the house as with a death-smell, and obliterated all definiteness of thought—she yielded without a question, and on the instant, to the will which Clifford expressed. For herself, she was like a person in a dream, when the will always sleeps. Clifford, ordinarily so destitute of this faculty, had found it in the tension of the crisis.

" Why do you delay so?' cried he sharply. " Put on your cloak and hood, or whatever it pleases you to wear! No matter what;—you cannot look beautiful nor brilliant, my poor Hepzibah! Take your purse, with money in it, and come along!"

Hepzibah obeyed these instructions, as if nothing else were to be done or thought of. She began to

wonder, it is true, why she did not wake up, and at
what still more intolerable pitch of dizzy trouble her
spirit would struggle out of the maze, and make her
conscious that nothing of all this had actually happened. Of course it was not real; no such black,
easterly day as this had yet begun to be; Judge Pyncheon had not talked with her; Clifford had not
laughed, pointed, beckoned her away with him; but
she had merely been afflicted—as lonely sleepers often
are—with a great deal of unreasonable misery, in a
morning dream!

"Now—now—I shall certainly awake!" thought
Hepzibah, as she went to and fro, making her little
preparations. "I can bear it no longer! I must
wake up now!"

But it came not, that awakening moment! It came
not, even when, just before they left the house, Clifford stole to the parlour-door, and made a parting
obeisance to the sole occupant of the room.

"What an absurd figure the old fellow cuts now!"
whispered he to Hepzibah. "Just when he fancied
he had me completely under his thumb! Come,
come; make haste! or he will start up, like Giant
Despair in pursuit of Christian and Hopeful, and
catch us yet!"

As they passed into the street, Clifford directed
Hepzibah's attention to something on one of the
posts of the front door. It was merely the initials
of his own name, which, with somewhat of his
characteristic grace about the forms of the letters,
he had cut there, when a boy. The brother and sister
departed, and left Judge Pyncheon sitting in the old
home of his forefathers, all by himself; so heavy and
lumpish that we can liken him to nothing better than
a defunct nightmare, which had perished in the
midst of its wickedness, and left its flabby corpse on
the breast of the tormented one, to be gotten rid
of as it might!

XVII

THE FLIGHT OF TWO OWLS

SUMMER as it was, the east wind set poor Hepzi-bah's few remaining teeth chattering in her head, as she and Clifford faced it on their way up Pyncheon-street and towards the centre of the town. Not merely was it the shiver which this pitiless blast brought to her frame (although her feet and hands, especially, had never seemed so death-a-cold as now), but there was a moral sensation, mingling itself with the physical chill, and causing her to shake more in spirit than in body. The world's broad, bleak atmosphere was all so comfortless! Such, indeed, is the impression which it makes on every new adven-turer, even if he plunge into it while the warmest tide of life is bubbling through his veins. What, then, must it have been to Hepzibah and Clifford,— so time-stricken as they were, yet so like children in their inexperience,—as they left the door-step, and passed from beneath the wide shelter of the Pyn-cheon-elm! They were wandering all abroad, on precisely such a pilgrimage as a child often meditates, to the world's end, with perhaps a sixpence and a biscuit in his pocket. In Hepzibah's mind there was the wretched consciousness of being adrift. She had lost the faculty of self-guidance; but, in view of the difficulties around her, felt it hardly worth an effort to regain it, and was, moreover, incapable of making one.

As they proceeded on their strange expedition, she now and then cast a look sidelong at Clifford, and could not but observe that he was possessed and swayed by a powerful excitement. It was this, in-deed, that gave him the control which he had at once, and so irresistibly, established over his movements. It not a little resembled the exhilaration of wine. Or it might more fancifully be compared to a joyous piece of music, played with wild vivacity, but upon a disordered instrument. As the cracked jarring note might always be heard, and as it jarred loudest amidst the loftiest exultation of the melody, so was there a continual quake through Clifford, causing him most to quiver while he wore a triumphant smile, and seemed almost under a necessity to skip in his gait.

They met few people abroad, even on passing from the retired neighbourhood of the House of the Seven Gables into what was ordinarily the more thronged and busier portion of the town. Glistening side-walks, with little pools of rain here and there along their unequal surface; umbrellas displayed ostentatiously in the shop-windows, as if the life of trade had concentrated itself in that one article; wet leaves of the horse-chestnut or elm trees, torn off untimely by the blast and scattered along the public way; an unsightly accumulation of mud in the middle of the street, which perversely grew the more unclean for its long and laborious washing;—these were the more definable points of a very sombre picture. In the way of movement and human life, there was the hasty rattle of a cab or coach, its driver protected by a water-proof cap over his head and shoulders; the forlorn figure of an old man, who seemed to have crept out of some subterranean sewer, and was stooping along the kennel, and poking the wet rubbish with a stick, in quest of rusty nails; a merchant or two at the door of the post-office, together with an editor, and a miscellaneous politician, awaiting a dilatory mail; a few visages of retired sea-captains at the window of an insurance office, looking out vacantly at the vacant street, blaspheming at the weather, and fretting at the dearth as well of public news as local gossip. What a treasure-trove to these venerable quid-nuncs, could they have guessed the secret which Hepzibah and Clifford were carrying along with them! But their two figures attracted hardly so much notice as that of a young girl, who passed at the same instant, and happened to raise her skirt a trifle too high above her ankles. Had it been a sunny and cheerful day they could hardly have gone through the streets without making themselves obnoxious to remark. Now, probably, they were felt to be in keeping with the dismal and bitter weather, and therefore did not stand out in strong relief, as if the sun were shining on them, but melted into the gray gloom, and were forgotten as soon as gone.

Poor Hepzibah! Could she have understood this fact, it would have brought her some little comfort; for, to all her other troubles—strange to say!—there was added the womanish and old-maiden-like misery arising from a sense of unseemliness in her attire. Thus, she was fain to shrink deeper into herself, as it were, as if in the hope of making people suppose that here was only a cloak and hood, threadbare and wofully faded, taking an airing in the midst of the storm, without any wearer!

As they went on, the feeling of indistinctness and unreality kept dimly hovering round about her, and so diffusing itself into her system that one of her hands was hardly palpable to the touch of the other. Any certainty would have been preferable to this. She whispered to herself, again and again—" Am I awake?—Am I awake?" and sometimes exposed her face to the chill spatter of the wind, for the sake of its rude assurance that she was. Whether it was Clifford's purpose, or only chance, had led them thither, they now found themselves passing beneath the arched entrance of a large structure of gray stone. Within, there was a spacious breadth, and an airy height from floor to floor, now partially filled with smoke and steam, which eddied voluminously upward, and formed a mimic cloud-region over their heads. A train of cars was just ready for a start; the locomotive was fretting and fuming, like a steed impatient for a headlong rush; and the bell rang out its hasty peal, so well expressing the brief summons which life vouchsafes to us, in its hurried career.

Without question or delay—with the irresistible decision, if not rather to be called recklessness, which had so strangely taken possession of him, and through him of Hepzibah—Clifford impelled her towards the cars, and assisted her to enter. The signal was given; the engine puffed forth its short, quick breaths; the train began its movement; and, along with a hundred other passengers, these two unwonted travellers sped onward like the wind.

At last, therefore, and after so long estrangement from everything that the world acted or enjoyed, they had been drawn into the great current of human life, and were swept away with it, as by the suction of fate itself.

Still haunted with the idea that not one of the past incidents, inclusive of Judge Pyncheon's visit, could be real, the recluse of the seven gables murmured in her brother's ear—

"Clifford! Clifford! Is not this a dream?"

"A dream, Hepzibah!" repeated he, almost laughing in her face. "On the contrary, I have never been awake before!"

Meanwhile, looking from the window, they could see the world racing past them. At one moment they were rattling through a solitude; the next, a village had grown up around them; a few breaths more and it had vanished, as if swallowed by an earthquake. The spires of meeting-houses seemed set adrift from their foundations; the broad-based hills glided away. Everything was unfixed from its age-long rest, and moving at whirlwind speed in a direction opposite to their own.

Within the car, there was the usual interior life of the railroad, offering little to the observation of other passengers, but full of novelty for this pair of strangely enfranchised prisoners. It was novelty enough, indeed, that there were fifty human beings in close relation with them, under one long and narrow roof, and drawn onward by the same mighty influence that had taken their two selves into its grasp. It seemed marvellous how all these people could remain so quietly in their seats, while so much noisy strength was at work in their behalf. Some, with tickets in their hats (long travellers these, before whom lay a hundred miles of railroad), had plunged into the English scenery and adventures of pamphlet novels, and were keeping company with dukes and earls. Others, whose briefer span forbade their devoting themselves to studies so abstruse, beguiled their little tedium of the way with penny-papers. A party of girls, and one young man, on opposite sides of the car, found huge amusement in a game of ball. They tossed it to and fro, with peals of laughter that might be measured by mile-lengths; for, faster than the nimble ball could fly, the merry players fled unconsciously along, leaving the trail of their mirth afar behind, and ending their game under another sky than had witnessed its commencement. Boys with apples, cakes, candy, and rolls of variously tinctured lozenges —merchandize that reminded Hepzibah of her deserted shop—appeared at each momentary stopping-place, doing up their business in a hurry, or breaking it short off, lest the market should ravish them away with it. New people continually entered. Old acquaintances—for such they soon grew to be, in this rapid current of affairs—continually departed. Here and there, amid the rumble and the tumult, sat one asleep. Sleep; sport; business; graver or lighter study; and the common and inevitable movement onward! It was life itself!

Clifford's naturally poignant sympathies were all aroused. He caught the colour of what was passing about him, and threw it back more vividly than he received it, but mixed, nevertheless, with a lurid and portentous hue. Hepzibah, on the other hand, felt herself more apart from human kind than even in the seclusion which she had just quitted.

"You are not happy, Hepzibah!" said Clifford, apart, in a tone of reproach. "You are thinking of that dismal old house, and of Cousin Jaffrey,"—here came the quake through him—" and of Cousin Jaffrey sitting there, all by himself! Take my advice— follow my example—and let such things slip aside. Here we are in the world, Hepzibah!—in the midst of life!—in the throng of our fellow beings! Let you and I be happy! As happy as that youth, and those pretty girls, at their game of ball!"

"Happy!" thought Hepzibah, bitterly conscious, at the word, of her dull and heavy heart, with the frozen pain in it. "Happy! He is mad already; and if I could once feel myself broad awake, I should go mad too!"

If a fixed idea be madness, she was perhaps not remote from it. Fast and far as they had rattled and clattered along the iron track, they might just as well, as regarded Hepzibah's mental images, have been passing up and down Pyncheon-street. With miles and miles of varied scenery between, there was no scene for her, save the seven old gable-peaks, with their moss, and the tuft of weeds in one of the angles, and the shop-window, and a customer shaking the door, and compelling the little bell to jingle fiercely, but without disturbing Judge Pyncheon! This one old house was everywhere! It transported its great, lumbering bulk, with more than railroad speed, and set itself phlegmatically down on whatever spot she glanced at. The quality of Hepzibah's mind was too unmalleable to take new impressions so readily as Clifford's. He had a winged nature; she was rather of the vegetable kind, and could hardly be kept long alive, if drawn up by the roots. Thus it happened that the relation heretofore existing between her brother and herself was changed. At home, she was his guardian; here, Clifford had become hers, and seemed to comprehend whatever belonged to their new position with a singular rapidity of intelligence. He had been startled into manhood and intellectual vigour; or at least, into a condition that resembled them, though it might be both diseased and transitory.

The conductor now applied for their tickets; and Clifford, who had made himself the purse-bearer, put a bank-note into his hand, as he had observed others do.

" For the lady and yourself?" asked the conductor. " And how far?"

" As far as that will carry us," said Clifford. " It is no great matter. We are riding for pleasure merely!"

" You choose a strange day for it, sir!" remarked a gimlet-eyed old gentleman on the other side of the car, looking at Clifford and his companion, as if curious to make them out. " The best chance of pleasure in an easterly rain, I take it, is in a man's own house, with a nice little fire in the chimney."

" I cannot precisely agree with you," said Clifford, courteously bowing to the old gentleman, and at once taking up the clue of conversation which the latter had proffered. " It had just occurred to me, on the contrary, that this admirable invention of the railroad with the vast and inevitable improvements to be looked for, both as to speed and convenience—is destined to do away with those stale ideas of home and fireside, and substitute something better."

" In the name of common sense," asked the old gentleman, rather testily, " what can be better for a man than his own parlour and chimney-corner?"

" These things have not the merit which many good people attribute to them," replied Clifford. " They may be said, in few and pithy words, to have ill-served a poor purpose. My impression is, that our wonderfully increased and still increasing facilities of locomotion are destined to bring us round again to the nomadic state. You are aware, my dear sir—you must have observed it in your own experience—that all human progress is in a circle; or, to use a more accurate and beautiful figure, in an ascending spiral curve. While we fancy ourselves going straight forward, and attaining at every step an entirely new position of affairs, we do actually return to something long ago tried and abandoned, but which we now find etherealized, refined, and perfected to its ideal.   The past is but a coarse and sensual prophecy of the present and the future.   To apply this truth to the topic now under discussion.—In the early epochs of our race, men dwelt in temporary huts, or bowers of branches, as easily constructed as a bird's nest, and which they built—if it should be called building, when such sweet homes of a summer solstice rather grew than were made with hands—which Nature, we will say, assisted them to rear, where fruit abounded, where fish and game were plentiful, or, most especially, where the sense of beauty was to be gratified by a lovelier shade than elsewhere, and a more exquisite arrangement of lake, wood, and hill.   This life possessed a charm which, ever since man quitted it, has vanished from existence.   And it typified something better than itself.   It had its drawbacks ; such as hunger and thirst, inclement weather, hot sunshine, and weary and foot-blistering marches over barren and ugly tracts, that lay between the sites desirable for their fertility and beauty.   But in our ascending spiral we escape all this.   These railroads —could but the whistle be made musical, and the rumble and the jar got rid of—are positively the greatest blessing that the ages have wrought out for us   They give us wings ; they annihilate the toil and dust of pilgrimage ; they spiritualize travel !   Transition being so facile, what can be any man's inducement to tarry in one spot ?   Why, therefore, should he build a more cumbrous habitation than can readily be carried off with him ?   Why should he make himself a prisoner for life in brick, and stone, and old worm-eaten timber, when he may just as easily dwell, in one sense nowhere—in a better sense, wherever the fit and beautiful shall offer him a home ?''

Clifford's countenance glowed as he divulged this theory ; a youthful character shone out from within, converting the wrinkles and pallid duskiness of age into an almost transparent mask.   The merry girls

let their ball drop upon the floor, and gazed at him.
They said to themselves, perhaps, that before his hair
was gray and the crow's feet tracked his temples, this
now decaying man must have stamped the impress
of his features on many a woman's heart.   But, alas!
no woman's eye had seen his face while it was
beautiful!

"I should scarcely call it an improved state of
things," observed Clifford's new acquaintance, "to
live everywhere and nowhere!"

"Would you not?" exclaimed Clifford, with
singular energy.   "It is as clear to me as sunshine—
were there any in the sky—that the greatest possible
stumbling-blocks in the path of human happiness and
improvement are these heaps of bricks and stones,
consolidated with mortar, or hewn timber, fastened
together with spike-nails, which men painfully contrive for their own torment, and call them house and
home!   The soul needs air; a wide sweep and frequent change of it.   Morbid influences, in a thousand-
fold variety, gather about hearths, and pollute the
life of households.   There is no such unwholesome
atmosphere as that of an old home, rendered poison-
ous by one's defunct forefathers and relatives.   I
speak of what I know.   There is a certain house
within my familiar recollection—one of those peaked-
gable (there are seven of them) projecting-storied
edifices, such as you occasionally see in our elder
towns—a rusty, crazy, creaky, dry-rotted, damp-
rotted, dingy, dark, and miserable old dungeon, with
an arched window over the porch, and a little shop-
door on one side, and a great, melancholy elm before
it!   Now, sir, whenever my thoughts recur to this
seven-gabled mansion—(the fact is so very curious
that I must needs mention it)—immediately I have a
vision or image of an elderly man, of remarkably
stern countenance, sitting in an oaken elbow-chair,
dead, stone-dead, with an ugly flow of blood upon his
shirt-bosom!   Dead, but with open eyes!   He taints
the whole house, as I remember it.   I could never

flourish there, nor be happy, nor do nor enjoy what God meant me to do and enjoy !"

His face darkened, and seemed to contract, and shrivel itself up, and wither into age.

" Never, sir !" he repeated. " I could never draw cheerful breath there !"

" I should think not," said the old gentleman, eyeing Clifford earnestly and rather apprehensively. " I should conceive not, sir, with that notion in your head !"

" Surely not," continued Clifford ; " and it were a relief to me if that house could be torn down, or burnt up, and so the earth be rid of it, and grass be sown abundantly over its foundation. Not that I should ever visit its site again ! for, sir, the further I get away from it, the more does the joy, the lightsome freshness, the heart-leap, the intellectual dance, the youth, in short—yes, my youth, my youth !—the more does it come back to me. No longer ago than this morning, I was old. I remember looking in the glass, and wondering at my own gray hair, and the wrinkles, many and deep, right across my brow, and the furrows down my cheeks, and the prodigious trampling of crow's feet about my temples ! It was too soon ! I could not bear it ! Age had no right to come ! I had not lived ! But now do I look old ? If so, my aspect belies me strangely ; for—a great weight being off my mind—I feel in the very hey-day of my youth, with the world and my best days before me !"

" I trust you may find it so," said the old gentleman, who seemed rather embarrassed, and desirous of avoiding the observation which Clifford's wild talk drew on them both. " You have my best wishes for it."

" For Heaven's sake, dear Clifford, be quiet !" whispered his sister. " They think you mad."

" Be quiet yourself, Hepzibah !" returned her brother. " No matter what they think ! I am not mad. For the first time in thirty years, my thoughts gush up and find words ready for them.   I must talk, and I will !''

He turned again towards the old gentleman, and renewed the conversation.

" Yes, my dear sir,'' said he, " it is my firm belief and hope, that these terms of roof and hearth-stone, which have so long been held to embody something sacred, are soon to pass out of men's daily use, and be forgotten.   Just imagine, for a moment, how much of human evil will crumble away with this one change !   What we call real estate—the solid ground to build a house on—is the broad foundation on which nearly all the guilt of this world rests.   A man will commit almost any wrong—he will heap up an immense pile of wickedness, as hard as granite, and which will weigh as heavily upon his soul, to eternal ages—only to build a great, gloomy, dark-chambered mansion, for himself to die in, and for his posterity to be miserable in.   He lays his own dead corpse beneath the underpinning, as one may say, and hangs his frowning picture on the wall, and, after thus converting himself into an evil destiny, expects his remotest great-grandchildren to be happy there !   I do not speak wildly.   I have just such a house in my mind's eye !''

" Then, sir,'' said the old gentleman, getting anxious to drop the subject, " you are not to blame for leaving it.''

" Within the lifetime of the child already born,'' Clifford went on, " all this will be done away.   The world is growing too ethereal and spiritual to bear these enormities a great while longer.   To me— though, for a considerable period of time, I have lived chiefly in retirement, and know less of such things than most men—even to me, the harbingers of a better era are unmistakable.   Mesmerism, now !   Will that effect nothing, think you, towards purging away the grossness out of human life?''

" All a humbug !'' growled the old gentleman.

" These rapping spirits, that little Phœbe told us

of the other day," said Clifford, "what are these but the messengers of the spiritual world, knocking at the door of substance? And it shall be flung wide open!"

"A humbug, again!" cried the old gentleman, growing more and more testy, at these glimpses of Clifford's metaphysics. "I should like to rap with a good stick on the empty pates of the dolts who circulate such nonsense!"

"Then there is electricity;—the demon, the angel, the mighty physical power, the all-pervading intelligence!" exclaimed Clifford. "Is that a humbug, too? Is it a fact—or have I dreamt it—that, by means of electricity, the world of matter has become a great nerve, vibrating thousands of miles in a breathless point of time? Rather, the round globe is a vast head, a brain, instinct with intelligence! Or, shall we say, it is itself a thought, nothing but thought, and no longer the substance which we deemed it!"

"If you mean the telegraph," said the old gentleman, glancing his eye towards its wire, alongside the rail-track, "it is an excellent thing;—that is, of course, if the speculators in cotton and politics don't get possession of it. A great thing, indeed, sir; particularly as regard the detection of bank-robbers and murderers."

"I don't quite like it, in that point of view," replied Clifford. "A bank-robber, and what you call a murderer, likewise, has his rights, which men of enlightened humanity and conscience should regard in so much the more liberal spirit, because the bulk of society is prone to controvert their existence. An almost spiritual medium, like the electric telegraph, should be consecrated to high, deep, joyful, and holy missions. Lovers, day by day,—hour by hour, if so often moved to do it,—might send their heart-throbs from Maine to Florida, with some such words as these,—' I love you for ever!'—' My heart runs over with love!'—' I love you more than I can!'—and, again, at the next message,—' I have lived an hour longer, and love you twice as much!' Or, when a good man has departed, his distant friend should be conscious of an electric thrill, as from the world of happy spirits, telling him,—' Your dear friend is in bliss!' Or, to an absent husband, should come tidings thus,—' An immortal being, of whom you are the father, has this moment come from God!'—and immediately its little voice would seem to have reached so far, and to be echoing in his heart. But for these poor rogues, the bank-robbers—who, after all, are about as honest as nine people in ten, except that they disregard certain formalities, and prefer to transact business at midnight, rather than 'Change-hours—and for these murderers, as you phrase it, who are often excusable in the motives of their deed, and deserve to be ranked among public benefactors, if we consider only its result—for unfortunate individuals like these, I really cannot applaud the enlistment of an immaterial and miraculous power in the universal world-hunt at their heels!"

" You can't, hey?" cried the old gentleman, with a hard look.

" Positively, no!" answered Clifford. " It puts them too miserably at disadvantage. For example, sir, in a dark, low, cross-beamed, panelled room of an old house, let us suppose a dead man, sitting in an arm-chair, with a blood-stain on his shirt-bosom —and let us add to our hypothesis another man, issuing from the house, which he feels to be over-filled with the dead man's presence—and let us lastly imagine him fleeing, Heaven knows whither, at the speed of a hurricane by railroad! Now, sir, if the fugitive alight in some distant town, and find all the people babbling about that self-same dead man, whom he has fled so far to avoid the sight and thought of, will you not allow that his natural rights have been infringed? He has been deprived of his city of refuge, and, in my humble opinion, has suffered infinite wrong!"

" You are a strange man, sir ! " said the old gentleman, bringing his gimlet-eye to a point on Clifford, as if determined to bore right into him. " I can't see through you ! "

" No, I'll be bound you can't ! " cried Clifford, laughing. " And yet, my dear sir, I am as transparent as the water of Maule's well ! But come, Hepzibah ! We have flown far enough for once. Let us alight, as the birds do, and perch ourselves on the nearest twig, and consult whither we shall fly next."

Just then, as it happened, the train reached a solitary way-station. Taking advantage of the brief pause, Clifford left the car, and drew Hepzibah along with him. A moment afterwards the train—with all the life of its interior, amid which Clifford had made himself so conspicuous an object—was gliding away in the distance, and rapidly lessening to a point, which in another moment vanished. The world had fled away from these two wanderers. They gazed drearily about them. At a little distance stood a wooden church, black with age, and in a dismal state of ruin and decay, with broken windows, a great rift through the main body of the edifice, and a rafter dangling from the top of the square tower. Further off was a farm-house, in the old style, as venerably black as the church, with a roof sloping downward from the three-storey peak, to within a man's height of the ground. It seemed uninhabited. There were the relics of a wood-pile, indeed, near the door, but with grass sprouting up among the chips and scattered logs. The small rain-drops came down aslant; the wind was not turbulent, but sullen, and full of chilly moisture.

Clifford shivered from head to foot. The wild effervescence of his mood—which had so readily supplied thoughts, fantasies, and a strange aptitude of words, and impelled him to talk from the mere necessity of giving vent to this bubbling-up gush of ideas —had entirely subsided. A powerful excitement had given him energy and vivacity. Its operation over, he forthwith began to sink.

" You must take the lead now, Hepzibah !'' murmured he, with a torpid and reluctant utterance. " Do with me as you will !''

She knelt down upon the platform where they were standing, and lifted her clasped hands to the sky. The dull, gray weight of clouds made it invisible; but it was no hour for disbelief ;—no juncture this to question that there was a sky above, and an Almighty Father looking down from it !

" Oh, God !''—ejaculated poor gaunt Hepzibah— then paused a moment to consider what her prayer should be—" O God—our Father ! are we not thy children? Have mercy on us !''

XVIII

GOVERNOR PYNCHEON

JUDGE PYNCHEON, while his two relatives have fled away with such ill-considered haste, still sits in the old parlour, keeping house, as the familiar phrase is, in the absence of its ordinary occupants. To him, and to the venerable House of the Seven Gables, does our story now betake itself, like an owl, bewildered in the daylight, and hastening back to his hollow tree.

The judge has not shifted his position for a long while now. He has not stirred hand or foot, nor withdrawn his eyes so much as a hair's breadth from their fixed gaze towards the corner of the room, since the footsteps of Hepzibah and Clifford creaked along the passage, and the outer door was closed cautiously behind their exit. He holds his watch in his left hand, but clutched in such a manner that you cannot

see the dial-plate. How profound a fit of meditation!
Or, supposing him asleep, how infantile a quietude
of conscience, and what wholesome order in the
gastric region, are betokened by slumber so entirely
undisturbed with starts, cramp, twitches, muttered
dream-talk, trumpet blasts through the nasal organ,
or any of the slightest irregularity of breath! You
must hold your own breath to satisfy yourself whether
he breathes at all. It is quite inaudible. You hear
the ticking of his watch; his breath you do not hear.
A most refreshing slumber, doubtless! And yet the
judge cannot be asleep. His eyes are open! A
veteran politician, such as he, would never fall asleep
with wide-open eyes, lest some enemy or mischief-
maker, taking him thus at unawares, should peep
through these windows into his consciousness, and
make strange discoveries among the reminiscences,
projects, hopes, apprehensions, weaknesses, and
strong points, which he has heretofore shared with
nobody. A cautious man is proverbially said to sleep
with one eye open. That may be wisdom. But not
with both; for this were heedlessness! No, no!
Judge Pyncheon cannot be asleep.

It is odd, however, that a gentleman so burthened
with engagements—and noted, too, for punctuality
—should linger thus in an old lonely mansion, which
he has never seemed very fond of visiting. The oaken
chair, to be sure, may tempt him with its roominess.
It is, indeed, a spacious and, allowing for the rude
age that fashioned it, a moderately easy seat, with
capacity enough, at all events, and offering no restraint to the judge's breadth of beam. A bigger
man might find ample accommodation in it. His ancestor, now pictured upon the wall, with all his English beef about him, used hardly to present a front
extending from elbow to elbow of this chair, or a
base that would cover its whole cushion. But there
are better chairs than this—mahogany, black walnut,
rosewood, spring-seated and damask-cushioned, with
varied slopes, and innumerable artifices to make them

easy, and obviate the irksomeness of too tame and
ease;—a score of such might be at Judge Pyncheon's
service.   Yes! in a score of drawing-rooms he would
be more than welcome.   Mamma would advance to
meet him, with outstretched hand; the virgin
daughter, elderly as he has now got to be—an old
widower, as he smilingly describes himself—would
shake up the cushion for the judge, and do her pretty
little utmost to make him comfortable.   For the
judge is a prosperous man.   He cherishes his
schemes, moreover, like other people, and reasonably
brighter than most others; or did so, at least, as
he lay abed, this morning, in an agreeable half-
drowse, planning the business of the day, and specu-
lating on the probabilities of the next fifteen years.
With his firm health, and the little inroad that age
has made upon him, fifteen years or twenty—yes, or
perhaps five-and-twenty!—are no more than he may
fairly call his own.   Five-and-twenty years for the
enjoyment of his real estate in town and country, his
railroad, bank, and insurance shares, his United
States stock—his wealth, in short, however invested,
now in possession, or soon to be acquired; together
with the public honours that have fallen upon him,
and the weightier ones that are yet to fall!   It is
good!   It is excellent!   It is enough!

Still lingering in the old chair!   If the judge has
a little time to throw away, why does not he visit the
insurance office, as is his frequent custom, and sit a
while in one of their leathern-cushioned arm-chairs,
listening to the gossip of the day, and dropping some
deeply-designed chance-word, which will be certain
to become the gossip of to-morrow!   And have not
the bank directors a meeting, at which it was the
judge's purpose to be present, and his office to pre-
side?   Indeed they have; and the hour is noted on
a card, which is, or ought to be, in Judge Pyncheon's
right vest-pocket.   Let him go thither, and loll at
ease upon his money-bags!   He has lounged long
enough in the old chair!

This was to have been such a busy day! In the first place, the interview with Clifford. Half-an-hour, by the judge's reckoning, was to suffice for that; it would probably be less, but—taking into consideration that Hepzibah was first to be dealt with, and that these women are apt to make many words where a few would do much better—it might be safest to allow half-an-hour. Half-an-hour? Why, judge, it is already two hours by your own undeviating accurate chronometer! Glance your eye down at it, and see! Ah! he will not give himself the trouble either to bend his head, or elevate his hand, so as to bring the faithful time-keeper within his range of vision! Time, all at once, appears to have become a matter of no moment with the judge!

And has he forgotten all the other items of his memoranda? Clifford's affair arranged, he was to meet a State-street broker, who has undertaken to procure a heavy per-centage, and the best of paper, for a few loose thousands which the judge happens to have by him uninvested. The wrinkled note-shaver will have taken his railroad trip in vain. Half-an-hour later, in the street next to this, there was to be an auction of real estate, including a portion of the old Pyncheon property, originally belonging to Maule's garden-ground. It has been alienated from the Pyncheons these fourscore years; but the judge had kept it in his eye, and had set his heart on re-annexing to the small demesne still left around the seven gables;—and now, during this odd fit of oblivion, the fatal hammer must have fallen, and transferred our ancient patrimony to some alien possessor! Possibly, indeed, the sale may have been postponed till fairer weather. If so, will the judge make it convenient to be present, and favour the auctioneer with his bid on the proximate occasion?

The next affair was to buy a horse for his own driving. The one heretofore his favourite stumbled this very morning on the road to town, and must be at once discarded. Judge Pyncheon's neck is too precious to be risked on such a contingency as a stumbling steed. Should all the above business be seasonably got through with, he might attend the meeting of a charitable society; the very name of which, however, in the multiplicity of his benevolence, is quite forgotten; so that this engagement may pass unfulfilled, and no great harm done. And if he have time, amid the press of more urgent matters, he must take measures for the renewal of Mrs. Pyncheon's tombstone, which the sexton tells him has fallen on its marble face, and is cracked quite in twain. She was a praiseworthy woman enough, thinks the judge, in spite of her nervousness, and the tears that she was so oozy with, and her foolish behaviour about the coffee; and as she took her departure so seasonably, he will not grudge the second tombstone. It is better, at least, than if she had never needed any! The next item on his list was to give orders for some fruit-trees, of a rare variety, to be deliverable at his country-seat in the ensuing autumn. Yes, buy them by all means, and may the peaches be luscious in your mouth, Judge Pyncheon! After this comes something more important. A committee of his political party has besought him for a hundred or two of dollars, in addition to his previous disbursements, towards carrying on the fall campaign. The judge is a patriot; the fate of the country is staked on the November election; and besides, as will be shadowed forth in another paragraph, he has no trifling stake of his own in the same great game. He will do what the committee asks; nay, he will be liberal beyond their expectations; they shall have a check for five hundred dollars, and more anon, if it be needed. What next? A decayed widow, whose husband was Judge Pyncheon's early friend, has laid her case of destitution before him in a very moving letter. She and her fair daughter have scarcely bread to eat. He partly intends to call on her to-day,—perhaps so—perhaps not,—accordingly as he may happen to have leisure and a small bank-note.

Another business, which, however, he puts no great weight on—(it is well, you know, to be heedful, but not over anxious, as respects one's personal health)—another business, then, was to consult his family physician. About what, for Heaven's sake? Why, it is rather difficult to describe the symptoms. A mere dimness of sight and dizziness of brain, was it?—or a disagreeable choking, or stifling, or gurgling, or bubbling, in the region of the thorax, as the anatomists say?—or was it a pretty severe throbbing and kicking of the heart, rather creditable to him than otherwise, as showing that the organ had not been left out of the judge's physical contrivance? No matter what it was. The doctor probably would smile at the statement of such trifles to his professional ear; the judge would smile in his turn; and meeting one another's eyes, they would enjoy a hearty laugh together! But a fig for medical advice! The judge will never need it!

Pray, pray, Judge Pyncheon, look at your watch, now! What—not a glance! It is within ten minutes of the dinner-hour! It surely cannot have slipped your memory that the dinner of to-day is to be the most important in its consequences of all the dinners you ever ate. Yes, precisely the most important; although in the course of your somewhat eminent career, you have been placed high towards the head of the table at splendid banquets, and have poured out your festive eloquence to ears yet echoing with Webster's mighty organ-tones. No public dinner this, however. It is merely a gathering of some dozen or so of friends from several districts of the state; men of distinguished character and influence, assembling, almost casually, at the house of a common friend, likewise distinguished, who will make them welcome to a little better than his ordinary fare. Nothing in the way of French cookery, but an excellent dinner, nevertheless! Real turtle, we understand, and salmon, tautog, canvas-backs, pig, English mutton, good roast-beef, or dainties of that serious kind, fit for substantial country gentlemen, as these honourable persons mostly are. The delicacies of the season, in short, and flavoured by a brand of old Madeira which has been the pride of many seasons. It is the Juno brand; a glorious wine, fragrant, and full of gentle might; a bottled-up happiness, put by for use; a golden liquid, worth more than liquid gold; so rare and admirable, that veteran wine-bibbers count it among their epochs to have tasted it! It drives away the heart-ache, and substitutes no head-ache! Could the judge but quaff a glass, it might enable him to shake off the unaccountable lethargy which—(for the ten intervening minutes, and five to boot, are already past)—has made him such a laggard at this momentous dinner. It would all but revive a dead man! Would you like to sip it now, Judge Pyncheon?

Alas, this dinner! Have you really forgotten its true object? Then let us whisper it, that you may start at once out of the oaken chair, which really seems to be enchanted, like the one in Comus, or that in which Moll Pitcher imprisoned your own grandfather. But ambition is a talisman more powerful than witchcraft. Start up, then, and, hurrying through the streets, burst in upon the company, that they may begin before the fish is spoiled! They wait for you; and it is little for your interest that they should wait. These gentlemen—need you be told it?—have assembled, not without purpose, from every quarter of the state. They are practised politicians, every man of them, and skilled to adjust those preliminary measures which steal from the people, without its knowledge, the power of choosing its own rulers. The popular voice at the next gubernatorial election, though loud as thunder, will be really but an echo of what these gentlemen shall speak, under their breath, at your friend's festive board. They meet to decide upon their candidate.

This little knot of subtle schemers will control the convention, and through it dictate to the party. And what worthier candidate—more wise and learned, more noted for philanthropic liberality, truer to safe principles, tried oftener by public trusts, more spotless in private character, with a larger stake in the common welfare, and deeper grounded, by hereditary descent, in the faith and practice of the Puritans— what man can be presented for the suffrage of the people, so eminently combining all these claims to the chief-rulership as Judge Pyncheon here before us?

Make haste, then! Do your part! The meed for which you have toiled, and fought, and climbed, and crept, is ready for your grasp! Be present at this dinner!—drink a glass or two of that noble wine!— make your pledges in as low a whisper as you will! —and you rise up from table virtually governor of the glorious old state! Governor Pyncheon, of Massachusetts!

And is there no potent and exhilarating cordial in a certainty like this? It has been the grand purpose of half your lifetime to obtain it. Now, when there needs little more than to signify your acceptance, why do you sit so lumpishly in your great-great-grandfather's oaken chair, as if preferring it to the gubernatorial one? We have all heard of King Log; but, in these jostling times, one of that royal kindred will hardly win the race for an elective chief-magistracy.

Well! it is absolutely too late for dinner! Turtle, salmon, tautog, woodcock, boiled turkey, South-Down mutton, pig, roast beef, have vanished, or exist only in fragments, with lukewarm potatoes, and gravies crusted over with cold fat. The judge, had he done nothing else, would have achieved wonders with his knife and fork. It was he, you know, of whom it used to be said, in reference to his ogre-like appetite, that his Creator made him a great animal, but that the dinner-hour made him a great beast. Persons of his large sensual endowments must claim indulgence, at their feeding-time. But, for once, the judge is entirely too late for dinner! Too late, we fear, even to join the party at their wine! The guests are warm and merry; they have given up the judge; and, concluding that the free-soilers have him, they will fix upon another candidate. Were our friend now to stalk in among them, with that wide-open stare, at once wild and stolid, his ungenial presence would be apt to change their cheer. Neither would it be seemly in Judge Pyncheon, generally so scrupulous in his attire, to show himself at a dinner-table with that crimson stain upon his shirt-bosom. By-the-by, how came it there? It is an ugly sight at any rate, and the wisest way for the judge is to button his coat closely over his breast, and, taking his horse and chaise from the livery-stable, to make all speed to his own house. There, after a glass of brandy and water, and a mutton-chop, a beef-steak, a broiled fowl, or some such hasty little dinner and supper all in one, he had better spend the evening by the fire-side. He must toast his slippers a long while, in order to get rid of the chilliness which the air of this vile old house has sent curdling through his veins.

Up, therefore, Judge Pyncheon, up! You have lost a day. But to-morrow will be here anon. Will you rise, betimes, and make the most of it? To-morrow! To-morrow! To-morrow! We that are alive may rise betimes to-morrow. As for him that has died to-day, his morrow will be the resurrection morn.

Meanwhile, the twilight is glooming upward out of the corners of the room. The shadows of the tall furniture grow deeper, and at first become more definite; then, spreading wider, they lose their distinctness of outline in the dark gray tide of oblivion, as it were, that creeps slowly over the various objects, and the one human figure sitting in the midst of them. The gloom has not entered from without;

it has brooded here all day, and now, taking its own inevitable time, will possess itself of everything. The judge's face, indeed, rigid and singularly white, refuses to melt into this universal solvent. Fainter and fainter grows the light. It is as if another double-handful of darkness had been scattered through the air. Now it is no longer gray but sable. There is still a faint appearance at the window; neither a glow, nor a gleam, nor a glimmer—any phrase of light would express something far brighter than this doubtful perception, or sense, rather, that there is a window there. Has it yet vanished? No! —yes!—not quite!—And there is still the swarthy whiteness—we shall venture to marry these ill-agreeing words—the swarthy whiteness of Judge Pyncheon's face. The features are all gone; there is only the paleness of them left. And how looks it now? There is no window! There is no face! An infinite, inscrutable blackness has annihilated sight! Where is our universe? All crumbled away from us, and we, adrift in chaos, may hearken to the gusts of homeless wind, that go sighing and murmuring about in quest of what was once a world!

Is there no other sound? One other, and a fearful one. It is the ticking of the judge's watch, which ever since Hepzibah left the room in search of Clifford, he has been holding in his hand. Be the cause what it may, this little, quiet, never-ceasing throb of Time's pulse, repeating its small strokes with such busy regularity, in Judge Pyncheon's motionless hand, has an effect of terror, which we do not find in any other accompaniment of the scene.

But listen! That puff of the breeze was louder; it had a tone unlike the dreary and sullen one which has bemoaned itself, and afflicted all mankind with miserable sympathy, for five days past. The wind has veered about! It now comes boisterously from the north-west, and, taking hold of the aged framework of the seven gables, gives it a shake, like a wrestler that would try strength with his antagonist.

Another and another sturdy tussle with the blast !
The old house creaks again, and makes a vociferous
but somewhat unintelligible bellowing in its sooty
throat—(the big flue, we mean, of its wide chimney)
—partly in complaint at the rude wind, but rather,
as befits their century and a half of hostile intimacy,
in tough defiance.   A rumbling kind of a bluster
roars behind the fire-board.   A door has slammed
above-stairs.   A window, perhaps, has been left
open, or else is driven in by an unruly gust.   It is
not to be conceived, beforehand, what wonderful
wind-instruments are these old timber mansions, and
how haunted with the strangest noises, which immediately begin to sing, and sigh, and sob, and shriek—
and to smite with sledge-hammers, airy, but ponderous, in some distant chamber—and to tread along the
entries as with stately footsteps, and rustle up and
down the staircase, as with silks miraculously stiff
—whenever the gale catches the house with a window open, and gets fairly into it.   Would that we
were not an attendant spirit here !   It is too awful !
This clamour of the wind through the lonely house ;
the judge's quietude, as he sits invisible ; and that
pertinacious ticking of his watch !

As regards Judge Pyncheon's invisibility, however,
that matter will soon be remedied.   The north-west
wind has swept the sky clear.   The window is distinctly seen.   Through its panes, moreover, we
dimly catch the sweep of the dark, clustering foliage, outside, fluttering with a constant irregularity
of movement, and letting in a peep of starlight, now
here, now there.   Oftener than any other object,
these glimpses illuminate the judge's face.   But here
comes more effectual light.   Observe that silvery
dance upon the upper branches of the pear-tree, and
now a little lower, and now on the whole mass of
boughs, while, through their shifting intricacies, the
moonbeams fall aslant into the room.   They play
over the judge's figure, and show that he has not
stirred throughout the hours of darkness.   They fol-

low the shadows, in changeful sport, across his unchanging features. They gleam upon his watch. His grasp conceals the dial-plate; but we know that the faithful hands have met; for one of the city-clocks tells midnight.

A man of sturdy understanding, like Judge Pyncheon, cares no more for twelve o'clock at night than for the corresponding hour of noon. However just the parallel drawn, in some of the preceding pages, between his Puritan ancestor and himself, it fails in this point. The Pyncheon of two centuries ago, in common with most of his contemporaries, professed his full belief in spiritual ministrations, although reckoning them chiefly of a malignant character. The Pyncheon of to-night, who sits in yonder arm-chair, believes in no such nonsense. Such at least was his creed some few hours since. His hair will not bristle, therefore, at the stories which—in times when chimney-corners had benches in them, where old people sat poking into the ashes of the past, and raking out traditions like live coals —used to be told about this very room of his ancestral house. In fact, these tales are too absurd to bristle even childhood's hair. What sense, meaning, or moral, for example, such as even ghost-stories should be susceptible of, can be traced in the ridiculous legend, that, at midnight, all the dead Pyncheons are bound to assemble in this parlour? And pray for what? Why, to see whether the portrait of their ancestor still keeps its place upon the wall, in compliance with his testamentary directions! Is it worth while to come out of their graves for that?

We are tempted to make a little sport with the idea. Ghost-stories are hardly to be treated seriously any longer. The family-party of the defunct Pyncheons, we presume, goes off in this wise.

First comes the ancestor himself, in his black cloak, steeple-hat, and trunk-breeches, girt about the waist with a leathern belt, in which hangs his steel-hilted sword; he has a long staff in his hand, such as gentlemen in advanced life used to carry, as much for the dignity of the thing as for the support to be derived from it. He looks up at the portrait—a thing of no substance, gazing at its own painted image! All is safe. The picture is still there. The purpose of his brain has been kept sacred thus long after the man himself sprouted up in grave-yard grass. See! he lifts his ineffectual hand, and tries the frame. All safe! But is that a smile?—is it not, rather, a frown of deadly import, that darkens over the shadow of his features? The stout colonel is dissatisfied! So decided is his look of discontent as to impart additional distinctness to his features; through which, nevertheless, the moonlight passes, and flickers on the wall beyond. Something has strangely vexed the ancestor! With a grim shake of the head he turns away. Here come other Pyncheons, the whole tribe, in their half-a-dozen generations, jostling and elbowing one another to reach the picture. We behold aged men and grandames, a clergyman with the Puritanic stiffness still in his garb and mien, and a red-coated officer of the old French war; and there comes the shop-keeping Pyncheon of a century ago, with the ruffles turned back from his wrists; and there the periwigged and brocaded gentleman of the artist's legend, with the beautiful and pensive Alice, who brings no pride out of her virgin grave. All try the picture-frame. What do these ghostly people seek? A mother lifts her child that his little hands may touch it! There is evidently a mystery about the picture, that perplexes these poor Pyncheons, when they ought to be at rest. In a corner, meanwhile, stands the figure of an elderly man, in a leather jerkin and breeches, with a carpenter's rule sticking out of his side-pocket; he points his finger at the bearded colonel and his descendants, nodding, jeering, mocking, and finally bursting into obstreperous, though inaudible laughter.

Indulging our fancy in this freak, we have partly

lost the power of restraint and guidance. We distinguish an unlooked-for figure in our visionary scene.
Among those ancestral people there is a young man,
dressed in the very fashion of to-day; he wears a
dark frock-coat, almost destitute of skirts, gray
pantaloons, gaiter boots of patent leather, and has
a finely-wrought gold chain across his breast, and a
little silver-headed whalebone stick in his hand.
Were we to meet this figure at noon-day, we should
greet him as young Jaffrey Pyncheon, the judge's
only surviving child, who has been spending the last
two years in foreign travel. If still in life, how
comes his shadow hither? If dead, what a misfortune! The old Pyncheon property, together with
the great estate acquired by the young man's father,
would devolve on whom? On poor, foolish Clifford,
gaunt Hepzibah, and rustic little Phœbe! But
another and a greater marvel greets us! Can we
believe our eyes? A stout, elderly gentleman has
made his appearance; he has an aspect of eminent
respectability, wears a black coat and pantaloons,
of roomy width, and might be pronounced scrupulously neat in his attire, but for a broad crimson stain
across his snowy neckcloth and down his shirt-bosom.
Is it the judge, or no? How can it be Judge Pyncheon? We discern his figure, as plainly as the
flickering moonbeams can show us anything, still
seated in the oaken chair! Be the apparition whose
it may, it advances to the picture, seems to seize the
frame, tries to peep behind it, and turns away with
a frown as black as the ancestral one.

The fantastic scene just hinted at must by no means
be considered as forming an actual portion of our
story. We were betrayed into this brief extravagance by the quiver of the moonbeams; they dance
hand-in-hand with shadows, and are reflected in
the looking-glass, which, you are aware, is always
a kind of window or door-way into the spiritual
world. We needed relief, moreover, from our too
long and exclusive contemplation of that figure in the

chair. This wild wind, too, has tossed our thoughts into strange confusion, but without tearing them away from their one determined centre. Yonder leaden judge sits immoveably upon our soul. Will he never stir again? We shall go mad, unless he stirs! You may the better estimate his quietude by the fearlessness of a little mouse, which sits on its hind legs, in a streak of moonlight, close by Judge Pyncheon's foot, and seems to meditate a journey of exploration over this great black bulk. Ha! what has startled the nimble little mouse? It is the visage of Grimalkin, outside of the window, where he appears to have posted himself for a deliberate watch. This Grimalkin has a very ugly look. Is it a cat watching for a mouse, or the devil for a human soul? Would we could scare him from the window!

Thank Heaven, the night is well-nigh past! The moon-beams have no longer so silvery a gleam, nor contrast so strongly with the blackness of the shadows among which they fall. They are paler, now; the shadows look gray, not black. The boisterous wind is hushed. What is the hour? Ah! the watch has at last ceased to tick; for the judge's forgetful fingers neglected to wind it up, as usual, at ten o'clock, being half-an-hour, or so, before his ordinary bed-time;—and it has run down, for the first time in five years. But the great world-clock of Time still keeps its beat. The dreary night,—for, oh, how dreary seems its haunted waste, behind us! —gives place to a fresh, transparent, cloudless morn. Blessed, blessed radiance! The day-beam,—even what little of it finds its way into this always dusky parlour—seems part of the universal benediction, annulling evil, and rendering all goodness possible, and happiness attainable. Will Judge Pyncheon now rise up from his chair? Will he go forth, and receive the early sunbeams on his brow? Will he begin this new day,—which God has smiled upon, and blessed, and given to mankind,—will he begin it with better purposes than the many that have been spent amiss? Or are all the deep-laid schemes of yesterday as stubborn in his heart, and as busy in his brain, as ever?

In this latter case, there is much to do. Will the judge still insist with Hepzibah on the interview with Clifford? Will he buy a safe, elderly gentleman's horse? Will he persuade the purchaser of the old Pyncheon property to relinquish the bargain in his favour? Will he see his family physician, and obtain a medicine that shall preserve him, to be an honour and blessing to his race, until the utmost term of patriarchal longevity? Will Judge Pyncheon, above all, make due apologies to that company of honourable friends, and satisfy them that his absence from the festive board was unavoidable, and so fully retrieve himself in their good opinion that he shall yet be Governor of Massachusetts? And, all these great purposes accomplished, will he walk the streets again, with that dog-day smile of elaborate benevolence, sultry enough to tempt flies to come and buzz in it? Or will he, after the tomb-like seclusion of the past day and night, go forth a humbled and repentant man, sorrowful, gentle, seeking no profit, shrinking from worldly honour, hardly daring to love God, but bold to love his fellow-man, and do him what good he may? Will he bear about with him, —no odious grin of feigned benignity, insolent in its pretence, and loathsome in its falsehood,—but the tender sadness of a contrite heart, broken, at last, beneath its own weight of sin? For it is our belief, whatever show of honour he may have piled upon it, that there was heavy sin at the base of this man's being.

Rise up, Judge Pyncheon! The morning sunshine glimmers through the foliage, and, beautiful and holy as it is, shuns not to kindle up your face. Rise up, thou subtle, worldly, selfish, iron-hearted hypocrite, and make thy choice whether still to be subtle, worldly, selfish, iron-hearted, and hypocritical, or to tear these sins out of thy nature, though they bring

the life-blood with them ! The Avenger is upon thee !
Rise up, before it be too late !

What ! Thou art not stirred by this last appeal?
No, not a jot ! And there we see a fly,—one of your
common house-flies, such as are always buzzing on
the window-pane,—which has smelt out Governor
Pyncheon, and alights, now on his forehead, now on
his chin, and now, Heaven help us ! is creeping over
the bridge of his nose, towards the would-be chief-
magistrate's wide-open eyes ! Canst thou not brush
the fly away? Art thou too sluggish? Thou man,
that hadst so many busy projects, yesterday ! Art
thou too weak, that wast so powerful? Not brush
away a fly ! Nay, then we give thee up !

And, hark ! the shop-bell rings. After hours like
these latter ones, through which we have borne our
heavy tale, it is good to be made sensible that there
is a living world, and that even this old, lonely mansion retains some manner of connection with it. We
breathe more freely, emerging from Judge Pyncheon's presence into the street before the seven
gables.

XIX

ALICE'S POSIES

UNCLE VENNER, trundling a wheelbarrow, was the
earliest person stirring in the neighbourhood, the day
after the storm.

Pyncheon-street, in front of the House of the Seven
Gables, was a far pleasanter scene than a by-lane,
confined by shabby fences, and bordered with wooden
dwellings of the meaner class, could reasonably be
expected to present. Nature made sweet amends
that morning for the five unkindly days which had
preceded it. It would have been enough to live for,

merely to look up at the wide benediction of the sky,
or as much of it as was visible between the houses,
genial once more with sunshine. Every object was
agreeable, whether to be gazed at in the breadth, or
examined more minutely. Such, for example, were
the well-washed pebbles and gravel of the side-walk;
even the sky-reflecting pools in the centre of the
street; and the grass, now freshly verdant, that crept
along the base of the fences, on the other side of
which, if one peeped over, was seen the multifarious
growth of gardens. Vegetable productions, of whatever kind, seemed more than negatively happy, in
the juicy warmth and abundance of their life. The
Pyncheon-elm, throughout its great circumference,
was all alive, and full of the morning sun and a
sweetly-tempered little breeze, which lingered within
this verdant sphere, and set a thousand leafy tongues
a-whispering all at once. This aged tree appeared to
have suffered nothing from the gale. It had kept its
boughs unshattered, and its full complement of
leaves; and the whole in perfect verdure, except a
single branch, that, by the earlier change with which
the elm-tree sometimes prophecies the autumn, had
been transmuted to bright gold. It was like the
golden branch, that gained Æneas and the Sybil
admittance into Hades.

This one mystic branch hung down before the main
entrance of the seven gables, so nigh the ground
that any passer-by might have stood on tiptoe and
plucked it off. Presented at the door, it would have
been a symbol of his right to enter, and be made
acquainted with all the secrets of the house. So
little faith is due to external appearance, that there
was really an inviting aspect over the venerable
edifice, conveying an idea that its history must be
a decorous and happy one, and such as would be
delightful for a fire-side tale. Its windows gleamed
cheerfully in the slanting sunlight. The lines and
tufts of green moss here and there, seemed pledges
of familiarity and sisterhood with Nature; as if this

human dwelling-place, being of such old date, had
established its prescriptive title among primeval oaks,
and whatever other objects, by virtue of their long
continuance, have acquired a gracious right to be.
A person of imaginative temperament, while passing by the house, would turn once and again, and
peruse it well :—its many peaks, consenting together
in the clustered chimney; the deep projection over
its basement-storey; the arched window, imparting
a look, if not of grandeur, yet of antique gentility,
to the broken portal over which it opened;—the
luxuriance of gigantic burdocks, near the threshold :
—he would note all these characteristics, and be conscious of something deeper than he saw.   He would
conceive the mansion to have been the residence of
the stubborn old Puritan, Integrity, who, dying in
some forgotten generation, had left a blessing in all
its rooms and chambers, the efficacy of which was
to be seen in the religion, honesty, moderate com-
petence, or upright poverty and solid happiness, of
his descendants to this day.

One object, above all others, would take root in
the imaginative observer's memory.   It was the
great tuft of flowers—weeds you would have called
them only a week ago—the tuft of crimson-spotted
flowers in the angle between the two front gables.
The old people used to give them the name of Alice's
Posies, in remembrance of fair Alice Pyncheon, who
was believed to have brought their seeds from Italy.
They were flaunting in rich beauty and full bloom to-
day, and seemed, as it were, a mystic expression that
something within the house was consummated.

It was but little after sunrise, when Uncle Venner
made his appearance, as aforesaid, impelling a wheelbarrow along the street.   He was going his matutinal rounds to collect cabbage-leaves, turnip-tops,
potato-skins, and the miscellaneous refuse of the
dinner-pot, which the thrifty housewives of the neighbourhood were accustomed to put aside, as fit only to
feed a pig. Uncle Venner's pig was fed entirely,

and kept in prime order, on these eleemosynary contributions; insomuch that the patched philosopher
used to promise that, before retiring to his farm, he
would make a feast of the portly grunter, and invite
all his neighbours to partake of the joints and spare-
ribs which they had helped to fatten. Miss Hepzibah Pyncheon's housekeeping had so greatly improved since Clifford became a member of the family,
that her share of the banquet would have been no
lean one; and Uncle Venner accordingly was a good
deal disappointed not to find the large earthen pan,
full of fragmentary eatables, that ordinarily awaited
his coming, at the back door-step of the seven gables.

" I never knew Miss Hepzibah so forgetful before," said the patriarch to himself.   " She must
have had a dinner yesterday—no question of that !
She always has one, now-a-days. So where's the
pot-liquor and potato-skins, I ask? Shall I knock,
and see if she's stirring yet? No, no—'t won't do !
If little Phœbe was about the house, I should not
mind knocking; but Miss Hepzibah, likely as not,
would scowl down at me, out of the window, and
look cross, even if she felt pleasantly. So I'll come
back at noon."

With these reflections, the old man was shutting
the gate of the little back yard. Creaking on its
hinges, however, like every other gate and door
about the premises, the sound reached the ears of
the occupant of the northern gable, one of the
windows of which had a side-view towards the gate.

" Good morning, Uncle Venner !" said the daguerreotypist, leaning out of the window.   " Do you hear
nobody stirring?"

" Not a soul," said the man of patches.   " But
that's no wonder. 'Tis barely half-an-hour past sunrise yet. But I'm really glad to see you, Mr. Holgrave ! There's a strange lonesome look about this
side of the house; so that my heart misgave me,
somehow or other, and I felt as if there was nobody
alive in it. The front of the house looks a good deal

cheerier, and Alice's Posies are blooming there beautifully; and if I were a young man, Mr. Holgrave, my sweetheart should have one of those flowers in her bosom, though I risked my neck climbing for it! Well! and did the wind keep you awake last night?"

"It did, indeed!" answered the artist, smiling. "If I were a believer in ghosts—and I don't quite know whether I am or not—I should have concluded that all the old Pyncheons were running riot in the lower rooms, especially in Miss Hepzibah's part of the house. But it is very quiet now."

"Yes, Miss Hepzibah will be apt to oversleep herself after being disturbed all night with the racket," said Uncle Venner. "But it would be odd, now wouldn't it, if the judge had taken both his cousins into the country along with him? I saw him go into the shop yesterday."

"At what hour?" inquired Holgrave.

"O, along in the forenoon," said the old man. "Well, well! I must go my rounds, and so must my wheelbarrow. But I'll be back here at dinnertime; for my pig likes a dinner as well as a breakfast. No meal-time, and no sort of victuals ever seems to come amiss to my pig. Good morning to you! And, Mr. Holgrave, if I were a young man like you I'd get one of Alice's Posies, and keep it in water till Phœbe comes back."

"I have heard," said the daguerreotypist, as he drew in his head, "that the water of Maule's well suits those flowers best."

Here the conversation ceased, and Uncle Venner went on his way. For half-an-hour longer nothing disturbed the repose of the seven gables; nor was there any visitor, except a carrier-boy, who, as he passed the front door-step, threw down one of his newspapers; for Hepzibah of late had regularly taken it in. After a while there came a fat woman, making prodigious speed, and stumbling as she ran up the steps of the shop-door. Her face glowed with fire-heat, and it being a pretty warm morning she bubbled and hissed, as it were, as if all a-fry with chimney warmth and summer warmth, and the warmth of her own corpulent velocity. She tried the shop-door;—it was fast. She tried it again, with so angry a jar that the bell tinkled angrily back at her.

" The deuce take Old Maid Pyncheon!" muttered the irascible housewife. " Think of her pretending to set up a cent-shop, and then lying abed till noon! These are what she calls gentlefolks' airs, I suppose! But I'll either start her ladyship, or break the door down!"

She shook it accordingly, and the bell, having a spiteful little temper of its own, rang obstreperously, making its remonstrances heard—not indeed by the ears for which they were intended—but by a good lady on the opposite side of the street. She opened her window, and addressed the impatient applicant.

" You'll find nobody there, Mrs. Gubbins."

" But I must and will find somebody here!" cried Mrs. Gubbins, inflicting another outrage on the bell. " I want a half-pound of pork, to fry some first-rate flounders, for Mr. Gubbins' breakfast; and, lady or not, Old Maid Pyncheon shall get up and serve me with it!"

" But do hear reason, Mrs. Gubbins!" responded the lady opposite. " She, and her brother too, have both gone to their cousin, Judge Pyncheon's, at his country seat. There's not a soul in the house but that young daguerreotype man, that sleeps in the north gable. I saw old Hepzibah and Clifford go away yesterday; and a queer couple of ducks they were, paddling through the mud-puddles! They're gone, I'll assure you."

" And how do you know they're gone to the judge's?" asked Mrs. Gubbins. " He's a rich man; and there's been a quarrel between him and Hepzibah this many a day, because he won't give her a living. That's the main reason of her setting up a cent-shop."

" I know that well enough," said the neighbour.
" But they're gone—that's one thing certain. And
who but a blood-relation, that couldn't help himself,
I ask you, would take in that awful-tempered old-
maid, and that dreadful Clifford? That's it, you may
be sure."

Mrs. Gubbins took her departure, still brimming
over with hot wrath against the absent Hepzibah.
For another half hour, or perhaps considerably more,
there was almost as much quiet on the outside of
the house as within. The elm, however, made a
pleasant, cheerful, sunny sigh, responsive to the
breeze that was elsewhere imperceptible; a swarm of
insects buzzed merrily under its drooping shadow and
became specks of light, whenever they darted into
the sunshine; a locust sang once or twice in some
inscrutable seclusion of the tree; and a solitary little
bird, with plumage of pale gold, came and hovered
about Alice's Posies.

At last our small acquaintance, Ned Higgins,
trudged up the street, on his way to school; and happening, for the first time in a fortnight, to be the
possessor of a cent, he could by no means get past
the shop-door of the seven gables. But it would not
open. Again and again, however, and half-a-dozen
other agains, with the inexorable pertinacity of a child
intent upon some object important to itself, did he
renew his efforts for admittance. He had doubtless
set his heart upon an elephant; or possibly, with
Hamlet, he meant to eat a crocodile. In response to
his more violent attacks, the bell gave now and then
a moderate tinkle, but could not be stirred into
clamour by any exertion of the little fellow's childish
and tiptoe strength. Holding by the door-handle,
he peeped through a crevice of the curtain, and saw
that the inner door, communicating with the passage
towards the parlour, was closed.

" Miss Pyncheon !" screamed the child, rapping on
the window-pane, " I want an elephant !"

There being no answer to several repetitions of the

summons, Ned began to grow impatient; and his little pot of passion quickly boiling over, he picked up a stone, with a naughty purpose to fling it through the window; at the same time blubbering and sputtering with wrath. A man—one of two who happened to be passing by—caught the urchin's arm.

" What's the trouble, old gentleman?" he asked.

" I want old Hepzibah, or Phœbe, or any of them !" answered Ned, sobbing. " They won't open the door; and I can't get my elephant."

" Go to school, you little scamp !" said the man. " There's another cent-shop round the corner. 'Tis very strange, Dixey," added he to his companion, " what's become of all these Pyncheons ! Smith, the livery-stable keeper, tells me Judge Pyncheon put his horse up yesterday, to stand till after dinner, and has not taken him away yet. And one of the judge's hired men has been in this morning to make inquiry about him. He's a kind of person, they say, that seldom breaks his habits, or stays out o' nights."

" O, he'll turn up safe enough !" said Dixey. " And as for old Maid Pyncheon, take my word for it, she has run in debt and gone off from her creditors. I foretold, you remember, the first morning she set up shop, that her devilish scowl would frighten away customers. They couldn't stand it !"

" I never thought she'd make it go," remarked his friend. " This business of cent-shops is overdone among the women-folks. My wife tried it, and lost five dollars on her outlay !"

" Poor business !" said Dixey, shaking his head. " Poor business !"

In the course of the morning there were various other attempts to open a communication with the supposed inhabitants of this silent and impenetrable mansion. The man of root-beer came, in his neatly-painted wagon, with a couple of dozen full bottles, to be exchanged for empty ones; the baker, with a lot of crackers which Hepzibah had ordered for her retail custom; the butcher, with a nice titbit which he fancied she would be eager to secure for Clifford. Had any observer of these proceedings been aware of the fearful secret hidden within the house, it would have affected him with a singular shape and modification of horror, to see the current of human life making this small eddy hereabouts ;—whirling sticks, straws, and all such trifles, round and round, right over the black depth where a dead corpse lay unseen !

The butcher was so much in earnest with his sweetbread of lamb, or whatever the dainty might be, that he tried every accessible door of the seven gables, and at length came round again to the shop, where he ordinarily found admittance.

" It's a nice article, and I know the old lady would jump at it," said he to himself. " She can't be gone away ! In fifteen years that I have driven my cart through Pyncheon-street, I've never known her to be away from home; though often enough, to be sure, a man might knock all day without bringing her to the door. But that was when she'd only herself to provide for."

Peeping through the same crevice of the curtain where, only a little while before, the urchin of elephantine appetite had peeped, the butcher beheld the inner door, not closed, as the child had seen it, but ajar, and almost wide open. However it might have happened, it was the fact. Through the passage-way there was a dark vista into the lighter but still obscure interior of the parlour. It appeared to the butcher that he could pretty clearly discern what seemed to be the stalwart legs, clad in black pantaloons, of a man sitting in a large oaken chair, the back of which concealed all the remainder of his figure. This contemptuous tranquillity on the part of an occupant of the house, in response to the butcher's indefatigable efforts to attract notice, so piqued the man of flesh that he determined to withdraw.

" So," thought he, " there sits Old Maid Pyncheon's bloody brother, while I've been giving myself all this trouble ! Why, if a hog hadn't more manners,

I'd stick him ! I call it demeaning a man's business
to trade with such people; and from this time forth,
if they want a sausage or an ounce of liver, they shall
run after the cart for it !"

He tossed the titbit angrily into his cart, and drove
off in a pet.

Not a great while afterwards, there was a sound
of music turning the corner, and approaching down
the street, with several intervals of silence, and then
a renewed and nearer outbreak of brisk melody. A
mob of children was seen moving onward, or stopping
in unison with the sound, which appeared to proceed
from the centre of the throng; so that they were
loosely bound together by slender strains of harmony,
and drawn along captive; with ever and anon an
accession of some little fellow in an apron and straw-
hat, capering forth from door or gateway. Arriving
under the shadow of the Pyncheon-elm, it proved to
be the Italian boy who, with his monkey and show
of puppets, had once before played his hurdy-gurdy
beneath the arched window. The pleasant face of
Phœbe—and doubtless too, the liberal recompense
which she had flung him—still dwelt in his remembrance. His expressive features kindled up, as he
recognized the spot where this trifling incident of his
erratic life had chanced. He entered the neglected
yard, (now wilder than ever, with its growth of hog-
weed and burdock,) stationed himself on the door-step
of the main entrance, and opening his show-box,
began to play. Each individual of the automatic
community forthwith set to work, according to his
or her proper vocation : the monkey taking off his
Highland bonnet, bowed and scraped to the by-
standers most obsequiously, with ever an observant
eye to pick up a stray cent; and the young foreigner
himself, as he turned the crank of his machine,
glanced upward to the arched window, expectant of
a presence that would make his music the livelier and
sweeter. The throng of children stood near—some
on the sidewalk, some within the yard; two or three

establishing themselves on the very door-step; and one squatting on the threshold. Meanwhile the locust kept singing in the great old Pyncheon-elm.

"I don't hear anybody in the house," said one of the children to another. "The monkey won't pick up anything here."

"There is somebody at home," affirmed the urchin on the threshold. "I heard a step."

Still the young Italian's eye turned sidelong upward; and it really seemed as if the touch of genuine, though slight and almost playful emotion, communicated a juicier sweetness to the dry, mechanical process of his minstrelsy. These wanderers are readily responsive to any natural kindness—be it no more than a smile, or a word, itself not understood, but only a warmth in it—which befalls them on the roadside of life. They remember these things, because they are the little enchantments which, for the instant —for the space that reflects a landscape in a soap-bubble—built up a home about them. Therefore, the Italian boy would not be discouraged by the heavy silence with which the old house seemed resolute to clog the vivacity of his instrument. He persisted in his melodious appeals; he still looked upward, trusting that his dark, alien countenance would soon be brightened by Phœbe's sunny aspect. Neither could he be willing to depart without again beholding Clifford, whose sensibility, like Phœbe's smile, had talked a kind of heart's language to the foreigner. He repeated all his music, over and over again, until his auditors were getting weary. So were the little wooden people in his show-box, and the monkey most of all. There was no response, save the singing of the locust.

"No children live in this house," said a schoolboy, at last. "Nobody lives here but an old maid and an old man. You'll get nothing here! Why don't you go along?"

"You fool, you, why do you tell him?" whispered a shrewd little Yankee, caring nothing for the music, but a good deal for the cheap rate at which it was had. " Let him play as long as he likes ! If there's nobody to pay him, that's his own look-out !"

Once more, however, the Italian ran over his round of melodies. To the common observer—who could understand nothing of the case, except the music and the sunshine on the hither side of the door—it might have been amusing to watch the pertinacity of the street-performer. Will he succeed at last? Will that stubborn door be suddenly flung open? Will a group of joyous children, the young ones of the house, come dancing, shouting, laughing, into the open air, and cluster round the show-box, looking with eager merriment at the puppets, and tossing each a copper for long-tailed Mammon, the monkey to pick up?

But to us, who know the inner heart of the seven gables, as well as its exterior face, there is a ghastly effect in this repetition of light popular tunes at its door-step. It would be an ugly business, indeed, if Judge Pyncheon (who would not have cared a fig for Paganini's fiddle, in his most harmonious mood) should make his appearance at the door, with a bloody shirt-bosom, and a grim frown on his swarthily-white visage, and motion the foreign vagabond away ! Was ever before such a grinding out of jigs and waltzes, where nobody was in the cue to dance? Yes, very often. This contrast, or intermingling of tragedy with mirth, happens daily, hourly, momently. The gloomy and desolate old house, deserted of life, and with awful Death sitting sternly in its solitude, was the emblem of many a human heart, which, nevertheless, is compelled to hear the trill and echo of the world's gaiety around it.

Before the conclusion of the Italian's performance, a couple of men happened to be passing on their way to dinner.

" I say, you young French fellow !" called out one of them,—" come away from that door-step, and go somewhere else with your nonsense ! The Pyncheon family live there ; and they are in great trouble just about this time. They don't feel musical to-day. It is reported all over town that Judge Pyn-cheon, who owns the house, has been murdered; and the city marshal is going to look into the matter. So be off with you at once!"

As the Italian shouldered his hurdy-gurdy, he saw on the door-step a card, which had been covered all the morning by the newspaper that the carrier had flung upon it, but was now shuffled into sight. He picked it up, and perceiving something written in pencil, gave it to the man to read. In fact, it was an engraved card of Judge Pyncheon's, with certain pencilled memoranda on the back, referring to various businesses, which it had been his purpose to transact during the preceding day. It formed a prospective epitome of the day's history; only that affairs had not turned out altogether in accordance with the pro-gramme. The card must have been lost from the judge's vest-pocket, in his preliminary attempt to gain access by the main entrance of the house. Though well soaked with rain, it was still partially legible.

"Look here, Dixey!" cried the man. "This has something to do with Judge Pyncheon. See!—here's his name printed on it; and here, I suppose, is some of his handwriting."

"Let's go to the city marshal with it!" said Dixey. "It may give him just the clue he wants. After all," whispered he in his companion's ear, "it would be no wonder if the judge has gone into that door, and never come out again! A certain cousin of his may have been at his old tricks. And Old Maid Pyncheon having got herself in debt by the cent-shop—and the judge's pocket-book being well filled—and bad blood amongst them already! Put all these things together, and see what they make!"

"Hush, hush!" whispered the other. "It seems like a sin to be the first to speak of such a thing. But I think with you, that we had better go to the city marshal."

"Yes, yes!" said Dixey. "Well!—I always said there was something devilish in that woman's scowl!"

The men wheeled about accordingly, and retraced their steps up the street. The Italian, also, made the best of his way off, with a parting glance up at the arched window. As for the children, they took to their heels with one accord, and scampered as if some giant or ogre were in pursuit, until, at a good distance from the house, they stopped as suddenly and simultaneously as they had set out. Their susceptible nerves took an indefinite alarm from what they had overheard. Looking back at the grotesque peaks and shadowy angles of the old mansion, they fancied a gloom diffused about it which no brightness of the sunshine could dispel. An imaginary Hepzibah scowled and shook her finger at them, from several windows at the same moment. An imaginary Clifford —for (and it would have deeply wounded him to know it) he had always been a horror to these small people —stood behind the unreal Hepzibah, making awful gestures in a faded dressing-gown. Children are even more apt, if possible, than grown people, to catch the contagion of a panic terror. For the rest of the day, the more timid went whole streets about, for the sake of avoiding the seven gables; while the bolder signalized their hardihood by challenging their comrades to race past the mansion at full speed.

It could not have been more than half-an-hour after the disappearance of the Italian boy, with his unseasonable melodies, when a cab drove down the street. It stopped beneath the Pyncheon-elm; the cabman took a trunk, a canvas bag, and a bandbox, from the top of his vehicle, and deposited them on the door-step of the old house; a straw bonnet, and then the pretty figure of a young girl came into view from the interior of the cab. It was Phœbe! Though not altogether so blooming as when she first tripped into our story—for in the few intervening weeks her experiences had made her graver, more womanly,

and deeper-eyed, in token of a heart that had begun
to suspect its depths—still there was the quiet glow
of natural sunshine over her. Neither had she for-
feited her proper gift of making things look real,
rather than fantastic, within her sphere. Yet we
feel it to be a questionable venture even for Phœbe,
at this juncture, to cross the threshold of the seven
gables. Is her healthful presence potent enough to
chase away the crowd of pale, hideous, and sinful
phantoms, that have gained admittance there since
her departure? Or will she likewise fade, sicken,
sadden, and grow into deformity, and be only another
pallid phantom, to glide noiselessly up and down the
stairs, and affright children as she pauses at the
window?

At least, we would gladly forewarn the unsuspect-
ing girl that there is nothing in human shape or substance to receive her, unless it be the figure of Judge
Pyncheon, who—wretched spectacle that he is, and
frightful in our remembrance, since our night-long
vigil with him!—still keeps his place in the oaken
chair.

Phœbe first tried the shop-door. It did not yield
to her hand; and the white curtain, drawn across the
window which formed the upper section of the door,
struck her quick perceptive faculty as something unusual. Without making another effort to enter here,
she betook herself to the great portal under the arched
window. Finding it fastened, she knocked. A reverberation came from the emptiness within. She
knocked again, and a third time; and, listening intently, fancied that the floor creaked, as if Hepzibah
were coming with her ordinary tiptoe movement to
admit her. But so dead a silence ensued upon this
imaginary sound, that she began to question whether
she might not have mistaken the house, familiar as
she thought herself with its exterior.

Her notice was now attracted by a child's voice,
at some distance. It appeared to call her name.
Looking in the direction whence it proceeded, Phœbe

saw little Ned Higgins a good way down the street,
stamping, shaking his head violently, making depre-
catory gestures with both hands, and shouting to
her at mouth-wide screech.

"No, no, Phœbe!" he screamed. "Don't you
go in! There's something wicked there! Don't—
don't—don't go in!"

But, as the little personage could not be induced
to approach near enough to explain himself, Phœbe
concluded that he had been frightened, on some of his
visits to the shop, by her Cousin Hepzibah; for the
good lady's manifestations, in truth, ran about an
equal chance of scaring children out of their wits,
or compelling them to unseemly laughter. Still, she
felt the more, for this incident, how unaccountably
silent and impenetrable the house had become. As
her next resort, Phœbe made her way into the garden,
where, on so warm and bright a day as the present,
she had little doubt of finding Clifford, and perhaps
Hepzibah also, idling away the noontide in the shadow
of the arbour. Immediately on her entering the
garden-gate, the family of hens half ran, half flew,
to meet her; while a strange Grimalkin, which was
prowling under the parlour-window, took to his heels,
clambered hastily over the fence, and vanished. The
arbour was vacant, and its floor, table, and circular
bench were still damp, and bestrewn with twigs, and
the disarray of the past storm. The growth of the
garden seemed to have got quite out of bounds; the
weeds had taken advantage of Phœbe's absence, and
the long-continued rain, to run rampant over the
flowers and kitchen-vegetables. Maul's well had
overflowed its stone border, and made a pool of
formidable breadth, in that corner of the garden.

The impression of the whole scene was that of a
spot where no human foot had left its print for many
preceding days—probably not since Phœbe's departure—for she saw a sidecomb of her own under the
table of the arbour, where it must have fallen on the
last afternoon when she and Clifford sat there.

The girl knew that her two relatives were capable of far greater oddities than that of shutting themselves up in their old house, as they appeared now to have done. Nevertheless, with indistinct misgivings of something amiss, and apprehensions to which she could not give shape, she approached the door that formed the customary communication between the house and garden. It was secured within, like the two which she had already tried. She knocked, however; and immediately, as if the application had been expected, the door was drawn open, by a considerable exertion of some unseen person's strength, not widely, but far enough to afford her a side-long entrance. As Hepzibah, in order not to expose herself to inspection from without, invariably opened a door in this manner, Phœbe necessarily concluded that it was her cousin who now admitted her.

Without hesitation, therefore, she stepped across the threshold, and had no sooner entered than the door closed behind her.

XX

THE FLOWER OF EDEN

Phœbe, coming so suddenly from the sunny daylight, was altogether bedimmed in such density of shadow as lurked in most of the passages of the old house. She was not at first aware by whom she had been admitted. Before her eyes had adapted themselves to the obscurity, a hand grasped her own, with a firm but gentle and warm pressure, thus imparting a welcome which caused her heart to leap and thrill with an indefinable shiver of enjoyment. She felt herself drawn along, not towards the parlour, but into a large and unoccupied apartment, which had formerly been the grand reception room of the seven gables. The sunshine came freely into all the uncurtained windows of this room, and fell upon the dusty floor; so that Phœbe now clearly saw—what, indeed, had been no secret, after the encounter of a warm hand with hers—that it was not Hepzibah or Clifford, but Holgrave, to whom she owed her reception. The subtle, intuitive communication, or, rather, the vague and formless impression of something to be told, had made her yield unresistingly to his impulse. Without taking away her hand, she looked eagerly in his face, not quick to forebode evil, but unavoidably conscious that the state of the family had changed since her departure, and therefore anxious for an explanation.

The artist looked paler than ordinary; there was a thoughtful and severe contraction of his forehead, tracing a deep vertical line between the eyebrows. His smile, however, was full of genuine warmth, and had in it a joy, by far the most vivid expression that Phœbe had ever witnessed, shining out of the New England reserve with which Holgrave habitually masked whatever lay near his heart. It was the look wherewith a man, brooding alone over some fearful object, in a dreary forest or illimitable desert, would recognize the familiar aspect of his dearest friend, bringing up all the peaceful ideas that belong to home, and the gentle current of everyday affairs. And yet, as he felt the necessity of responding to her look of inquiry, the smile disappeared.

" I ought not to rejoice that you have come, Phœbe," said he. " We meet at a strange moment !"

" What has happened?" she exclaimed. " Why is the house so deserted? Where are Hepzibah and Clifford?"

" Gone ! I cannot imagine where they are !" answered Holgrave. " We are alone in the house !"

" Hepzibah and Clifford gone?" cried Phœbe. " It is not possible ! And why have you brought me into this room, instead of the parlour? Ah, something terrible has happened! I must run and see!"

"No, no, Phœbe!" said Holgrave, holding her back. "It is as I have told you. They are gone, and I know not whither. A terrible event has, indeed, but not to them, nor, as I undoubtingly believe, through any agency of theirs. If I read your character rightly, Phœbe," he continued, fixing his eyes on hers, with stern anxiety, intermixed with tenderness, "gentle as you are, and seeming to have your sphere among common things, you yet possess remarkable strength. You have wonderful poise, and a faculty which, when tested, will prove itself capable of dealing with matters that fall far out of the ordinary rule."

"Oh, no; I am very weak!" replied Phœbe, trembling. "But tell me what has happened!"

"You are strong!" persisted Holgrave. "You must be both strong and wise; for I am all astray, and need your counsel. It may be you can suggest the one right thing to do!"

"Tell me!—tell me!" said Phœbe, all in a tremble. "It oppresses—it terrifies me, this mystery! Anything else I can bear!"

The artist hesitated. Notwithstanding what he had just said, and most sincerely, in regard to the self-balancing power with which Phœbe impressed him, it still seemed almost wicked to bring the awful secret of yesterday to her knowledge. It was like dragging a hideous shape of death into the cleanly and cheerful space before a household fire, where it would present all the uglier aspect, amid the decorousness of everything about it. Yet it could not be concealed from her; she must needs know it.

"Phœbe," said he, "do you remember this?"

He put into her hand a daguerreotype; the same that he had shown her at their first interview in the garden, and which so strikingly brought out the hard and relentless traits of the original.

" What has this to do with Hepzibah and Clifford?" asked Phœbe, with impatient surprise that Holgrave should so trifle with her at such a moment. " It is Judge Pyncheon ! You have shown it to me before !"

" But here is the same face, taken within this half-hour," said the artist, presenting her with another miniature. " I had just finished it when I heard you at the door."

" This is death !" shuddered Phœbe, turning very pale. " Judge Pyncheon dead !"

" Such as there represented," said Holgrave, " he sits in the next room. The judge is dead, and Clifford and Hepzibah have vanished ! I know no more. All beyond is conjecture. On returning to my solitary chamber last evening, I noticed no light, either in the parlour, or Hepzibah's room, or Clifford's ; no stir nor footstep about the house. This morning there was the same death-like quiet. From my window I overheard the testimony of a neighbour, that your relatives were seen leaving the house in the midst of yesterday's storm. A rumour reached me, too, of Judge Pyncheon being missed. A feeling which I cannot describe—an indefinite sense of some catastrophe or consummation—impelled me to make my way into this part of the house, where I discovered what you see. As a point of evidence that may be useful to Clifford, and also as a memorial valuable to myself—for, Phœbe, there are hereditary reasons that connect me strangely with that man's fate—I used the means at my disposal to preserve this pictorial record of Judge Pyncheon's death."

Even in her agitation, Phœbe could not help remarking the calmness of Holgrave's demeanour. He appeared, it is true, to feel the whole awfulness of the judge's death, yet had received the fact into his mind without any mixture of surprise, but as an event pre-ordained, happening inevitably, and so fitting itself into past occurrences that it could almost have been prophesied.

" Why have you not thrown open the doors and called in witnesses?" inquired she, with a painful shudder. " It is terrible to be here alone!"

" But Clifford!" suggested the artist. " Clifford and Hepzibah! We must consider what is best to be done in their behalf. It is a wretched fatality that they should have disappeared! Their flight will throw the worst colouring over this event of which it is susceptible. Yet how easy is the explanation to those who knew them! Bewildered and terror-stricken by the similarity of this death to a former one, which was attended with such disastrous consequences to Clifford, they have no idea but of removing themselves from the scene. How miserably unfortunate! Had Hepzibah but shrieked aloud—had Clifford flung wide the door and proclaimed Judge Pyncheon's death—it would have been, however awful in itself, an event fruitful of good consequences to them. As I view it, it would have gone far towards obliterating the black stain on Clifford's character."

" And how," asked Phœbe, " could any good come from what is so very dreadful?"

" Because," said the artist, " if the matter can be fairly considered, and candidly interpreted, it must be evident that Judge Pyncheon could not have come unfairly to his end. This mode of death has been an idiosyncrasy with his family, for generations past; not often occurring, indeed, but when it does occur, usually attacking individuals about the judge's time of life, and generally in the tension of some mental crisis, or perhaps in an excess of wrath. Old Maule's prophecy was probably founded on a knowledge of this physical predisposition in the Pyncheon race. Now, there is a minute and almost exact similarity in the appearance connected with the death that occurred yesterday and those recorded of the death of Clifford's uncle thirty years ago. It is true there was a certain arrangement of circumstances, un-necessary to be recounted, which made it possible—nay, as men look at these things, probable, or even certain—that old Jaffrey Pyncheon came to a violent death, and by Clifford's hand."

" Whence came those circumstances?" exclaimed Phœbe; " he being innocent, as we know him to be!"

" They were arranged," said Holgrave—" at least such has long been my conviction—they were arranged, after the uncle's death, and before it was made public, by the man who sits in yonder parlour. His own death, so like that former one, yet attended with none of those suspicious circumstances, seems the stroke of God upon him, at once a punishment for his wickedness, and making plain the innocence of Clifford. But this flight—it distorts every thing! He may be in concealment, near at hand. Could we but bring him back before the discovery of the judge's death, the evil might be rectified. '

" We must not hide this thing a moment longer!" said Phœbe. " It is dreadful to keep it so closely in our hearts. Clifford is innocent. God will make it manifest! Let us throw open the doors, and call all the neighbourhood to see the truth!"

" You are right, Phœbe," rejoined Holgrave. " Doubtless you are right."

Yet the artist did not feel the horror which was proper to Phœbe's sweet and order-loving character, at thus finding herself at issue with society, and brought in contact with an event that transcended ordinary rules. Neither was he in haste, like her, to betake himself within the precincts of common life. On the contrary, he gathered a wild enjoyment—as it were a flower of strange beauty, growing in a desolate spot, and blossoming in the wind—such a flower of momentary happiness he gathered from his present position. It separated Phœbe and himself from the world, and bound them to each other, by their exclusive knowledge of Judge Pyncheon's mysterious death, and the counsel which they were forced to hold respecting it. The secret, as long as it should continue such, kept them within the circle of a spell, a solitude in the midst of men, a remoteness as entire as that of an island in mid-ocean; once divulged, the ocean would flow betwixt them, standing on its widely-sundered shores. Meanwhile, all the circumstances of their situation seemed to draw them together; they were like two children who go hand in hand, pressing closely to one another's side, through a shadow-haunted passage. The image of awful Death, which filled the house, held them united by his stiffened grasp.

These influences hastened the development of emotions that might not otherwise have flowered so soon. Possibly, indeed, it had been Holgrave's purpose to let them die in their undeveloped germs.

"Why do we delay so?" asked Phœbe. "This secret takes away my breath! Let us throw open the doors!"

"In all our lives, there can never come another moment like this!" said Holgrave. "Phœbe, is it all terror?—nothing but terror? Are you conscious of no joy, as I am, that has made this the only point of life worth living for?"

"It seems a sin," replied Phœbe, trembling, "to think of joy at such a time!"

"Could you but know, Phœbe, how it was with me, the hour before you came!" exclaimed the artist. "A dark, cold, miserable hour! The presence of yonder dead man threw a great black shadow over everything; he made the universe, so far as my perception could reach, a scene of guilt, and of retribution more dreadful than the guilt. The sense of it took away my youth. I never hoped to feel young again! The world looked strange, wild, evil, hostile; —my past life, so lonesome and dreary; my future, a shapeless gloom, which I must mould into gloomy shapes! But, Phœbe, you crossed the threshold; and hope, warmth, and joy came in with you! The black moment became at once a blissful one. It must not pass without the spoken word. I love you!"

"How can you love a simple girl like me?" asked

Phœbe, compelled by his earnestness to speak. "You have many, many thoughts, with which I should try in vain to sympathize. And I,—I, too,— I have tendencies with which you would sympathize as little. That is less matter. But I have not scope enough to make you happy."

"You are my only possibility of happiness!" answered Holgrave. "I have no faith in it, except as you bestow it on me!"

"And then—I am afraid!" continued Phœbe, shrinking towards Holgrave, even while she told him so frankly the doubts with which he affected her. "You will lead me out of my own quiet path. You will make me strive to follow you, where it is pathless. I cannot do so. It is not my nature. I shall sink down and perish!"

"Ah, Phœbe!" exclaimed Holgrave, with almost a sigh, and a smile that was burthened with thought. "It will be far otherwise than as you forebode. The world owes all its onward impulses to men ill at ease. The happy man inevitably confines himself within ancient limits. I have a presentiment that, hereafter, it will be my lot to set out trees, to make fences,—perhaps, even in due time, to build a house for another generation,—in a word, to conform myself to laws, and the peaceful practice of society. Your poise will be more powerful than any oscillating tendency of mine."

"I would not have it so!" said Phœbe, earnestly.

"Do you love me?" asked Holgrave. "If we love one another, the moment has room for nothing more. Let us pause upon it, and be satisfied. Do you love me, Phœbe?"

"You look into my heart," said she, letting her eyes drop. "You know I love you!"

And it was in this hour, so full of doubt and awe, that the one miracle was wrought, without which every human existence is a blank. The bliss, which makes all things true, beautiful, and holy, shone around this youth and maiden. They were conscious of nothing sad nor old.   They transfigured the earth, and made it Eden again, and themselves the two first dwellers in it.   The dead man, so close beside them, was forgotten.   At such a crisis there is no death; for immortality is revealed anew, and embraces everything in its hallowed atmosphere.

But how soon the heavy earth-dream settled down again !

"Hark !" whispered Phœbe.   "Somebody is at the street-door !"

"Now let us meet the world !" said Holgrave. "No doubt the rumour of Judge Pyncheon's visit to this house, and the flight of Hepzibah and Clifford, is about to lead to the investigation of the premises.   We have no way but to meet it.   Let us open the door at once."

But to their surprise, before they could reach the street door—even before they quitted the room in which the foregoing interview had passed—they heard footsteps in the further passage.   The door, therefore, which they supposed to be securely locked —which Holgrave, indeed, had seen to be so, and at which Phœbe had vainly tried to enter—must have been opened from without.   The sound of footsteps was not harsh, bold, decided, and intrusive, as the gait of strangers naturally would be, making authoritative entrance into a dwelling where they knew themselves unwelcome.   It was feeble, as of persons either weak or weary ; there was the mingled murmur of two voices, familiar to both the listeners.

"Can it be?" whispered Holgrave.

"It is they !" answered Phœbe.   "Thank God— thank God !"

And then, as if in sympathy with Phœbe's whispered ejaculation, they heard Hepzibah's voice more distinctly.

"Thank God, my brother, we are at home !"

"Well !—Yes !—thank God !" responded Clifford. "A dreary home, Hepzibah !   But you have done well to bring me hither !   Stay !   That parlour-door is open. I cannot pass by it! Let me go and rest in the arbour, where I used—oh, very long ago, it seems to me, after what has befallen us—where I used to be so happy with little Phœbe!"

But the house was not altogether so dreary as Clifford imagined it. They had not made many steps—in truth, they were lingering in the entry, with the listlessness of an accomplished purpose, uncertain what to do next—when Phœbe ran to meet them. On beholding her, Hepzibah burst into tears. With all her might, she had staggered onward beneath the burden of grief and responsibility, until now that it was safe to fling it down. Indeed, she had not energy to fling it down, but had ceased to uphold it, and suffered it to press her to the earth. Clifford appeared the stronger of the two.

"It is our own little Phœbe!—Ah! and Holgrave with her," exclaimed he, with a glance of keen and delicate insight, and a smile, beautiful, kind, but melancholy. "I thought of you both, as we came down the street, and beheld Alice's posies in full bloom. And so the flower of Eden has bloomed likewise, in this old, darksome house to-day!"

XXI

THE DEPARTURE

THE sudden death of so prominent a member of the social world as the Honourable Judge Jaffrey Pyncheon created a sensation (at least in the circles more immediately connected with the deceased) which had hardly quite subsided in a fortnight.

It may be remarked, however, that of all the events which constitute a person's biography, there is scarcely one—none, certainly, of anything like a similar importance—to which the world so easily reconciles itself, as to its death. In most other cases and contingencies, the individual is present among us, mixed up with the daily revolution of affairs, and affording a definite point for observation. At his decease, there is only a vacancy, and a momentary eddy—very small, as compared with the apparent magnitude of the ingurgitated object—and a bubble or two, ascending out of the black depth, and bursting at the surface. As regarded Judge Pyncheon, it seemed probable, at first blush, that the mode of his final departure might give him a larger and longer posthumous vogue than ordinarily attends the memory of a distinguished man. But when it came to be understood, on the highest professional authority, that the event was a natural, and—except for some unimportant particulars, denoting a slight idiosyncrasy—by no means an unusual form of death, the public, with its customary alacrity, proceeded to forget that he had ever lived. In short, the honourable judge was beginning to be a stale subject, before half the county newspapers had found time to put their columns in mourning, and publish his exceedingly eulogistic obituary.

Nevertheless, creeping darkly through the places which this excellent person had haunted in his lifetime, there was a hidden stream of private talk, such as it would have shocked all decency to speak loudly at the street-corners. It is very singular, how the fact of a man's death often seems to give people a truer idea of his character, whether for good or evil, than they have ever possessed while he was living and acting among them. Death is so genuine a fact that it excludes falsehood, or betrays its emptiness; it is a touchstone that proves the gold, and dishonours the baser metal. Could the departed, whoever he may be, return in a week after his decease, he would almost invariably find himself at a higher or lower point than he had formerly occupied, on the scale of public appreciation. But the talk or scandal,

to which we now allude, had reference to matters
of no less old a date than the supposed murder, thirty
or forty years ago, of the late Judge Pyncheon's
uncle. The medical opinion, with regard to his own
recent and regretted decease, had almost entirely
obviated the idea that a murder was committed, in
the former case. Yet, as the record showed, there
were circumstances irrefragably indicating that some
person had gained access to old Jaffrey Pyncheon's
private apartments, at or near the moment of his
death. His desk and private drawers, in a room
contiguous to his bedchamber, had been ransacked;
money and valuable articles were missing; there was
a bloody hand-print on the old man's linen; and, by
a powerfully welded chain of deductive evidence, the
guilt of the robbery and apparent murder had been
fixed on Clifford, then residing with his uncle in the
House of the Seven Gables.

Whencesoever originating, there now arose a theory
that undertook so to account for these circumstances
as to exclude the idea of Clifford's agency. Many
persons affirmed that the history and elucidation of
the facts, long so mysterious, had been obtained by
the daguerreotypist from one of those mesmerical
seers, who, now-a-days, so strangely perplex the
aspect of human affairs, and put everybody's natural
vision to the blush, by the marvels which they see
with their eyes shut.

According to this version of the story, Judge Pyncheon, exemplary as we have portrayed him in our
narrative, was, in his youth, an apparently irre-
claimable scapegrace. The brutish, the animal in-
stincts, as is often the case, had been developed
earlier than the intellectual qualities, and the force
of character, for which he was afterwards remarkable. He had shown himself wild, dissipated,
addicted to low pleasures, little short of ruffianly in
his propensities, and recklessly expensive, with no
other resources than the bounty of his uncle. This
course of conduct had alienated the old bachelor's

affection, once strongly fixed upon him. Now it is averred—but whether on authority available in a court of justice we do not pretend to have investigated—that the young man was tempted by the devil one night to search his uncle's private drawers, to which he had unsuspected means of access. While thus criminally occupied, he was startled by the opening of the chamber-door. There stood old Jaffrey Pyncheon in his night-clothes! The surprise of such a discovery, his agitation, alarm, and horror, brought on the crisis of a disorder to which the old bachelor had an hereditary liability;—he seemed to choke with blood, and he fell upon the floor, striking his temple a heavy blow against the corner of a table. What was to be done? The old man was surely dead! Assistance would come too late! What a misfortune, indeed, should it come too soon, since his reviving consciousness would bring the recollection of the ignominious offence which he had beheld his nephew in the very act of committing.

But he never did revive. With the cool hardihood that always pertained to him, the young man continued his search of the drawers, and found a will, of recent date, in favour of Clifford—which he destroyed—and an older one, in his own favour, which he suffered to remain. But before retiring, Jaffrey bethought himself of the evidence, in these ransacked drawers, that some one had visited the chamber with sinister purposes. Suspicion, unless averted, might fix upon the real offender. In the very presence of the dead man, therefore, he laid a scheme that should free himself at the expense of Clifford, his rival, for whose character he had at once a contempt and a repugnance. It is not probable, be it said, that he acted with any set purpose of involving Clifford in a charge of murder. Knowing that his uncle did not die by violence, it may not have occurred to him, in the hurry of the crisis, that such an inference might be drawn. But when the affair took this darker aspect, Jaffrey's previous steps had already pledged him to those which remained. So craftily had he arranged the circumstances, that at Clifford's trial his cousin hardly found it necessary to swear to anything false, but only to withhold the one decisive explanation, by refraining to state what he had himself done and witnessed.

Thus Jaffrey Pyncheon's inward criminality, as regarded Clifford, was indeed black and damnable; while its mere outward show and positive commission was the smallest that could possibly consist with so great a sin. This is just the sort of guilt that a man of eminent respectability finds it easiest to dispose of. It was suffered to fade out of sight, or be reckoned a venial matter, in the Honourable Judge Pyncheon's long subsequent survey of his own life. He shuffled it aside, among the forgotten and forgiven frailties of his youth, and seldom thought of it again.

We leave the judge to his repose. He could not be styled fortunate, at the hour of death. Unknowingly, he was a childless man, while striving to add more wealth to his only child's inheritance. Hardly a week after his decease, one of the Cunard steamers brought intelligence of the death, by cholera, of Judge Pyncheon's son, just at the point of embarkation for his native land. By this misfortune Clifford became rich; so did Hepzibah; so did our little village maiden, and, through her, that sworn foe of wealth and all manner of conservatism—the wild reformer—Holgrave!

It was now far too late in Clifford's life for the good opinion of society to be worth the trouble and anguish of a formal vindication. What he needed was the love of a very few; not the admiration, or even the respect, of the unknown many. The latter might probably have been won for him, had those on whom the guardianship of his welfare had fallen deemed it advisable to expose Clifford to a miserable resuscitation of past ideas, when the condition of whatever comfort he might expect lay in the calm of

forgetfulness. After such wrong as he had suffered,
there is no reparation. The pitiable mockery of it,
which the world might have been ready enough to
offer, coming so long after the agony had done its
utmost work, would have been fit only to provoke
bitterer laughter than poor Clifford was ever capable
of. It is a truth (and it would be a very sad one,
but for the higher hopes which it suggests) that no
great mistake, whether acted or endured, in our
mortal sphere, is ever really set right. Time, the
continual vicissitude of circumstances, and the invari-
able inopportunity of death, render it impossible. If,
after long lapse of years, the right seems to be in our
power, we find no niche to set it in. The better
remedy is for the sufferer to pass on, and leave what
he once thought his irreparable ruin far behind him.

The shock of Judge Pyncheon's death had a per-
manently invigorating and ultimately beneficial effect
on Clifford. That strong and ponderous man had
been Clifford's night-mare. There was no free
breath to be drawn, within the sphere of so malevolent an influence. The first effect of freedom, as we
have witnessed in Clifford's aimless flight, was a
tremulous exhilaration. Subsiding from it, he did
not sink into his former intellectual apathy. He
never, it is true, attained to nearly the full measure
of what might have been his faculties. But he
recovered enough of them partially to light up his
character, to display some outline of the marvellous
grace that was abortive in it, and to make him the
object of no less deep, although less melancholy interest than heretofore. He was evidently happy.
Could we pause to give another picture of his daily
life, with all the appliances now at command to
gratify his instinct for the Beautiful, the garden
scenes, that seemed so sweet to him, would look mean
and trivial in comparison.

Very soon after their change of fortune, Clifford,
Hepzibah, and little Phœbe, with the approval of the
artist, concluded to remove from the dismal old

House of the Seven Gables, and take up their abode,
for the present, at the elegant country-seat of the
late Judge Pyncheon. Chanticleer and his family
had already been transported thither, where the two
hens had forthwith begun an indefatigable process of
egg-laying, with an evident design, as a matter of
duty and conscience, to continue their illustrious
breed under better auspices than for a century past.
On the day set for their departure, the principal personages of our story, including good Uncle Venner,
were assembled in the parlour.

"The country-house is certainly a very fine one,
so far as the plan goes," observed Holgrave, as the
party were discussing their future arrangements.
"But I wonder that the late judge—being so opulent,
and with a reasonable prospect of transmitting his
wealth to descendants of his own—should not have
felt the propriety of embodying so excellent a piece
of domestic architecture in stone, rather than in
wood. Then every generation of the family might
have altered the interior to suit its own taste and
convenience, while the exterior, through the lapse of
years, might have been adding venerableness to its
original beauty, and thus giving that impression of
permanence which I consider esential to the happiness of any one moment."

"Why," cried Phœbe, gazing into the artist's
face with infinite amazement, "how wonderfully your
ideas are changed! A house of stone, indeed! It is
but two or three weeks ago, that you seemed to wish
people to live in something as fragile and temporary
as a bird's nest!"

"Ah, Phœbe, I told you how it would be!" said
the artist, with a half-melancholy laugh. "You find
me a conservative already! Little did I think ever
to become one. It is especially unpardonable in this
dwelling of so much hereditary misfortune, and
under the eye of yonder portrait of a model conservative, who, in that very character, rendered himself so long the evil destiny of his race."

"That picture !" said Clifford, seeming to shrink from its stern glance. "Whenever I look at it, there is an old, dreamy recollection haunting me, but keeping just beyond the grasp of my mind. Wealth, it seems to say !—boundless wealth !—unimaginable wealth ! I could fancy that, when I was a child, or a youth, that portrait had spoken, and told me rich secret, or had held forth its head, with the written record of hidden opulence. But those old matters are so dim with me, now-a-days ! What could this dream have been?"

"Perhaps I can recall it," answered Holgrave. "See ! There are a hundred chances to one, that no person, unacquainted with the secret, would ever touch this spring."

"A secret spring !" cried Clifford. "Ah, I remember now ! I did discover it, one summer afternoon, when I was idling and dreaming about the house, long, long ago. But the mystery escapes me."

The artist put his finger on the contrivance to which he had referred. In former days, the effect would probably have been to cause the picture to start forward. But, in so long a period of concealment, the machinery had been eaten through with rust; so that, at Holgrave's pressure, the portrait, frame and all, tumbled suddenly from its position, and lay face downward on the floor. A recess in the wall was thus brought to light, in which lay an object so covered with a century's dust that it could not immediately be recognized as a folded sheet of parchment. Holgrave opened it, and displayed an ancient deed, signed with the hieroglyphics of several Indian sagamores, and conveying to Colonel Pyncheon and his heirs, for ever, a vast extent of territory at the eastward.

"This is the very parchment, the attempt to recover which cost the beautiful Alice Pyncheon her happiness and life," said the artist, alluding to his legend. "It is what the Pyncheons sought in vain, while it was valuable; and now that they find the treasure, it has long been worthless."

"Poor Cousin Jaffrey! This is what deceived him," exclaimed Hepzibah. "When they were young together, Clifford probably made a kind of fairy-tale of this discovery. He was always dreaming hither and thither about the house, and lighting up its dark corners with beautiful stories. And poor Jaffrey, who took hold of everything as if it were real, thought my brother had found out his uncle's wealth. He died with this delusion in his mind!"

"But," said Phœbe, apart to Holgrave, "how came you to know the secret?"

"My dearest Phœbe," said Holgrave, "how will it please you to assume the name of Maule? As for the secret, it is the only inheritance that has come down to me from my ancestors. You should have known sooner (only that I was afraid of frightening you away) that, in this long drama of wrong and retribution, I represent the old wizard, and am probably as much of a wizard as ever he was. The son of the executed Matthew Maule, while building this house, took the opportunity to construct that recess, and hide away the Indian deed, on which depended the immense land-claim of the Pyncheons. Thus they bartered their eastern territory for Maule's garden-ground."

"And now," said Uncle Venner, "I suppose their whole claim is not worth one man's share in my farm yonder!"

"Uncle Venner," cried Phœbe, taking the patched philosopher's hand, "you must never talk any more about your farm! You shall never go there, as long as you live! There is a cottage in our new garden —the prettiest little yellowish-brown cottage you ever saw; and the sweetest-looking place, for it looks just as if it were made of gingerbread—and we are going to fit it up and furnish it, on purpose for you. And you shall do nothing but what you choose, and shall be as happy as the day is long, and shall keep

Cousin Clifford in spirits with the wisdom and
pleasantness which is always dropping from your
lips!"

"Ah! my dear child," quoth good Uncle Venner,
quite overcome, "if you were to speak to a young
man as you do to an old one, his chance of keeping
his heart another minute would not be worth one
of the buttons on my waistcoat! And—soul alive!
—that great sigh which you made me heave, has
burst off the very last of them! But never mind! It
was the happiest sigh I ever did heave; and it seems
as if I must have drawn in a gulp of heavenly breath,
to make it with. Well, well, Miss Phœbe! They'll
miss me in the gardens, hereabouts, and round by
the back-doors; and Pyncheon-street, I'm afraid, will
hardly look the same without old Uncle Venner, who
remembers it with a mowing field on one side, and
the garden of the seven gables on the other. But
either I must go to your country-seat, or you must
come to my farm—that's one of the two things certain; and I leave you to choose which!"

"O, come with us, by all means, Uncle Venner!"
said Clifford, who had a remarkable enjoyment of
the old man's mellow, quiet, and simple spirit. "I
want you always to be within five minutes' saunter
of my chair. You are the only philosopher I ever
knew of, whose wisdom has not a drop of bitter
essence at the bottom!"

"Dear me!" cried Uncle Venner, beginning partly
to realize what manner of man he was. "And yet
folks used to set me down among the simple ones,
in my younger days! But I suppose I am like a
Roxbury russet—a great deal the better, the longer
I can be kept. Yes; and my words of wisdom, that
you and Phœbe tell me of, are like the golden dande-
lions, which never grow in the hot months, but may
be seen glistening among the withered grass, and
under the dry leaves, sometimes as late as December.
And you are welcome, friends, to my mess of dande-
lions, if there were twice as many!"

A plain but handsome dark green barouche had now drawn up in front of the ruinous portal of the old mansion-house. The party came forth and (with the exception of good Uncle Venner, who was to follow in a few days) proceeded to take their places. They were chatting and laughing very pleasantly together; and—as proves to be often the case, at moments when we ought to palpitate with sensibility —Clifford and Hepzibah bade a final farewell to the abode of their forefathers, with hardly more emotion than if they had made it their arrangement to return thither at tea-time. Several children were drawn to the spot by so unusual a spectacle as the barouche and a pair of gray horses. Recognizing little Ned Higgins among them, Hepzibah put her hand into her pocket and presented the urchin, her earliest and staunchest customer, with silver enough to people the Domdaniel cavern of his interior with as various a procession of quadrupeds as passed into the ark.

Two men were passing just as the barouche drove off.

" Well, Dixey," said one of them, " what do you think of this? My wife kept a cent-shop three months, and lost five dollars on her outlay. Old Maid Pyncheon has been in trade just about as long, and rides off in her carriage with a couple of hundred thousand—reckoning her share, and Clifford's and Phœbe's—and some say twice as much! If you choose to call it luck it is all very well; but if we are to take it as the will of providence, why I can't exactly fathom it!"

" Pretty good business!" quoth the sagacious Dixey. " Pretty good business!"

Maule's well, all this time, though left in solitude, was throwing up a succession of kaleidoscopic pictures, in which a gifted eye might have seen foreshadowed the coming fortunes of Hepzibah and Clifford, and the descendant of the legendary wizard and the village-maiden, over whom he had thrown Love's web of sorcery. The Pyncheon-elm, moreover, with what foliage the September gale had spared to it, whispered unintelligible prophecies. And wise Uncle Venner, passing slowly from the ruinous porch, seemed to hear a strain of music, and fancied that sweet Alice Pyncheon—after witnessing these deeds, this by-gone woe, and this present happiness of her kindred mortals—had given one farewell touch of a spirit's joy upon her harpsichord, as she floated heavenward from the HOUSE OF THE SEVEN GABLES!

THE END

EVERYMAN'S LIBRARY AND EVERYMAN PAPERBACKS: A Selection

BIOGRAPHY

ESSAYS AND CRITICISM

FICTION

HISTORY

RELIGION AND PHILOSOPHY

SCIENCES: POLITICAL AND GENERAL

TRAVEL AND TOPOGRAPHY